SUMMER
DOCTOR

SUMMER
DOCTOR

CHARLES H. KNICKERBOCKER

DOUBLEDAY & COMPANY, INC.
GARDEN CITY, NEW YORK

author's note:

Some years ago I wrote a novel about life on an island off the coast of Maine. In a prefatory note I claimed that this island was not real. Since I live on an island off the coast of Maine, readers didn't believe me. More recently I wrote a novel about doctors, and I claimed that the doctors in that novel were not real. Since I am a practicing physician, readers didn't believe me. The present novel concerns a doctor on an island off the coast of Maine. This time I make no claim beyond stating that this is a novel, a work of fiction. Readers may believe whatever they like.

C.H.K.

dedicated to

Bill Berger,
with gratitude

Contents

Part 1

September 1953

"WHERE IS THIS JUNIPER ISLAND?" Jake swirled his glass, as the ice cubes tinkled, and cocked an eyebrow at me. He looked like a large loose-jointed leprechaun.

"You haven't heard of it?" I said.

"Has anyone?"

No longer, perhaps. A generation earlier, Juniper Island was famous, a select and highly fashionable summer resort off the coast of Maine, midway between Boston and Canada.

"Beautiful as ever, but not fashionable any more," I said. "The older wealthy families are vanishing. Young millionaires don't care to summer on remote islands surrounded by a view."

"Just you and the fog and the sea gulls?" said Jake.

"There are a few of the rich summer people left," I said. "And there's a year-round population of several hundred souls. The natives are lobster fishermen: a proud, tough, stubborn, cantankerous, independent breed. I think they need a doctor. They never had one before."

"Why you, Dan?"

"Why not?"

Jake ticked off the disadvantages for me on his fingers: "No money in the winter. No hospital. No coverage. No professional associates. No opportunity for advancement. Isolation. Loneliness. Primitive conditions. Primitive people. You're a city boy and you'll be lost out there."

"I'm a country boy at heart," I said. "I need elbow room and space in which to grow. I want to lead my own life without somebody peeking over my shoulder all the time. I want to get back to fundamentals."

"Dan, I never thought of you as a pioneer."

"I'm not," I said. "There's a bridge connecting Juniper Island to the mainland. I can escape at any time."

Jake and I were drinking together in the Officers' Club at Fort Meade, Maryland. The following day we would be officially separated from the Medical Corps of the Army of the United States. I had never been in private practice and neither had Jake. We had interned together and joined the army immediately after our internship.

"Korea has something to do with this, I suppose?" said Jake.

Jake and I had served two years in that unattractive land.

"I don't mind if I forget."

"Neither do I," said Jake. He was headed for the surgical residency that had been waiting for him for the last two years. "What happened to internal medicine?"

At one time I had also planned residency training. "I don't know," I said. "Maybe our profession is too specialized. Nobody treats the whole patient any more."

"There is still room for the family physician."

"Not in the suburbs," I said. "The general man is nothing but a feeder to the specialists."

"What's the matter with the suburbs?"

"They give me creeping palsy and slow suffocation," I said. "It seems to me the whole country is becoming one vast suburb coast to coast."

"Not where you're going."

"That's why I'm going there," I said. "No status to maintain. To hell with the Joneses. No crab grass for me, no smog, no traffic problems. I won't spend half my life looking for a place to park."

"Instead, you'll be chopping ice from the well."

"No competition. I won't be cutting throats with the guy next door. Juniper Island is ten miles long and three miles wide."

"No place to hide?"

"Who wants to hide?"

"You," said Jake. "You're running away. You are fifty years too late. You will bury yourself before your time."

"The last stronghold of the rugged individualist," I said. "I'll lead my own kind of life my own way, and find myself."

"Something's lost?" said Jake.

"Yes, I think something is," I said. "We've gotten out of touch with basic things. We've forgotten how to live."

"Soft because of indoor plumbing and electricity?"

"There's plumbing and lights on the island," I said. "Likewise sunsets and the moon rising out of the ocean and the sound of surf, green spruces, white birch trees, sparkling blue water, brilliant sun, air crisp and cool as chilled wine."

"Sounds like you're in love."

"I spent a summer there when I was a boy," I said. "I admit I fell in love with the natural beauty of the place. It's God's country, Jake."

"And the winter lasts from September till June."

"I've never been there in the winter," I admitted.

"And what does the young lady think about all this?"

"She doesn't," I said. "So, she's not going, but I am."

"Stubborn."

"I'm of Dutch descent, and I have short thumbs."

"And the wedding's off?"

"Rain check," I said. "Some other year."

"Well," said Jake. "It's all right by me. You've looked this place over very carefully and decided this is where you want to live and practice medicine. This is your decision. You have my blessing, son."

"Thanks, Pop, but I haven't," I said. "I've not been there since I was a boy."

"Maybe the place has changed."

"So have I."

"You've been corresponding with the Chamber of Commerce and the local medical society and so forth?"

"Nope."

"You've lined up a home and office suite?"

"No, I haven't."

"You're just going to arrive?" said Jake. "Without investigation of any kind?"

"Exactly," I said. "First, I'm going to get all that back pay we accumulated overseas and turn the check into cash."

"Better get a bodyguard. There's several thousand bucks."

"I'll get a few civilian clothes and then I'm going to buy a car. In cash. I have in mind a Thunderbird convertible."

"You've savings in reserve for your house and office and your office furnishings?"

"The G.I. mortgage for the house. And I'll have an office in my home of course. I don't need much equipment. I'll be starting small."

"Sounds pretty informal and dangerous to me. How do you know that this is a promising location? Can you make a living there?"

"I'm young and smart and well trained," I said. "Damn it, I can make a living anywhere."

"Lots of places, sure," said Jake. "But why Juniper Island?"

"Because I want to live out there. Okay?"

Jake eyed the remains of melted ice cubes in his glass. "Doc," he said, "you know what I think? You want my professional evaluation of your case?"

"Not especially," I said.

"You've popped your cork."

"I'm a loner," I said, "not an organization man."

"This," he said, "is a form of minor suicide."

"This remains to be seen," I said.

"You're trying to get lost on Juniper Island."

"The lost and found department."

"I hope you find whatever it is you're looking for."

"So do I," I said.

* * *

I thoroughly enjoyed my trip from Maryland to Maine. The weather was clear and cool, the traffic light. In the expressways around the metropolitan centers, I gave my new Thunderbird convertible free rein. She was a purring smooth beauty of a car, and I was in love with her. She was an extravagant gesture. The roads on Juniper Island would be narrow and winding, full of potholes and frost heave in the spring, and I would have no real need for such a fast and fancy car. It was part of the gesture I was making. Perhaps I wanted to prove that I didn't have to bury myself at the end of the earth if I didn't want to. Perhaps I wanted the means for a fast getaway in case Jake and my parents and a young lady of my acquaintance happened to be right. They all thought my decision on a remote and isolated location was impulsive, immature, and foolish. So was the purchase of this automobile. Well, maybe so, but I knew I was dissatisfied with the pattern of living that was shaping up for me, and Korea wasn't the only reason. I wanted to take a long running jump into a nice cold ocean and clear my head. Impulsive? Sure. Immature? Of course. But sometimes, I think, you've got to take a chance and do some wild and foolish thing. Otherwise, how can you tell that you're alive at all?

When I hit New England, with the climate getting cooler and clearer by the mile, I slowed down. Entering Maine, I took Route 1 along the coast. I passed through Kittery and York, Ogunquit, Biddeford, and Bath, Brunswick, Kennebunk, Wiscasset, Damariscotta. The towns were pretty as their names: white colonial houses, elms, views out over the bay. Finally I found myself in a place called Rockport Falls. From here, there should have been a bridge to Juniper Island, according to the map, according to my boyhood memory, but I couldn't find it. So I hailed a passer-by, a whiskery lobsterman with a distinctive fish aroma, a suspicious attitude, and a rough piratical to-hell-with-you look about him.

"Hey," I said, "where's Juniper Island?"

He stared at me, hostile and suspicious. Finally he waved a horny hand towards the water.

"Setting out yonder in the bay where she's always been," he said. "We ain't moved her recently."

"How do I get there?"

"Can you swim?"

"What do you mean?"

"You'll never make it setting down," he said.

It didn't seem to me that we had established communication. "I want to go to the island," I said, as plainly as I could.

"I don't recommend it, buddy," he said. "There's nothing on Juniper that ain't better represented somewhere else."

"I'll be the judge of that," I said. "Never mind. If I follow along the shore, I'll surely find the bridge."

"Want to bet?"

"Why not?"

"Blew down."

"Beg pardon?"

He addressed me slowly and carefully as if speaking to an idiot. "The Juniper Island bridge blew down. Hurricane, couple of years ago, right around this particular season of the year. If you look real close you can see a couple of pilings sticking up out of the water. That's all there's left of her."

I looked real close. I saw the remains of a few old battered pilings sticking up out of the mud. Maybe I didn't want to go to Juniper Island after all.

"Who are you visiting out there, mister?"

"Nobody," I said. "I don't know a soul."

"Didn't figure so," he said. "I live on the island myself, born and bred there, and I don't know you, and everybody knows everybody on Juniper Island. What's your business?"

I wasn't sure it was his business, but I said, "I'm considering living out there myself."

"For the summer season?"

"Year round," I said.

"Why?"

"To practice my profession. I'm a doctor."

"Horse, tooth, eye, osteopath, or regular?"

"Regular," I said.

My friend looked dubious. "Don't know. We never had a doc out there before. Don't exactly see the need for one myself."

"How many people you got out there?"

"Three hundred and seventy-one," he said, "unless Mrs. Wellington's come through in the last couple of hours, which I don't know about, in which event there's three hundred and seventy-two."

"Maybe she had twins," I suggested helpfully.

"That's a fact. Twins do run in the family," he said.

A good ratio of patients to the physician is in the neighborhood of seven hundred and fifty to one. I wasn't quite so sure that this would be a favorable location. Especially without a bridge.

"She's crowded in the summertime," he said. "Couple of thousand folks,

I guess. The summer is only ten weeks long, but that's plenty long enough. We're always happy to see 'em come, but we're more than happy to see 'em go, brother, I can tell you that."

Two thousand people would keep one doctor hopping. Ten hectic weeks of business and forty-two weeks of lazy leisure: that wouldn't be so bad. In fact I thought I might enjoy it.

"Any money out there?"

"Plenty in the summertime," he said. "Lots of them folks is millionaires, you understand, and millionaires appreciate their privacy. That's why they stay with us."

"And the rest of the year you starve."

"Nope," he said. "We're eating regular. We go lobster fishing, most of us. There's six, eight, ten thousand dollars, maybe even fifteen, for a guy who ain't afraid of a little wind and weather. And if you're living on an island, friend, you can't fret and fuss too much about the weather."

No, I could see that you couldn't.

"Sometimes we're cut off for days at a time," he said.

Well, if I wanted privacy, this was it.

"Of course, you'd need a boat," he said.

"And I could surely get along without a Thunderbird," I said.

"Thunderbird," he said. "Five thousand dollars' worth of automobile, ain't she?"

"Brand new," I said.

"Pretty," he said. He kicked reflectively at the right front tire. "I'd admire me a bus like this."

"You wouldn't have much use for her on Juniper."

"Nope," he said. "But I could go riding around on the mainland with the top down. Maybe I'd go to Boston. Honking at the girls."

"Yeah," I said. "Girls always look twice at a car like this."

"Yes indeed." My friend turned contemplative, as if doing a little serious thinking for himself. "Doc, I got a boat. Worth two or three times that sum when she was new. Of course, she ain't exactly new any more."

"Just so long as she floats," I said.

"Oh, she floats, real good. There ain't scarcely any kind of wind or weather that vessel of mine can't get through. Good engine in her too. Doc, I'll tell you what: I'll make a deal with you. Swap your car for my boat, even stephen, sight unseen."

"Wait a minute," I said. "I've made no final decision about Juniper Island. There must be dozens of communities along this part of the coast with a greater population who need a doctor worse than you do."

"Oh, we could keep you plenty busy, Doc, I'm sure."

"Furthermore," I said, "I haven't seen your boat but you're looking at my car."

"Yeah, I see her, but how do I know she runs?"

"Without seeing your boat, how do I know she floats?"

"Some things, Doc, you gotta take on faith."

"Not five thousand dollars' worth of property," I said, "which is all the property I own."

"Fair enough. You got a point," he said. "Okay, come along with me."

So I got out of the car and went along with him, out onto the end of the municipal pier.

"There she is, Doc," he said, pointing downward. "Ain't she a beauty?"

There, indeed, she was, but not exactly a beauty: twenty-eight feet of dirty leaky old fishing boat. She lay low in the water amidships, with a high superstructure, big bluff bows, and a dirty triangular canvas sail at the stern. There was an encrustation of barnacles and trailing tendrils of green slime at the water line and I doubted if she'd been out of the water in ten years' time.

"I'll concede she ain't a yacht, and she's getting along in years like the rest of us," he said, "but she's a tough strong vessel, sound as the American dollar."

There were several feet of dirty water sloshing around in the bilges. I declined to comment on the soundness of the American dollar. The vessel bore the name of *Mary Jane*.

"Your wife?" I asked him.

"Had me a couple or three but not at the present time," he said.

"I meant Mary Jane."

"One was Susan; one was Evelyn; and one was Pamela, as near as I can recollect."

"And who was Mary Jane?"

"Her I don't care to recollect," he said. "Come aboard."

I scrambled down a ladder as an overpowering aroma rose to meet me from the *Mary Jane*. I identified the source: a barrel of chopped chunks of decaying fish. This was what the fishermen called "chum"; they used it to bait the lobster traps.

"You get so you don't hardly notice that," he said.

The time never came for me when I could hardly notice the smell of chum. I breathed through my mouth as my friend demonstrated the advantages of the *Mary Jane*. Also he introduced himself. His name was Cyrus Lunt. In turn I said that my name was Dr. Daniel van Dine, age twenty-six, unmarried, general practitioner by trade.

"Speaking of the trade . . ." said Cyrus Lunt.

"This boat is older than I am," I said. "My Thunderbird is brand new."

"Conceded."

"And I'm rather fond of the car."

"You can't get to Juniper without a boat."

"I'm not sure I want to go to Juniper."

"Son, I can tell by the look of you: you're a stubborn man. You'd already made your decision before you came. You're not the kind of man to change his mind."

"I haven't been out there in twenty years," I said. "Just one summer, when I was a boy."

"No time like the present, Doc. I'll run you out. We'll have a look around."

"Furthermore, I haven't got a place to live," I said. "No house, no office suite."

"Matter of fact, I got me a house which I ain't terribly fond of any more. Tell you what, Doc, if it'll give you peace of mind, I'll throw in the house on the side."

"Perhaps we better have a look at it," I said.

"Sure thing! Easily arranged."

Cyrus Lunt spun the flywheel and the engine roared into life. Scrambling deftly as a spider in a web, he cast off the mooring lines. We headed outward into the choppy waters of the bay. The wind was from the north with a cutting-tool edge and I was glad for the shelter of the cockpit despite heavy gasoline fumes, which hinted at danger from carbon monoxide gas. The outer bay was rough. Whitecaps whisked off the curling tops of blue-green waves. Once we were in motion the stink of chum was wafted rearward in our wake where a flock of gulls picked it up and relished it, squawking to each other in delight. A cloud of these graceful powerful white birds followed us all the way to the island. The old *Mary Jane* rolled and bucked and yawed, creaking loudly, but she handled this moderate sea without strain and I thought she could probably weather a hurricane. Conversation was difficult over the noise of the engine, but Cyrus Lunt was hollering at me, describing the oceanography of the half mile of choppy water we were crossing. It was what the fishermen call a "reach," a narrow shallow channel running between a chain of islands on the one hand and the mainland on the other.

We approached Juniper. I could see green spruces and white birch trees, granite ledges, occasional glimpses of emerald lawn, rooftops and chimneys of rambling summer mansions, and the fishing village crowding all sides of a deep indentation of a harbor. It looked much as I remembered from my boyhood, except that everything was smaller and older and lonelier and faintly run-down at the heels. Cyrus picked his way through a cluster of mooring posts, floats, lobster cars, anchored dories, and other fishing boats, now and then lightly sideswiping another vessel in a neighborly sort of way. He throttled down the engine and the *Mary Jane* glided in to that particular one of a mad conglomeration of jetties, piers, floats, and docks that she called home.

We scrambled up a ladder and walked through the village. I doubt if anything had changed here in a century. It was a salty and earthy mess of a village, untidy as the wind-blown hair of some old mad lady. At the edge of town, on a rise of ground, slightly on an angle like a top hat on a tipsy drunk, was the house of Cyrus Lunt. It was creaky and old. The porch sagged; the timber was rotting; the roof leaked; the plaster was cracked; and the house hadn't seen a coat of paint in twenty years. But, somehow or other, I fell instantly in love with it. I could tell home at a single glance. If I wanted a fancy house I should have gone to the suburbs. Cyrus Lunt could tell that I had risen for the bait.

"She ain't a castle, Doc."

"Castles I don't need," I said.

"She gives you a kind of a cozy feeling, right in here," he said, sentimentally touching his bosom. "Sort of a setting-down, take-it-easy, make-yourself-comfortable, living little old place, ain't she, Doc?"

"Badly in need of repairs," I said.

"Ain't we all?" said Cyrus Lunt.

"Well . . ."

"House and boat for the car, Doc, even up," he said. "I'm taking a financial licking here, but I got a soft heart, and it would make me feel proud to give a fine young feller a good start in life."

"And furthermore, you fell unrationally, unreasonably, and romantically in love with the Thunderbird."

"And you been struck with the house. Just look at that view."

The house wasn't worth very much, but it was indeed a million-dollar view. From the front porch, which sagged, the hillock tumbled downward. Over to the left was a tiny jewel of a crystal lake; to the right, a proud virgin stand of forest; in the middle distance, the picturesque fishing village and the harbor; beyond was the sparkling reach and still farther the soft blue hills of the mainland.

"I do need a house and I do need a boat," I said. "Provided, of course, I decide to settle here at all."

"And I do need a Thunderbird, provided I don't decide to give up the finer sporting things in life and roll right over and die."

"On the other hand," I said, "the car is in perfect condition, which cannot be said for either house or boat."

"It's no small matter to deprive a workingman of his home and his means of earning a livelihood at the same time," said Cyrus Lunt. "I was born upstairs, sonny, and married twice downstairs and my grandfather died beside the kitchen stove. It takes a lot of living to make a house a home and nothing but gas and oil to drive a car."

"It's hard to put a price on sentiment," I said, "but of course you understand that the sporting life comes high."

"I'm a working fisherman. What would I do without a boat?"

"No," I said, "it's not a wise transaction. Why don't you take me back to Rockport Falls?"

Silently, we went back across the reach together. I got into the Thunderbird. I touched the horn. It gave a pleasant sporty two-toned blast. Two long-legged young ladies in slacks, walking down the main street of Rockport Falls, turned around and stared, not at Cyrus Lunt and me, but at the car. Cyrus kicked the right front tire again.

"Goes pretty rapid, does she, Doc?"

"Hundred and twenty miles an hour. No strain," I said.

"Hell on gas, I suppose."

"Runs entirely on her reputation," I said.

"Not very practical," he said.

"No, and not a very promising location."

"The county courthouse is just around the corner, Doc," said Cyrus Lunt. "Won't take more than five or ten minutes to formalize the deal. That is, providing you got clear title to this automobile."

"I presume you have clear title to the house and boat?"

"Doc, we'll both regret it."

"No doubt," I said. "So why don't we get this over with, fast, before common sense takes over and we change our minds?"

The transaction was quickly and casually accomplished at the county courthouse nearby. I handed Cyrus Lunt the keys to the Thunderbird and he gave me house and boat keys.

"Doc," he said, staring at his new shiny acquisition, "how do I start this thing?"

"Put the key in the ignition. Turn it. Put the lever in the drive position. Step on the gas. By the way, how do I start the *Mary Jane?*"

"Brother," he said, "if you can handle this machine, you can handle the *Mary Jane.*"

He started the car, sounded the horn, and the last I saw he was zooming down Main Street, waving at the girls. I took my luggage to the *Mary Jane,* managed to start her, and managed to get her safely across the reach, although we did a bit of wandering. When I reached the harbor mouth I ceased my navigational attempts and let one of the grinning fishermen tow me in and tie me up. There was a crowd of curious bystanders around the wharf. I pushed through them and carried my belongings to my new home, conscious of following eyes. I settled myself and then I wandered down to the grocery store to lay in some provisions. It was a true general country store, a dark cluttered museum smelling of horehound, molasses, smoked fish, and long winter underwear. You could buy almost anything here except, possibly, a Thunderbird.

"You the new doc?" asked the man behind the counter.

These things get around. I had only just arrived, but I was well known. I told the man my name and was informed that his was Wellington.

"You just transacted business with Cyrus Lunt and got yourself his boat and house."

The transaction had just been accomplished, and Cyrus Lunt was on his way to Boston in the Thunderbird, to the best of my knowledge. I didn't see how Wellington could have known all this. Obviously the island's grapevine was a long strong hardy plant and I suspected that this general store was at the root of the vine. Perhaps the sea gulls carried messages.

"Yes," I admitted. "I own Mr. Lunt's house and boat and he owns my Thunderbird."

"Roof leaks," said Wellington. "Foundations ain't much good."

"I've noticed," I said.

"The *Mary Jane's* quite liable to sink at any time."

"I intend to make repairs," I said.

"Thunderbird," said Wellington. "That's one of them new fancy souped-up models put out by the Ford Motor Car Company, ain't she? Runs about five thousand per?"

I acknowledged this for a fact.

"Mister," said Wellington, "you've been took!"

I later discovered that Cyrus Lunt had taken only a brief joy ride in my automobile and then had sold her later in the day and with the money had been able to purchase for himself another boat and another house on Juniper Island. The house and the boat were smaller than mine, but newer and in better shape. Young men didn't care for island life and were gradually drifting to the cities, leaving only the old-timers behind, so fishing boats were lying on beaches for lack of men to use them, and you could have picked up half the houses in the village for back taxes alone. Nevertheless, I was satisfied. I liked the house and boat I had, and, after all, on Juniper Island, who needs a Thunderbird?

"Are you really a doc?" Wellington asked me.

"Sure," I said. "Why not?"

"Sonny, you look a little young to me!"

There are times in the career of any young physician when he wishes it were the days of old Vienna when every young physician grew a beard for just this reason.

"Got my credentials in my bag," I said.

"I'll accept your word," said Wellington. "What's new for the liver, Doc?"

"That depends on the liver," I said.

"I feel a mite run down and poorly at this season of the year. Think maybe I need a tonic?"

"I think maybe you need a good physical checkup first."

"Well, if you think so, go ahead," said he.

"Mr. Wellington," I said, "I would rather not do a physical examination in the middle of your grocery store. This is the sort of thing to be done in the office, when I have an office, but it will be two or three weeks before I am equipped and open for business. Can you wait?"

"In the office, I suppose you'll charge me three to five dollars for the job?"

"Very possibly."

"I can wait, sonny."

So I took my groceries home without examining Mr. Wellington's liver. Cyrus Lunt's possessions were still all over the house, just as he had left them, but I figured somebody would pick them up sooner or later. I cooked supper for myself. I'm not such a bad cook if I don't lose the can opener.

After supper I stoked my pipe and sat out on my own front porch, enjoying the pleasures of the property owner. The sun was sinking in a blaze of screaming red and orange cloud while other sectors of the sky were an astonishing light clean blue. The wind had dropped and the reach was a glassy mirror, reflecting red and orange sunset overtones. Weary lobster boats chugged homeward towards the harbor. In the crystal air a few gulls, feathers dusted pink, were wheeling to some island nest.

In the cities, I thought, the crowds were fighting their way to the suburbs. In the hospitals, evening admissions and emergencies were beginning to pour in. Suburban doctors were just starting on a hectic round of pre-supper house calls. And here was I, sitting on my own porch with nothing to do. How had I earned such a luxury? Doctors are too busy for peace, quiet, and the sunset. Doctors are brusque and tired, overwhelmed, too busy to think. How can they help others who themselves have never learned to live?

The burnished copper ball of the sun dipped below the western hills. I saw a bat angulating through the dusk. I heard a field mouse squeak: it was quiet enough for that. Beneath the inky surface of the ocean, unseen marine creatures were eating each other and, when not eating or being eaten, were spawning to produce the food for the next generation. Life feeds on life. Lots of violence and bloody death going on out there, and all so quietly! In my generation, doctors and patients worry about the significance of pain and suffering. Couldn't a man understand these things better while looking at the sunset? The sun goes down, the moon comes up, the tides rise and fall, no matter what happens to the individual.

I found myself thinking of the poet Robinson Jeffers, once a favorite of mine before I had become ashamed to admit that I like poetry. This poet, I had read, carved himself a rock house in a cliff overhanging the ocean, where he lived a hermit existence. I suppose this is the equivalent of island life. In his solitude, the poet had spawned a dark and bitter philosophy: that the beauty of nature is marred only by the destructive futility of the human equation; that nature is heartbreakingly beautiful and will so remain even when there are no more human hearts to break. Is this why people live on islands? To get as close as possible to the beauty in the few precious moments that remain?

These thoughts were too dark and bitter. I was young, full of energy and faith in the future and myself. Furthermore, I have a sense of humor and an appreciation for the ridiculous absurd. As long as man can laugh at himself, things can't be too grim. From what I had seen of islanders, such as Cyrus Lunt and Mr. Wellington, there was humor in the life out here: another good reason for choosing Juniper Island. I knocked out my pipe on the porch railing and went upstairs to bed.

I had inherited a feather bed and I sank into it as if into some tropical lagoon. At first it was frightening, as if I might drown in my own bedding, but then a delicious warmth and luxury crept over me. No man could have insomnia in a feather bed. I closed my eyes and fell asleep like an anchor dropped into the harbor.

* * *

Along towards morning I was awakened by a knocking and a banging on the house. At first I thought it might be a shutter flapping in the wind, but I could distinguish distant voices:

"Doc, hey, Doc!"

I swam out of my feather bed and lurched to the window, shivering. My watch told me it was 3:00 A.M. It was black as the proverbial pit and cold as that appendage of a nun which I shouldn't mention in mixed company. Down below was a cluster of men, some bearing flashlights and lanterns. I identified one as Cyrus Lunt. I realized fishermen got up early and I wondered if Cyrus Lunt had chosen this as the appropriate time to move his various belongings, which were scattered all over the house.

"Hey, is that you up there, Doc?" he called.

"Present and accounted for," I said sleepily.

"Put on your gear and come below," said another of them, whom I identified as Wellington from the general store. "We got business for you."

"My office equipment hasn't come," I said. "I'm not open for business."

"Doc, this ain't my liver; it won't wait a couple or three more weeks," said Wellington.

"Poor old feller's kinda blue and frothy around the lips," said Cyrus Lunt.

It sounded like a heart attack, which certainly wouldn't wait two or three weeks. I put on my clothes and went downstairs. They were waiting on the porch. All hands began speaking at once.

"Ninety-three if he's a day."

"Some specialist told him he had a leaky heart."

"Yep. They said he wasn't going to live and never to set foot in a lobster boat and claimed he'd be dead in a month, and this was around the time my cousin Zachary got married, which was twenty-three years ago, as near as I can recollect."

"Stubborn old coot. Wouldn't take advice from no man."

"Didn't even own a motorboat. Did all his fishing from a dory."

"It was me who thought to look for him. Noticed his dory bumping around the harbor and the poor old feller just setting there, looking stiff, not caring where he was going!"

"Boys," I said, "I'll do what I can, but I don't even have a stethoscope." They looked at one another. Said Cyrus Lunt: "Neither do we, Doc."

What did they do in my profession before Laënnec invented the stethoscope? I guess they rolled up a paper tube. I had a mental picture of the antique print: the Edwardian physician with his neat spade beard, delicately applying an ear to the chest of a prim blushing damsel who was looking the other way. And what if I did find a failing heart? I had no digitalis. Was I supposed to go into somebody's garden, looking for a late-blooming foxglove plant? The fact of the matter was that I could provide nothing but moral support, but at least I could do this. We all went clumping down to the harbor through the darkness. A dory was pulled ashore on a beach at the harbor mouth. In it was the poor old man, bolt upright, stiff and blue, still grasping the oars in rigid white waxy hands. I didn't need a stethoscope for this.

"The poor old man is dead," I said.

"We kinda figured so," said Wellington.

"Yeah," said Cyrus Lunt. "We go on the assumption round these parts that when a feller isn't breathing he's more than likely to be dead."

I remembered how comfortable I had been in my feather bed. "If you knew he was dead, why bother me?" I asked.

"One thing a doctor's good for," said Wellington. "He can sign the death certificate."

I was wondering if they thought that was all a doctor was good for: to sign the death certificate.

* * *

I had work to do while waiting for my drugs, equipment, supplies, instruments, and office furnishings to arrive. There was plenty of fixing to do on the house. I papered and plastered and painted and puttered with cement. The house obviously appreciated my attentions and grew in grace and beauty despite her age.

I also had to fix up my boat, the *Mary Jane*. For this job, it would be necessary for me to get her out of the water, and I didn't know how to go about it. I selected my spot, a sheltered cove just to the east of the harbor where the beach rose sharply to a sunlit meadow. I anchored the *Mary Jane* in the cove and left her overnight while wondering how to pull her from the water. When I returned the following morning, there was the *Mary Jane*, sitting in the meadow on rollers, next to a cow. The fishermen hadn't accepted me yet, but likewise they hadn't turned me down, and they didn't want me to go away mad. They knew I could never get a boat out of the water, so they did it for me, prior to breakfast.

I spent the next few days in the meadow working on the *Mary Jane*, observed by the cow. I scraped off ten years' accumulation of barnacles and slime. I replaced some rotten timbers and caulked up the cracks. I painted her, spick and shiny as a yacht. When I was finished I left her in the meadow. I was hoping my friends would put her back into the water. Several nights passed, but the *Mary Jane* remained in the meadow.

Finally Wellington said to me one day in the general store: "Doc, that meadow you're occupying ain't a municipal parking lot."

"It isn't?" I said innocently.

"That meadow belongs to a nephew of mine. He pays taxes on her regular every few years, whenever they get after him."

"Indeed," I said.

"Yep, and my nephew thinks that if you're converting that vessel into a permanent tourist cabin on his meadow you ought to be paying your share of the tax."

"I was hoping somebody might help me put her back into the water."

"Doc, there's only one way you'll ever get that vessel back into the water."

"What's that?" I said.

"Push," said Wellington.

I returned to the meadow. I noted that the tide was high. There was a pile of logs that the boys had used as rollers when hauling her out for me. I laid a string of logs from the boat down the beach to the water, and then I pushed. At first nothing happened, but I really put my back into the job, and the old *Mary Jane* rolled smoothly over the lip of the meadow and down the declination of the beach, entering the water with a soft splash. I would have been proud of the job except for one feature. I had forgotten to hang onto the mooring line. The *Mary Jane* drifted quickly towards deep water, heading in the general direction of Portugal. I debated swimming for her, but the Atlantic is deathly cold in late September and a swimmer soon goes under from the shock. Fortunately a lobster boat happened by and lassoed the maverick and towed her into the harbor for me. I had given them something to talk about at the general store.

"Pushed her in, by God, and didn't even think to hang onto the mooring line!"

Would they ever trust a doctor who was so obviously lacking in ordinary common sense?

* * *

The day started early on Juniper Island. Long before dawn the harbor resounded with the putter-put-put of marine engines, and shadowy vessels with red and green riding lights worked their way out into the reach, each vessel surrounded by its own cloud of raucous gulls. The weather was clear and fine, and this was the time to lay in a supply of lobsters against a long hard winter when you couldn't get into a boat.

I wonder who first discovered that lobsters are edible? They don't look promising in the natural state. But, when boiled alive in brine, the lobster contains a sweet chewy flesh with an exotic flavor, the best eating morsel that I know. Lobster goes well with ballrooms and pink champagne but it also goes fine with a bonfire and beer. I have heard it said that lobster meat is aphrodisiac, but I guess I won't explore that subject any further.

At one time, I understand, lobsters were so common along the coast of Maine that people used them for fertilizer on potato fields, and the man who ate lobster was too poor to eat anything else. Later there were lobster canneries, and fishermen sold lobsters to the canneries at a penny apiece, no matter what the size. With newer methods of transportation and refrigeration, it became possible to ship the lobster live to great distances, and since that time it has remained a highly desired luxury food. Lobstering is speculative; the price swings rather widely; but in general it's a good living though a tough one.

There's no easy way to catch a lobster. You can't hook them or net them or trawl for them; they won't spawn in captivity and can't be "farmed." They are caught as they have been for centuries: in a lobster trap.

The trap is an oblong box of wooden slats with space between the slats for circulation of the brine. At one end of the trap is a funnel of knotted cordage, pointing inward. The lobster crawls through the funnel with no difficulty to get at the decaying fish chunks inside. Presumably he could crawl out again through the narrow end of the funnel if he could figure what to do with his claws, but he is a stupid slow-witted creature and this problem is beyond him. So he stays in the trap until the fisherman is ready to pull him up.

The lobster prefers a rocky bottom and the best catch is had in dangerous locations, in tricky waters near reefs, rocks, and ledges. Lobstering, therefore, is somewhat dangerous and most fishermen have an inner suspicion that sooner or later they will drown. They are fatalistic about it, and most of them have never learned to swim. Among the speculative features of the trade is the problem of what to do before a storm. If a man leaves his string of traps in the water the storm may blow them away and he will lose his capital investment. On the other hand, if he pulls them from the water he tends to lose several days of fishing.

Most of the lobstering is done by old-timers. Youngsters tend to drift away to the cities for an easier living. It's cold and rough on the water, and there's no time and a half for overtime in a lobster boat. But for those of the proper temperament, there seems to be a lot of satisfaction in the trade. A man pits his strength and his skill against the ocean under beautiful surroundings.

According to the old expression, the fisherman lives in God's pocket. I have not heard this said about those who live in tenements.

* * *

I went over to the library one afternoon. It was my intention to study the history and tradition of my new island home. I thought I might serve my patients better if I understood their heritage.

The island had a rather good-sized library. It was supported largely by the summer colony but, perhaps surprisingly, fishermen are great readers when the weather keeps them out of the boats. They don't go for biography or non-fiction of any kind; a fisherman holds no esteem for facts. A tall story, a good juicy yarn, fast and funny, full of liquoring and good eating and wenching, of cloaks and swords, adventure and romance—this is the stuff to accompany the pipe, the slippers, and the glass beside the fire on a cold winter night.

A sign on the librarian's desk identified her as Miss Winkle. Do I need to describe a librarian? Miss Winkle was of intermediary age, not as young as she used to be but not quite yet at middle age: a sweet shy thing, pale, wide-eyed, wistful, and a little dusty around the edges—in other words, a librarian.

"I'm Dr. van Dine," I said. "New to the island."

"I'm glad you've come. We need a doctor here," she said.

"May I have a library card?"

"You won't need one," she said. "A fisherman might borrow your boat and gear, or steal your lobsters, or cheat you blind in a real estate transaction if the deed would stand up in court, but he would never steal a book. We have no problem with late returns except in the summer, I'm afraid. The natives hate to be in debt, even at a penny a day."

I smiled. "You sound as if you enjoy island life."

"A library is a library anywhere," she said.

"Don't you ever get out of it?"

"I blink in the sunshine. What sort of reading material are you after, Doctor?"

"History," I said.

"In the basement. History in general, or anything in particular?"

"The history of this island, if it has any."

"It has plenty. I hope you don't mind dust."

I followed her towards the basement. I observed that she wore flat loafers, which gave her a sort of slouch, and gray cotton stockings. She had some librarian spread but not enough, in my mind, to require a girdle.

"What time does the library close?" I inquired.

"Five o'clock except on Saturdays when we're open to nine."

"How about cocktails at my place at five-twenty?" I said. "We can discuss good books."

She put a finger across pursed lips and said, "Shush!"

"There's nobody here but you and me," I said.

"This is a library, Doctor," she replied. "Do you want any specific title, or shall I leave you to browse around by yourself?"

"I'd rather browse around with you."

"The Juniper Island section is over here. The most complete and accurate study was done by a local minister, now dead. It is authentic and scholarly, but some find the style a little heavy. The point of view is Victorian and somewhat overmoral."

"Just like you," I said.

"The most readable history was done by a man from the summer colony. I don't recommend it to old ladies. It is racy in style and some of the passages are questionable."

"Just like me," I said, "and yet I note that the two volumes sit side by side together on the shelf in perfect harmony. Five-twenty?"

"I'll leave you down here," she said. "Don't bump your head."

Watching her go up the stairs, I did manage to bump my head on an over-hanging shelf. I have a certain weakness for librarians. They may not be as colorful as chorus girls but they're safer and more literate. The atmosphere in the basement was chilly and damp. I sneezed twice. I went back upstairs with the two recommended titles underneath my arm.

"May I take them out?" I inquired of Miss Winkle at the desk.

She nodded.

"But not the librarian?" I said.

"The books are due in fourteen days," she said.

"Within fourteen days or sooner, I shall return," I said, taking the literature home with me but not Miss Winkle.

At home, I settled down for the afternoon with the history of Juniper Island. According to one of the books, the island was first discovered by Henry Hudson, who stopped here to ship a mast. According to the other, it was discovered by a drunken Indian, and there has been a drunken Indian here ever since. Both books agreed on the original owner, one Colonel Swan.

Swan was born in Scotland in the eighteenth century and came to America as a stowaway at the ripe old age of eleven. By the time he was sixteen he was a millionaire, thanks to an inheritance from a wealthy bachelor by whom he had been employed. Swan was one of those who dumped the tea into Boston Harbor and he was wounded at Bunker Hill. After the Revolutionary War he acquired vast tracts of timberland, Juniper being one of his holdings for this purpose.

Swan knew most of the prominent citizens of the day, among them Lafayette, and once he went to France to visit Lafayette. On this occasion he spent a wild night at the gaming tables and in the morning somebody claimed that Swan owed him two million francs. Swan denied it. He was a wealthy man who could easily have afforded to pay the debt but he re-fused to do so as a matter of principle and was thrown into debtor's prison. He could have bought his way out at any time, and in fact he often paid off the debts of fellow prisoners but never his own. He stayed in jail for more than twenty years. Finally released when the jail was thrown open during a revolution, Swan spent one night of freedom in a party with his old friend Lafayette, but then he voluntarily returned to prison, where he stayed until his death.

Old Colonel Swan was a typical Juniper Islander, it seemed to me. A fighter for freedom but a man so proud and stubborn that he surrendered his own freedom voluntarily on a matter of principle.

I could not resist making a certain parallel between myself and Colonel Swan. I had surrendered the possibility of a promising professional career in favor of island life and this was a matter of principle with me. I am proud of being a doctor, proud of being well trained and modern in my thinking, and I keep myself up to date with medical progress. But I have a private opinion that doctors don't do what we like to pretend we do. There is a small lurking suspicion within me that cries "fool" at medical pretensions. This philosophy is not compatible with the teaching hospital or the suburban clinic.

I think, for example, that we seldom really heal or cure, and that our fancy rituals and formalized techniques often make the illness worse. Of course we have our minor miracles. The miracle drugs are wonderful; new diagnostic techniques are very clever; we can extirpate and transpose human tissue in ingenious ways. But the drugs are tricky to handle; although we can often diagnose the present condition, we frequently cannot predict the future; and surgery will often substitute one disability for another.

The rituals, the drugs, the techniques come and go. What is modern today is obsolete tomorrow. Medicine is not truly a science nor should it be mechanical manipulation with a knife or a pill. The good physician can only be a humanist, I think. The gift is not so much to be clever with the knife or pill but to make a suffering patient smile. The doctor ought to be able to tell his patients that death is as normal as life, that pain is as natural as pleasure, and that the greatest human strength is the ability to laugh and endure in the face of adversity. They're not very good at this in the big teaching hospital or the busy suburban clinic. I thought I could do it better on an island by myself.

At this point my cosmic thinking was interrupted. That's one refreshing thing about my profession: whenever your thinking gets bombastic and overblown, some earthy matter brings you down with a bump.

Coming down out of the clouds, I heard a small voice call, "Help!"

It was a child, a small dirty disheveled urchin, who had wandered into my house.

"Hello, there," I said.

"Are you really a doctor, mister?" I couldn't tell if the urchin was a boy or girl.

"Sure," I said. "Don't you believe it either?"

"Then you better come along with me."

"All right. Somebody sick?"

"Is having a baby sickness?"

"No," I said. "That's natural."

"Then, mister, she's dying natural."

"Your mother?" I inquired.

"Nope. I haven't got a mother."

I wondered if this urchin had sprung spontanteously from the granite ledges of Juniper Island. "What's your name, dear?"

"Martha."

This solved a problem. The urchin was female. "How old are you, Martha?"

"Going on thirteen."

This was surprising. She didn't look more than eight or ten years old. "The Widow Gideon's gone," said Martha. "So you better hurry."

"And who is the Widow Gideon?"

"She's a dirty fat old Indian woman and most of the time she's drunk. She's the midwife on the island. Mister, you better rustle up your bustle and come along with me."

I rustled up my bustle and went along with Martha. We went down into the village and Martha tugged me into a small dark dirty loft over a fish storage shed. There was a bed in the room, entirely surrounded by women, kids, and dogs. I pushed my way through the crowd. The woman was in labor, obviously, and she was bleeding. A glance informed me that the infant was arrested in the breech position; I could just see the feet as the presenting part. The light was poor; dirt and germs were everywhere; I had no instruments or drugs; the only anesthesia available was a bottle of gin; it was several years since I had delivered a baby and I had never delivered one except in the sterile precision of a hospital maternity suite. I couldn't recall the details of breech extraction, but this was no time for details. I just grabbed hold of the baby's feet and pulled. It came out, scrawny and blue, and I thought it was dead. I cut the cord with a pair of old rusty scissors somebody handed me after tying it off with what must have been a bit of old fishing line, and then I tossed the child in the direction of the nearest woman. I was surprised to hear it give a lusty howl. I had no time to consider the infant, for the mother was still bleeding. Shuddering at the thought of germs and dirt and postpartum infection, I had no choice except to reach right in with my bare hands and do a manual extraction of the placenta. I tried to tell one of the women how to squeeze down on the uterus through the lower belly, but she was already doing it. The woman with the baby had already presented it to the mother's breast. I saw no point in this, since it was too early for milk, but I have subsequently read that this old country trick, like many old country tricks, has a firm foundation in fact. Suckling stimulated contraction of the uterus, thereby decreasing postpartum bleeding, which was exactly what we had in mind. The bleeding stopped. I was afraid that the patient might have died and I went around to the front end to investigate. Far from dead, the mother grinned up at me cheerfully.

"Boy or girl, Doc?"

"I don't know," I said.

A murmur of disapproval went around the room: a hell of a doctor who couldn't tell the difference between a boy and a girl.

Martha, my young urchin friend, piped up and said, "Let me take a look, Doc, I can tell!"

Everybody laughed at this, and my mood of tension was broken. I decided that everything was under control, that mother and baby would survive. I did think it advisable that they should both be hospitalized for observation. The nearest hospital was in Rockport Falls on the mainland. The mother firmly vetoed the suggestion.

"We'll be okay, Doc. The Widow Gideon will look after us."

It didn't seem to me that this Widow Gideon had been looking after them very well this far.

"Thanks, Doc," said Martha.

"Any time," I said.

"You done a real fine job," said Martha. "Nearly as good as the Widow Gideon."

I took my departure, thinking about the Widow Gideon. It sounded as if she might be my professional competition on the island, and I wasn't sure Juniper would be big enough for both of us. I decided to find out more about her, so I went to the fountainhead of local wisdom, Wellington of the general store.

"Indian woman," Wellington informed me. "Member of the Wabanaki tribe; they got a reservation twenty miles to the east of here. The Widow Gideon got kicked off the reservation long time back. They don't permit them Indians to drink unless they forfeit their tribal privileges and become American citizens."

"A drinking woman?" I inquired.

"Brother, that old fat squaw's got the most extraordinary taste for gin. There's only one thing she likes better, I suppose."

"What's that?"

"White men. She's married six or eight of them in her day. They don't seem to last very long; all of 'em dead, poor souls; the widow wears them out, that's my opinion. I recollect the last of 'em, poor Gideon; he looked mighty peaked and tuckered just before the end."

"And this woman delivers babies when she isn't drinking gin or getting married?"

"Yeah. She's a midwife, legal and registered. I understand they don't license midwives in this state any more, but they let the old-timers keep on going. I don't know what we'd do on the island without her, as a matter of fact."

Wellington directed me to the widow's house, which stood alone on the eastern seaward exposure of the island, some distance from the village and from the summer colony as well. I found her at home. The Widow Gideon was an enormous person, big-boned and globular. She had a copperish complexion, opaque dark brown eyes, and stringy black hair. She was surrounded by a loud perfumery of gin and was obviously a creature of enormous appetites. She had a certain regal, though raffish, elegance. I was reminded of a gypsy queen. There were no grunts, no Indian "hows" in her speech; she spoke a good Juniper Island twang.

"Madam," I said, "I am the new doctor here."

"Howdy, Doc, welcome aboard!"

"I understand that you're a licensed midwife."

"There's the license hanging on the wall."

It was an official-looking document, dated nearly a generation earlier, and I had no reason to doubt its authenticity.

"Madam, I will concede that you have the legal right to deliver babies."

"Reckon I've pulled out five thousand of them in my time. How about yourself?"

She had the clear edge on me in experience; I had delivered perhaps fifty babies during my internship.

"As one professional to another, I won't criticize your technique," I said. "But I certainly question your judgment on the case I delivered this afternoon. The infant was arrested in the breech position and the mother was bleeding. The placenta had begun to separate. You know what the placenta is, of course."

"We call it the afterbirth," she said.

"You had left the scene. The woman could have bled to death. If you were having trouble, why didn't you call for me?"

"No trouble, sonny. She was in good shape when I left. Figured she'd hold for another hour or two. Most of them breeches hang up for quite some length of time."

"Why did you leave?"

"Had something more important to do."

"What's more important than a bleeding woman with a baby on the way?"

"A bleeding woman with two babies on the way," she said.

"Beg pardon?"

"Twins. Coming fast."

"Oh," I said.

"I came right back after them twins was delivered and found you'd finished the job. What did you use to tie that cord? Bit of old fishing line?"

"It was all I had," I said.

"In my experience, when it comes to midwifery, it pays to be extra clean."

"My equipment hasn't come."

"Feel free at any time to borrow mine," she said. "They say you didn't wash your hands."

"I didn't have time," I said lamely.

"Son," she said, "when you've been at this business as long as I have, you'll find it always pays to take your time and wash your hands."

I was defeated. My face must have showed it, I suppose.

"Cheer up, sonny," she said. "Everything turned out just fine. Would you care to join me in a nip of gin?"

"Some other time," I said.

And I went home. Perhaps there was room on Juniper Island for the Widow Gideon. I wasn't quite so sure about myself. It had been a tiring afternoon, and I was in need of a nip of gin, but underneath my own roof. The gin was waiting for me there, already mixed with vermouth in a pleasant ratio of four to one, already poured in a glass.

"You're late, Doctor." It was Miss Winkle.

"Oh," I said. "You decided to come after all."

"I thought the invitation was genuine," said Miss Winkle. "Since you weren't in, I took the liberty. We're informal on Juniper Island, except in the summertime. What's the matter, Doctor? You look as if you'd been run over by a truck."

"I was. They call it the Widow Gideon."

"A man would be well advised to stay away from the Widow Gideon."

"So I understand."

"You wanted to know the history of Juniper Island, Doctor," said Miss Winkle. "You've just met some of it, in person. She's a rowdy old ruffian, loose around the moral edges, and she drinks too much, of course. Another martini?"

"Please," I said. "Delicious."

"She's got a heart of gold. I can't judge her competence as a midwife, but she can't be too bad. Plenty of babies have been born here, and I can't remember a maternal death. But she's more than just a midwife. She takes care of all the sick, all the old folk, all the lonely people on the island."

"And practices medicine without a license," I said.

"Maybe she does," said Miss Winkle. "But the nearest doctor is on the other side of the reach, and doctors don't enjoy boating on stormy winter nights, and sometimes no boat can get across the reach. What are you going to do?"

"I am going to practice medicine," I said, "and do my best to prevent the Widow Gideon from doing the same."

"Doctor, she's a Juniper Island institution."

"Give me time," I said. "I just arrived."

Miss Winkle smiled at that. She had a pretty smile. "Doctor," she said, "you are interested in history?"

"Yes."

"Then let me tell you an Indian legend. The Widow Gideon told it to me. She came to me one winter night with hot soup when I was in bed with the flu. The widow belongs to the Wabanaki tribe. The name means 'those who dwell nearest to the sunrise.' Once there were hundreds of thousands of Wabanaki in this area. Now only a few of them are left. The Wabanaki tribe began to vanish when Glooskap went away."

"Who?"

"Glooskap, the great and good god of the Wabanaki. His name means 'liar.'"

"This is good?"

"Glooskap was able to tell the truth and a lie at the same time. To an Indian, this is good. A doctor might think so too."

"See what you mean," I said.

"When Glooskap first came to the land nearest to the sunrise there were no people here. All the animals in the forest were alike, the same size and shape, all equally good and equally bad."

"Monotonous," I said.

"Glooskap mixed them up and gave them each identity. He made the moose belligerent and dumb, the bear strong and tricky, the deer swift and curious, the beaver cautious and busy, the chipmunk garrulous and cheeky. He gave the porcupine a set of quills and the skunk a distinctive smell. One day Glooskap created in his own image. He gave it the belligerency of moose, the strength of bear, the swiftness of deer, the caution of beaver, and the cheekiness of chipmunk. This was the Wabanaki brave. Glooskap took the quill of porcupine and made it into an arrow and gave it to the brave. He gave him fire. He taught him how to cure and smoke tobacco, to grow maize and potatoes, to predict the weather, and to understand the speech of animals."

"But the nights were lonely and cold and the Wabanaki brave complained," I said. "So Glooskap took his own image and rounded it out. He added the dumbness of moose, the trickiness of bear, the curiosity of deer, the busyness of beaver, the garrulosity of chipmunk, and the smell of skunk, and he created the Widow Gideon."

"That's when the trouble began," said Miss Winkle. "During the cold winter night, Wabanaki brave and squaw shared the same blanket, and nine months later Wasis came along."

"Whatsis?"

"No, Wasis, the baby god. Wasis was very powerful. He ate from his mother and borrowed his father's strength and refused the gifts of Glooskap. Naturally Glooskap went away mad, and he has never returned. Wasis was stubborn and mischievous and selfish, equally good and bad. He accepted gifts from strangers, which no baby should ever do. Strange people with pale faces and a new god came out of the sunrise, bearing such curious gifts as alcohol, pants, gunpowder, treaties, taxes, tuberculosis, and cruelty to animals. Wasis put on pants and made treaties, paid his taxes, used alcohol and gunpowder, and contracted tuberculosis. So now there aren't many Wabanaki Indians left."

"What's the moral?" I said. "That squaw and brave should occupy separate blankets on cold winter nights?"

"To endure without Glooskap in the land nearest to the sunrise, one must develop a high resistance to tuberculosis."

"And also to taxes, alcohol, gunpowder, and pants."

"It's time for a tipsy librarian to go home," said Miss Winkle. "I am no surviving Wabanaki. My tolerance to alcohol is not high."

"How about your resistance to pants?"

"I'm afraid to trust it," she said.

"Why don't you stay for supper?" I said. "If I can find the can opener?"

"I am very much afraid I have stayed too long."

"You show good sense in avoiding my cooking," I said. "But please stay. One more drink."

"I've had one too many."

"I like your stories," I said. "You're an interesting, complicated, and slightly silly sort of person, Miss Winkle. I want to know you better."

"Only when tipsy," she replied.

"Tell me another story," I said. "I'll have one more drink and catch up with you. Tell me about the Trojan War."

"Why?"

"Because I'm interested in history."

"Well . . ." she said. "This is not proper for a librarian."

"On Juniper Island, I think, one can afford to do away with propriety. At least, I hope so. That's why I came here."

"The Trojan War is a very complicated subject. For this I will need another drink, which will be two too many, and then I'll hate myself in the morning."

"You can blame it all on me," I said. "I am quite proper too, in my fashion."

She regarded me owlishly. "Yes, I suppose you are, and I don't understand it. Why aren't you married, Dr. van Dine?"

"Dan."

"Well, Dan?"

I mixed up two more martinis. "That subject is far more complicated than the Trojan War. How about yourself? You weren't born to be a librarian."

"Once upon a time," she said, "there were three dames. One was powerful. One was wise. One was beautiful. The powerful one was greedy and she also wanted to be beautiful. The wise one was vain and hoped that beauty was more than just skin deep. The beautiful one, of course, was dumb. They were jealous of each other. They competed with each other and got into an argument, as three such dames are apt to do. A nice young boy was passing by, and they seized on him to judge the competition."

"An innocent bystander."

"Men usually are," she said. "The competition was not fair. This is frequently the case when jealous women are concerned."

"Bribery," I said.

"The young man had to choose between power, brains, and beauty. Being young, he chose beauty, of course."

"Which started the war," I said. "If I remember correctly, Paris struck the great Achilles in the heel and was later himself struck down by a poisoned arrow."

Miss Winkle took a sip of her martini. "If he was middle-aged he would have chosen power, I suppose."

"And if he was old he would have chosen wisdom," I said. "Three ages of man. And yet I have the feeling that man doesn't make the choice. Woman chooses him."

"So?" said Miss Winkle, finishing the martini. "Then what's the matter with you?"

"No ambition," I said. "Lack of zeal. I am good for nothing, I'm afraid."

"If I don't go home now I will soon be telling you what you are good for."

"I found the can opener," I said.

"You'll find all sorts of things if you keep looking," said Miss Winkle. "Thanks for the gin. Good night."

Miss Winkle weaved in the direction of the door and vanished out of it. In a moment her head popped in again.

"One thing you're good for: a doctor, right here, on Juniper Island," she said before vanishing again.

The next time the head popped in she said, "Don't let the Widow Gideon vanquish you, nor the hostility, stubbornness, and pigheaded pride of the inhabitants. Remember you need fortitude to survive in the land nearest to the sunrise now that Glooskap has gone away."

The next time her head appeared I said, "Please don't play jack-in-the-box. You're making me giddy."

"And furthermore, remember, although we do need you, we also need the Widow Gideon."

"Miss Winkle," I said, "if you'd only . . ."

"One last word," she said. "Please don't play doctor any more until your equipment and supplies arrive, or you'll make some horrible mistake. Remember, we have done without a doctor on Juniper Island for several centuries. We can last a few more days."

"I hope my equipment will arrive in the morning, and then I'll really begin to operate," I said. "In the meantime . . ."

But she was gone again. I went to the door and hollered out into the darkness, "Miss Winkle! Oh, Miss Winkle!"

But Miss Winkle was making like Glooskap. She did not return. In the morning my supplies arrived and I was too busy to think of Miss Winkle. I was in business at last.

Part 2

The First Winter

THE OFFICE WAS READY: shiny instruments of stainless steel, clever diagnostic gadgets, enough surgical supplies and pharmaceuticals to stock a corner drugstore. There was only one small difficulty: nobody rang the office bell.

A fisherman slipped on a piece of kelp and broke his ankle; the Widow Gideon trussed him up in a splint. An infant developed high fever in the night; the mother called Wellington of the grocery store, who brought over a proprietary known as Save the Baby; it worked and the baby was saved. If a man got gas pains around the heart he took a swig of hot whiskey. If a woman developed cramps of the lower belly she brewed hot ginger tea. If somebody died they called the undertaker. Nobody thought to call for me.

I said to Wellington, "I'm ready for your liver now."

"Feeling better, thanks just the same," said Wellington. "Reckon I'll let her go till spring."

I said to Cyrus Lunt, "You look sick today. You ought to see a doctor."

"Yeah," said Cyrus Lunt. "I'll make an appointment with one of them specialists at the clinic in Rockport Falls."

When I returned the history books to the library I said to Miss Winkle, "Don't you ever get migraine headaches?"

"Aspirin works very well," she said.

When I finally got my first patient it was a doll. The urchin named Martha brought it in to me; some of the stuffing was extruded from one of the feet.

"Mister, can you fix my doll?"

"I'll try," I said. "Please bring the patient into the examining room."

I laid the doll on my examination table.

"She's awful brave. She won't cry," said Martha.

"I'll be gentle," I said. "What's her name?"

"She ain't got one."

I applied my stethoscope to the chest of the doll. "Can't hear a thing," I said. I tried to examine the throat but the mouth, being only a stitching of red cotton yarn, wouldn't open. "Nothing here," I said. I shook the doll's head. "Nothing inside at all but fluff," I said.

Martha giggled.

"Ah," I said. "Here's the trouble: stuffing extruding from the right great toe."

"Serious, Doc?"

"You brought her just in time."

I gravely painted the toe of the doll with red Merthiolate antiseptic and sutured it with my surgical needle and thread. I put on a prominent bandage.

"Good as new," I said.

"I know what," said Martha. "I'm going to name her Dan."

"You can't do that," I said.

"Why not?"

"It's a boy's name."

"It's your name, ain't it?"

"Yes."

"Then it's good enough for her," said Martha. "How much do we owe you, Doc?"

"How much have you got?"

Martha examined the grubby contents of a pocket: two pennies, an old dead starfish, and a used piece of chewing gum.

"The fee is a penny," I said. "Now you run right down to Wellington's store and get a penny lollipop for Dan. That's his reward for bravery. He didn't cry a bit."

"She," said Martha.

"And in case she's still too sick for lollipops, give it to the mother instead. That's you."

Martha giggled again. "You're funny, Doc," she said. "Don't go away. I'll be back with some more business for you pretty soon."

Martha was back within the hour with another patient, a live one this time, a male urchin somewhat smaller and grubbier than Martha.

"It's the same sort of case, Doc, and I reckon you can handle it," said Martha. "You done such a fine job on Dan."

"I'll try," I said.

"This here is my brother John. Go into the examination room, John, and let Dr. Dan fix you up good and proper."

"Don't want to," said John sullenly.

"John's a sissy, Doc," said Martha. "All the time, he cries."

"He isn't crying now," I said.

"He doesn't dare," said Martha. "You go on into that examination room peaceable and prompt, John, or I'm going to let you have it again."

John went into the examination room, prompt and peaceable. I looked him over. He had a bruise and abrasion of the right lower leg. It looked suspiciously as if somebody might have kicked him in the shin.

"How'd you get hurt, John?" I asked.

"He don't know," said Martha.

"I was asking John," I said.

"I don't know," said John.

I washed and cleaned the abrasion and put on a dressing.

"Poppa gave me three dollars for the fee," said Martha. "Is that enough?"

"Yes," I said, "but . . ."

"See you later, Doc," said Martha, departing, taking her brother.

She was back shortly with a child of her own size. "This here is William, who lives next door to me," said Martha. "He thinks he's pretty tough."

"He looks pretty tough," I said.

"Doc, she hit me," said William.

"Martha!" I said reproachfully.

"With a pop bottle, Doc," said William. "Right on the head. Got me a bump."

"Tell him you earned it," said Martha.

"Reckon I earned it, Doc," said William.

I examined William's head, and he had certainly earned himself a bump. There was nothing to be done for it, so I dismissed him, but I managed to collar Martha before she could escape.

"Young lady, you're a bad girl."

"Yeah?"

"Yeah. You kicked your brother in the shin and hit your neighbor with a pop bottle. You know that isn't proper, respectable, or ladylike."

"I done it for you, Dr. Dan."

"Well, please don't!" I said.

"How you going to make a livelihood without patients ringing on your office bell?"

"Martha, I don't need you to supply me with patients," I said. "One more episode of this kind, and I'll tell your father."

"Poppa knows all about me," she said.

"Well then, if he won't spank you, I will," I said. "Now git!"

She got. I must confess that I was a little sorry that she did not come back.

*　*　*

The foliage developed fire: leaves of scarlet, crimson, magenta, sharp yellow, flaming orange. There was a mellow smoky smell in the air and the sun was pale. The fishermen left their boats and put on flaming checkered flannel shirts to match the foliage, oiled their guns, and called the dogs, who were already calling to them. Hunting season had arrived in the state of Maine.

A couple of the local gentry, father and son, jumped the mark and went deer hunting a couple of weeks before the season. Fish and game laws are something islanders study carefully only in order to violate. It's legal if you don't get caught, according to the local point of view.

They chose a small neighboring island, uninhabited by man but populated by a small family of deer. The son took position at the edge of a meadow. The father went into a dense thicket of alder scrub in order to rouse up the deer and drive it in the direction of the son. The father had a mild chronic intestinal complaint, a form of colitis, and conditions of excitement often brought on an attack of diarrhea. Having faced this situation before in other seasons, he came prepared. Whenever he went hunting, he always carried a few sheets of toilet paper with him. He smelled deer shortly after the deer smelled him. Feeling the familiar rush of gas pains in the belly, he paused to relieve himself. The flash of white toilet paper looks not unlike the white tail of a deer when viewed at a distance in the shimmering light of late afternoon in autumn. The son raised his gun and fired. The father gave a cry and collapsed. The horrified son discovered the horrifying situation and he summoned help. For some reason, perhaps because the Widow Gideon was otherwise engaged, they called for me.

I found the man lying where he had fallen. He was in poor condition. The blast had shattered his upper femur and severed the femoral artery on that side. I gave him a couple of bottles of plasma and worked over him for quite a while before I dared to move him. My Korean battlefield experience and modern equipment stood me in good stead. A majority of the male population of Juniper had gathered on the scene before I was finished and my heroics were performed before a sizable audience. Finally we improvised a stretcher out of boat hooks, belts, and shirts; we took him to the water, out to a boat in a dory, and over the reach to the hospital in Rockport Falls. Fortunately the patient managed to survive. He didn't even lose his leg, although this was owing to the skill of the surgeon at Rockport Falls and not to me. As we were crossing the reach I overheard a conversation between Wellington and Cyrus Lunt.

"Young Dr. Dan done a damn fine job!"

"Sure did. If I ever have me a bad shooting accident, brother, I want to call on him."

I thought my reputation on the island was established, but still the office bell didn't ring. They'd call on me whenever there was a bad shooting accident, but shooting accidents are rare. For anything else, of course, they'd call the Widow Gideon.

* * *

I believe it always rains on Hallowe'en, a cold blustery miserable night when dead leaves scurry along the pavement like witch feet and branches scratch at the window like the fingers of skeletons. I bought a large pumpkin at Wellington's store and carved the most horrible face I could conjure. I laid in a supply of apples, nuts, and goodies for the little ones.

The crowds of little hobgoblins went around, tricking and treating, far more scared themselves than they were liable to scare anybody else. Not very many of the small ones rang my bell. It was my thought that they, and perhaps their parents, were still afraid of me, and I found this depressing. They were not afraid of the Widow Gideon. Small spooks always ended the evening at her house, although it was isolated and remote and not far from the cemetery. She fed them large quantities of strange Indian food and entertained them with dubious Wabanaki witchcraft. Some years, I believe, the Juniper Island P.T.A. attempted to declare the widow's place off limits. According to rumor, small spooks sometimes came home smelling of gin.

Late that night, when all spooks, large and small, should have been in bed, I had a frightening experience of my own. It started with the usual knocking at the door. A young fisherman with a lantern summoned me to attend his father, whom he believed to be dying of a heart attack. The patient was in serious condition, in shock, with severe chest pain. At first glance it seemed like the very common coronary heart attack, but the pain was too severe and showed unusual radiation downward. Despite clinical evidence of shock, I found blood pressure in the right arm high. I thought to try it on the other arm where blood pressure was lower, and then I tried it in the legs, where I found no pressure at all. I thought I knew the diagnosis: the so-called dissecting aneurysm of the aorta. In this condition, the lining of the great arterial trunk splits and tears along the longitudinal axis of the vessel. The condition is extremely painful, progressive, and almost invariably fatal. There is no specific treatment. All I could hope to do was alleviate the patient's pain. He was a courageous man. He remained fully conscious and despite his agony was able to smile and joke with me, though fully aware that he was dying in the most painful manner. I gave him morphine and morphine and still more morphine, up to the level of tolerance and beyond it. After some hours he lost consciousness and almost immediately died. I thought it more than likely I had killed him with the morphine. If my diagnosis was correct, my action was fully justified. If a condition is fatal, the doctor can scarcely be criticized for relieving the patient's pain at the risk of hastening the end. On the other hand, if this was some other condition such as a coronary where the patient had good expectation of returning to active useful life if he could survive the initial acute attack, I might have made a serious error.

For my own piece of mind, I wanted to be sure and I felt I had to ask permission from the wife to do an autopsy.

She was waiting in an adjacent room with her son. I felt sure she must have known her husband had been a dying man, as he knew it himself, and I thought she knew that he had died from the silence in the next room and the fact that I had finally quit the bedside. I therefore gently asked her for the autopsy permission. She didn't answer me. Her face turned gray and beads of cold perspiration burst out on her forehead, so that her face looked much the same as her husband's had done. She clapped a hand to her left breast. Her son put out an arm to support his mother, but she seemed to drop out from under it, sliding to the floor where she lay motionless. I bent down and groped for a pulse at her wrist but could find none. I tore open the front of her dress and applied my stethoscope to her chest and heard no sounds. Apparently she also had died: a heart attack from emotional stress, presumably, a cardiac arrest. In a case of this kind, where a heart abruptly stops without the premonitory warnings of organic disease, the patient can sometimes be revived by cardiac massage. Cardiologists speak of "hearts too good to die." If prompt action is taken, some of these people will live normally for years. What I had to do was brutal, but I knew I had to do it. I reached in my bag, pulled out my surgical tools, and, with my largest scalpel, I opened the woman's chest with a slashing butcher stroke. I spread the rib cage as well as I could, slid my bare hand inside, grasped the heart with my fist, and squeezed it. Under my fingers, I could feel the heart muscle recover tone, and the heart picked up a spontaneous beat for a few minutes. She breathed a number of times and once I thought her eyelids were flickering open. The recovery was brief, however. The heart went flabby again and I couldn't start it. She too was dead. I quit trying and stood up, dripping with her blood. The son had been staring at me, wide-eyed and aghast.

"Sorry," I said inadequately.

"Doc, you ought to be." Each word was cold and distinct as a funeral bell.

"Mister, I didn't enjoy myself," I said. "But I couldn't just leave her dead without a try. Some people have been saved this way."

"Dead's dead, it appears to me. Maybe you like cutting people up."

"In her case, I was trying to save a life. In his case, I need to know the cause of death. I can't help him, but this could help the next such case I see. Now I must ask your permission to do an autopsy on both of them."

He tore open his shirt and thrust his bare chest at me. "Want to carve on me, Doc?"

"You don't understand."

"Reckon I don't. We need a doctor in this town, but I ain't sure we need a butcher here."

I would have preferred him to spit at me. I gathered up my bloody instruments. I saw no way to communicate with him.

I was shaken by this episode, and I didn't eat or sleep very well for the next few days. Hallowe'en had passed. Ghouls and hobgoblins had returned to the shadows, and the Indian summer sun was warm but it didn't warm me. On the day of the double funeral, I was sitting on my front porch. I could hear the church bell tolling each year for each of the separate lives. My eyes were down. I was aware that a small friend had joined me on the porch, but I couldn't look at her.

"Hello, Dr. Dan," said Martha.

"Hello," I said.

"Don't care much for funerals, so I didn't go," she said.

"Me neither."

"I hear tell you had yourself a pretty rough time, Dr. Dan."

"I hear tell they're discussing butchery down at Wellington's store," I said.

"Not around me, they're not!" said Martha ferociously. "They wouldn't dare! Doc, you ain't going to get paid for that case."

"I didn't expect it."

"So therefore I collected your fee for you and brung it over, even though it ain't in cash."

"Martha, please stop interfering in my business."

"I only try to help."

"I understand but I don't want your help," I said, "especially in this particular case."

"Well," said Martha, "if that's the way you feel, Dr. Dan, I guess we'll have to drown him!"

"Drown whom?"

"Doc, you'll never know what I'm talking about if you won't take a look at us."

I looked at her for the first time. In one hand she held the end of a piece of rope; at the other end of the rope was an object.

"This here is a dog," she said.

Indeed, it did look like a dog, although God only knows what kind of a dog. It was a puppy in the gangling affectionate stage. The bloodlines were, to put it mildly, mixed.

"Martha, where in the hell did you get that dog?"

"Used to belong to him and her, them two they're ringing the funeral bell for."

"Take him home."

"Ain't got a home any more."

"How about the son?"

"He hates dogs almost as bad as doctors. This poor feller ain't got any place to go."

"Why don't you take care of him?"

"Can't," said Martha. "Got to take care of Poppa and John. I also got two dogs and a cat and a goldfish and a turtle and a little alligator from Florida occupying the bathtub. Poppa says we ain't got no more room. Besides, Doc, this is your fee. If you don't take him we'll have to drown him, I suppose. You could learn to love him, Doc. He ain't much to look at, I agree, but he's got a friendly nature."

"I wouldn't want you to drown him."

"Poppa'll be glad to do it."

"Dog, are you in the mood to be drowned?"

He looked at me and started to wag, commencing at the tip of the tail and working upward until his whole hindquarters were involved. Then he leaped at me and tried to lick my face.

"He knows that he belongs to you," said Martha. "He won't be any trouble. You can feed him anything and he'll sleep most any old place. When he's six months old you gotta get him a license. Poppa'll gladly pay the license fee if you can't afford it, Dr. Dan."

"I can afford the fee," I said. "What's his name?"

"He ain't got one, so far as I know."

Martha left the porch. I took the rope off the dog's neck, hoping he would run along after Martha, but he preferred to stay with me.

"All right," I said. "You win. This is your home. Come in." He came in with me. "Care for a bite to eat, chum?"

This dog was always interested in a bite to eat. I fed him my lunch, which I hadn't had the heart to eat myself.

"Partner, you need a name," I said. "I ought to call you Butcher, or Cardiac Arrest, or Dissecting Aneurysm of the Aorta."

He didn't seem to care for any of these names.

"You look like a slob to me," I said.

At this he gave an affectionate leap.

"Slob?" I said.

He leaped again.

"That's a hell of a name!" I said. "Can't we do any better?"

He didn't think so, apparently. From that moment on, he only answered to the name of Slob.

* * *

Still insecure from my moment of butchery, I was called upon to perform similar bloody heroics almost immediately. The patient was a child with a severe acute tracheobronchitis, what most people call "the croup." The parents had ignored it for a couple of days, hoping it would go away, but the child was becoming progressively and rapidly worse. They decided to take her to the clinic in Rockport Falls. The father was just starting the engine of his boat when emergency conditions developed. The child was strangling. She fought for breath; her face was blue; each gasp seemed likely to be the last. The usual crowd of helpful bystanders was hanging around the wharf. One of them ran for the Widow Gideon. Another ran for me. Perhaps I was in better running condition than the Widow Gideon; at any rate, I got there first.

The emergency was extremely real. The child's larynx was almost closed from infection and edema and she was on the verge of strangulation. Despite the urgency of the moment, I did take time to explain to the parents what was necessary as an immediate life-saving measure: a tracheotomy, an incision into the windpipe below the point of obstruction. There was no argument from them. The urgency was obvious, even to the most casual observer. Taking just a moment longer, to douse my hands in alcohol and pull on sterile gloves, I did the tracheotomy on the deck of the fishing boat. As I cut through the cartilage ring of the trachea, the child gulped in fresh sweet air through the incision. Instantly she became less blue. She gave a totally angelic smile, which in itself was enough to compensate me for my long hard training years even if I did nothing else in my professional career; then she fell placidly and normally asleep.

I rode across the reach with her, in order to be sure the tracheotomy remained open. We delivered her to the hospital in good condition. They kept her there, of course, for steam inhalation and antibiotics. Within a couple of days they were able to close the tracheotomy, and the child was home in ten days with nothing to show for her experience except a tiny scar on the neck.

"Well, Slob," I said to my dog when I got home that night, "Dr. Dan did a good job for a change."

At the grocery store, I imagine, they were saying, "Young Doc's a good man with kids as well as gunshot wounds."

There were no more gunshot wounds, but now the kids began to come. The Widow Gideon delivered them. After that, when necessary, Momma dragged them in to me. There were the infants, puking and mewling in their mothers' arms, which, if male, frequently pissed on the examiner the moment the diaper was removed. There were the toddlers, sweetly smiling, curious, and unafraid. There were middlers, awkward, shy, and inarticulate, and an occasional teen-ager with pimples, giggles, and confusion.

I had no office nurse. In the beginning I couldn't afford one, and later on I didn't want one. Slob became my receptionist, taking permanent position in my waiting room, greeting the kids. He loved children and they, for the most part, loved him. Slob might not have been the most hygienic medical receptionist but nothing will soothe a frightened child more effectively than an affectionate easygoing old fleabag of a hound. A few of the children were afraid of dogs. Slob was sensitive to this, and he left such ones strictly alone. This became a valuable indicator to me. If the young patient wasn't playing with Slob when I looked into the waiting room, I knew that I would have to see beyond the superficial illness to the neurosis, psychosis, or behavior problem underneath. Often I didn't have to look beyond the mother.

Very occasionally Slob would growl at a child. The mother would complain, but Slob was always right. I get along fine with kids, even spoiled brats, but there is an occasional child who is just plain no damned good: the bullies, the thieves, the liars, the wise guys, and the psychopaths. If Slob ever growled at a child, he was beyond my help. If male, he would know the inside of the county jail at Rockport Falls before he reached fifteen. If female, she would have borne a problem child of her own before she reached this age.

Once, Slob bit a patient. This was a mean young psychopath off a Boston fishing trawler that had stopped at Juniper Island for repairs. Slob had frightened him away, so I did not know at the time what the patient wanted from me. I couldn't permit this sort of thing and I resolved to keep the dog out of the waiting room. Later I discovered that Slob was right again. From my office the patient had gone to the clinic in Rockport Falls and there he pulled a gun on the examining physician. He was after narcotics. Slob was reinstated in the waiting room.

Although a skillful diagnostician of children, Slob was sometimes erratic with adults. He could be fooled by superficial appearance. For example, he growled at the first adult to enter my waiting room. The man did indeed look ominous, sardonic, lean, and cadaverous, dressed entirely in black, like a character out of Edgar Allan Poe. His face was familiar but I couldn't quite place him. He looked as if he should have been an undertaker, except that all Maine undertakers I have ever met have been plump, pleasant, very cheerful men.

"Don't mind the dog," I said. "He's not dangerous."

"Once I threatened to drown this animal and perhaps he remembers me," said my patient. "I don't feel as if I needed an introduction, Doctor. I am the father of the strange child known as Martha."

"Martha's Poppa?" I said. "Welcome. Martha is my best friend on the island, I believe."

"And she is very fond of you. You might never suspect it, but the child is intelligent, and she is literate although she prefers the island idiom and peppers her conversation with *ain'ts*. How will we ever get her into Vassar?"

"Whenever Martha wants to go to Vassar, nothing will keep her out," I said. "I'm afraid I don't know your last name. Martha has never told me."

"Drinkwater."

Suddenly I placed him. "Are you Rufus Drinkwater, the anthropologist?"

"My field is technically known as comparative osteology. I'm surprised that you would have heard of me."

"I think you lectured to my class when I was a freshman in medical school."

"Possibly. I used to do some teaching, although I gave up all that sort of thing some years ago."

Yes, I knew about him. Drinkwater was perhaps the leading authority in his rarefied specialty. He studied bones, the skeletal structure of various races of man, of prehistoric man, of the anthropoids. From his lecture, I recalled that he had done a good deal of medicolegal work. Studying a single bone, he could not only determine whether it was animal or human but could often reconstruct the race, sex, weight, height, and age. He had done some truly remarkable work in identification. Once, given only a femur, he was able to draw a face accurate enough to identify a missing person. In another case, he spent weeks sifting through the contents of an entire municipal dump looking for the bones of a missing heir, and he found them.

"I am trying to write an authoritative textbook on my field, Doctor. I have been at it for the past ten years, and it will take me at least another ten," he told me. "Juniper Island is a good place for this sort of work. Nobody ever bothers me. I only need a steady supply of bone, which the post office is happy to deliver to me as long as they don't discover the contents of my boxes and my crates. I dispose of my material in the bay. The local sheriff suspects me of being a mass murderer, and I realize that I look the part, but he's never been able to prove his case. Doctor, I have a problem with Martha, and I came for your advice, since she is such a good friend of yours."

"I'll gladly help if I can."

"She looks like a boy, and she acts like a boy, but she isn't. As a matter of fact, she's almost thirteen years old."

"I know."

"She is a very good little mother to my son but has no mother of her own. My wife died many years ago. It is impossible for an abstract and intellectual person like myself to be of much guidance to the child and we will soon be facing a problem that I don't know how to manage. Martha soon will become a woman."

"You're thinking of the menarche?"

"Yes. Do you think the child should be told?"

"I do."

"So do I," said Drinkwater, "and this is beyond me. All I know of the human organism is the bone."

"I'll try to explain things to her whenever a logical opportunity arises."

"I would greatly appreciate it, Doctor. What is your fee?"

"There'll be no charge," I said.

"Nonsense," he said. "Although I have lectured in medical schools, I have no medical degree and am not entitled to professional courtesy."

"Martha is a friend of mine."

"Nevertheless you have to eat."

"All right," I said. "Three dollars."

He gave me ten and refused to accept any change. Martha appeared in the waiting room later that afternoon.

"Poppa said you wanted to have a talk with me."

"Sure," I said. "If you're interested."

"About the facts of life?"

"Some people call it that," I said.

"Birds, bees, flowers, and all that sort of gurry?"

"Grown-up men and women and how babies are born is more to the point," I said.

"You mean sperms and ovaries and falling off the roof?"

"Yes," I said. "Have you, by the way?"

"Yep."

"Then maybe you know all about it."

She proceeded to tell me, at some length and in detail, what she knew about the subject, which was considerable. She used the island colloquialisms, but her knowledge was specific and exact.

"Have you been looking in your father's books?" I asked her.

"Poppa's got no books like that," she said. "He don't know nothing about anything excepting bones, and I reckon he knows everything about that."

"How did you find out all these things?"

"From the Widow Gideon," she said. "Anything else you want to know?"

"I guess not," I said.

"There's a couple more questions Poppa told me to ask."

"All right."

"Can you play bridge?"

"Yes," I said, "when I can find time."

"And do you drink whiskey?"

"When I have the time," I said.

"Well," she said, "if you've got the time, Dr. Dan, you come over to our house Friday night at eight o'clock. Poppa needs a fourth for bridge."

I was over at the Drinkwater house Friday night at eight o'clock for bridge that week, and almost every week thereafter. The other two members of the group besides Drinkwater and myself were Willie Harpswell and Josiah Brown.

Willie was the artist, a painter of some reputation. He painted marine scenes in such a way that you could scarcely recognize the sea, the rocks, and the sky. His style was wild and violent, and Willie himself had a certain wild violence in him. Willie, as he promptly told me when I met him, was insane: a manic-depressive. Once a year or so he had spells of hyperactive mania and he would take off for the city on a china-smashing, woman-shocking binge that sometimes landed him in jail. These spells didn't last very long and he would return to Maine in a couple of weeks quite rational. Once or twice a year his mood would swing in the opposite direction, into a psychotic depression state, and he would stay in bed for days in a deep black inactive gloom. His depression states, like his manias, were brief and self-limited. He cheerfully accepted and understood his insanity and refused to seek psychiatric help.

"It's me," he said. "Without my interesting lunacy, I'd be just like anybody else."

During his long stretches of normality, Willie was intensely productive, filling canvas with violent globs of color, attempting to match the dynamic restless moods of the ocean outside his picture window. Willie ground his own pigments from materials found locally, and he guarded his professional secrets. He often painted on canvas that had once been part of the brown weather-beaten triangular sail on the stern of a lobster boat.

Willie didn't live on Juniper Island. Juniper was too crowded and civilized for him. Willie lived alone on a tiny island of his own, originally called Hog Island and still so recorded on the charts, although everybody called it Harpswell Island in honor of Willie. Harpswell Island was a quarter of a mile to the south and west of us, a small high knoll of granite, no more than a few acres big. Willie came to Juniper Island every Sunday morning for church, and every Friday night for bridge, but otherwise he kept to himself. People didn't often try to land on Harpswell Island; it was quite possible that Willie might take a shot at you. The only boat he owned was a sturdy high-sided dory. Wind and wave never bothered him, and he would go rowing in any sort of weather. He was a small fat man with a red face, wind-blown hair, and a wild eye, but he had great courage and muscular strength, and the fishermen admired him.

Willie played bridge as he painted and rowed: with reckless violence. He was an exciting partner and a dangerous opponent, and it was fun to play with him. Drinkwater played a conservative game, deadly on defense, cautious on his bidding, using a mathematician's knowledge of probability to compensate for relative blindness to the personality factors of the game. I play just well enough to get by. Our fourth man, Josiah Brown, was totally unpredictable. Joe knew all the latest fads and conventions; he would frequently quote the book at you and then, with equal frequency, forget to follow his own rules.

I was disconcerted when I was introduced to Joe, for he always wore the dress of a minister, black clerical garb and round starched collar. I had some reservations about bridge and whiskey with a minister, but it was explained to me that the man was no longer in the ministry. He once had been but had resigned. He was in fact a lobsterman, although he wore his clerical clothing even in a fishing boat. The fishermen naturally called him "Holy Joe."

"I lost my faith quite suddenly," he explained to me. "There was a man in my congregation who was a thoroughly good man. He attended all the services, gave liberally to the church, was a good father, husband, and provider, and had no obvious vices, sins, or weaknesses. One afternoon his only daughter was raped and murdered in a sex crime. His wife was so disturbed that she committed suicide. And the very same week the man himself learned that he had incurable cancer. Next door to him was a notorious wife-beater, profligate, and drunkard. And this fellow, that week, won a hundred thousand dollars in a box-top lottery. I searched the Bible for a justification of these events and could find no satisfactory answer. The best I could do was in the Book of Job, where the answers seem more confusing than the problem. How can the futility of the human equation and the obvious injustice of pain and suffering be reconciled with the existence of a benign and loving deity? I tried to preach a sermon on this subject in the church. It suddenly seemed to me that I talked too much. In fact, all preachers preach too much. Said the Lord to Job, 'Who is this that darkeneth counsel by words without knowledge? . . . Where wast thou when I laid the foundations of the earth? Declare, if thou hast understanding!'

"Well, I had no understanding, so who was I to declare? Don't all ministers counsel without knowledge and declare without understanding? Suddenly, I could preach no more. I stared at the congregation and they stared at me and squirmed. There were five minutes of terrible restless silence in the church. Then I walked out and never finished my sentence. The bishop was understanding. He planned to send me to a home for broken-down clergymen. Feeling far from broken down, I offered my resignation and it was accepted, of course. Then I spent a year of Sundays, visiting every type and variety of church, listening from the other side of the pulpit. All of the priests, preachers, ministers, and rabbis were men of good faith, earnest, devout, and sincere. Some were learned and some inspired and some merely enthusiastic, even the few who seemed, like myself, to have lost their convictions. But not one of them could resist a tendency to exhort. Each of them seemed to imply, 'Think as I think, if you wish to be saved!' However, each of them thought differently. All, probably, are right. Otherwise it would be most confusing on Judgment Day. But the sum total of the argument is this: if each man's conviction is correct but different, each man must work out his own conviction for himself. Therefore, you cannot learn conviction in a church. Most people consider this a blasphemy, and for this, Doctor, I apologize. I have no intention to shock or offend, and above all I have no intention to exhort, but my God is a free-speaking, free-thinking liberal deity Who expects man to reason and to think. I feel so deeply on this subject, I can't keep a clean tongue in my head. Obviously, I have no business in the pulpit."

"Then why do you wear the clerical garb?" I was forced to inquire.

"To remind myself that, even in a lobster boat, I must continue to search and to think."

"Did you choose lobstering for any particular reason?"

"Perhaps," he said. "My father is a rich man, and I don't need to work at all, but I think better when my hands are occupied. Fishing is difficult and therefore good discipline for me. Fishing is useful and therefore I don't waste my time."

"He works as hard as the rest of them," Drinkwater explained. "In fact, harder. Most of the men are in church on Sundays while Joe is on the water. On Easter Sunday, even on Christmas if the weather permits, he's the only man in a boat."

"I'm eccentric and just a wee bit mad, like everybody else out here," he said. "All us islanders are hiding, for some reason or other. In my case, fishing seems especially appropriate. Recall the twelve apostles. Were they preachers? Mystics? Religious scholars? Well versed in the religious arts and crafts?"

"We've heard all this before, Doc," said Willie Harpswell. "Joe is trying to say that the apostles, also, were only fishermen."

"Exactly," said Joe. "I'll bid three clubs."

The transition from theology to bridge was a little abrupt for me, but I returned my concentration to the game. I passed. Drinkwater tried a cautious three no-trump. Josiah jumped to a small slam in clubs. Willie Harps-well doubled. Willie made a killer of an opening lead, and we set them fourteen hundred points.

"I don't wish to be blasphemous, but I am quite sure that the apostles did not play bridge," said Drinkwater pointedly.

"Leave all blasphemy to me and confine your thoughts to bridge and bones, Professor," said Joe.

"Your bridge is terrible," said Drinkwater.

"True," said Joe, "but it may improve," and on the following hand he bid and made seven spades.

These three men were more than my constant Friday night companions. They were my first regular adult patients. At least, two of them were: Willie Harpswell was what you might call an "anti-patient" and perhaps this amounts to the same thing. He didn't believe in doctors and made frequent pointed comments about my profession, but I noticed that he frequently asked my advice on medical matters, veiled as a hypothetical question. Willie would have liked regular medical attendance but he was afraid that one of us might stumble on some way to cure his manic-depressive state. He was convinced that his condition was in some way related to his artistic talent. He would have been horrified to wake up some morning sane and unable to paint. Maybe he was right. I would not wish to cure a man at the risk of killing his sole accomplishment or genius.

Drinkwater had hypertension and he reported to me regularly once a month for a blood pressure reading. Personally, I feel that far too much attention is paid, by doctors and patients alike, to the problem of high blood pressure. I could practice just as good medicine, and my patients would live just as long, and more happily, if I threw away my blood pressure machine, but I don't dare. In Drinkwater's case, his hypertension was solely and exclusively a measure of personal loneliness. His wife had died soon after the birth of his second child, and it was then that he retired to Juniper Island. He convinced himself that this was for the purpose of writing his book, but I was not convinced that he ever would, or should, finish it. He was a lonely man and the degree of his lonesomeness was reflected by the readings on my machine. I gave him pills, because he expected them, and after a time the readings were much lower, but I did not ascribe this to the medication. Seeing me in the office and playing bridge with us on Fridays, he wasn't as lonely. Therefore his blood pressure fell. Only a research man would ascribe the improvement to the medicine.

"Holy Joe" Brown was a hypochondriac and came dashing into the office frequently with a new fascinating imaginary disease. He kept me busy trying to disprove his own diagnoses. It was no great difficulty to find the source of his complaints, and he was well aware of this.

"If I ever really find my faith, I'll lose all my symptoms and my diseases and my fears, and I will become a thoroughly healthy man and promptly die of boredom and disappointment."

"If you ever find it," I said, "you'll also remove that costume and put on coveralls and a flannel shirt like everybody else."

"Or else return to the pulpit," he said.

"Maybe. Why don't you go to church? You don't have to listen to the exhortation. You can close your ears and go to sleep like everybody else."

"The Devil gave me open ears and sermons make me mad," he said.

A curious man. Each of my three bridge companions was, in his way, a psychological cripple, I suppose, and perhaps the same could be said for every inhabitant of Juniper Island. And yet I don't know that Juniper Island was in any way unique in this respect. Most physicians could tell you that Horatio Alger and Cinderella are rather rare, that most people have to compensate for disability and failure of a kind. In a time and country where a man is measured by success, where a man is measured by what he does and not what he is, one tries to hide the disability. But my own impression is that failure is more interesting and more significant than success and that man's greatest strength lies in his ability to compensate.

* * *

It sometimes seems that Thanksgiving falls at the wrong season of the year. The Pilgrim fathers were grateful for the harvest. Today, the harvest is taken for granted. We go down to Wellington's store, or the neighborhood equivalent, and plunk down a few dollars on the counter and take home frozen turkey, frozen cranberries, and a frozen pumpkin pie. This is the current harvest. We then proceed to eat ourselves into a state of semi-coma out of gratitude. Our most fatal vice isn't drinking or smoking or even driving automobiles; it's eating. We fork ourselves to death with saturated fats.

It might be more logical on Juniper Island to have Thanksgiving in the spring. Surviving winter is our problem. To have Thanksgiving when the skies are getting leaden and the wind is cold and a few absent-minded snowflakes are sifting through the air seemed a little premature and risky to me.

I bought a small turkey and a frozen pumpkin pie at Wellington's. The turkey lasted nearly a month. This was a far cry from my boyhood with the groaning board, with aunts, uncles, and faintly distant cousins all over the place.

Immediately after Thanksgiving the commerciality of the Christmas season was thrust upon us, even on a remote island off the coast of Maine. I bought my presents early as I always do. A necktie for Dad, which he wouldn't wear. A luxurious bed jacket for my mother, which would please her but which she wouldn't wear because it was too luxurious. For Wellington at the grocery store, a bottle of scotch. The same for Cyrus Lunt, although I don't know why, except perhaps I might want another house or boat someday. A pipe for Drinkwater. Willie Harpswell was a tough one until I had an inspiration and bought him a new set of oars. For Holy Josiah Brown, a copy of the book entitled *The Screwtape Letters*. I nearly bought a doll for Martha until I realized this might have been a fatal error; I substituted a set of lacy lingerie in black after first getting clearance from her Poppa so that my intentions should not be misunderstood. I nearly forgot Miss Winkle of the library; I got her a pen and pencil set. I did forget June until the last moment; June was the young lady in New York with whom I had some sort of loose understanding. My mother and father thought that June and I were practically engaged. I'm not sure what June thought we were. Just a few days before Christmas, I got her a bottle of Wellington's best perfume and sent it air mail; I imagine it wasn't very good and perhaps it smelled like halibut.

The weather grew colder as Christmas Day approached. The thermometer was well below freezing at night and not far above in the daytime. The skies remained leaden; the waters of the reach were the same sullen leaden color; but still it didn't snow. It seemed a shame to go this far north and have a bare Christmas.

I went to the midnight service on Christmas Eve. The little church was packed. I sang the familiar carols loudly and remembered boyhood Christmases. Only Slob was waiting at home underneath my small Christmas tree. When I was an intern, I wondered why we had so many drunks on Christmas Eve, but now I was beginning to understand. When I came out of church after the service it was snowing: the beginning of a heavy fall, small dry granular flakes hissing down out of a black windless night. I encountered Willie Harpswell outside the church.

"Merry Christmas, Doc."

"The same to you, Willie. Do you plan to row home through this blizzard tonight? Won't you get lost on the bay?"

"No more than always, Doc. Tonight I've got to finish my portrait of a hanging man."

"A hanging man on Christmas Eve?"

"It's just another night, without children in the house," said Willie.

On a stone portico not far from the church door I saw Josiah Brown, just sitting there.

"Well, Joe," I said, "did you break down and finally go to church?"

"This is as far as I can get," he said. "I like to listen to the bells."

At that moment the bells began pealing from the clock tower in the darkness not far over our heads. We were too near and the bells were too loud; there was a jangling in my eardrums and on the lower notes my bone marrow was reverberating.

"Bells interest me," said Joe when the clarion had stopped.

"I'm not sure I like them," I said. "They're pretty in the distance, and they can sound jubilant and joyful, but there's no warmth and no color in the overtones."

"I know what you mean," said Joe. "An unearthly lack of human timbre and of sympathy. Always a trace of the Devil in the middle of organized religious joy."

"As your physician, Joe, I should warn you not to sit too long on a cold stone bench at midnight in a blizzard. You'll have pneumonia on Christmas Day."

"My faith shall keep me whole. Merry Christmas, Doc."

It wasn't such a bad Christmas for me after all. I woke bright and early, just as the sun was coming up. The snow had fallen heavily in the night and now had stopped: several clean virginal inches of the stuff sparkling gaily in brilliant sunshine. Slob was barking fit to kill with a joyful note in his clarion. I brushed frost from my bedroom window and saw a scene straight from Currier and Ives. There, astonishingly, was an old-fashioned sleigh, drawn by a sad old horse in a blanket of dull red wool. I didn't know Drinkwater owned a horse. He was getting out of the sleigh and loading his arms full of Christmas packages, a tall dark cadaver in black overcoat with fur-lined collar, dark scarf, and fur ear muffs. Martha was pounding towards the house, closely followed by her younger brother, John. There would be children in my house that day! I slipped on my bathrobe hastily.

"Doctor, I hope you don't object," said Drinkwater, plodding in with his packages. "I consider this an imposition. I think every family should have Christmas morning to itself, but Martha insisted, so here we are."

"Splendid. I'm delighted," I said. A disturbing thought then occurred to me. The packages in Drinkwater's arms contained my present to him and to Martha but none for John. Drinkwater read my mind.

"Taken care of, Doctor," he said behind his hand. "I noticed the omission when I was checking the labels on the packages and corrected it. If you don't mind, you have given John a jackknife. Probably this will give you business, because I imagine he will lacerate his finger within the hour."

Yes, the boy did just that, and I had to take a couple of stitches, but the day was otherwise unmarred. Drinkwater appreciated the pipe, and I wouldn't attempt to describe Martha's expression on opening the box of lingerie. Wellington dropped by in the afternoon with a turkey for me, which was a nice gesture, even though Slob and I had just finished working on turkey soup and turkey hash from Thanksgiving. The best Cyrus Lunt could do was a drink from the bottle I had given him, but this was very generous from a man like Cy. Josiah Brown telephoned me later in the day.

"No pneumonia, Doc, and thanks for the gift," he said. "But do you think this book is for me? I am not a demonologist."

"Read it," I said. "Maybe you are."

The day was over before I could fully savor it, and then almost immediately it was New Year's Eve.

* * *

Our island New Year's Eves are pretty tame affairs. There's no place in particular to go. Some folks have quiet parties in their own homes; many go to bed as if it were just another night. One year is much like the next on Juniper Island.

Accustomed to a wilder sort of night, I was at loose ends with myself, alone with Slob in the house and finding him a rather dull companion. I was delighted when my doorbell rang around eleven o'clock.

"Maybe business," I thought. "A good accident case or a heart attack: anything to break the monotony."

It was my friend from the library, Miss Winkle.

"Oh, hello," I said. "Come in."

"Hello." She stood at the door awkwardly, not attempting to enter.

"Having problems? Come on into the office," I said. "Feeling sick?"

"No."

"Then what's the matter?"

"This is not a professional visit, Doctor."

"My name, in case you may have forgotten, is Dan."

"Dan," she said, "I'm bored."

"So am I."

"Screaming mimis, and four-wall fever. It isn't proper to intrude on you at such an hour, but . . ."

". . . you want a drink?"

"I do."

"You have come to the proper establishment," I said. "Me too."

So at last she entered and sat down in the living room while I mixed up the drinks. Slob put his head in her lap. He approved of her. Still, drinks or no, there was awkwardness between us. She sat primly and stiffly and silently in the chair. I didn't know how to start up conversation.

"Miss Winkle . . ."

"I have a first name too."

"Oh yes?"

"Betty."

"Good. Well, Betty, I . . ."

"Yes?"

"Ready for another drink?"

"We've scarcely started this one yet."

"True. I could turn on the radio. Would you care to dance?"

"Not especially," she said.

"Well . . . Read any good books recently?"

"I only read the dust jackets."

Clunk! Social unease lay between us like glue. So I tried again. "Another new year."

"Yes," she said. "Too many already."

And, clunk, that silence again. Maybe she wasn't ready for another drink. By then, I was. I got it. Then I, too, sat in silence. After all, this dame had come barging into my place, and this was all her own idea, and if she had something to say, let her say it. I had tried to give her all of my encouragement. If she wanted to sit there, silent, stiff, like a clam, well okay!

"You ever seen a stiff clam?" I said.

"I beg your pardon?" she said absently.

"Let it go."

I lit a fire in the fireplace. Maybe this would warm us up. Merry pleasant flames crackled up through the birch logs. I had some dried seaweed. I put it on top. Blue-green coloration was added to the flame, from the copper salts, and just a little flicker of red. What was that? I tried to remember my chemistry. Calcium? Strontium? The burning weed gave off sea smell: faintly acrid, briny, distant aroma of clam flat at low tide. Now we were back to clams again.

"Who is she?" At long last the mountain, having labored, had produced a mouse. Miss Winkle was pointing at a picture on my mantelpiece. I still couldn't think of this librarian as Betty: still Miss Winkle, the stiff, the anti-social.

"Well," I said, "maybe that's my mother."

"And maybe it's your fiancée."

"The lady's name," I said, "is June."

"Pretty."

"The lady or the name?"

"The name," said Miss Winkle. "I can't tell much from a picture alone. And you love her very deeply, I suppose."

"What gives you the right to make suppositions?"

"Oh," she said. "Touchy!"

"I am not touchy!" I said in a touchy and irritable manner. Miss Winkle was down to the ice cubes now. I made her another drink, without objection. And freshened my own. I was boozing rather rapidly, even for a New Year's Eve. And put another log on the fire. And seaweed. And sat down again.

"Happy days," I said.

Miss Winkle nodded.

"Tell me a story," I said. "All about Glooskap and Whatsisname."

"Wasis."

"The same to you."

"Thanks, Dan, for the drink," she said. She had scarcely touched the second. "And the company. Happy New Year."

She got up and started putting on her coat.

"Damn it, Betty . . ."

"Yes, Dan?"

"Nothing," I said. "Happy New Year to you."

"Just like last year," she said. "Just the library."

She perched dangerously on the arm of the chair and began drawing on her snow boots. I believe I had already noted that she had shapely legs. My original impression had not been mistaken. And I was thinking that there hadn't been a hell of a lot of female in my life recently. June was too far away. I got up, went over, kneeled down, and, daringly, pulled off a snow boot.

"Once upon a time," I said, "there were two Russians on a train. You know, the long train ride from Moscow to Siberia. Takes about five days. There were no sleeping accommodations. Just sitting space. In compartments. Our two friends were alone in the compartment together. One was a male. The other female. He sat and stared at her, and she sat and stared at him, and the wheels went clickety-clack, and the long miles went slowly by. Train service isn't very good in Siberia, I understand. Late in the first day the man said to the woman, in Russian, 'Hello.' Late in the second day the woman said to the man, 'Hello.' On the morning of the third day the man got up and grabbed her ferociously and said, in Russian, of course, 'Enough of this love-making! Take off your clothes!' "

"Thanks, Dan, but I can take off the other snow boot all by myself," said Miss Winkle.

"And the coat?"

"And the coat."

So I turned on the radio, and we danced. Not very well. Miss Winkle was stiff. But after a few minutes the room was hot from the fire, and we were both warm, and a bit perspiry, and breathing hard. Miss Winkle's color had risen.

"Thanks, Dan," she said, and she disengaged herself from my arms, sat down, polished off the remains of a lukewarm drink at a gulp. "You're kind to me. Why? Are you more or less kind to everybody? Thank you for the pen and pencil set."

"Oh dear," I said. "And when I think of what I gave young Martha Drinkwater!"

"Exactly what I mean."

"Don't understand," I said, but I thought I did. Everybody knows everything on Juniper Island. So the story of Martha and the lingerie had gone all around, and Miss Winkle must have assumed I thought she was just the pen and pencil type. Seems I had put my foot in it again. With women I often do.

"I was a backward child," I said.

"I'm too forward, and it does me no good," said Miss Winkle. "Once upon a time there was a tribe called the Amazons. They, as you may have heard, were female."

"And rather tough ones, so I understand."

"Too tough to bother with romance and men, except just seasonally for biological purposes, when they swept down from the hills, kidnaped by force a few promising men, returned to the hills, used them sufficiently, then killed them. In nine months, only the female infants were spared. Males were put to the sword."

"I think," I said, "that they amputated the right breast, in order to be better able to swing a sword."

The bells began ringing at that moment. It was midnight. I got up and firmly kissed Miss Winkle on the lips. She kissed me back, just momentarily, and then removed her lips to use them for a little more talk.

"Actually, Amazons are obsolete," she said. "One does not seize a man by force. Even seasonally."

"Miss Winkle, you talk too much," I said.

I tried to kiss her again, but she almost conked me on the forehead, with her forehead, bending down with Amazonian determination, putting on her boots. Then she put on her coat. Then headed for the door. I don't know women very well, but I did comprehend that she was not going to be stopped this time, so I didn't try. I made a bet with myself that she would pause at the door for an exit line. To be certain of getting the last word. She met my expectations.

"Dan, I'm sorry, but I just get so God damned sick of that library!" she said, and she burst out of the door before I could notice that she might begin to cry. Or maybe I was dreaming.

"Good night, and happy New Year, Betty," I called out after her. "Please come again." But naturally she was gone and didn't hear me. "Women are strange," I said to Slob.

He seemed to agree with me.

"Impossible. Nuts. Screwy."

Slob wagged the tip of his tail.

I cleaned up the glasses. I indulged in a short fast nightcap. I put Slob to bed, wishing him the best of seasonal greetings, and I went upstairs myself.

Maybe, I was thinking, I should look up Miss Winkle sometime at my convenience. Maybe in the spring.

Part 3

Spring (if you could call it that)

"MISSED SPRING LAST YEAR," said Cyrus Lunt. "Didn't happen to look out my window between ten and eleven o'clock on the twenty-third of May."

The truth of the matter is that on Juniper Island we have only three seasons. I struggled through February, a cold nasty month, with much respiratory disease and no money. March was a little better, but not much, and a great deal longer. After the long climb up the hill of March, it was April. This, in my definition, should have been spring, but the air was cold and the wind was sharp and the sun was pale. There was only enough hint of springtime to be a disillusionment. Whoever spoke of April as the cruel month must have spent his time on Juniper Island.

Still, nevertheless, there was spring cleaning to be done before the summer visitors were with us. I decided to clean a couple of old hornet nests and cobwebs out of the attic of my life. For example, June, and I don't mean the month: a young woman of my acquaintance. Occasional letters dribbled back and forth between us.

"Why don't you come and visit me in New York?" June wrote.

"Can't," I fired back on a postcard.

"Why in the hell not?" came her postcard back.

So I wrote a long letter describing the obligations of a practicing physician to his patients. I said that if she had any intentions of marrying me this would imply that she would live where I lived, which happened to be Juniper Island, since I did not practice medicine in New York. I suggested that unless she wanted to visit the island we'd better call the whole thing off. I thought this might solve the problem. June loved to ankle down Park Avenue in stilt heels, and stilt heels would stick in the mud in April on Juniper. I didn't think she'd come.

But she telegraphed right back: COMING READY OR NOT.

Well, I wasn't ready, but I did my best. I cleaned my little house from stem to stern. The *Mary Jane* was already in the water with a fresh coat of paint. I even gave Slob a bath. It was his first and he didn't care for it. He was convinced that it would cause him, like the sow, to perish of the measles in the spring, but afterward he looked as fluffy as a spring lamb and felt very proud of himself.

June arrived one day earlier than I had planned. I was down at the harbor, chewing the fat with the boys, when Cy Lunt's boat tied up after a voyage from Rockport Falls. He hollered at me:

"Hey, Doc, you got company!"

"Huh?"

"A dame. Some dame!" With his hands, Cy drew the two double hemispheres in air that classically described the figure of the female. I thought I recognized the proportions.

"Where is she?" I asked.

"Sitting on the dock in Rockport Falls with steam coming out of her ears," he said.

"Why didn't you bring her over?"

"She didn't ask."

June wasn't the sort of woman who enjoyed a wait. I jumped into the *Mary Jane* and whipped across the reach at full throttle. It was a pretty nice day considering. Although the wind was cold, the sun was bright and the sky a deep dazzling blue. The ocean was a screaming combination of deep purple, loud green, and shocking violet, a more violent mixture of the blue-green spectrum than even Willie Harpswell would have dared to paint. I found her on the wharf at Rockport Falls. I couldn't see steam coming out of her ears, but I could tell even at a distance that her mood was not serene. The usual gang was not on the wharf. A lascivious April wind was taking indecent liberties with the edges of her skirt, and I'm sure the boys were watching at a distance, but they didn't dare to get too close. June might have been wearing a sign: DANGER! HIGH EXPLOSIVES!

I clambered up the ladder and walked across the wharf towards her. Her eyes flicked at me and then flicked away. At first glance she hadn't recognized me. Then she looked again.

"You?" she said.

"Who else?" I said. "You was expecting, maybe, Cary Grant?"

"But you've grown a beard!"

True, so I had! Beard cultivation is a reasonable hobby on an island in the wintertime.

"Like it?" I said.

Stupid question. She stared at my beard as if expecting to see rats, lice, and history come crawling out of it.

"And your clothes!" she said.

Clothes? I was wearing a flannel shirt and coveralls and hip-length fisherman's boots. Did she expect me to come across the cold and windy reach in white tie and tails?

"Dan, are you a practicing physician? You look like a fisherman."

I was tempted to reply, as Holy Joe Brown would have replied, "So did

Peter, James, and John, Andrew, Philip, and Bartholomew, Matthew, Thomas, and the other James, Thaddaeus, Simon, and Judas Iscariot."

But I restrained myself. Sometimes I couldn't be sure of June's sense of humor. She was smart and exquisitely groomed as usual. I think there's a shop in New York called the Tailored Woman. If so, June got her clothing there.

"Where is this Juniper Island of yours?" she inquired.

I waved a horny hand in the direction of the ocean. "Setting out yonder where she's always been. We ain't moved her recently."

"Funny! Where's the bridge?"

"What bridge?"

"The one they've got so clearly indicated on the map. How can I get that thing out there without a bridge?"

"That thing" was a Thunderbird convertible, parked nearby. "Once I had me one of those," I said. "Don't do a bit of good on Juniper Island. Suggest you trade her in, lady, for a boat."

"What's the matter with you, Dan?"

"Me? Nothing. Why?"

"Have you gone native? Are you living on the beach?"

"Oh," I said. "Well, ma'am, I ain't seen civilization for quite some spell."

"Obvious."

"Darling, there isn't any bridge, and we go across by boat. Let me get your luggage. Do you have a coat? You'll find it's cold on the water, and it might not be a bad idea to change your shoes. High heels may be sort of tricky for scrambling down the ladder."

She looked very dubious. I transferred her luggage to the *Mary Jane.* We locked up the Thunderbird. Then I scooped her up in my arms and carried her down the ladder to the *Mary Jane* and dumped her on the deck.

"This ain't a yacht, lady, but I reckon she will get us there."

"Stop it, Dan!"

I grinned. "Okay. Darling, you look wonderful."

She gulped and choked and finally was able to say, "Well, so do you, if only you would shave the beard."

I tossed a yellow oilskin in her direction. "You better put this on," I said. "Maybe not fashionable, but you'll find it cold and wet when we get in motion."

She put on the mackintosh. It was much too big and swamped her. She stopped looking like a tailored woman and started looking like a small fuzzy peach in a large yellow ocean. Then she grinned at me, so I kissed her. I started the engine and we crossed the reach. We couldn't speak well over the engine roar, but we grinned and winked at each other. Once she asked, by gesture, if she could take the wheel, and I let her for a few minutes, but the *Mary Jane* didn't respond to her city fingertips and started wandering all over the bay. When we docked at Juniper, I scooped up June again to carry her up the ladder. Cyrus Lunt was peering down at us from overhead with a bawdy grin.

"Let me give you a hand, Doc. Pass her on up to me," he said.

"No, thanks, I wouldn't trust you for the job," I said.

"Don't blame you none," he said, and he pursed his lips and gave a wolf whistle.

To my surprise and delight, June puckered up and whistled right back at him.

"I didn't know you could do that," I said.

"Haven't tried it for years," she said. "Who is that cute horny old man?"

"You just stay away from him," I said.

"So this is Juniper Island!"

"The best we can do for it," I said.

"I think I like it here," she said.

"Fine. So do I."

"The people are such characters: so dirty, so wind-blown, so primitive. And the village is quaint and picturesque. The whole darn place is arty."

"June, don't," I said.

"Don't what, darling?" She seemed genuinely puzzled.

"Don't condescend," I said. "Don't patronize."

"But . . ."

"They're not characters," I said. "There's nothing quaint or picturesque, and the only arty thing about the whole damn place is you."

"But . . ."

"These are proud people, my dear, and tough and strong," I said. "You have to fight to survive at all in a place like this in the wintertime."

"Yes, surely, but . . ."

"If you start patronizing them, you're patronizing me, and we don't permit it," I said. "We may be wind-blown, but we can spit in your eye, even against the wind."

"Well, Dan, don't get violent!"

"We're plain-spoke people round these parts."

"Yes," she said. "So I see."

No more conversation between us until we got to the house. Slob, greatly to my surprise, growled at June. I had to lock him in the cellar. As I've said, Slob's judgment was erratic where adults are concerned.

I took June's things upstairs and showed her the bedroom just across the hall from mine. I left her to primp and freshen up. When she came downstairs again, I was pleased to see that she had changed to slacks and sweater. This didn't do her figure any harm: quite a chunk of woman, actually, and I wondered what I had ever done to deserve it.

"Dan, is that a feather bed?" she inquired.

"Yes."

"I never slept in one."

"At first it's frightening; you sort of fall right in, but then you begin sleeping like a log. Drink before supper?"

"Sure."

"Martini?"

"Fine. But, Dan, don't feel you have to entertain me. Don't let me keep you from your patients."

I had to laugh at that.

"No patients?" she said.

"Just every now and then."

The martinis were crisp and cold, and June was a crisp-looking woman and I sat, admiring her. I wondered why I had deprived myself of her so long. Just because I was a physician in a primitive location didn't mean I had to be living like a monk. June was no nun; this I knew from previous experience. But she was thinking of something else and was studying me rather carefully.

"Dan?"

I didn't care for her tone of voice: an entering-wedge approach, the woman about to talk serious on touchy things.

"Dan, you make a living here?"

"In the summer," I replied. "The millionaires, you know."

"But you haven't been here in the summer yet."

"Just around the corner," I said.

"In other words, you haven't made a . . ."

"No, not yet," I said.

"Dear," she said, "I guess I more or less understand. Korea was pretty tough for you. You don't talk but I can tell."

"Yeah."

"And coming out of that, maybe, you wanted to be alone for a while. A vacation and a rest. Peace, quiet, beautiful scenery, primitive people who won't bother you very much. It's understandable."

"Very," I said.

"So aren't you feeling a little better now?"

"Feeling fine," I said.

"So," said she, "when are you coming back to work?"

I got up and walked to the window and looked out over the bay. "June, this is my work. They need a doctor here."

"Do they?"

"They are slowly beginning to find out."

"And slowly you are falling apart at the seams."

"I am not convinced," I said, "that money means a God damned thing."

"Of course not, dear, and I have plenty, so that needn't worry you. Could I please have another drink?"

Another round for two, and then I said, "I couldn't live in New York."

"It must be nice here in the summertime," she said.

"Which is only ten weeks long."

"Rather grim in February, I suppose."

"And not too salubrious in April. You want to go back right now?"

"Dan," she said, "I didn't come all this way to pick a fight with you."

"And why did you come all this way?"

"At least I expect to spend the night," she said obliquely.

Spend the night, huh? Well, okay, who am I to complain? *Pourquoi pas?* And all that sort of thing.

"By the way," I said. "Can you cook?"

"Me?"

How many a man has married a woman and never even asked that question?

"Because there aren't any restaurants, exactly, and all I've got is a can opener," I said.

"You look well nourished. You must have put on ten pounds. I'll take a chance," she said.

"Actually," I said, "I've got a couple of chicken lobsters and a lovely mess of clams."

"Clams?"

"No?"

"They give me the hives," she said. "I feel like a nice juicy steak."

"I'll run right down to Wellington's," I said.

"Dan, I don't want to put you out."

"Not in the least," I said. "The store is just around the corner."

I went down to Wellington's, feeling some relief at being out of my own house and out of immediate contact with the rather perplexing person staying there. I bought a steak.

"Party night tonight, Doc?" said Wellington.

"I rather imagine the grapevine has told you all about it," I said.

Wellington gave me a bawdy wink. "Don't do nothing I wouldn't do, Doc."

"I imagine that would be difficult," I said.

By the time I got back home with the steak June had changed her clothes again: a filmy frothy black sort of evening gown. No wonder her luggage was so heavy. For what I presumed might be a short visit of a day or two or three, this dame had brought along most of her equipment. She had let Slob out of the cellar and negotiated an uneasy truce with him.

"You let this hound into your waiting room?" she inquired.

"Couldn't do without him," I said.

"Oh, we'll have to change all that," she said.

Oh, you will? I thought. Maybe Slob will have something to say about that. Maybe me too.

"Got any candles?" June asked me. "Wouldn't it be nice to eat by candlelight?"

Yes, I had candles. They were rather necessary on Juniper Island. We lost our electricity with some frequency.

"And how about a good red wine to go with the steak? A burgundy, Dan?"

"Sorry," I said. "The nearest state liquor store is in Rockport Falls, and I couldn't get over there before it closed. In desperate emergency, you can get a bottle from Wellington, but it isn't exactly legal, and I don't like to break the law. We'll have to get along on the staples: gin and vermouth, scotch, bourbon, and rum. And beer, of course. The cellar's pretty strong in those departments."

"Oh, all right, but we really should stock up on a few choice imported wines, don't you think?" The lady was taking charge. "Dan," she said, "the wallpaper in your waiting room must be fifty years old. The whole office suite looks like an abandoned museum. Really, we ought to redecorate the whole damn thing. The office of a professional man must look professional. And you don't work in the office dressed like that, I trust?"

"Sure I do."

"But, Dan, you look like a fisherman."

"So do all my patients," I said.

"I was poking through your closets, dear. You need a whole new wardrobe. And, obviously, you'll shave your beard by summertime."

"June?"

"Yes, dear?"

"Nothing," I said. "I'll start cooking the steak."

The steak was reasonable. After dinner we settled in the living room, well nourished. June had asked about doing the dishes, like a good guest. Like a good bachelor, I left 'em in the sink. I lit a fire in the fireplace, adding some of my dried seaweed, and June was pleasantly enchanted by the magic color in the flame. We turned on the radio and danced. June was a fluid smooth dancer and made me feel awkward, as usual. The room was hot from the fire but June lost none of her cool composure and not a single fleck of powder. Not as Miss Winkle from the library had done, and why should I be thinking of Miss Winkle at a time like this? June wanted a weak scotch and water; I sucked on a beer. We sat and rested in opposite chairs beside the fire.

"Would this be the logical time for a brass tack?" I asked.

"Do you really think so, darling?" said June languidly.

Her perfume was distracting me but I said, "I think so. June, what do you want out of me?"

"What do you mean?"

"Could you be a doctor's wife out here?"

"It might be fun in the summertime," she said. "I suppose the millionaires have a social life."

"I suppose they do, but that's only ten weeks out of the year."

"I'm willing to go along with the experiment for a little while," she said. "Until you get it out of your system."

"Experiment?"

"Isn't it? This scarcely strikes me as a permanent arrangement."

"I don't know why not."

"Dan, you have a tremendous potential of raw material. We could develop it."

"We?"

"Surely I'm included in your plans. You could reach the top of your profession. We can work it out together."

I lit a cigarette and tossed the pack to June. "What's tops in my profession, just for instance?"

She exhaled twin streams of smoke from her nostrils and I was thinking that she looked like a miniature dragon. "Well, professor in a medical school or something of the kind."

"I don't like politics," I said. "I'm not a teacher and I have no leanings towards research."

"All right. Then chief of medicine in some busy city hospital. Aren't you pretty keen at diagnosis?"

"Ninety per cent of the clinical diagnosis is the history," I said. "And history merely means knowing your patient. Out here, I know my patients because I live with them. In the city, they depend on X rays and a battery of laboratory tests. This is deceptive. The clinician may rely on tests but he forgets who's working in the lab. Often it's some damn fool hysterical girl, just out of a six-month lab technician course, who doesn't know a monocyte from a wedding ring and is only thinking of the wedding ring. Damn it, if I need a blood count out here, I do it myself, and then I damn well know it's right!"

"Don't you get along with people very well?"

"I get along with patients fine," I said, "but I'm impatient with educated fools."

"It was my impression that modern medicine was a co-operative venture and that the day of the rugged individualist was done."

"Not entirely," I said. "One good man is better than a pack of mediocre morons."

"I've heard of false modesty but never of false arrogance," said June.

"False pride, perhaps?"

"Dan, you sound like a snob. Do you really think you practice a better brand of medicine out here than they do in the city?"

"At times," I said. "I'll give you an example. Last week I saw a man who had recently been discharged from a famous teaching hospital with a diagnosis of anemia. His doctor was the head of the hemotology department, a famous expert who has written a book. I use his book, as a matter of fact. He's an important man, maybe so important that he doesn't have time for his patients any more. He never even did a rectal."

"Huh?"

"To be plain-spoke like an islander, June, the professor never stuck his index finger up the patient's ass. I'm only a country boy. I did."

"What's that got to do with anemia? Isn't this a condition of the blood?"

"In this case, the anemia was caused by cancer of the rectum. The professor missed it. He's too busy writing books."

"That's what I mean," she said. "Your ability is equal to that of the professor, but it's being wasted here. I haven't even heard the telephone ring since I came into the house. Perhaps you don't have a phone."

"We're not that primitive," I said, "but country people tend to distrust telephones. They'd rather come around in person."

"Which they don't do very often."

"From time to time, I'm a real handy guy to have around," I said. "We had a bad storm in February, for instance, and nobody could get across the reach in a boat. We were cut off for three days. During that time I had a case of lobar pneumonia, and the man would have died if I hadn't been here with my penicillin. I also had an acute appendix. I did the appendectomy in the patient's home with the father pouring the ether and the mother handing me the hemostats. Obviously, surgery should be done in the operating room, but we had no other choice, and the kid did very nicely, as a matter of fact. Also, one of the boys down at the waterfront was eating peanuts and happened to inhale a peanut into a major bronchus. He almost strangulated. This man should have been bronchoscoped, but I don't have a bronchoscope, and I couldn't use one if I did. However, there was an overhead pulley and a rope on the dock. I tied the end of the rope around the patient's ankles and I got some of the boys to help me. We yanked on the other end of the rope so that we jerked the patient off his feet and hung him in the air, upside down. He was mad as a hornet and opened his mouth to start cussing me, and out popped the peanut. Crude and brutal, I agree, but it worked. And you say they don't need me here on Juniper Island? Three days, June, and three lives saved."

"There would be more people needing you in other places."

"Is a doctor measured by the volume of his practice?" I said. "Is a life worth more in the city than on Juniper Island?"

"Since doctors are in short supply, I think they should be located where they are most needed."

"I'm needed here," I said. "My practice is growing all the time. I had to gain their confidence, and I've been willing to wait."

"For the rest of your life, Dan?"

I got up and walked to the window and looked out at the darkness. I could see the red and green riding lights of some late fishing vessel on the reach.

"I like it here," I said. "I can see why you wouldn't. There's nothing much out here for you."

"Except yourself," she said.

"That's my point," I said. "June, you can do better in the city."

"May I be the judge of that?"

She crossed the room to me, standing directly in back of me, touching me. She put her arms around my waist, rested the point of her chin on my right shoulder, and nibbled at my right ear lobe.

"Perhaps you're not interested in me?" she whispered in my ear.

She knew the answer to that as well as I, but I was still fighting. "You can't change me," I said.

"I have certain weapons," she replied.

This was obvious. "If you succeeded, are you sure you'd like the change?"

"I'll let you know," she said.

"I think you're taking advantage of me," I said.

"This is my intention," she replied. "Now, isn't it about time to go to bed?"

From his corner by the fire, Slob growled.

"Shut up!" I said.

"Why, Dan, what a thing to say!"

"I was speaking to the dog," I said.

"Sooner or later, that dog has got to go!"

She took me by the hand and started pulling me towards the stairs and I found I wasn't pulling back.

* * *

I was up early the following morning. June was a late sleeper and I didn't expect her on deck till noon. I made a couple of house calls and gave a vaccination in the office. Then, because it was warm and bright for April, I went out to tackle the garden: at least, I hoped it would be a garden by summer; at the moment it was a jungle of weeds and alder bushes.

"Morning, Dr. Dan."

I had acquired a small observer and companion. "Good morning, Martha," I said to her.

"Say," said Martha, "what happened to your beard?"

"Shaved it off last night."

"How come?"

"I'm not in the mood for beards."

"Bet I know," said Martha. "I'll bet she made you shave it off."

"Beards tickle and she has a tender skin," I said.

"Where is she now, Doc?"

"In bed."

"Your bed?"

"Martha!" I said.

"Doc, you're blushing."

"Not from embarrassment," I said. "I've told you a thousand times to keep your nose out of my affairs!"

"If I was a little older, Doc, would you sleep me in your bed?"

"Before you're very much older, you're going to get the licking of your life!"

"Poppa paid you cash money to teach me the facts of life," she said. "Ain't this a fact?"

"The lady and I have a grown-up understanding," I said. "We may get married."

"But you ain't married yet?"

"No."

"Doc, is it legal, proper, ethical, and ladylike to bundle with a feller prior to that time?"

"Often not considered so," I said.

"Then she ain't a lady," Martha stated.

"You're working on the basis of supposition and not demonstrated fact."

"You're the fact man, Doc," she said. "Tell me it ain't so!"

"I'll only tell you it's none of your business," I said.

"Reckon not," she said. "I don't particularly want to be a lady, Doc. Don't strike me as being any fun. You remember William, who lives next door to me?"

"The one who thinks he's pretty tough?"

"Yeah. I kind of admire William, though I don't know why, and I suppose I might have to marry William one of these days, if you wouldn't marry me."

"I'm too old for you," I said.

"That leaves William. There ain't much choice on Juniper Island."

"Later on," I said.

"Yeah. But since I got no particular ambitions to be a lady, Doc, I reckon I'll start bundling with William. He wants to. He's done already asked."

"Absolutely not!" I said.

"Why not? Reckon I'm old enough already."

"Because," I said, "you are going to be a lady. I'll see to that personally, even if your Poppa doesn't."

"Don't see the percentages," she said. "Men don't admire ladies. They fancy the other kind."

"The other kind we fancy, but it's the lady we marry," I said. "And that's the entire point, my dear."

"So that's the reason you ain't going to marry the dame upstairs?"

"I haven't decided yet."

"So in the meantime you figure you'll have a little sporting pleasure while you're thinking on the subject?"

"Martha, you're too young for this," I said, "but I did promise your father to teach you what I can. When children ask these certain questions, I don't think the adult should be evasive. It's better to give an honest answer, even though the answer may be over your head, so I'll do my best. The lady and I have a serious relationship. We aren't fooling around for sport or pleasure. We don't know yet whether we should marry or not. It's a very serious problem and we want to be thoroughly sure before we make a serious mistake. We are just trying to get to know each other very well. Can you understand?"

"Yep. And you advise that I should get to know William very good before I marry him?"

"Certainly."

"So I better start going to bed with him, right?"

"Absolutely not."

"I'm too young?"

"Absolutely."

"And you're not?"

"Well . . ." I said.

"Doc," she said, "what's the age limit for that?"

This conversation was out of my control and I was very happy that it was interrupted at this moment. June, in negligee, leaned out of the upstairs window and called down to me.

"She ain't wearing many clothes," said Martha.

"She doesn't need to. Take a look! Can't you see she's beautiful?"

"You take a look, Doc. Can't you see she's a bitch?"

"Dan dear," called June, "I'm ready for my coffee now."

"She's bigger than me," said Martha, "but that's the only difference. Them parts is standardized, just like a Ford motorcar."

"You run along, right now," I said to Martha.

"Dan, please bring me up a cup of coffee!" called June.

"Doc," said Martha, "there's a ring in your nose, and she's tugging it."

"One more word out of you, my young friend, and I'm going to haul down your blue jeans and give you the spanking I should have given you weeks ago," I said.

"Doc, you wouldn't dare."

"Wouldn't I?"

"Nope," said Martha. "On account of I'm wearing them black French pants you gave me Christmastime, and I'd just as soon tell her up there who give 'em to me as not!"

"Dan," called June.

"Coming!" I called back, and I quickly went into the house.

I took June up her cup of coffee. She was back in bed by then. I kissed her good morning.

"Dan, you're dirty," said June.

"Good clean farmer's soil," I said.

"Who was that little brat down there?"

"A gadfly, general pest, nuisance, and occasional friend of mine, when she minds her own business, which isn't very often."

"You choose strange friends."

"And you make good enemies," I said.

"What do you mean by that?"

"Nothing," I said. "What do you want to do this morning? There isn't much left of it."

"Same thing you want to do," she said, "but since the brat is still lurking on the lawn, wouldn't it be wise to pull down the shade?"

* * *

I managed to get June out of the house by afternoon, and we went for a walk. We passed Martha, still lurking. Wellington leaned out of the general store as we passed and smiled at us. Cyrus Lunt was with him and he gave me a bawdy wink.

"We're under close observation, Dan," said June.

"Small-town hobby," I said. "Essentially harmless. They get vicarious pleasure out of watching the neighbor's small downfallings and petty vices. If we were in trouble, they'd be the first to rush out and give us a hand, no questions asked."

"I'm a small downfalling and petty vice of yours?"

"I didn't mean that the way it sounds."

"And how do you mean it?"

"The men envy me. Martha is jealous of you, and maybe some of the older women too. That's all I meant," I said.

"That's the trouble with a little town," she said. "Eyes in every window, and ears over the back fence. In the city, nobody cares."

"And when you're in trouble, nobody cares," I said.

"The official agencies are always on duty."

"I'm more than an official agency. I am Dr. Dan, their friend."

"In the city, your professional reputation is the only thing that counts," said June. "The patients know nothing and care less about your personal affairs."

"And the doctor doesn't know his patients as people," I said. "And therefore he can't help them very much."

"Isn't that obsolete?" said June. "The good old family doctor who may know the family but knows nothing about modern diagnosis and therapy?"

"It's possible to keep yourself up to date," I said, "even way out here."

"But easier to drift with the tide, like the rest of them."

"At the moment, the tide is high. Look!" I said, pointing to the ocean. It was a delicate shy lavender color that afternoon.

"I see a lot of salt water. What about it, Dan?"

"I wouldn't feel alive if I couldn't see the water every day," I said. "I've never seen it the same color twice. It has the brilliance and the passion, the vitality and confusion, the moods, the whims, the fascination, the danger, the hint of fecundity that man finds attractive in a woman. I see the dynamic restlessness of life out there and also the cold impartiality of death. If I looked at the ocean long enough, I might be able to understand the significance of suffering and pain."

"Then, Dan, perhaps you'd better marry the ocean," she said.

We walked home. June went upstairs and changed her clothes: the tailored woman again. She called to me to carry down her bags.

"Leaving already?" I said.

"Haven't I stayed long enough?"

"Couldn't you stay another night?"

"Although this may surprise you, Dan, I'm aiming for a somewhat higher relationship than that."

"Well," I said, "so am I."

"I've not necessarily given up on you," she said. "You need more time out here. I may come back for you."

"I may be wearing a beard."

"I don't think so, Dan. I don't really think you are that type."

I took June across the reach and put her things into the Thunderbird. I was pleased to see that nobody had siphoned off the gas or stolen the hubcaps. She started the engine and I kissed her good-by.

"Dan, I really understand what you're after," she said. "Maybe it isn't obsolete. Perhaps you'll find it out here and be a very happy man. But there's more to it, according to my way of thinking. Lazy peace of mind isn't everything. I'm not sure a man has the right to bury his talents, and I don't think anybody has the privilege of dying before his time."

"Not quite dead," I said. "Not yet."

"No," she said, "and not yet certain in your mind, so maybe I'll be seeing you again."

"Sure thing," I said.

But I didn't really think so. She departed in one direction in the Thunderbird and I in the other in the *Mary Jane*.

Part 4

May

WE HAD A BRISK LITTLE SNOWSTORM on the first of May. Memorial Day, on the other hand, was muggy and hot and the foliage had burst into full summer exuberance. My medical practice followed a similar pattern. In early May, I was no busier than I had been in the winter; by the end of the month my time was fully occupied. Part of this was owing to increased confidence of the inhabitants in me. Part of it was seasonal. More than doctors are willing to admit, more than politicians and labor leaders can seem to understand, medical care is a luxury and not a necessity. Juniper Islanders have no money in the winter and defer all luxuries till spring.

My practice had begun with emergency cases, like that of all doctors in a new location, but you can't make a living on emergencies alone. The true emergency is relatively rare. I had only ten or fifteen in the first six months. Furthermore, emergencies don't pay very well. One might think the victim of an accident or medical catastrophe would be among the most grateful of patients, but my experience has been otherwise. The patient has been in good health until suddenly struck down by catastrophe. Like the prophet Job, he resents it. He has considered himself a reasonably good and righteous man, give or take a few minor sins, and he finds it utterly unreasonable and incomprehensible that he should have been the victim of a thunderbolt. His first reaction is to scream for help. First he screams at God but receives no immediate reply so then he calls for human aid. Help is slow in coming. The doctor may arrive within five minutes, but five minutes can be an eternity to the man in pain. When the immediate emergency is over the patient is saddled with an illness he did not expect and cared for by a doctor whom he did not choose. After recovery, he often is not as strong and healthy as he was before; he carries scars and disabilities. Like Job's, his attitude is sullen, resentful, and hostile, and it is very easy for him to transfer the blame to the physician in the case. Young doctors respond to the challenge and excitement of the emergency, but older men prefer the regular steady grateful patients. You need the latter to build a practice on.

My first regular patients were children. I enjoyed pediatrics. Children need a lot of medical attention; they're easy to treat and handle, if you're not afraid of them; they respond well to therapy. Mothers are grateful and so, for that matter, are the kids. Of course, there are ugly moments in pediatrics. It is disturbing when a child develops disability: a twisted leg from polio, a distorted heart valve from rheumatic fever, blindness following meningitis. On the other hand, children adjust to disability better than adults. Mothers love their disabled children most, and a loved child can compensate for anything. The most awful combination of the life-and-death equation is the child with the progressive fatal illness. Fortunately these are rare, but I remember several: acute leukemia, cancer of the kidney, sarcoma of bone, cystic fibrosis of the pancreas. In every such case, however, the memory of the human dignity and strength outweighs the tragedy. The dying child is not afraid and becomes quite visibly an angel: you can almost see the halo and the wings. Care of the dying child seems to bring forth in mother and father, even in the most unpromising human material, something of the grace and dignity of a Mary and a Joseph at the foot of the cross.

At first I was happy to consider myself a pediatrician, but I noticed that pediatrics rather rapidly lost its charm. The vast bulk of the work is routine and tedious. I never lost my enjoyment of the small patient himself but too much of the time was spent treating the anxious mother. I like young women but I find the situational neurosis of harried young motherhood a screaming irritation and a crashing bore. Many children, incidentally, share the same opinion. Young mothers have my sympathy. They are exhausted, with good reason, and frustrated, with good cause. Wet diapers and colic in the night are not exactly equivalent to candlelight and wine although the one is the inevitable result of the other. But too many of the young mothers were psychologically unequipped for motherhood. They badgered their children and nagged them and created an atmosphere of hostility and uneasy guilt. Such mothers bored and irritated me, and for this reason the element of my pediatric practice failed to grow after a promising beginning.

I like young women and I was disappointed that so few of them came to me as patients. The Widow Gideon still did all the obstetrical work. The women went off the island for their gynecology. I finally decided that this might be because I did like women. The strange conclusion came to me that most obstetricians and gynecologists do not really like women. Daily professional contact with the female pelvis might tend to destroy romance. Would a young woman choose a doctor who really didn't like her? Yes, sometimes I think so. I have a feeling that pregnant females, women in labor, females with pelvic diseases are afraid of, fed up with, and momentarily disgusted by certain of the messier mechanical aspects of being a woman. I think this may produce unconscious selection of a doctor who unconsciously shares the same opinion.

Once past the dangerous reef of menopause, however, ladies quite naturally gravitated in my direction. Middle-aged and geriatric females became the backbone of my practice on Juniper Island.

From the point of view of physical disease, geriatric ladies are pretty tough. If a woman can survive the complex problem of having sex and raising babies—or the even more complex problem of not having sex or raising babies—she is very likely to survive into extreme old age. She consistently outlives her husband and often her children too. Physically strong and tough, she does not, however, consider herself well. She has myriad complaints. These are largely incurable and she knows it. She doesn't come to the doctor to be cured. She comes for tender loving care, which she doesn't get from her husband very much, or from her children either. Tender loving care of the female geriatric patient is not difficult to supply. You don't give medicine or treatment of any kind; you just listen. You don't agree or disagree. You don't even open your mouth. Some doctors can't listen to old ladies and others can do so only by controlling extreme irritation but this comes easily enough for me. Therefore, old ladies have always been the bread and butter of my trade.

Old gentlemen are the salt and savor. I knew the fishermen would be the last to consult me professionally, but I couldn't feel established until they did. Old men are fully as neurotic as their female counterparts and carry a far wider variety of serious organic disease but they reject tender loving care. They don't want to be babied and they don't want to be advised. They live on nothing but cussedness and pride, and this you can't take away from them. You can't deprive them of the little pleasures of their lives. If you try to stop their smoking or their drinking or change their patterns of eating, wenching, or their daily work, one of two things will happen. They will either reject your advice, in which case they will not come back; or they will accept your advice, in which case they will begin to die, although it will take a little time to bury them. An old woman may live without pleasure and zest, but a man who stops enjoying life will not long survive. My more sophisticated colleagues in the city often try to enforce upon geriatric males a list of those nasty little sensible restrictions. You don't see very many vigorous lusty old men in the city. On Juniper Island they thrive. Sensible men fill the cemeteries.

When Wellington of the grocery store finally consulted me about his liver, I figured I had it made. Mr. Wellington did have a liver, a rubbery and resilient old organ, good for another twenty or thirty years of heavy Saturday drinking. I didn't advise him to stop drinking. Absorbing alcohol is what a tough old liver is good for. I only told him that I had great confidence in the long-range endurance of his liver, and this was all he wanted to know. A tonic was not necessary. He started feeling better immediately.

Quite incidentally, I discovered that Mr. Wellington had the gout. I had usually considered gout to be a rich man's disease. Wellington was a key figure in the economy of the island; a good deal of cash passed through his hands in both directions, but he wasn't rich. Being a monopoly, he could and did charge outrageous prices for the groceries. Having also the public responsibilities of a monopoly, he could not deprive any citizen of groceries. Consequently, he made a lot of money in the summer and carried most of the community on credit in the winter. In the long run, I suspect, he broke approximately even.

It was diet, not money, that gave Wellington the gout. He ate almost nothing but lobster and steak. The heavy Saturday night drinking was another factor in the case. I could control his symptoms with medication: colchicine and Benemid. I could have stopped his symptoms only by stopping the lobster, steak, and alcohol. But I had to consider the patient's needs as well as his pathology. He, his liver, and his gout were going to survive for another generation in reasonable equilibrium. If I advised him to straighten up and be a teetotaling vegetarian, I'd have never seen him again and therefore been unable to give him relief with colchicine and Benemid. In the unlikely event he had accepted my advice, he would have sold his store, promptly retired, and died a resentful irritable death within a couple of months, I think.

Cyrus Lunt consulted me too. His problem was peptic ulcer. Like most of the men, he was a considerable user of nicotine, alcohol, and caffeine, and these three substances have a notoriously bad effect on the peptic ulcer. A conservative therapist would have tried to make him cut them out. I knew in the first place that he had no intention of cutting them out. More importantly, though, this was not the true cause of his disease. Cyrus Lunt was a born wheeler and dealer. His occupation was making sharp negotiations. Wheelers and dealers have no visible conscience, but almost invariably they develop peptic ulcer. Their stomach acids are their conscience, I believe. I could heal Cy's ulcers quite readily with milk and cream, Malcogel, Pro-Banthine. They would flare up again each time he cut a sharp corner on a deal. This, I was sure, would happen whether or not he indulged in his caffeine, nicotine, and alcohol. I could scarcely plant in Cyrus Lunt a conventional conscience. I put the problem frankly, man to man, and tried to see if I could make him honest. He made a valiant effort. For quite some period of time his deals were honorable. No more ulcers, although his fleshly indulgences remained the same, but instead he developed alarming giant hives and urticaria out of sheer frustration. I could manage his ulcers better than his urticaria, so by mutual consent we permitted him to return to wheeling and dealing.

* * *

About ten per cent of the natives on Juniper Island seemed to be named Lunt. Cyrus claimed to have no relatives in the generations before, after, or contemporaneous with him, but obviously there was mutual blood. All the Lunts were wheelers and dealers in one fashion or another. About ten per cent of the natives were Wellingtons; the keeper of the grocery store admitted this relationship; hard-working industry and heavy Saturday drinking were characteristic of Wellington blood. All the rest of the natives, the remaining eighty per cent, were named Rast. There were so many Rasts all over the place that I could never keep 'em apart. I developed a system of nomenclature, biblical in inspiration, as a means of identification.

The old patriarch of the tribe, obviously, I thought of as Adam. He was in his middle nineties, nearly blind and nearly deaf and nearly paralyzed from a series of little strokes. His blood pressure was Mount Everest in height; his arteries were solid calcified pipes; I imagine his diet was straight cholesterol. He had several obvious cancers, and diabetes which he never bothered to control, and in general had enough disease to kill ten other men, but he went lobstering every day. Old Adam Rast was a gentle and soft-spoken man. In general, one thinks that physical strength means toughness and roughness, but not in Adam's case. Adam was an excellent example of the willow that bends in contrast to the oak that breaks.

One very cold morning old Adam Rast fell overboard in the middle of the reach. Like most of the fishermen, he could not swim. Most healthy young men die within minutes from shock and exposure in the cruel arctic temperature of our northern ocean. Adam, of course, survived. He was unable to clamber up the high sides of his boat, and panicky struggling would have finished him, so he didn't struggle. He didn't even waste his energy screaming for help with nobody to hear him; he just hung onto the side of the boat and waited. He waited several hours before somebody noticed him. You certainly would have expected old Adam to develop severe pneumonia at the very least, but he didn't even get a sniffle.

Adam Rast had three sons. Very naturally, I thought of them as Cain, Abel, and Seth.

Cain, of course, was a bad man, and Abel was a good man, although, in this instance, Cain was no murderer. He was only a thief. He was supposed to be a lobsterman, but if he had any traps of his own, nobody could ever find them. Also, it might have seemed unusual that Cain always went lobstering after dark. Of course, Cain was stealing lobsters from everybody else, and everybody knew it. I wondered why they didn't do anything about it.

"Doc, he's no damn good," they said. "Why should we bother with him?"

"You could put him in jail," I said.

"You figure that would change the nature of his ways?"

"No, but it would stop him from stealing your catch."

"Only for sixty or ninety days at a time, Doc, according to the mood of the judge."

"Sooner or later the judge would get fed up with him and put him away for good."

"Doc, he's a relative to most of us. You can't put a relative away for good, just because you don't happen to like him."

Cain consulted me with a stubborn chronic skin rash, an itching eczema that had covered most of his body most of his life. I prescribed the usual medicated lotions and greases which work quite well in most cases, but they didn't work. Cain knew it wasn't going to work. Since his relatives would not punish him, since he could not change the nature of his ways, since his relations didn't like him, and since he didn't even like himself, he was punishing himself: with his fingernails.

Cain's brother, whom I thought of as Abel, was a righteous man, community leader, deacon of the church. He didn't smoke or drink, and he was the island's only vegetarian. There was even a rumor that he offered daily prayer for the suffering of the lobsters that he had to catch. But Abel had a single vice and I found it astonishing. Although a highly proper man in his seventies, he could not leave young women alone. Since the better young women are reserved for the better men of appropriate age, Abel was left with the other kind. Approximately twice a year he consulted me for venereal disease.

And we had a Seth, the old-age son of Adam whom everybody seems to forget, and I knew nothing about him except that he had a lot of sons. I could never discover who was the mother of these sons. Which seems to remind me that, whenever I read my Genesis, I come to a confusion. The Lord created Adam and the Lord created Eve, and they had a couple of sons. Cain killed Abel and left Eden and went to the land of Nod, where he took a wife. Who was she? Where did she come from, if Eve was the only woman alive? Well, it seems to me I've heard of somebody named Lilith who, some people used to think, was Adam's first wife, created before Eve, who refused to submit to Adam and whom Adam for this reason threw out of the garden and who has been hostile to little children ever since. Was Lilith whom Cain married? I would think she was the only one available.

Well, at any rate, after a certain time Adam had another son named

Seth, and after a certain length of time Seth took a wife. Who was she? Where did she come from?

Well, enough of the biblical analogy, which has become too confusing for me. All I mean to imply is that on Juniper Island, as in Eden, there were one or two women whose origins have not been satisfactorily accounted for. This brings strongly to my mind, of course, the Widow Gideon.

* * *

My most unexpected patient in the month of May was the Widow Gideon herself. I suspected the unusual when I first heard her come into the waiting room. Slob was making strange noises, almost as if he was trying to speak; it is said that the Wabanaki Indian can understand the speech of animals. And through the office door filtered her aroma: a strong acrid scent that intermingled gin, unwashed clothing, strange herbs, and unusual foods. I opened the office door. She almost seemed to fill the waiting room. I invited her into the office; when she sat in the patient's chair, that bit of furniture creaked and I was afraid that it might buckle.

Her opening gambit took me by surprise: "Doc, do you believe in cancer?"

"What do you mean?"

"Just what I said. Some folks think there's such a thing as cancer."

"Well, of course," I said. "Cancer is one of the most common and probably the most frightening of human diseases. I see it too often. It's either the second or the third most common cause of death."

"What are the other two?"

"Heart disease and accidents."

"Them I believe in," she said.

"That's very kind of you," I replied. "Are you trying to say you don't believe in cancer?"

"No." She stared at me with muddy and rather stupid opaque brown Indian eyes. "I seen lots of folks die on Juniper Island," she said at last.

"And none of them dying of cancer, I suppose."

"No. Ain't no such article."

"Okay by me." I didn't want to start an argument. She outweighed me by at least a hundred pounds.

"What causes cancer?" she asked next.

"Nobody knows."

"What is cancer?"

"I'm not sure anybody knows that exactly," I said.

"Then how in the hell, Doc, can you believe in something you don't know nothing about?"

"I know nothing about God," I said, "but I believe in Him."

"That's a right smart, right tricky little answer, sonny," she said. "Of course, you and me don't happen to believe in the same kind of God. I know all about the gods of my particular Indian tribe. My tribe has known them very well since long before you people came. Of course, your God is stronger than ours. We got a kind of weak puny miserable kind. But Indians don't get cancer. Indians don't get nothing we don't believe in, see what I mean?"

"I suppose."

"Tell me more about this cancer thing you believe in, Doc. What's she like?"

"The original name means crab. You know what a crab is, of course? I'm sure you believe in them?"

"Crabs I understand," she said.

"It's a Latin word. The people who spoke Latin, the Romans, had a number of deities, just like your people, and perhaps they were weak and puny too, since they seem to have died away. The Roman nation became extinct, just as your Wabanaki nation did, but we remember the language. Latin is better suited for definition and description than any language we have invented since. Cancer is hard and ugly and greedy and it stretches out grasping claws to tear up anything soft and tender in the vicinity. I think it's a rather good descriptive word. We don't know much about cancer, but it seems to be some disturbance in the process that controls the growth of cells. Madam, perhaps you don't believe in cells, but we like to think of them as the tiny building blocks out of which flesh is formed. You can see them very well under the microscope. Every cell has its own shape and structure, its own particular function. Cell growth is under some marvelous orderly control that may or may not be the influence of God; I rather think this is one of God's functions and one of the most miraculous. When every cell is functioning and playing its distinctive role in the organism as a whole, we have the orderly and beautiful miracle of the functioning human body. In cancer, something gets out of control. One single cell, first, goes wild. It starts growing, wild and crazy, like a spark in a meadow of dry grass. It is stronger and wilder and crazier than neighboring cells still under natural control, as evil always seems to be stronger and wilder and crazier than orderly virtue. The malignant creature devours orderly neighbors and, not content with that, it spreads to other parts of the body and destroys them too. In time, on account of this destruction, the whole body dies. This is also typical of evil, it seems to me: to destroy not only orderly good but its own source of life, so that it destroys itself along with the good, leaving nothing but death and putrefaction."

"This thing is a devil," she said.

"You could call it that, I guess."

"I do believe in the Devil," said the Widow Gideon.

"So do I."

"What do you do about this cancer, Doc?"

"Cut it out or burn it out," I said. "What else would you do with a devil?"

"You done convinced me, Doc. I believe in you, so maybe you better have a look at this."

She put her hand at the edge of a loose deep neckline, did some mysterious adjustments to straps and buckles inside, and scooped out of her dress one of the most massive and pendulous breasts I have ever seen. Jut below the areola was a ragged ulceration the size of a half dollar.

"Looks like it," I said. "Would you mind if I examine?"

"Help yourself, son. I never met a man your size I was afraid of yet."

"That's not what I mean," I said.

"I know what you mean. Poke and feel around to your heart's content if you think it'll do us any good."

I palpated the lesion. The edges were hard as stone, and there wasn't very much doubt in my mind. I palpated other segments of the breast, finding no evidence of local spread, and I examined the supraclavicular area and the axilla and I found no evidence of enlargement of lymph nodes to suggest distant metastasis. I thought this was almost undoubtedly malignancy of the breast, but in this particular organ, with the lesion in the center before there is local invasion and distant spread, the outlook following treatment is relatively good. Many of these cases will live five years before recurrence, and a number of them are cured.

"I'm almost sure this is the devil you have in mind," I said.

"Doc, how can you be proof-positive sure?"

"Biopsy," I said.

"What's that?"

"Cut out a little piece. Look at it under the microscope. That way you can tell for sure."

"What next?"

"Remove it," I said. "Surgery."

"Cut out all of me?"

"All on that side and a little more around the edges," I said. "And sometimes, after that, X ray too. Exactly what they do depends on how things look under the microscope."

"No fun," she said.

"The devil's death is worse."

"Doc, I ain't afraid of pain. No Indian is."

"I have heard that legend."

"Not a legend. This is factual truth. My people don't feel pain, Doc. There's no word for it in the Wabanaki tongue. We hurt a little, of course, but hurting is only part of being alive. So therefore, Doc, start cutting this part of me out right now."

"Not I. I am not equipped for this and I lack the surgical training. You need a good modern surgeon in a good modern hospital operating room."

"Don't care for hospitals."

"I don't blame you," I said. "But it's the only way."

"Hell, Doc, if you won't do this job for me, I reckon I'll go home and hack her off myself. May I borrow one of your knives?"

Damned if I didn't think she'd do it! "Madam, no, please!" I said. "Let me refer you to the surgeons in Rockport Falls?"

"Do they understand cancer same as you? Do they know it for a crab and a devil?"

"Not necessarily," I said, "but they know how to handle it far better than I, madam, I absolutely promise and guarantee."

She finally permitted me to persuade her to be referred to the surgeons in Rockport Falls. They performed radical mastectomy. On the phone, they informed me that the lesion was localized and that pathological study of the specimen revealed no evidence of spread. Good news! This meant that she had an excellent chance of a cure.

She was gone from the island approximately a month. Originally, I had resented the presence of the Widow Gideon on Juniper Island and hoped to deliver all the babies myself. During the month she was gone, however, I found myself hoping there would be no babies to be delivered. There were three. The first was spontaneous and easy and there was really nothing to the job. The husband could have delivered it and in fact he almost had by the time I arrived but I still found myself wishing I was somewhere else. In the next case, there was uterine inertia and the baby hung up. Mid-forceps extraction was indicated. I did my damnedest to persuade the mother to go to Rockport Falls but she absolutely refused. Since I had not been doing obstetrics, my office equipment did not include a pair of forceps. I was stuck. Then I had the inspiration to go over to the Widow Gideon's house. Forceps too modern for an Indian midwife? Says who? They had obstetrical forceps way back to the days of ancient Egypt. The Widow Gideon had a pair. Made of wood. She made them herself. With grave doubts about sterility and reservations about the mechanics of this crude homemade instrument, I boiled it up and used it. Worked fine, naturally. But I decided that island obstetrics really was not for me and I made a firm resolution to deliver no more babies. I told Wellington of my decision, which was equivalent to setting up a large bill-board in the center of the village.

"Don't blame you none, Doc, this is woman's work," said Wellington. "I sure hope the widow gets back pretty soon."

So did I. "I'm sending them all to Rockport Falls until she does," I said.

"Sometimes they won't send."

"They got to," I said, "because sooner or later I'm going to kill a mother or a child, and I don't need this on my conscience. I get into enough trouble doing the things I know and understand."

My point of view was perfectly acceptable to the citizens. There was one more baby case before the widow got back. The husband was sent to ring my bell.

"Send her to Rockport Falls."

"Doc, she won't go."

"Sir, she's got to go, because I refuse to take the case. A doctor has the legal right to turn down any case if he wants to."

"Doc, it ain't a matter of legal rights, it's a matter of female stubborn-ness. You ever tried to argue with a woman?"

"Damn it."

"Don't do no good to swear at 'em neither."

So, damn it, I went along. I wasn't needed. The baby was already in the mother's arms when we arrived. The placenta was out; cord cut and tied. She was alone. She'd done the job herself.

"Matter of fact, Doc," the husband told me later on, "she didn't really want you. She waited until she knew it was the proper time and then she sent me over to your place just to get me out of the house. She had every full intention of doing the thing herself. That's the true and real reason, Doc. I don't try to argue much against female stubbornness. In one way or another, though often in an upside-down position, the stubborn woman turns out to be correct."

Probably so. I was, however, relieved when the Widow Gideon came back. So were all pregnant women on Juniper Island. The Widow Gideon looked fine, big as a blimp, strong as a draft horse, as usual. There was only one thing about her that attracted momentary attention all over the island.

"Damn it, Doc, she's lopsided," said Wellington. "If you know what I mean, and if you don't know what I mean, all you've got to do is take a look at her."

Sure I knew what he meant. Most women, following mastectomy, wear a prosthetic device in the brassiere which conceals the loss of the breast. The Widow Gideon refused one. So her bosom was enormous on the one side and missing on the other.

"Doc," said Wellington, "she changed her Indian name."

"What is it?"

"Damned if I know. I couldn't say it. Some tongue-twisted Indian word about fifteen and a half syllables long, but I know what it means in English. She told me."

"Yes?"

"Her new name means: One-Mound Momma!"

I had to laugh at this.

Wellington peered around the dark corners of the store to be sure there were no innocents or females listening and then he whispered to me: "Doc, tell me the truth: how much do you think that damn thing weighed? Twenty or thirty pounds?"

"That's enough!" I said. "Keep a clean tongue in your head! How would you like it if somebody made a dirty joke about your anatomy?"

"Sorry, Doc," said Wellington. "Didn't mean no harm by it. I was just curious, that's all."

"You can find better objects for your curiosity," I said.

Still, despite myself, I couldn't help wondering. Yes, twenty pounds at least would be my guess!

* * *

And even Miss Winkle consulted me professionally during the month of May.

"Dan," she said, "I really do have migraine headaches and aspirin doesn't do the trick any more. Do you have something better?"

I gave her Cafergot, which worked very well.

"Dan, when you first came to the island you took one look at me and knew I had migraine. How could you tell?"

"Miss Winkle," I said, "do you have a morbid fascination with the pathology of disease?"

"I'm a woman. I read. Don't all reading women have an acute and morbid interest in pathology? And my name is Betty, in case you may have forgotten."

"Betty, I try to be an honest man. You ask me a question and I'll give you an honest answer, if you really want to know. Are you sure?"

She gave me a weak smile. "Will it hurt?"

"Perhaps."

She put stamina into her smile. "You can't tell me any dirty secrets about myself that I don't already know. I try to conceal it. I'm only mortified that I am so transparent. I want you to tell me where my slip is showing."

"Okay, but don't get mad," I said. "And just because I say it doesn't mean that it is true. This is merely an observation of mine. They don't teach it in school, and I never read it in a book. I've stored up a quantity of little hints and clues and minor quirks I've noticed in people that tell me the kind of people they are, which in turn tells me the kind of diseases they may develop."

"You ought to write a book of your own."

"I couldn't. Not that kind of a book. And if I did my medical associates wouldn't accept my observations, since I don't do controlled experiments, since I have no specialized credentials or qualifications. The only kind of book that I could write would be a light humorous little memoir of no particular consequence about some of the crazy fascinating wonderful people I have met."

"Maybe it would show what a crazy wonderful person you are."

"I blush."

"It's true. You know it. People automatically like you, Dan."

"Only because I like them," I said.

"Oh, come now!"

"All right, true, I'm a conceited little jerk, and I don't mind tootling my own trumpet now and then, but I am honest enough to know that the only person fascinated by Dr. Daniel van Dine is Dr. Daniel van Dine himself."

"And women," she said.

"Oh?" I said. "This is news. I wish I could believe it. They conceal their fascination fairly well from me."

"The Widow Gideon thinks you're God Almighty on a crutch."

"This would be a dandy compliment if I didn't happen to know that the Widow Gideon doesn't believe in God."

"Little Martha Drinkwater thinks you're Santa Claus."

"And grownups don't happen to believe in Santa Claus," I said.

"And then there's that woman."

"Which?"

"I believe her name is June."

"Oh," I said.

"And me. So why do I have migraine headaches, Dr. Dan?"

Darn it! I didn't really want all this embarrassing discussion over me, but I had purposely steered things in this direction, not in order to feed my vanity (which is, of course, enormous), but in order not to embarrass her. This was a patient in the office now. This was not a young woman drinking with me before the fireplace on New Year's Eve. When patients ask me embarrassing questions I always, God damn it, try to answer them. And I often hurt their feelings in the process. If they didn't know me as friend and neighbor, know that I am really harmless, they wouldn't come back. If I practiced in the suburbs I couldn't get away with it. I'd have to polish up a pretty sequence of palatable half-truths and evasions. And I wouldn't like it. I couldn't live with myself without at least a reasonable margin of reliability.

"What's the matter, Dan?"

"Oh. I beg your pardon?"

"You just fell into a trance or something."

"Sorry," I said.

"Look," said Betty Winkle, "if you don't want to tell me why I'm not a woman, don't. That's the reason for the migraine, isn't it?"

"No, as a matter of fact. Exactly the contrary," I said.

"What do you mean?"

"There's a certain type of woman prone to migraine headaches," I explained. "She's small, fragile, often petite. She's tense and highly strung. She likes high heels, and when she walks you can hear the heels go clitter-clatter like staccato on a beaten gourd. She is pretty, smart, and cold. Her temperament is brittle. Men are a little afraid of her, afraid to touch her for fear she'll break; they tend to think she's frigid. She drives them away. Actually she's afraid of her own impulses, afraid to let herself go, knowing that she would always go too far, and so she doesn't go anywhere at all. Sometimes, therefore, she hates herself. Then she develops migraine. I think of the migraine type as ultrafeminine."

"Thanks very much," she said.

"I'm sorry," I said. "But you asked."

"Thanks for the pills. I hope they work. What's the fee?"

"Three bucks."

She paid me.

"How about cocktails tonight?" I said. "In the office, Betty, I must tell the patient what's wrong with her. This is part of the job. At night, I'll tell a woman what's right with her. This is part of the fun."

"Since I'm now a patient, it might be best to keep our relationship on the purely professional level."

"I'd regret it."

"In any other relationship, I might regret it," she said.

"Why not give it a try?"

"Because you're right, of course," she said. "Because I've tried it before, at the wrong time. Because whenever I try it I choose the wrong man. The right man is invariably attached."

"I am attached to a hound dog," I said. "That's all."

"May the two of you be happy together," said Miss Winkle, and she left the office suite.

Put my foot in it again! No wonder young women never consult me in the office! I'm only good for geriatric ladies and difficult old men and one-mounded Indian squaws. Fine right have I to be conceited! Me with my major liabilities showing down the middle, deep, wide, and broad! No wonder I have to hide on an island by myself. In any civilized locality I would know I was incompetent.

I closed up the office. It was the end of the day and I was tired. It had been a long hard day. A long hard month as well, and summer was just around the corner, and summer was the time I had to make a living in.

Part 5

Summer

As a summer resort, Juniper Island had seen better days. The island had its moment of high fashion, fame, and distinction during the first two decades of the twentieth century. At the turn of the century, a wealthy railroad tycoon named Somerset had discovered the place accidentally when his yacht took shelter in the harbor during a summer storm. Entranced by the scenic beauty of the island and, like so many millionaires, seeking peace and privacy, Somerset bought the western half of the island from the original fishermen owners. He cut this territory up into a dozen sizable plots for his friends.

On the choicest location, a hill that dominated the western side of the island, Somerset erected a castle, a genuine medieval castle that he imported from Europe, stone by stone. It had thirty bedrooms for a family of three plus fifty maids and butlers plus fifty horses with a groom for every horse. He even built a miniature cog railway on the place.

The castle was named Somerset House. Although it burned down in the mid-1930s, it had been reconstructed and still was the most prominent attraction of the western side of Juniper Island: enormous, archaic, out of place. The original Somerset committed suicide there in 1929, jumping off a battlement shortly after the stock market crash. His only son, apparently an eccentric with hermit tendencies, lived there year round by himself without benefit of maids and butlers. He considered himself a native; he even bought a fishing boat and went lobstering now and then. This man had died before I came to Juniper, and Somerset House had recently been bought by a wealthy sport who was to become a patient of mine.

In the vicinity of Somerset House was a cluster of other enormous mansions and estates, all built around the same time, all cavernous, obsolete, and ugly. One was built in the form of a Moslem mosque; another was a Spanish villa of pink and yellow stucco, now rain-streaked and badly faded; a third was an enormous structure in ivy-covered colonial red brick; a fourth was famous on account of its twenty-one bathrooms, the fixtures of which had once allegedly been made of platinum.

In the fashionable early decades Juniper Island must have been quite something in the summertime: bridle paths, horses, carriages, footmen in livery, floating palaces of yachts at anchor, a polo field, pink champagne, candle-illuminated ballrooms, caviar, truffles. The older fishermen still recalled a fabulous party given at Somerset House in 1912 for President William Howard Taft. A carnival midway had been erected for the occasion at the edge of the property, complete with ferris wheel, roller coaster, merry-go-round, and the rest of it. On the little lake in the center of the island, then part of the Somerset property, small-scale reproductions of the *Nina,* the *Pinta,* and the *Santa Maria* were built to ferry the guests across. On the other side of the lake was a snow run, genuine snow brought from Labrador, although it was a hot summer day; and a sleigh pulled by reindeer. The great banquet hall of Somerset House had been transformed into a forest: live trees in pots, live birds flying loose in the trees. Each menu cover was a signed original sketch by a contemporary famous artist. For entertainment at the mid-point of the banquet, they had a Broadway show with the original cast brought from New York for the day.

Such things aren't seen any more, certainly not on Juniper. The wealthy aristocracy was nearly extinct; the stock market crash of '29 had been a mortal wound to them; inheritance and income taxes did the rest. Many of the vast summer mansions had been torn down; the rest were sagging and weary and waterlogged and soon would follow. Perhaps a dozen of the original estates were still occupied each summer, last traces of a fabulous bygone day that would never come again. As the few remaining specimens of trumpeter swans are carefully guarded and protected and preserved, so we protected our few remaining summer millionaires on Juniper Island.

The bridge connecting Juniper Island to Rockport Falls on the mainland had been built in the mid-1930s. It was an expensive job, a formidable engineering feat, paid for only in part by the taxpayer: the majority of the expense had been donated by a few of the millionaires in the hope that a link to civilization would restore a fashionable tinge to the summer colony. The effect was not what they intended. Across the bridge in quantity came, not millionaires and the socially elite, but common garden-variety middle-class tourists. This produced an entirely different summer economy for Juniper Island. Commercial property sprang up to cater to the tourists: filling stations, hotels, motels, restaurants, drugstores, lunch stands, curio shops, antique shops. This phase of tourist invasion lasted well through World War II and during the war the island economy was further boosted by the presence of a naval radio station on Juniper. At the end of the war the radio station was decommissioned. In the autumn of 1950 the tourist phase stopped abruptly; in a hurricane that year, the bridge buckled in the center, collapsed, and washed away. Overnight, Juniper was again remote, primitive, and isolated. When it became apparent that the bridge would not be rebuilt, hotels, motels, shops, and filling

stations were torn down. Tourists went where highways could take them
and not to Juniper Island.

We still had a summer economy just the same. There were the few remaining millionaires of course; then we had a new type of visitor, professional people and executives who were nautical by inclination. A
considerable number of modern and attractive summer cottages and camps
were built. These new summer guests had to come to Juniper by boat,
and boats were what they came for: the new American class who put their
excess luxury dollars on the water. We had an active yacht club that con-
ducted sailing races for various classes of sailboats several times each summer week. These were ideal waters for pleasure boating: none better. The
broken coast line made a great variety of fascinating channels, coves,
harbors; the string of islands provided calm, almost landlocked water for
miles along the reach. The western side of Juniper was sheltered and
provided excellent anchorage. Boats dotted the waters everywhere: canoes,
skiffs, dories, kayaks; sloops and knockabouts; yawls and ketches; noisy
little outboards; Chris-Craft, cabin cruisers, occasional imposing schooners
and sizable motor yachts. The fishermen grumbled about the congestion.
They claimed the traffic scared the lobsters away and likened the
reach on a warm summer day to Times Square. Actually, the lobstering
was done on the outer seaward exposure of the island where reefs, rocks,
and ledges made the going too hazardous for the pleasure boats. Many of
the fishermen put on captain's hats and sailed the boats for summer people;
many others turned an extra dollar in the care and maintenance of the
pleasure boats. Everybody profited directly or indirectly from the summer
trade. The island was an exciting, crowded, busy little spot from mid-
June till after Labor Day.

As long as there are lobsters in the ocean, there will always be fishermen on Juniper Island. As long as the natural beauty of the coast remains
unspoiled, there will always be summer visitors. The summer beauty of
the island is an exotic luxuriant many-sided thing. The essence of the appeal lies in contrast, I should think: intermingling of incredible blues
and greens; lazy July in contrast with mellow August and sharp September; soft misty fog alternating with cold crystal clarity; pink granite, olive
kelp, white barnacles; soft dappled waters of the lake; green forest, blue
sky, puffs of high cloud; screaming sunsets; full moons rising blood red out
of the ocean. And surrounding everything, the restless dynamic mass of
the sea. Summer folk tried to spend as much time on the water as the most
ambitious fisherman. There isn't a house on Juniper Island, from the empty
grandeur of the most imposing summer palace to the meanest little tar-
paper shack in the village, that doesn't have at least a pinhole view of

water. Memory of Juniper Island, to anybody who has ever been there, is memory of ocean.

I expected my practice to increase when the summer came, but I was unprepared for the rush of business that almost overwhelmed me. The telephone began to ring in June and hardly stopped till Labor Day; at times I was afraid the thing might melt from the heat. Apparently every summer visitor went down to Wellington's for groceries the moment he stepped off the boat, and the first thing Wellington told each of them was that we had a smart new young doc on the island who had performed miracles with his liver and his gout; and then each visitor seemed to remember some disability, disease, or complaint he had forgotten to tell his family physician about and straightaway called me.

Sudden change came over every native in June as he abandoned pleasant easygoing winter ways and prepared to greet and cheat the summer folk. I changed too. Fishermen would wash up and discard long winter underwear. I stopped dressing like a fisherman and started wearing business suits. I cleaned my waiting room and filled it full of magazines. I thought of ejecting Slob from his station in my waiting room, but I didn't have to. He himself put on a summer face. He left the house, and I scarcely saw him till fall. Slob spent the summer scrounging for food. He was hell on picnics and would turn up just as predictably as ants as soon as an egg salad sandwich was removed from a glassine envelope anywhere on the island. When there weren't picnics, there were the rear entrances and garbage pails of the summer estates. Slob was eating like a hog and he began to fatten up like one.

I was gratified to be as busy as all doctors seem to be. It was nice to make a living for a change. It was refreshing to be in professional demand. And yet, on the other hand, I resented it. I was doing volume business now, like the suburban men: five minutes to the patient, a quick look, a quick prescription, and five dollars please. I didn't get to know these people and they didn't know me. I was caught temporarily on the assembly line of modern American medicine.

Vacation trade is, for the most part, mechanical and easy. I came to the conclusion that the American vacation is an exhausting and harrowing experience and it is surprising that people survive it. The vacationing American travels too far and too fast and gulps his entertainments in undigestible overdosages. I saw painful sunburn, heat exhaustion, sunstroke from exposure of a pale city skin on the first day in the sun. I saw innumerable bruises, contusions, and sprained ankles from walking on wet slippery rocks in high heels or rubber soles. There's a scenic little cliff at the northeast tip of the island; every week somebody managed to fall over it. Meals were apt to be eaten by exhausted people in hot crowded little joints, and I saw plenty of nausea, vomiting, vertigo, syncope, and bursts of tourist diarrhea. Not content to consume one small lobster, a visitor is inclined to consume three large ones with a side order of steamed clams and plenty of beer; this flares up the gall bladder and the coronary arteries. A man who hasn't gotten off the seat of his pants in eleven months will not be content to play a few easy holes of golf his first day on the course; he's got to try thirty-six and wonders why he has a heart attack. A woman who hasn't seen the sun in eleven months spends the first day on the water from dawn till dusk and faints when she steps off the boat. People swim in icy water immediately after eating and sometimes drown. The tender skins of infants are exposed to unshaded brilliant sun and that night run temperatures of 106 degrees. The American seems to leave his common sense at home when he goes on a vacation trip.

Treatment of the wounded and exhausted traveler can be summed up in two little words: rest and relax. This is sometimes difficult to achieve.

"How can I rest, Doc, how can I relax? I've only got two weeks. You'll spoil my vacation!"

The first part of the summer, the romantic month of June, always brought me a particular type of patient with a particular and delicate type of problem: the honeymooner. I have reached the conclusion that the honeymoon is harrowing and dangerous for those who are chaste, innocent, and moral; only the previously immoral can enjoy themselves. Honeymoon cystitis of the woman, phimosis and balanitis in the male: I see several cases every June. If either newly married partner has emotional instability, neurosis, or psychosis, there's nothing like a honeymoon to bring it out.

The people who streamed into my offices in summer knew me no better than I knew them. Many of them, accustomed to the crisp sterile streamlined efficiency of the suburban clinic, took one look at me and my cozy little house and immediately tagged me as an ignorant sloppy primitive young quack who had probably obtained his medical license under false pretenses. With this type of patient, I never attempted any salesmanship. I didn't want their business any more than they wanted my attendance. We put up with each other only long enough to solve the immediate problem at hand. There were other summer patients quite willing to accept my credentials and advice who were nevertheless under the domination of the family physician back home. Sometimes that man back home was giving them excellent treatment and sometimes his advice was appallingly neglectful or ignorant, but I did not attempt to impose on the relationship. I always did what the doc back home would have done, which pleased the patient, even if it did not always please me. Often, even for the simplest and most obvious of problems, I was asked to phone the doctor at home; I was glad to do it; invariably I received gracious courtesy and full backing from the man at the other end of the line.

There were a few of the passing summer folk who, taking one look at me and my humble quarters, instantly saw in me the doctor they had been looking for all of their lives. These people became regulars of mine on the spot, returning year after year; some of them phoned me for advice periodically when they got home; a number of them corresponded with me regularly; and there was one who, although she lived in an Eastern city surrounded by the best physicians in the world, came to Juniper Island whenever she got sick to consult me at any time of year. These patients pleased me although I did not reckon my own stock so high. They all could have found as good or better physicians in their own neighborhood. But maybe this was proof that my type of obsolete family physician isn't completely obsolete today!

Then there were the few millionaires to contend with. Millionaires are really only people with too much money. Some of them I got along with fine. Some I got along with only when I had to, and some I didn't get along with at all. My first call to a summer estate fell into this latter class. It was an elderly fierce old tiger of a dame, planted in a large bed in an empty room the general size of the waiting room at Grand Central Station. As I humbly entered the room a large summer housefly buzzed through the door with me and began bumbling around on the ceiling.

"Young man, kindly swat that fly," she told me.

"Madam, I'm a physician, not an exterminator," I replied.

"Kill the creature instantly," she said.

"If you don't mind, I'm a doctor, and I'm busy, and I'd rather examine you, I don't have the time to swat flies."

"Gross impertinence," she said. "Get out of here, young man."

Gratefully, I got out. She received all further medical attention from one of the less distinguished practitioners in the Rockport Falls area who came out to the island two or three times a day. If there were flies in the room, I presume he swatted them. I know he was paid fifty dollars a call. I also know that he gave her morphine every visit; she was an addict; that was all she wanted a doctor for.

One hazard in treating the socially elite was my obvious youth and inexperience. Some of the millionaires were prone to calling in city specialists over my head, flying them to Juniper at enormous expense. This I could understand, but this I did not especially enjoy, because when the specialist arrived I was expected to become second cook and bottle washer and bedpan carrier, which took a lot of time, and I had other things to do. I especially recall a young man, one of the richest young men in the world and one of the world's most heroic alcoholics, who was dying very young of cirrhosis. The city specialist was world famous. He arrived with a complete clinical laboratory, fully equipped and fully staffed, and entertained himself by studying the patient's water balance and blood electrolytes, as if the patient were a laboratory animal. Perhaps this study advanced the progress of medical science, but it killed the patient. Each time the doc desired to add a few more interesting electrolytes he did so with intravenous infusions, and the patient died of a wet lung, pulmonary edema. The specialist drowned him just as surely as if he had stuck the patient's head in the bathtub. I have a few heroic drinkers with cirrhosis among my fishermen. The only way they drown is to fall overboard in the bay. If I can keep 'em off the bottle reasonably, they survive, and if I can't, they don't, and I don't care any more about electrolytes than they do. But of course I'm not world famous. Mr. Specialist was paid fifty thousand dollars for one week's work. I followed him around all week, saying, "Yes, sir!" and admiring the beauty of electrolytes. I got a thousand bucks. Really, though, I can't complain. I earned almost ten per cent of my first year's income on this single case.

At the end of that week, however, I was absolutely pooped, so I went into the library. It was five o'clock in the afternoon, closing time, but the joint was packed with summer types: fat men in shorts; fatter women in shorter shorts; delicate little old lavender ladies; elderly old gentlemen with floppy white panama hats.

"Miss Winkle," I said, "throw 'em out."

"Dr. Dan, these aren't natives. I can never throw 'em out."

"After five o'clock."

"I can't close until they leave of their own accord."

"Why not?"

"Because their money supports this institution and pays my salary," she said. "One does not bite the feeding hand."

"I do."

"Yes, Dan, but most people can't afford to be as independent as you."

"I'm tired of millionaires. They bore me," I said. "I'm going to close up shop for you."

So I went to each patron in the library and reminded him that it was closing time. I cleaned out the joint in three minutes flat.

"You shouldn't have done that, Dan," said Miss Winkle. "There'll be complaints to my board of trustees."

"You can blame it on me. The notorious nonconformist and troublemaker. In kindergarten I flunked follow-the-leader. I hate people on beautiful July afternoons. I'm rich enough. Betty, I made a thousand bucks this week. On average, that's fifty-two thousand dollars a year."

"I don't like the change."

"Beg your pardon?"

"In the winter you were a pretty nice guy. Now you're a snob and slightly arrogant and you don't seem to like people any more."

"Blame it on the money. It happens all the time," I said. "Come along."

"Where?"

"Follow me."

"I passed the course in kindergarten," she said, and she locked up the library. I took her to the *Mary Jane*. I had stowed a picnic supper aboard and a Thermos of martinis. We set forth into the beautiful peaceful crowded waters of the reach.

"This yellow stuff is sunshine," I said. "Don't blink. Uncork the jug."

"It must be wonderful to spend a vacation here," she said. "But what if there's a medical emergency, Dan?"

"What if the ship sinks? What if somebody sets off an atom bomb?"

"You like to shirk responsibility. I don't think the good Lord ever intended you to be a great success."

"Agreed. I have no ambition. I came to Juniper Island under the impression that the place was uninhabited and now I find it's full of sick people all the hell over the place."

"You don't like sick people, Dan?"

"There's a limit," I said. "There are only just so many aches and pains, tensions, anxieties and itches, colics and hemorrhages, fits, cramps, and intimations of mortality that a man can stand at any given time. Show me one more infected black-fly bite and I'll scream. One more person tells me that he's going to die and I'll agree with him. I'm pooped. I'll do better work tomorrow if I take the evening off. If I was in the office tonight, my ears would be closed, and my heart would be made of stone, and I'd be giving out pills by the numbers. This God damn profession isn't as glamorous as your reading might lead you to suppose. Go report me to Hippocrates! I lost my dedication several hours ago."

We were passing the golf course on our left. It was populated as by a colony of ants.

"You know they had a hell of a slam-bang party here in 1912 for President William Howard Taft," I said.

"I've heard of it."

"In the afternoon he played a little golf. And you know what? They say he took twenty-eight strokes on the seventeenth hole."

Betty Winkle laughed.

"By the way," I said, "when are you going to marry me?"

She didn't seem to hear me.

"Shall I repeat the question?"

"Would you like another martini, Dan?"

"My answer is yes," I said. "Do I presume your answer is the same?"

"What happened to June?"

"This is July."

"Don't be evasive," she said.

"You see, I need some help in the office suite. Slob has left me. Last time I saw him, he was twenty pounds overweight, chewing on the remains of a prime rib roast."

"Just like President Taft."

"And I figure the best way to get a receptionist is to marry one."

"I already have a job," said Miss Winkle.

"There are fringe benefits," I said.

"Look," she said, "have you forgotten June in April?"

"That sounds like the title of a song."

"And it must have been a beautiful melody. She was in your bed what, Dan, three days?"

"For Pete's sake, you sound like little Martha Drinkwater," I said.

"Neither Martha nor I, who have both unfortunately fallen under the dubious spell of your questionable charms, Dr. Dan, can begin to approve of your April shenanigans with that woman."

"What shenanigans?" I said. "As if it was any of your business."

"If either I or Martha Drinkwater or both intend to marry you, this is very definitely a matter of our business, isn't it?"

"Nothing happened," I said, and I twisted the wheel sharply to the right to avoid a large submerged floating object.

"Nothing that wouldn't happen again next time she comes into the vicinity," said Betty.

"Now hold it," I said. "I refuse to be a defendant in the case."

"Plead guilty and get it over with."

"Maybe I'm innocent."

Betty Winkle laughed.

"Yes?" I said aggressively, on the verge of starting an argument.

"Reminds me of a story," said Betty.

"May I share the joke with you?"

"Once upon a time," she said, "there was this young dame."

"Beautiful, I presume?"

"Naturally. She was walking along a deserted country road when she heard a voice say, 'Hi, good-looking!' There was nobody in sight, nothing but an ugly little toad hopping along the road beside her. Again came the voice: 'Hey, babe, what are you doing tonight?' She could still see nothing but the toad and she said to it, 'That couldn't have been you speaking.' The toad said, 'Sure, it was me!' The girl said, 'But toads can't talk.' He said, 'I'm not really a toad. Actually, I'm a handsome young prince but I met a witch who turned me into this repulsive little object you see in the dust.' 'That's too bad,' said the girl. 'Is there any way you can get turned back into a prince again?' 'Only if some beautiful young girl takes pity on me and takes me home and puts me on her pillow for the night.' So the girl did take pity on the toad, scooping him out of the dust and taking him home. She put him on her pillow for the night. In the morning her father looked into the bedroom, and there was the girl in bed, and beside her a handsome young prince."

"Oh," I said.

"Well," said Miss Winkle, "the father didn't believe that story any more than you do."

It seemed to me that I got the point of Miss Winkle's anecdote and it also seemed to me that she had left me no reply. So I did not pursue the subject further.

I anchored the *Mary Jane* off one of the smaller uninhabited islands in the bay. In my dory, I rowed our picnic and Miss Winkle and me in to shore. I put bottles of beer in the ocean water to cool. I built a small fire on the rocks. We roasted hot dogs and marshmallows and consumed peanut butter and jelly sandwiches. It was a lovely soft summer night. A three-quarter moon cast a shimmering silver carpet to the horizon. After supper we sat beside the fire, sipping beer and watching the moon.

"I probably won't get married anyway," I said.

"Why not?"

"Probably I'm not the type. I'll be twenty-seven next week. How old are you?"

"This isn't the sort of question a lady should be required to answer on a night like this."

"I'm your doctor. A lady must be frank with her physician."

"You didn't ask me the question in the office. I'm older than you are, Dan."

"But not much?"

"Enough," she said.

There was only the slightest trace of briny chill off the water. Miss Winkle and I could very well have been alone on the face of the globe.

"Please don't, Dan," she said suddenly.

I hadn't done anything yet. I was just thinking of it. "Why shouldn't I?"

"It wouldn't make things easier for me."

"Since when has it been the ambition of a man to make things easier for a woman?"

"It ought to be."

"What dream world are you living in?" I said.

"I inhabit a library, surrounded by dreams incorporated in print and paper and cloth and glue."

"What do you have against romance?" I said. "In the flesh, I mean?"

"Nothing, if by romance you mean pleasant dabbling at a distance. I don't permit myself close contact."

"What's wrong with physical togetherness?"

"I like to watch the bonfire," she said. "I'm not going to put my naked hand in the flame. I burn."

"Burned before?"

"Yes. Don't go waving torches at me."

"Women are asbestos-lined," I said. "Only men are inflammable. Like moths, we fly into the flame. Women can handle fire. Such are the techniques of getting a husband. Any woman can get married if she chooses. It's only a question of fire control."

"What kind of a man do you get that way?"

"What kind do you want?"

"Not one so easily trapped by a physical technique."

"I believe we're all the same."

Miss Winkle suddenly reached out and grabbed a stick out of the fire. She thrust the blazing end at me. I jumped. I didn't think she really intended to burn me but the fire brought out menacing highlights in her eyes, and I didn't quite trust her expression.

"Hey, watch it!" I said. "Don't set me on fire. There isn't a doctor in miles!"

She laughed and threw the firebrand into the ocean. It hissed and went out. "This is my point," she said.

"Don't follow."

"You don't want to be burned either, Dan."

"Self-preservation," I said.

"Nearly twenty-seven years old, in a profession that surrounds you with women, but still quite single and not to be had. In other words, Dan, you don't want to marry me or anybody else. And I'm not like that woman, June. I don't play with fire for the fun of it. I wasn't born yesterday, and I'm not easily fooled. I happen to be out here with you not because of my overwhelming attractiveness, but because I'm the only one available. If others were around, I wouldn't rate a second glance. Let's go home."

She got up, washed out the Thermos, dumped some water on the fire, gathered up our debris and garbage, and got into the dory. I pushed off and we started rowing back to the *Mary Jane*.

"I didn't hear any argument from you on the subject," she said.

"As all Casanovas know, what a man can't get by persuasion and suggestion he can never win by debate."

"I didn't exactly call you a Casanova."

"I'm a man of persistence and patience, Betty. You can't break a bucking filly hastily. I'll get a saddle on her yet."

"I'm a bit afraid of you, Dan."

"Essentially, I'm harmless."

"You know what?" she said. "It's my impression you don't really care for women. Perhaps you can't see beyond the petticoat."

"I'm always interested in seeing beyond a petticoat," I said.

"Well, exactly. It may be difficult for you to appreciate a woman as a person above and beyond any female lure she might happen to possess for you. A passing moment of pleasure, maybe, but not connected with the main business of your life, which, of course, is medicine."

"You sound more like Martha Drinkwater all the time," I said.

"Sometimes I think men resent the power that a woman may have over them and try to take a cheap revenge."

"I'm glad we've come around to generalities," I said. "Men in general and not me in particular."

"Particularly, Dan, I was thinking of you."

I was glad that it was dark and that she couldn't see my face. The oars creaked and clunked in the rowlocks as I pushed the heavy dory through inky gelatinous water.

"That's rather a rough remark out of a gentle personality," I said.

"Dan, you started this. I was contented until you came along. You have no right to unsettle me."

"I have a distinct and definite purpose in mind," I said. "I'm not giving up so easily. Resistance merely whets the appetite."

"All of my training, all of my upbringing, my personal philosophy is dead set against that purpose you have in mind."

"What? Marriage?"

"Who said anything about that?"

"Me."

"A useful word at this stage of the game, but I've no evidence to believe such honorable motivations."

"You've no evidence to distrust me."

"Well, there's this woman from New York. And my own female intuition. I suppose you don't believe in that."

"Give me the benefit of the doubt," I said. "My basic object is education, Miss Winkle. I once said you were a silly and complicated sort of person. I want to know you better."

"Which can be accomplished perfectly well by conversation," she said.

"I'm not convinced of that."

"Well, you don't have to make love to your patients in the office, and you know them pretty well."

"You get to know a person by building a bridge of communication between yourself and them. For every two types of individuals, a different sort of bridge. For young man and woman, mutually attractive, there's always a block. You can't build your bridge until you dynamite the block."

"Build over it, around it."

"Doesn't work."

"Why should you want to know me anyway, Dan? I'm just an ordinary middle-aged librarian. What could you possibly learn from me?"

"Many things. After all, you're older than I."

"Miaow!"

"Well," I said, "you scratched me a few minutes ago."

Miss Winkle trailed her hand in the water on the dark side of the dory. Her hand, and my oar on that side, stirred up whorls of phosphorescence, cold forked greenish sparks under the surface of the water.

"This is my only kind of fire, Dan," she said.

"Don't hold yourself in so tight, Betty. You cut yourself off, and this is the reason you are lonely. Relax and live and let yourself go and things develop naturally."

"I don't want things developing out of my control. I don't play the game that way."

"As a matter of fact," I said, "you don't play the game at all."

We approached the looming hull of the *Mary Jane*. We touched with a soft bump. I scrambled aboard the larger vessel and made fast the dory. Then I reached down and helped Miss Winkle into the *Mary Jane*. I think we were both aware of the necessary physical contact. She broke free.

"Dan, it takes me days and days and days in the library to recover from these periodic jousts with you."

"Someday you won't recover. I'm willing to wait."

"I've heard of sunburn," she said. "Is there such a thing as moonburn? Blisters, shock, and fever from overexposure of a tender skin to moonlight on a night like this?"

"There's a word," I said. "Lunacy."

"I must use oils, greases, and lotions to toughen up the skin. It wouldn't do to walk into the library covered with a silverish glow."

"Most becoming," I said.

"Get me out of the moonlight, Dan. Please take me home."

And I did. She thanked me at the door of her apartment. She did not invite me in. When I got back to my house I found a note sticking in my screen door. I was requested to make a call to Somerset House as soon as I got back, no matter how late it might be. Whenever a doctor returns from any expedition, there seems to be a call waiting for him. No wonder doctors have messy personal lives. We never have time to work out domestic problems.

I got my bag and set off for Somerset House. In the winter I needed no transportation, for everybody lived just around the corner from me. The summer estates were spread all along the shore, some as far as nine miles away. We had tarred roads on the island, and some of the summer people had automobiles. I had even seen a Thunderbird. But a bicycle was adequate for my purposes.

Somerset House was the medieval castle. I crossed a drawbridge over a dry moat and knocked on a great oaken door. It was opened by a footman in livery. He escorted me down a succession of echoing stone corridors and into a large den where the owner of the place, one Michael Vladimir, awaited me. He was a thin, suavely dark and handsome man wearing a red velvet smoking jacket with a white silk ascot. He nursed the remains of a highball, staring moodily into the fire.

I knew the man by reputation. He was enormously wealthy and noted for his sagacity in sharp real estate negotiations, a sort of upper-class Cyrus Lunt. He was even better known as a sort of upper-class Abel Rast, for he too had petticoat fever. Apparently trying to break the record of a Tommy Manville, the man had been married and divorced any number of times to the tune of front-page publicity.

"You're the doctor? You look young."

"In the winter, I tried to hide my youth behind a beard," I said.

"I suppose some woman made you shave it off?"

"Yes, sir."

"Please call me Mike. Everybody does."

"My name is Dan."

"Would you care for a drink, Dan?"

As a matter of policy, I almost never accept anything at the patient's home: food, coffee, or a drink. To accept hospitality takes the physician off the professional level and reduces him to the status of a guest. On this occasion, however, I accepted a gin and tonic. It was my feeling that this patient would confide in me more readily over a drink.

"Are you married, Dan?"

"No."

"If you read the papers, you know that I am. My current marriage is two weeks old. My current wife is upstairs in a hysterical fit. In the morning, she calls her lawyers and starts divorce proceedings. I know the pattern."

"Do you want me to see her?"

"Are you any good at handling hysterical women?"

"Frankly, no," I said.

"Neither am I. No, Dan, I'm your patient. To tell you the truth, I doubt if you can help me."

When a patient makes this remark he is usually correct. "I'll try," I said. "What's the trouble?"

"The obvious trouble. I'm tired of this marital merry-go-round. What's the matter with me?"

"I don't know you," I said. "I can hardly make a diagnosis on such casual acquaintance."

"I'm a pathological type. You must have encountered it."

"Not often," I said.

"No. To marry a harem requires money, and most men of my type don't have it. I know the words to describe the condition: immaturity, hostility, revenge, masochism, obsession, psychological impotence. Knowing the words doesn't do me any good."

"I'm not a psychiatrist," I said.

"I'm not convinced psychiatrists can do any good," he said. "I've seen enough of them."

"There's a very obvious question that I would want to ask."

"Sure. Why in the hell do I marry them? I know they all marry me for only one purpose and live with me only enough to set up the alimony. My women are all alike. Why don't I rent them for the night? Why do I buy them at such an enormous price?"

"Maybe that type of woman isn't rentable."

"Don't be ridiculous. Of course they are," he said.

"All right. I'll bite. Why? So you enjoy publicity?"

"Of course I enjoy publicity, but I could hire press agents. Them I wouldn't have to marry."

"It's some type of psychological revenge mechanism. I don't know on whom you take revenge. A mother or stepmother? A favored older sister?"

"Or myself?"

"Yes," I said. "Very possibly. Would I be correct in saying that all your wives are young, shapely, and physically beautiful, greedy, stupid, and emotionally cold?"

"You read the papers, Dan," he said. "Strangely enough, I believe that I value the institution of marriage more than I value the woman concerned. Or, to put it more crudely, perhaps, I can't be satisfied in a rented woman until I have paid full purchase price and bought her."

"These women satisfy you?"

"For a few nights, yes. I love honeymoons. I've been most of my life on one."

"Is physical satisfaction such an important thing?"

"I don't know. Isn't it?"

"I don't know," I said. "I'm sure you were right. I can't help you. But I'll give you my honest opinion, for what it might be worth."

"It's worth a hundred-dollar fee."

"Not that," I said.

"That's what I'll pay," he said.

"Mike, you remind me of an alcoholic."

"I drink, but this is not my problem, Dan."

"I know," I said. "I only mean that your disease is similar. It is a fatal fascination with the seeds of your own destruction. Your need to painfully destroy yourself is greater than your need for the love, friendship, and respect of others. I've never been able to cure an alcoholic unless he really wanted to be cured. After that, it's simple."

Mike Vladimir looked at me. "Have you ever done surgery without anesthesia?"

"Only when we're cut off out here in a winter storm," I said.

"I suppose you think I should be upstairs with my wife."

"You would be," I said, "unless you were also looking forward to the next divorce."

"You're a painfully frank young man," he said. "Would you mind if I was painfully frank with you?"

Yes, I minded, but this was part of the job, part of the way I was earning a hundred-dollar fee.

"I know why you're not married," he said. "You don't like women either."

This was the second time that night somebody had pointed out this fact to me. I didn't bother to debate with him.

"Thanks," he said. "My secretary will send you the check."

"The service wasn't worth the fee."

"On the contrary," he said. "It was to me."

I departed and bicycled home through the moonlight. The first thing in the morning, Mike rang me on the telephone.

"Dan, I took your advice."

"I wasn't aware I had given any," I said.

"I went upstairs and spent the night with her. Wow! Best night since my second honeymoon."

"And when's the divorce?"

"Not this week, at any rate," he said. "I may need you again next week. But the honeymoon drunkard has decided he wants to be cured, and you said it was easy after that."

"Time will tell."

"I'm sending down your hundred dollars by messenger."

The messenger arrived: a long-legged, full-breasted, empty-faced, exquisitely groomed creation. First she gave me a kiss. Then she laid a hundred-dollar bill on my desk. Finally, as if further identification was required, she said:

"I am Mrs. Vladimir."

"Thank you. Want a receipt?"

"Doc, how'd you do it?"

"I'm not exactly sure what I did," I said.

"For the first time, last night, I got the impression that he really likes me."

"And you're not divorcing him?"

Her reply was the same as her husband's: "Not this week, at any rate."

She hauled out a cigarette holder at least a foot long, planted a cigarette in the end of it, lit the thing at arm's length, and regarded me with sleepy feline eyes. I was reminded of a leopard about to spring out of a tree on some helpless tethered goat below.

"Doc," she said, "you know it's tough to be a girl like me."

"Indeed?" I said.

"Yeah. Nobody understands me."

I studied a pair of sleek hips, snugly encased to the bursting point in a pair of yellow slacks, and luscious mammary development trying to burst through a tight purple sweater, and the predatory mouth set in the gorgeous but empty face. It seemed that anybody could understand this one at a single glance. I didn't say so.

"You know," she said, "I like you. You're sweet."

"Not when you really get to know me," I said.

"Why don't you drop around to the castle for cocktails? Almost any night at five o'clock. Sometimes Mike is there. Sometimes he isn't."

"I'm pretty busy," I said.

"See you around."

"If I see you," I said, "I'll certainly look."

Mike himself appeared at the office later in the day.

"What did you think of her?" he asked me.

"Some dish!"

"I mean, beyond the obvious superficials."

"To tell you the truth, Mike," I said, "she frightened me. I wouldn't be convinced that your hold on her was permanent. She invited me up for cocktails some evening when you wouldn't be around."

"She has a generous nature."

"Yes. And such a supply of goodies to be shared!"

"I found her in a chorus line. What happens to girls like that when they get old, I wonder? I can't visualize Dolores as a little old lady, exactly."

"They fatten up," I said. "You can't recognize them."

"I've enjoyed what you call the goodies, Dan, but be honest with me: could anybody make a wife out of material like that?"

"I don't know."

"What does a man go looking for when he wants to find a good wife?"

"This they don't teach in medical school," I said.

"You seem like a very sensible and wise young man for your age."

"At an age when most men are married," I reminded him, "I'm not."

"I'm not discussing you, Dan. I'm discussing me. I happen to be the patient in this case."

"Well, it all depends on what happens to lie underneath the supply of goodies."

"I think she's stupid," said Mike.

"Maybe. On the other hand, perhaps people don't understand her. This, at any rate, seems to be her own diagnosis."

"What's to understand?"

"Maybe that's her trouble," I said.

"I suspect that she is sweet and gentle, patient, easygoing, and sympathetic."

"Not bad qualifications for a starter," I said.

"And greedy."

"So are all of us when faced with temptation," I said. "A woman faced with your bank account. A man faced with a figure like that."

"To tell you the honest-to-God truth, Dan, I really don't know her very well. I know what she looks like without any clothes. Aside from that, you know her as well as I."

"She's your wife, and I have spent exactly two minutes with her, and I know her as well as you do."

"You suggest that I get to know her better before I decide whether to keep her or let her go?"

"I thought it was the wife who made this decision in your case."

"Perhaps I could alter this decision if I really tried," he said. "As I did last night."

"Perhaps."

"Thanks, Dan. You help me. Is a hundred dollars enough again for this visit?"

"Too much," I said.

"Look, if money embarrasses you, why don't I keep you on a retainer basis? So much each week throughout the summer? Then I can feel free to call on you at any time."

"No," I said.

"Why not? You can't make a living here in the wintertime."

"Mike, frankly, I want to be free to turn you down at any time."

A flush spread across his handsome face, and I was afraid I might have hurt his feelings. "I wasn't trying to buy you, Dan. I know you're not a chorus girl."

"You can call me any time, Mike, and I'll see you any time I can. But suppose a fisherman broke his leg at a time you wanted me?"

"I see your point, of course," he said. "My small problem, these two-humped camels I keep passing through my needle's eye, are scarcely important if somebody happens to be sick."

"Your problem is as important to you as a broken leg to a fisherman," I said.

"Thanks. I am glad you do appreciate this fact."

"Sickness comes in many shapes and forms, but I must feel free to handle every problem according to my own judgment and on my own priority scale. Otherwise, Mike, I would be no good to you, or a broken-legged fisherman, or anybody else. You could probably find a doctor you could hire full time, if you want one."

"And that kind of doctor would be just as good for me as the kind of woman I could buy for a wife."

"Maybe she loves you," I said. "Or wants to, at least."

This, apparently, was an astonishing suggestion that had never occurred to him. "You mean Dolores," he said, "or all of them?"

"Maybe each of them, in their fashion. They are not identical, even though they may look identical."

"Doesn't sound logical," he said. "Why are they so greedy? Why do they leave so quick?"

"They are not unaware of money, obviously; I never knew a woman who was," I said. "But I also never knew a woman who married for money alone."

"They don't all marry for love."

"No. Many marry for security. And many more marry out of pity, I believe. Has it ever occurred to you how many beautiful women marry men who are crippled in some manner or another?"

He winced. "Surgery without anesthesia again."

"They don't divorce you for money," I said. "After all, wouldn't they have more money as your wife than they could ever get in alimony?"

"I keep telling them this," he said. "As my wife, they control the entire capital. The alimony can only be a small portion of the interest."

"They're not after that money, Mike. Really they're after you. Before the ceremony, they think they can have you, can win where so many before them have failed. Immediately afterward, something happens and they know they must run."

"Mental cruelty," he said. "And yet I swear I have never been as cold and cruel as they have been to me."

"Men can tolerate coldness in a woman but never indifference. Women expect indifference to alternate with passion, but frigidity in a man will make a woman sick."

He got up quite suddenly, dropped a hundred-dollar bill on the top of my desk, and left the office, almost on the run. I didn't know if I was helping this man. I surely didn't think I was earning the fee. But I felt obliged to offer him what I could. I did think he was sick. I thought he deserved treatment just as much as anybody else, and I think a doctor must attempt to treat the patient even when groping in the dark. A therapeutic program may not be found in any book, but this is no excuse to turn the patient down.

*   *   *

Drinkwater rang me on the telephone.

"I haven't checked your blood pressure since the beginning of the summer," I said to him.

"You're busy. It's not important. My blood pressure can wait till fall."

"Nonsense. Of course you're important."

"Dan, I once heard you say that you could practice just as good medicine, and your patients would do just as well, if you threw your blood pressure machine away."

He had me there. "I miss our bridge games," I said.

"So do I," said Drinkwater, "but we did agree it would be best to stop playing bridge till fall. You couldn't get Willie Harpswell over to Juniper in the summertime. He sticks to his solitary little private island like a barnacle. You know he hates people. Especially summer people."

"Sometimes I agree with him," I said. "Juniper is certainly different in the summer. I can scarcely wait till Labor Day."

"We endure it," said Drinkwater. "It's only ten weeks. The winter here is plenty long enough."

"Funny. I haven't even seen Holy Joe Brown since the summer began, and he used to be running into my office several times a week. Did I offend him?"

"Of course not. He's just busy."

"Doing what?"

"Being a character," said Drinkwater. "You'd be surprised what a kick it gives the summer folk to see him working a lobster boat dressed like a clergyman. There's somebody else you haven't seen this summer."

"Who?"

"Martha."

True. I had not seen Martha for many months, it seemed to me. Although I hadn't thought of it before, I missed her. Little Martha Drinkwater was close to being my favorite person on Juniper Island.

"What's she doing?"

"Running around," he said. "Making a lot of noise. Acting like a brat. Bothering summer people. She's reverting to infancy. For a while there, Dr. Dan, I thought you were helping her grow to be a woman."

"I'm just as glad she isn't growing up too fast. I like her the way she is."

"You wouldn't like her now. She's just as smart-alecky and pushy and dirty and unattractive and spoiled as she was before you came to Juniper."

"One last fling," I said. "A few more months and she'll be a woman from then on, and go to Vassar, and you'll be very proud of her."

"You did not offend Holy Joe Brown," said Drinkwater, slowly and rather distinctly.

It took me a moment to get his point. "You mean I have offended Martha? Gee, I wouldn't intend to. I'd rather cut off my arm."

"I don't know," said Drinkwater. "But she never walks down your way any more. Always the other way. She doesn't mention your name. And if I do, she turns off her hearing aid, if you know what I mean."

I was perplexed. "What the hell did I do?"

"This is the question, Dan. Are you so busy with rich people from the castle and beautiful women that you don't have time for your friends any more?"

And before I could reply, Drinkwater hung up. I was unhappy and distressed. Maybe I hadn't offended Holy Joe Brown, but there was Martha and, more than that, Martha's Poppa too. What had I done? I thought back carefully, trying to remember the last time I had seen the child. When was it?

The last time I saw little Martha Drinkwater she was lurking on the lawn. She was lurking in the vicinity of the rose garden. Only at that time there weren't roses: nothing but alder scrub and weeds. It was in April. Upstairs was a woman named June.

Oh, my God!

* * *

I searched all over the island before I found Martha. I finally located her on the uninhabited eastern side of Juniper. She had clambered down into a sheltered hidden cove and was examining the contents of a tide pool on the rocks. With some difficulty and small lacerations, I scrambled into the cove myself and made my way towards her over wet slippery seaweed.

She must have heard me coming, but she didn't look up. She was a ragged, disheveled urchin in blue jeans, sneakers, and a flannel shirt. If I hadn't known her I could not have been certain whether she was boy or girl. I sat down near her and cleared my throat. She still refused to acknowledge my presence. This would have informed me she was female, if I hadn't known.

"Miss Drinkwater, I presume," I said at last.

"Poppa sent you out for me," she said, without looking up.

I lit myself a cigarette. "Care for a smoke?" I said.

"Are you kidding? What are you, some kind of humorist?"

"I'm a very serious person," I said.

At that, she looked up. "You're always making jokes and poking fun at things. Don't you know, other folks got feelings?"

"I can't afford to let people's injured feelings get me down," I said. "I'm a doctor, and my world is filled with injury and pain. Perhaps even more, this world is full of broken dreams, and ships that never come in, and things that aren't quite fair. My defense against this mass of suffering is laughter. I try never to laugh at people, Martha. I laugh at myself and at the foolish stubborn pride I share with everybody else. You'll understand when you're old enough."

"When I'm old enough to smoke?"

"Those old enough to smoke are old enough to make love," I said. "Otherwise you'll stunt your growth."

She returned her attention to the tide pool, plunging her elbow deep into the cold clear water.

"If you gave me a cigarette Poppa would skin you alive," she said.

"Nobody skins me alive," I said, "not even your formidable Poppa."

"I know somebody who did." She might have been addressing a passing small green crab, not me.

"In the first place, you don't know her," I said. "In the second place, my skin is perfectly intact, as you can see if you look at me, and in the third place——"

"——you haven't been fair with that Miss Winkle from the library."

"Good," I said. "You approve of Miss Winkle."

"I don't!"

"Why not? She's shy and sweet and pleasant and sensible and——"

"Half dead, she is!" said Martha.

"Oh no! You don't know Miss Winkle either."

"Who cares?"

"I guess you do," I said, "judging from your present frame of mind."

"Don't care about nothing, nobody, nowhere, and nohow!"

"Suit yourself."

Silence reigned. She fished her pool. I looked over the water to the horizon. It was a humid afternoon in early August. The water was an insipid misty wishy-washy shade.

"What do you see out there, Doc?" said Martha at last.

"Everything important with one exception," I said. "The most important thing of all."

"What's that?"

"People," I said.

"I don't like people. They're no damn good."

"I disagree with you."

"People ain't good for much unless they mind their own affairs."

"Again I disagree," I said. "People are no damn good only when exclusively occupied with their own affairs. The thing of no importance, Martha, is the busyness."

"You think it's better to lay around, goofing off, like you're doing this afternoon?"

"There is a time for everything," I said, "including goofing off."

"There's somebody else I don't like," she said. "That dame from the castle. The one with sweaters and pants, if you know what I mean."

"I know who you mean. Dolores Vladimir."

"You just stay away from her, Dr. Dan."

"Why?"

"Because you're a man and can't control yourself."

"Oh," I said, "I can if I try."

"Oh," said Martha, "then men don't want to try."

"There are some things you don't completely understand about men."

"And you understand all about women, I suppose?"

"No," I said. "None of us want to. Why spoil all the fun and mystery?"

"This gives you an alibi. Then you don't have to explain yourself."

"Why should I have to explain myself?"

"I know," she said sadly. "It's none of my business. I'm supposed to keep my little nose out of your affairs. You've told me a million times. I've been keeping it out for months now, haven't I?"

"That's not what I meant," I said.

"And what do you mean, Dr. Dan?"

"No man, no woman, should have to apologize for the way they are. If you can change yourself for the better, try and do it. You should never justify yourself for the evil that you do, especially to others. But you must learn to live with yourself in peace, exploiting the assets, limiting the liabilities. Nobody has to apologize. Everybody has to try to understand."

"Can't do it," she said. "Maybe I don't want to grow up. Especially not to be a woman."

"You'd rather be a man?"

"Nope. Not nothing. Just me."

"Just you is just right," I said. "Are you bashful?"

"What do you mean?"

"I mean there's nobody around in miles."

"There's a guy named Rast in a lobster boat out there."

"Nobody named Rast would mind," I said. I suddenly kissed her on the cheek. "Now, watch yourself, and keep up your guard, because I'm a man and can't control myself," I said.

"You're laughing at me, Doc."

"No."

"I can see that twinkle in your eyes."

"That twinkle is a healthy thing."

"You didn't mean nothing by that kiss. Of course Rast wouldn't mind. Poppa wouldn't mind if he was here. You don't mean nothing at all."

"Martha, I love you. I do mean that. And I promise to control myself. Around Miss Winkle. Around Dolores Vladimir."

"Around that dame called June?"

"She isn't here."

"Lucky for you."

"Someday," I said, "I wish you could get to know her."

"How can I do that? If she ain't coming back?"

"Someday maybe she will," I said. "In the meantime, we must cope with this particular day when she won't. And this particular day is a hot one, and I personally would enjoy an ice cream soda down at Wellington's."

"Dr. Dan," she said, "I'd love an ice cream soda down to Wellington's."

So we marched down to the village together and had an ice cream soda. That night, Drinkwater called me on the telephone.

"Thank you, Dan."

"My pleasure."

"Tonight, she took a bath for the first time this summer. *Mirabile dictu*, she's wearing a dress. She's taken off those damn blue jeans and sneakers. I think I'll throw them away."

"I'm glad you weren't watching this afternoon," I said. "You might not approve of the pass I made at your daughter."

"I'd like nothing better than to have you as a son-in-law, but hadn't you better wait a few more years?"

"I'll always be too late," I said. "Don't they come in that style ten or fifteen years older?"

"I hope you find her, Dan," said Drinkwater. "And actually, this is Martha's true desire. Only she doesn't know it yet."

* * *

I wasn't finished with the problem of Mike and Dolores Vladimir. I was summoned to the castle again late at night. Mike was in his den, nursing a highball, staring at the fire.

"Apologies," he said. "I hope I didn't drag you away from a sick fisherman. But, for all your wise and helpful advice, I don't think we've gained an inch. She's upstairs, indulging in hysteria. Tomorrow she consults her lawyers. I know the pattern."

"Well, maybe we better get this over with," I said.

"You think I should let her go?"

"If you go through the same performance every week or two, you haven't much ground for a solid and sustaining relationship."

"I'll buy that," he said. "The hundred-dollar fee is adequate?"

"Just for thirty seconds?" I said. "And agreeing with the decision that you'd already made?"

"I told you it would be less embarrassing to have you on a retainer basis."

"And I wanted to be free to turn you down."

"You're fed up with me," he said. "Next time I call, you won't come."

"No, I won't, not unless I feel I can contribute something postive to the problem."

"Divorce is positive."

"Hardly," I said.

"All right. And what would you do to earn your fee?"

"This time, I should be talking to Dolores."

"All right. Let's go upstairs."

"Alone," I said.

He looked at me suspiciously.

"What's the matter?" I said. "Don't you trust me alone with your wife?"

"I'm not quite sure. No offense," he said.

"What difference would it make, if she's not going to be your wife next month?"

"That's true," he said.

"If you can still be jealous, there may be something here worth salvaging."

"Suit yourself. The butler will show you the way."

The butler showed me the way. I knocked on the door and identified myself. A muffled voice inside told me to enter, and I did. The lady was in bed. The covers were pulled up to her chin. She had been crying and there was neither beauty nor greed on her face. She looked like a sullen little girl, put to bed without any supper.

"What do you want?" she said.

"I don't know. I'd like to help. If I can."

"How come? For a hundred-dollar fee?"

"Yes, or for no fee at all. The money isn't important."

"It isn't?"

"Do you think so?" I said.

"Without the money, I'd hardly be in this pickle of a mess."

"What pickle of a mess would you be in?"

She began to cry. I let her alone, sitting silently and patiently until she reached the Kleenex stage.

"Feeling better now?" I asked.

She nodded, snuffling and blowing her nose.

"Okay," I said. "So what are we going to do about this problem? Any time, you can get this divorce. I imagine your terms will be just like the others: no better and no worse. Next year by this time, somebody else will have him. In two years he won't even remember your name. He won't remember whether you were number eight or number ten. You lasted longer than some and not as long as others."

"I'm not just like all the rest of them. I'm me."

"And what's so different?" I said.

She started to cry again.

"You'd save this thing if you knew how to go about it, wouldn't you?" I said.

Through Kleenex, she nodded.

"Strangely enough, so would he," I said. "So what are you going to do?"

She blew her nose again. "There's only one thing I know," she said.

"Does it work?"

"Just for a little while," she said.

"Put together a lot of little whiles," I said, "and you get a long while."

"Yes," she said, "but what do you do in the mornings?"

It seemed to me I heard an echo, a lonely cry through the long unhappy centuries: what do you do in the mornings?

"There's only one answer to that," I said. "Like all important things, it's simple."

"Yeah?"

"Yeah. You've got to try and learn to like the other guy. That's all."

"I could like him," she said, "if we didn't happen to be married."

"Okay, so become unmarried and the best of friends."

"Then I'd never see him again," she said.

"This is the possibility. You'd see his alimony check."

"I don't want his alimony check."

"Good," I said. "I'll tell Mike. This one is on the house. He will be pleased. For this will mean one extra marriage he can afford before the capital runs out."

"You're horrid!"

"I've often suspected so," I said.

"But you may be right."

"This is how I earn my fee," I said.

She took the Kleenex away from her nose. "May I say something to you, Doc? You won't get mad?"

"This is also how I try to earn a fee."

"You might be wrong."

"It's happened before," I said.

"Because how could you know about all these things, Doc? You're not married."

"Good-by, Dolores," I said, and I went downstairs.

"Solved?" said Mike.

"Go on upstairs. She's ready for you. Plenty of goodies, I suspect."

"What the hell kind of solution is that?" said Mike.

"Don't ask me. I'm only a doctor," I said. "I'm not married."

"Maybe you should have been a pimp."

I passed my hand over my eyes. It was late; I had a headache; I needed sleep.

"Excuse me, Dan. I didn't mean that," said Mike. "I got so wrapped up in my own problems, I wasn't thinking of yours. I don't know how you doctors put up with this sort of thing. People must say the damnedest things to you without thinking what they mean. They forget that a doctor is a human being, with problems of his own."

"Your sort of problem will never trouble me."

"No." He smiled. "Which is worse? No wife or an even dozen?"

"There's nothing like that at home, waiting upstairs for me."

"And you thank heaven for that," said Mike.

"But if there was," I said, "I wouldn't waste my time downstairs chatting with a bachelor. Even for the pleasure of calling him a pimp."

"Will you forget that, please?"

"Unless you hurry, she may no longer be there."

"Thank you, Dan."

"Good night, Mike. Don't do anything I wouldn't do."

Making my way home on my bicycle, I was wondering whether I could survive till Labor Day.

*　*　*

This patient came from the estate next door to Somerset House, the one shaped like a Moslem mosque. The problem: diabetes. The complication: diabetic acidosis and impending coma. He was a young man and he had been diabetic since childhood. He was pretty sick and the problem was a complex and serious one, as diabetic coma always is. I gave insulin and stood by for some hours and managed to pull him out of it.

Two days later he was back in coma again. And again that Saturday. And still again the following week. This was getting monotonous.

"What the devil does he do between times?" I asked the patient's mother. "Fill himself full of candy bars?"

"He just got married this summer," she said, as if that would explain everything.

"And she feeds him chocolate ice cream sodas?"

"Have you met his wife?"

"No."

"I'll introduce you."

This was another long-legged, full-breasted, gorgeous, empty-faced creature. She should have been in the movies. If Dolores Vladimir was Marilyn Monroe, this creation was Elizabeth Taylor, raven dark where Dolores was silver blonde, but otherwise they came from the same mixing pot. In the winter there wasn't a pretty woman on Juniper. Fishermen's wives tend to run short, plain, and stringy. I would hardly consider Betty Winkle a beautiful woman, although I may have noted that she had good legs. But now, in the summer, these dishes seemed to spring up from behind every granite ledge. Or maybe the trouble was with me. So pressed and busy, I had no choice except to live like a busy eager monk. Of course, I hadn't gotten anywhere with Betty Winkle. And June was in New York.

"Do you understand now?" said the mother of the patient after having led me away.

Yes, I did think I understood. The patient was a sallow timid gentle quiet individual with a weak chin. His mother stood six foot one with the same approximate silhouette as the Widow Gideon. There was no father on the scene. Divorce had occurred a number of years ago.

"And when was the diabetes first picked up?" I inquired.

"When Sonny was thirteen."

"When were you divorced from Sonny's father?"

"When Sonny was twelve," she said. "It was a stormy time for several years and then we took him to the Joslin Clinic. They straightened him out."

Dr. Joslin was a remarkable man. A specialist in the best sense of the word, which meant he was the best kind of family physician, as the really good specialist so often is.

"No more trouble until that creature married him," said Sonny's mother, "and she married him for the money, of course. Not that I mind that. It was more or less expected. And Sonny is very much in love with her, I guess. Certainly he was overwhelmed. You don't have to tell me that this sort of female is overwhelming to a certain kind of male, and I have always known that Sonny is weak. So was Sonny's father. That woman is just more woman than the boy can handle. This is the trouble, Doctor. It isn't candy bars."

I guess I was looking at Sonny's mother a little too closely.

"And you're thinking, me too," she said.

Poor Sonny, caught in a tug of war between two women, each more than he could handle. No, this wasn't candy bars.

She gave me a rather sardonic smile. "Perhaps we should call a truce?" she said. "We'll each let Sonny go. Then, without either of us, perhaps he can stay out of acidosis."

"Unfortunately," I said, "Sonny needs you."

"And her?"

"Sonny has to prove, somehow or other, that there's a man inside, underneath the chin."

"At the cost of his life? People sometimes die in diabetic coma, Doctor."

"Unfortunately, yes. Life is such a little thing to throw away for the price of self-respect."

"I'm not proud of what I've done to Sonny. I can truly say I tried to do my best. I know that I tried too hard. I never cared for the mother spider. I watched myself develop into one."

"It's not entirely your fault, Mrs. West," I said.

"Partly Sonny's. He should have broken free."

"Mr. West must also take his share of the blame," I said.

"Him!"

Mr. West had broken free. Spider mothers may defend their young, but they eat their mates, unless Mr. Spider is fast on his feet.

"Doctor, you wouldn't know it to look at me now, but I was beautiful when I was her age. Sonny was a beautiful baby. I wonder what happened to his chin?"

*   *   *

Mike Vladimir called me on the telephone. This time, he was calling for social and not professional considerations. I was invited to cocktails at Somerset House.

"You'll be there?" I asked him.

"Sure," said Mike. "You don't think I'd trust you alone with my wife? By the way, we have a house guest. I think you've met her before."

"Who is it?"

"You'll find out at five o'clock."

I didn't own a tuxedo and I was wondering how to dress for cocktails at Somerset House. I considered a flaming orange sports shirt, Hollywood style. I settled for my dark blue Sunday suit. It was too heavy for the muggy August heat and was covered with dust by the time I reached Somerset House on my bicycle. For the first time in nearly a year I regretted that I didn't own a Thunderbird.

Mike wore a flaming orange sports shirt with green pants. Dolores wore snug-fitting pants of gold lamé and a pink transparent blouse.

"We weld her into the pants," Mike confided to me behind his hand. "It takes a can opener to get her out."

The house guest made an appearance, dressed in cool gray slacks and a silver blouse. When I saw her my jaw must have dropped. I was glassy-eyed with shock.

"June!"

"You was expecting, maybe, Marilyn Monroe?" said June.

"Anybody but you. I thought you were in New York," I said. "Why didn't you write? What are you doing here?"

"I've known Mike for a long time," she said.

I wasn't entirely pleased that Mike Vladimir should have been included in June's list of long-term intimates and doubt must have registered on my face.

"Dan, it is possible for me to have known a young woman without having been married to her," he said.

"Don't look so punchy, Dr. Dan," said June. "I've no intention of becoming wife number thirteen."

"Bad luck," said Mike, with a grin.

"Besides, Dolores might have something to say on the subject," said June.

Dolores was on the verge of saying something, but nothing came out. Since I had been invited for cocktails, I grabbed one off the butler's passing silver tray. June sat down on a sofa. As if by tacit agreement, Mike and Dolores drifted over to the other side of the room. I joined June on the sofa. She appraised me.

"No beard," she said. "And I see you're wearing a business suit."

"Quite prosperous this summer, thanks to the problems of such people as Mike Vladimir," I said.

"He tells me you've helped him a great deal, that you're popular and highly regarded by the summer colony."

"Just how well do you know Mike?" I inquired.

She thought it over. "Nearly as well as I know you, Dan," she said.

I studied the implications of this remark. In one sense, I really didn't know June at all. If this was what she meant!

"Why are you staying here?" I asked.

"Because Mike was kind enough to invite me and because the accommodations are very luxurious."

"More luxurious than mine, but I bet I've got something he doesn't have."

"What's that?"

"Feather beds," I said.

"I always wanted to sleep in a feather bed."

"Huh?"

"Well, Dan, I really didn't get much sleep, as you may recall."

I looked at her; she looked at me; the gray iris of her pupils grew wider and wider, and finally she laughed. It was a husky, intimate sort of laugh; both Dolores and Mike glanced in our direction.

"Let's sneak out of here," I said.

"Dan, I'm a guest. I can't sneak out of here."

"Or else you don't want to."

"I'm being very well entertained."

"At my expense, I suspect," I said, leaving the sofa, going over to Dolores and Mike. "Hope I'm not interrupting anything," I said to them.

"What's to interrupt?" said Mike. "We're married."

Now that I was in close proximity to those snug gold lamé pants, I found it difficult to keep my eyes raised to proper levels. "Mike, how well do you know June?"

"We've been acquainted for many years. How well does one know a woman of this kind?"

"Meaning what?" I said.

"Meaning that all the eggs aren't in one basket, I guess. Besides, I like the simple kind."

Dolores seemed to be working up a protest but it didn't come. Both Mike and I together seemed to be eying gold lamé. The butler passed with his silver tray. I snatched a martini in each hand and drank them quickly in close succession. This was a mistake. I was dry and dusty from the road. The martinis were only glowing pleasantly in my stomach but if all that concentrated alcohol reached my dehydrated brain simultaneously, it might put me on the rug. I asked the butler for a glass of water to dilute the stuff. Then I went to the sideboard where a spread of delicate and delicious eatables was on display, and I gobbled down some food. I was aware that the three others were watching me. I thought my antidote would be sufficient but a slight vertigo had already seized my balance center.

"What's the matter? Am I on display? Am I the star of the show?" I heard myself saying, too loudly.

Dolores and June took a quick glance at each other and both of them glanced at Mike. Dolores murmured something about powdering the nose and she and June went upstairs together.

"A little warm and stuffy in here, isn't it, Dan?" said Mike, taking my arm. "Why don't we step out on the terrace? There's always a cool breeze off the water, even on a day like this."

After a few deep inhalations I was all right. "I'll make the next one a long gin and tonic," I said. "As a thirst quencher to the dehydrated man, the martini carries hidden menace."

"So I have also discovered."

The flagstoned terrace was on the lip of a granite cliff and commanded a magnificent panorama of the bay, the mainland, and the distant hills. Mike and I strolled back and forth.

"Mike," I said, "why did June come here?"

"Because we invited her."

"Why did she accept? Does my presence on Juniper have anything to do with this?"

"You better ask her," said Mike.

"You seem to know her pretty well. What do you think? Would June make a good wife for a man?"

Mike gave an explosive laugh. "Good God Almighty!" he said. "Don't ask me!"

"You know what?" I said darkly. "I think it's a trick. I think she wants to drag me out of here, away from Juniper Island, back to New York."

"That's funny," said Mike.

"What?"

"Last night at supper she said she'd like to live out here."

"A trick and a trap," I said.

"Then defend yourself at all times, and keep up your guard," said Mike. "The ladies are coming back."

The ladies returned. Before June could subject me to any wifely scrutiny I told her, "I have recovered. I am fine."

June pointed a shapely finger out over the bay, where a two-masted sailing yacht was beating out of the reach towards the ocean. "Isn't that beautiful?" she said. "Looks like a living creature rejoicing in her freedom."

June wandered to the far end of the terrace, as if to get closer to the schooner, and Mike had drifted in the other direction, to inspect his gardens. This left me with Dolores.

"Love those man-trapping pants," I said.

"Mine," said Dolores, "or hers?"

"It was yours I had particular reference to."

"She is very lovely."

"Of course."

"Say, Doc," said Dolores, "would you mind if I asked you a personal question?"

I always mind persons asking such questions. "Shoot," I said.

"What have you got against marriage anyway?"

A very strange question out of her, it seemed to me. "Nothing," I replied.

"Don't you like women at all?"

"On the contrary."

"You don't act that way," she said.

At this particular moment the butler came out on the terrace and said there was a telephone call for me. I took it. Somebody had fainted down at the waterfront. Could I come along?

I apologized to host and hostess in the name of emergency, promising to return, and I bicycled back to the village. The patient had something real, an attack of paroxysmal tachycardia rather than the simple syncope I had been expecting, and it took some time for me to bring her out of it. It was several hours before it was safe to leave her. I was tempted not to return to Somerset House, it being nighttime and long after supper by then, but my visit with June had been strangely inconclusive, and I was afraid she might escape if I didn't go back.

Her voice in the darkness stopped me before I reached the drawbridge. I dismounted from the bicycle. She was alone, seated on a bench in the gardens at the edge of the property.

"Waiting for me?" I said.

"I didn't think you were coming back."

"Sorry," I said, "but the case was more difficult than I anticipated. I just stopped off at my place for a bite to eat and came back as quick as I could."

"That's nice."

It was a tropical summer night, the air hot and still, the moonless sky dotted with sparkling stars.

"I'll say it quickly, before there's another interruption," I said. "I'm lonely, June. Will you marry me?"

"When?"

"Tonight. Any time. As soon as possible," I said.

There was a very long pause. I couldn't see her face. There must have been a party on a yacht in the bay just off shore: I could hear laughing and singing. In the castle, somebody must have been listening to television; faintly, I could hear that.

"May I ask you something first?" said June at last.

"Something personal?"

"How many other women have you asked to marry you this summer?"

"None," I said rapidly, and then I added, "Well . . ."

"Yes, Dan?"

"Only one," I said.

"She turned you down?"

"She didn't say yes; she didn't say no; she hasn't said anything yet."

"A rather good reply under the circumstances, Dan."

"Well, damn it . . ."

"Yes?"

"Damn it, how does a fellow know where he stands?" I said.

"Don't you first have to determine where you stand?" she said. "I mean, you can't exactly marry both of us. Not at the same time. Even Mike Vladimir has to make decisions."

"She's a librarian," I said.

"Not the one at the local island library?"

"Miss Winkle is the name."

"I took out a detective story for light summer reading yesterday."

"She isn't much to look at," I admitted. "She's shy. But she's got a good sense of humor and she's something of a screwball in her own quiet way, and I've grown quite fond of her."

"She's older than you are."

"She has migraine headaches. I believe she's afraid of marriage."

"You have a lot in common."

"Now, June . . ."

"Good night, Dan. It's been fun seeing you again."

"Now wait . . ."

"I'm waiting," she said, but she wasn't; she was striding across the drawbridge at a fast long-legged gait; I came hurrying along behind her.

"When will I see you again?" I said at her back.

"I don't know."

"How long will you be around?" I asked her shoulders.

"I don't know."

"Damn it, June . . ."

She stopped, whirled around, and I almost ran into her. "If you please, don't swear at me, Dan."

"Well, I'm sorry."

"If you can't make up your own mind, please don't blame me," she said. "It seems to me I've given you every reasonable latitude and opportunity. You can't expect me to wait indefinitely. I have a certain amount of personal pride myself, you understand."

"Okay."

"Okay. So we understand each other."

It didn't seem to me that I understood much of anything.

"So, good night," she said with some finality.

I heard her high heels clatter over the drawbridge and the great oaken door go slam. There wasn't much left for me but to go on home on my bicycle.

I was kept busy the following morning. I didn't get around to phoning Mike Vladimir till noon.

"She's gone, Dan," Mike informed me. "Packed up bright and early and away by ten o'clock."

And that was that, I guess. I was tired of the summer. I was looking forward to Labor Day.

Part 6

Autumn

OUT OF THE HUMIDITY, the muggy heat and mists, a northeast wind arose. Gray clouds gathered, obscuring the sky, and the sea was gray. The wind bore an icy hint of Labrador and gathered white foam and scud off the top of curling gray-green waves. The tides were very high. Rain fell heavily. Cold air and rain, driven by the wind, pierced the loose framework of summer cottages and mansions like arrows. Summer people huddled in front of open fires and thought of going home. Fishermen started their furnaces. Boatyard men started putting pleasure yachts to bed. Children gathered up their pencils and their books. Summer was over.

For a week, the last few days of August and on into September through Labor Day, the chill blustery northeast storm continued. It was what the fishermen called a "line storm," although everybody else called it Carol. I'm not sure where the name "line storm" comes from, but it meant two things to me. The rain, driven by the wind, seemed to fall into dotted, almost horizontal lines. And this particular type of seasonal storm seemed to divide the seasons, summer and autumn, as sharply as a line. Fishermen chewed their pipes and wagged their heads and spoke knowingly of an equinox. I'm sure they could not have defined an equinox but I know what it meant to them: this same sudden shifting of seasons without any zone of transition. The fishermen welcomed it. Summer was the season of money, and for the next nine months there would be no loose money on Juniper Island. The coming of autumn meant that cold harsh man-hating winter was soon to follow. Summer was beautiful and winter was severe, and the winter was too damn long on Juniper Island, but the summer was also too damn long. To live by choice on an isolated island implies that the resident values peace, privacy, and solitude. There is no peace, privacy, and solitude on Juniper Island in the summertime. Money cannot buy these things.

The summer visitors, welcomed like long-lost cousins and returning prodigal sons in the month of June, could sense that their welcome had expired, and they were in a hurry to depart. The weather was formidable; the fishermen were unfriendly; another vacation had gone. It was time for them to go back home, back to school and work, and they looked forward to it. They couldn't seem to go fast enough, and every fisherman was anxious to give them a pushing hand in going. The population of the island dropped from two thousand to four hundred during the week of Labor Day.

And when the scene was cleared, the line storm stopped. Brilliant sunshine washed away the rain. Summer visitors will never know it, but they leave too soon. The most gorgeous weather along the coast of Maine is reserved for three fall months. Natives know it very well. This weather is just too damned lovely and delightful to be wasted on work and summer people. The natives stop working. They live and enjoy themselves.

The days are brilliantly clear; the sun is bright; the air is crisp and sharp; the sky and water are incredible rich luxurious shades of violet, purple, emerald, and azure. Blood courses tingling through the veins. A man rejoices in the feeling that he is alive.

I felt rain-washed, dawn-pure, reborn, full of the sense of anticipation of adventure, as if I were just coming to Juniper Island for the first time to find myself, to find whatever it was that I was missing in the suburbs.

But I was a year older. A little less innocent. I wouldn't try to drive across the reach in a Thunderbird convertible this year, nor would I feel naïve and stupid when encountering a Cyrus Lunt about to cheat me on a real estate transaction. I had had a good summer financially, and I wasn't as much in debt, though more in debt than when I had arrived the year before. But I owned some things that nobody could mortgage and nobody could cheat away from me. The inhabitants had also gained from my presence. They no longer had to wonder what a doctor was good for. They had discovered that he was something of more value than just a signer of the death certificate. I didn't envy the fact that the Widow Gideon still delivered all island babies. I knew that she could deliver them better than I could, although she was nothing but an obese stupid opaque drunken one-mounded Indian squaw. If I hadn't happened to come to Juniper, she wouldn't be here this year. She and I had caught a crab together.

Some of the things I was looking for, I seemed to have found on Juniper Island. Exactly what they were I could not precisely define; how I had found them I was not exactly sure; but I knew what I was doing in my professional work. Before I came to Juniper I didn't.

Some other of the missing links, it seemed to me, were further away than ever. I was about to become reconciled to being a full-time bachelor. There was something else, more fundamental and more obscure, that seemed to be lacking. I was brought up on fairy tales and fantasy and Puritan romanticism, like everybody else who has been brought up at all. I was told, as we have all been told, and had been firmly encouraged to believe, that my life would have a plot. It would have a beginning of promise, a fighting middle as I battled between the choices of good and evil, and a conclusion of some kind. The ending might be happy or sad, depending on whether the balance of my free choices had added up in the red or the black, but it would at least be final and conclusive. I would live happily ever afterward or else, like the flying Dutchman, damned. Either way would bring its own satisfaction, since I would be reaping harvest from the seeds I had sown.

That second autumn on Juniper it was occurring to me that the plot seemed to be lacking. No resolution of conflict was in sight. Each day brought its little battles and I fought them out, sometimes well and sometimes badly, and I went to bed at night, tired enough from the battling to sleep very soundly. The morning, however, seemed to have brought no progress: neither gain nor loss, not even an inch. More little engagements remained to be fought, fundamentally the same battles, although never exactly on the same terrain.

Was I, Alice, running hard to stay in the same place? As I ran, the scenery flowed by me and I was standing still. A treadmill. An aging horse.

Well, I thought, I really have no complaint. I paid the purchase price, I suppose, and I have to accept the merchandise, for the complaint department is closed. This must be what takes place when the young man of promise, with the keen sense of history, decides to live fifty years prior to his day and bury himself prior to his time. I've learned the trick of relative happiness, or at least satisfaction in daily routine: you live your life in day-tight compartments, one day at a time, without looking forward or back. You live like an old hound dog. But can you, and should you, a human being who once had plans and zeal and ambitions, learn to savor the satisfactions like an old hound dog? I wonder. I am still not sure.

As soon as the line storm cleared, when there were no more egg salad sandwiches being taken out of glassine envelopes, when there were no more kindly chefs and butlers giving out soup bones in back of summer estates, Slob returned to me. At suppertime there was a small scratching at the kitchen door.

"Well," I said, "that sad begging expression of the eyes is familiar, and I have seen that sloppy variety of nobility before, but do you really think you should be recognized, dog?"

Only somewhat sheepishly, he wagged the tip of his tail.

"You ever heard the story," I said to him, "of the man who was sent down to the grocery store for a loaf of bread and didn't come back for twenty years?"

From his expression, I was given to understand that Slob had heard the story. Furthermore, I suppose, when the man came back and finally laid the loaf of bread on the table, he was accepted into the family bosom without comment and given supper as if he had never been away. Probably, they never even asked him where he'd been. Probably, that was why he had gone away in the beginning.

"But there's one thing about the story I don't understand," I said to Slob as I let him in. "The loaf of bread: was it twenty years stale? Or was it fresh baked and freshly bought?"

Hell, Slob's expression informed me, I'm not human; I don't know these things; I'm only a hound dog of doubtful origins, considerably fatter and somewhat older than when you last saw me. I had a hell of a summer, Dr. Dan. How about you? I had the God damnedest things to eat and I suspect, here and there all over the island pretty soon, there are going to be litters!

"But you see, my sensual and greedy canine friend," I said, "it makes all the difference in the moral of the story. Because, if that loaf of bread was twenty years stale, it meant the poor man didn't really intend to go away and had been faced with temptation that he could not overcome, but the fact that he was lugging a stale loaf all over the world for twenty adventurous years meant that basically he always intended to come back. Otherwise he would have given it to some destitute prostitute in Singapore. See what I mean? On the other hand, if he bought that bread just before he got back, it means he had first intended to leave for good, but now he really wanted to return."

This was too complicated for Slob. He laid his head in my lap. Said a voice at the kitchen door, a young female voice, "Do you always talk to yourself like that, Dr. Dan?"

"Hello, Martha," I said. "I wasn't talking to myself. I was talking to Slob."

"You think he can understand you?"

"I don't think he can understand me," I said. "I know he can."

"But that story you were telling was awful kind of complicated, wasn't it?" she said. "I mean for a dog?"

"True."

"So, really, weren't you trying to tell that story to yourself?"

"Also true," I said.

"I know what prostitute means."

"In a sense, I'm happy for your education," I said. "In another sense, I'm sad."

"A woman couldn't hardly get through life without knowing what that word meant."

"Wouldn't it be nice if she could!"

"But a fact of life is a fact, Dr. Dan, and it ain't necessarily nice."

"With a fact, ethics have no place."

"What's ethics?"

"Oh, this younger generation," I said. "They understand prostitution but not ethics."

"Did you understand an ethic when you was my age?"

"Still don't, Martha," I said. "Slob does. I don't. This is one of the harder things for humans."

"Why don't I stay for supper, Dr. Dan? Can you cook?"

"If I don't lose the can opener," I said.

"How about a scallop stew?"

"I love it," I said, "but I have no scallops."

"I do." For the first time I noticed that Martha was carrying a paper bag in her hand.

"But what about your Poppa and John?"

"Done already cooked supper for them."

"Have you eaten?" I asked.

"Nope. Figured I was going to eat with you. You reckon Slob likes scallops?"

We looked at Slob. He wagged himself vigorously. There was no doubt whatever. Slob liked scallop stew.

"You're spoiling me," I said, spooning up the delicious scallop stew. "I'll never again enjoy my own cooking after this."

"You shouldn't have to cook for yourself, Dr. Dan. Not a busy important person like yourself."

"Busy only in the summer, only ten weeks out of fifty-two," I said. "And in no meaning of the word important."

"Important to your patients and your friends, Dr. Dan."

"So is every physician, no matter how unimportant he may be."

"And therefore we got to take care of you."

"We?"

"Yeah. Me, Poppa, and John; the Widow Gideon; Slob; Cyrus Lunt; Wellington down to the grocery store; all them characters named Rast. All us proud people who don't necessarily leave a place as soon as the temperature gets a little cold. You're a valuable man, Dr. Dan. We don't want you to go away!"

"Why should I ever go away?"

"We can't pay you very much in the wintertime."

"Sweetie," I said, "you pay me plenty."

"Your own kind of folk don't seem to care very much about you."

"This is my own kind of folk," I said.

"We figured you was a dead duck when she came back again."

"Who? June?"

"But then she took one look at you and went away again."

"You see?"

"Don't worry, Dr. Dan. You won't be lonely here this winter," said Martha. "Not if there's anything we can do about it."

* * *

Slob took position in my waiting room as if he had never been away. The kids came in, for shots and examinations prior to school. Martha was headed for high school this year. We had a little elementary school on the island, but for the high school grades the children were transported to Rockport Falls. I therefore didn't see as much of Martha during the working week.

Soon after Labor Day, Wellington made an appointment at the office.

"Feel a mite run down and poorly at this season of the year," said Wellington. "Reckon it's my liver again, don't you?"

"Or too much summer visitors," I said.

"Gee, Doc, I'm delighted to see 'em come, but I'm even more delighted to see 'em go," said Wellington. "Guess I need a tonic."

"If you were truly concerned about your liver, you wouldn't drink so much beer on Saturday nights," I said.

"Doc, you sound just like my wife."

"Women seem to understand these things," I said. "Have you ever noticed? How the wives outlive their husbands ten or fifteen years?"

"Doc, you call that living?" he said. "What is there about women anyway? They always seem to resent it when a feller has a little fun. Fun ain't nothing a woman hankers after, it always seems to me, and whatever she can't enjoy, she don't seem to want the other feller to enjoy. Know what I mean?"

"It's mysterious," I said. "It has something to do with the survival and perpetuation of the race."

"Doc, if you want to look at it that way, living is very dangerous. It's bound to kill you in the end. Living is a fatal sort of thing. Take a drink and you die of liver disease. Smoke and you get cancer of the lung. Eat and you get fat and you get the gout, and if the gout won't kill you, fatness does. Everybody knows that womanizing weakens a man. Go out in a lobster boat and you're likely to freeze or drown. If you don't go out in a lobster boat, you don't eat and you die of starvation. If you step into an automobile, you have a fatal accident. If you don't step into an automobile, somebody else runs over you. In a thunderstorm, if you take shelter under a tree, you're liable to be lightning struck. If you don't take shelter under the tree, you get sopping wet and catch pneumonia. Seems to me, Doc, there's only one answer to this thing."

"What's that?"

"Don't never get out of bed at all."

"That won't work," I said. "Didn't you know that most everybody dies in bed?"

"True. So what the hell, I say! Take a chance. I ain't going to get out of this thing alive anyway. So I might just as well enjoy myself."

"No argument," I said.

"A pity my wife can't see things that way."

"If she did," I said, "she wouldn't be much of a wife."

* * *

There was a call from Cyrus Lunt in the middle of the night. He was a pretty sick man. His pain was extreme. His belly was as hard and rigid as a board; I could have stood on it. There was no particular doubt about the diagnosis. One of his recurrent peptic ulcers had ruptured, and surgery was indicated. Nothing I could do but give him something to relieve his pain and get him quickly over to the clinic in Rockport Falls.

"Thanks, Doc," he breathed to me sleepily when the intravenous morphine had taken hold.

"You'll be okay," I said. "They'll fix you up in no time. But they may have to remove part of your stomach, you know."

"That part of my stomach ain't doing me any particular good, is it, Doc?"

"Certainly not at the moment," I said.

"Serves me right. It's my own fault. You done warned me plenty of times about this."

"Cutting corners on a business deal, I suppose?"

"Doc, business is business, and it ain't love nor sentiment, right?"

"Well . . ." I said.

"What I mean to say is: you're dealing with a businessman, and he's dealing with you, and he's going to get away with every penny that he can, and he knows it, and you know it, and rules was made to be broken, and both of you know it, right? It's a game, and in every game somebody's got to win or lose, right? I mean, hell, Doc, this is America, and capitalism has been working fine for us for a couple of hundred years, and we built this system on enterprise and independence and them laws of supply and demand. Business is business. You just can't get away from it."

"Honesty is honesty, and there are certain things you can't get away with either," I said.

"I ain't dishonest. It's only I'm a businessman," he said.

"Don't talk so much."

"If you don't mind, Doc, talking keeps my mind off the belly, and if you really want to know, Doc, my belly hurts like hell."

"Keep talking," I said.

"I know you're right," he said. "That's what I mean: this is all my own damn fault. Businesswise, I'm shrewd, and usually I can get away with it, you know? But inside of me, I ain't so shrewd. Just when I'm feeling happy about what I done to the other feller, inside I'm feeling unhappy about what he's done to me. Damn son-of-a-bitching businessman, you know what he made me do? He's made me do something which would make my mother cry. That is, Doc, if my mother was alive, and if she could ever find out about what I'm doing, which she never can, thank God, and may her blessed soul rest in peace!"

"She was only trying to make you honest, so she could be proud of you."

"Doc, I'm honest," he said. "I got just one problem. I ain't exactly ethical."

"It's a rather fine difference, and when you get out of the hospital I'd like to ask you to define your terms."

"Doc, maybe I won't get out of the hospital. Maybe I'm going to die."

"Unlikely, if we can get you over there quick enough," I said.

"Well, sooner or later I'm going to die. I ain't exactly the immortal type."

"I was just discussing this problem with Wellington," I said.

"Got neither kith nor kin, but one hell of a lot of money in the bank. You know what I'm going to do with it, after I'm deceased?"

"It's the general impression that you can't take it with you," I said.

"I'm referring to my last will and testament, Doc. It's all laid down legal, in black and white. I'm giving my money to the poor: the widows, the bums, the drifters, and the fatherless children."

"You old rascal," I said. "That's where you got your money in the first place: from the widows, the bums, the drifters, and the fatherless children."

He gave me a weak grin. "Well, Doc, ain't it honest of me to give all that money back?"

"It would have been more ethical not to take it in the first place."

"If it hadn't been me, it would have been some other businessman, Doc. The fool and his money is soon parted, as you may have heard. You might say I've been keeping the money in trust for them."

"You might say it. I wouldn't."

"Doc, I'm no good," said Cyrus Lunt. "My own father told me that, and he should have known. He was no good neither."

Cyrus Lunt was still talking when they put the ether to him, and he came out of anesthesia talking fast, and he was back on Juniper in a couple of weeks, saving money for the widows and the fatherless children, in his own peculiar fashion.

* * *

And then there was the residual problem of Miss Winkle. She made an appointment in the office early in October.

"Dan, what were those wonderful pills you gave me for the migraine?"

"Cafergot."

"They surely worked," she said. "You know, I haven't had a headache since you prescribed that medication?"

I thought this one over. "You're taking the pills regularly every day?"

"No. Only as directed, Dan."

"And what were my directions?"

"I should take a pill whenever I felt a headache coming on," she said.

Logic doesn't seem to apply to women, but I thought I'd try it on for size. "You take a pill whenever you feel a headache coming on. But you haven't had any headaches since I prescribed the pills. Therefore, you haven't taken any pills. So how can you say they're wonderful?"

"I consulted you with migraine, and I've had no headaches since I consulted you. What more does the patient require?"

So much for logic! Then she got around to telling me what she had really come for.

"Dan, I'm going away."

"Where?"

"I don't know," she said. "I'll have a vacation first. Then I'll find another job. This is one advantage to being a librarian. The job is dull and it doesn't pay much, but we're always in demand."

"You'll get more salary elsewhere?"

"I doubt it."

"The work will be more interesting in a larger town?"

"The work will be the same."

"You'll find more social opportunities, more recreation, a wider circle of friends?"

"You know damn well I have no recreation, no friends, and no social life," she said.

"If I weren't on Juniper Island," I said, "would you stay?"

She refused to answer this one.

"Betty," I said, "Cafergot didn't cure your headaches, but you want to know something? I did."

"Better some kinds of pain than others," she said obliquely.

"Come now!" I said. "You have a sense of humor and a sensible outlook on things. Don't try to tell me you are suffering from the pain of a broken heart?"

"Now, Dan," she said. "I don't want to puncture your ego or lacerate your pride, but you don't break all female hearts. You seem to intrigue certain leggy types and sweater-filling varieties, some of the innocent and some not so innocent, but this doesn't imply you have done any injury to me. At a certain time of life a woman must come to terms with herself. I'm an old maid and a librarian. What about it? Within the limitations which I cannot alter, I accept myself. This is my life and I like it. You have almost nothing to do with it."

"As you wish," I said.

"Dan, you're not getting any younger," she went on. "One of these mornings you might take a long cool look at yourself in the shaving mirror. What are your objectives and your goals? Is treating sick people enough for you? Do you ever plan to have a family of your own? Unless you're willing to commit yourself, you also may find it is too late."

"Betty, will you——"

"Is there anybody in the waiting room?"

"Only Slob," I said.

"Well, he can keep a secret. And things that happen in the office are kept in professional confidence, correct?"

"Correct."

"Then put this in the files," she said. She startled me with a kiss. It was a frank, honest, and erotic kiss. "Don't react," she said. "Sit still."

"I'm sitting," I said.

"Dan," she said, "there's nothing I'd like better than what you've had in mind. My inhibitions are not as impregnable as you may suppose. I've been tempted to enjoy a small affair with you. I think I would enjoy it. But what would it prove, Dan? We are not in love. Without love, there could be no marriage. Without marriage, there could be no children. Without children, what's the point? Small pleasures, physical satisfactions, grotesque acrobatics lacking grace and dignity. Is this sufficient recompense for ashes in the morning? Not for me, Dan. And really, I think, not for you. Can you really tell me different?"

"But . . ."

"If you could only say it without that conjunction, Dan."

"Don't you set standards impossibly high? If I look around, Betty, really, there's not a saint in the crowd."

"I'd rather be right than President," she said.

"Epitaph for wallflowers," I said.

"As long as there are walls," she replied, "there might as well be flowers. Better than weeds."

"If you could tell me this, before breakfast, in the morning, I'd accept it," I said. "Otherwise, this is nothing but the ignorance of innocence."

"Dan, you can't marry both of us."

"It doesn't look from here as if I were going to marry either of you," I said. "And since Martha is too young, and the Widow Gideon is too old, and Slob is nothing but a dog, perhaps I'd better go away."

"Would she marry you if you really asked her?"

"How about you?"

"I'm trying to tell you," she said. "Haven't I?"

"I can hear two voices speaking. Which do I believe? Look, Betty, it wouldn't be so bad."

"But, Dan, would it be any good?"

"There's only one answer to that."

"Your favorite answer," she said. "How can you tell till you try? This can't be a matter of trial and error, a hit-or-miss proposition."

"It's never anything else," I said.

"Sorry. I wouldn't enter the transaction on that basis. Therefore I won't enter it at all. The ways of the Michael Vladimirs are not those of grace and dignity."

"Everybody keeps throwing Mike Vladimir at me," I said.

"And you would register injury and protest if it were pointed out to you how much you resemble Michael Vladimir?"

"I would ignore the remark," I said, "since I don't!"

"And you're twenty-seven years old, my young friend, and what are you waiting for? Please don't tell me this was lack of opportunity."

"The same thing you have been waiting for, perhaps."

"The impossible ideal?"

"Well, maybe not," I admitted. "The implausible probability would be nearer."

"And besides, you enjoy independence and fight against giving it up."

"You're a wonderfully honest person, Betty," I said. "I love you for this. Really and truly I do."

"You wouldn't if I cheated on myself."

"You can't. That's just it!"

"That's it, Dan," she said. "So you have no right to test me. You've no business trying to unsettle me."

"I'll quit," I said. "I guess I'll have to love you from afar."

"At closer range, you wouldn't. This I know. I am very sure of it now."

"Just friends," I said. "Can two people who won't marry, who can't cheat, and who will not take advantage of nature's peculiar and unsettling little game, really be in love with each other at a distance in some funny sterile oddball sort of way?"

"Wouldn't it be nice if we could?"

"I believe we can," I said.

In my mind there was a sudden illumination, as if a searchlight had been turned on. I had made a discovery. Perhaps Miss Winkle also made a discovery, for she gave me a beautiful smile. Then she kissed me again. This kiss was on the cheek and definitely unerotic; it might have been defined as a sisterly kiss.

"Now I won't have to go away," she said.

"I never had a sister."

"Brother, you don't have one now!" she said.

I'm not sure I liked what I had discovered. "What I do have now," I said, "is a headache."

"I suggest Cafergot."

"Good old Dr. Dan, the ancient family physician, confirmed old bachelor, fond of children, pets, and middle-aged ladies. Won't I look sporty in a floppy white panama hat?"

Miss Winkle spoke a rude Anglo-Saxon word.

"Why, Miss Winkle!" I said.

"Dan, you've fought a valiant battle, but you're going to lose. I give you six or eight more months."

I wasn't sure we were speaking of the same thing. "Will it hurt?" I asked.

"Yes, I believe it will."

"Then I don't want to," I said.

She smiled. "I know. But you've got to."

Six or eight more months? How could a middle-aged librarian know this?

* * *

Glorious October: I think of it as the golden month. There's goldenrod in the fields; the sunshine is melted honey; the foliage flames with orange, red, and gold. The days are warm and mellow, the nights sharp and cool. A man feels alive and full of energy and only slightly sad.

Several nights a week, when she got back from school in Rockport Falls, little Martha Drinkwater came over to my house and cooked supper for me. I enjoyed her company and her cooking. After supper we washed the dishes together, and then I would light a fire in the fireplace. Martha would curl up in an armchair on one side of the fire, doing her homework, and on the other side, me with my pipe and slippers, catching up on the professional literature, learning what they were doing in the city hospitals these days. Slob snored on the tiles between us, just as close to the fire as he could get. Every now and then Martha would interrupt me with a question about the quadratic theory or Caesar's Gallic Wars, which I would attempt to answer from the depths of shadowy learning long forgotten. It was most domestic and rewarding. Yet I didn't think I should monopolize so much of her company. I protested to her father one night during our weekly bridge games.

"Dan, she enjoys it, and you're a good influence on her," said Drinkwater.

"Yeah," I said, "but I have the feeling that she's taking care of me. I'm not exactly a cripple, or anything."

Drinkwater, my partner, smiled at me across his cards. Willie Harpswell and Holy Joe Brown were also smiling. I looked at my hand.

"I'll open with three no-trump," I said.

I had a good hand, but this was an outrageous overbid. I had only eighteen high-card points, rather than the twenty-four I should have had, and there was weakness in the club suit. Everybody passed. Willie Harpswell had the opening lead and, with his usual shrewd ferocity, he led a club. I lost the first five tricks and was down before I could get started, but at least the play distracted attention from the previous conversation. I was among friends. We were all psychological cripples here.

I saw a lot of Betty Winkle that October. I frequently picked her up at the library at closing time and walked her home. Sometimes when Martha wasn't coming we had dinner together. We shared several Sunday afternoons.

One Sunday we were lying side by side together in a field, watching high puffs of cloud against a brilliant blue sky. Around us the reds and oranges and scarlets and crimsons of the foliage shone forth almost blindingly.

"Nature has the right idea," said Betty. "She goes out to face decay and death, dressed in her best fiery strumpet clothing."

"But she's not an old maid," I pointed out. "Mother Nature has already known the pain and power of creative reproduction."

"Isn't it fashionable, in these Freudian times, to dig up old hostilities and conflicts to explain why people act?"

"Freud was a genius," I said. "His discoveries truly rank with those of Einstein and Columbus. But I think it is a mistake to explain all human conduct and motivation in the Freudian idiom. There are many other elements to human psychology, as Freud himself would be the first to recognize. If he were alive, I think he would be appalled at the mess of murky muck being peddled under his name."

"I was engaged to be married once," said Betty. "Nine years ago. I knew this man exactly two weeks, Dan, if you can believe it. We were both on furlough. He was in the army and I was a WAC. He was killed at Normandy. Isn't it foolish of me to hold up the memory of a man I never knew as the impossible standard for rejection of every man I have met since?"

"Most doctors, I think, consider marriage as the normal human relationship. Therefore, every unmarried woman or man beyond a certain age we would tend to consider abnormal. But I wonder! It seems to me that marriage is a social condition and not a psychological necessity. In fact, successful marriage requires suppression of certain basic drives. Marriage is a compromise for the socially mature. The immature marry by droves, and we see the results in our offices."

"This dead man has been my alibi, and I use his ghost as my excuse not to marry, but, Dan, if this guy had come back I wouldn't have married him either. I recognize that marriage is a give-and-take relationship. I can take it, but I haven't anything to give. I've been working away, trying to discover myself, trying to find some sense of my own individual unity and integrity. If I gave away any single stone, the whole damn arch might collapse. This isn't very brave of me, but I suspect a safe and comfortable coward is in better shape than the hero in a panic state."

"All men are bachelors at heart," I said. "The male instinct is love 'em and leave 'em and find somebody else."

"A fact that the female knows and finds disturbing and vaguely disgusting. She knows that the man is interested only in her body and never in herself as a personality."

"If the female is to reproduce, she requires the support of marriage and the home. Therefore she sets marriage as the price of her consent. To satisfy desire of the moment, the male must meet the price or settle for a cheaper article of goods. Women with a cheaper price can give temporary pleasure but never lasting satisfaction, since they themselves are not satisfied. But to obtain satisfaction with the woman of his choice, the man must compromise: he must give up his independence and he must give away his freedom of selection, variety, and choice which is part of his maleness. This is the tragedy of sex, although actually it isn't a tragedy: it's more like a comedy of errors. Was it Shaw who called it a cruel little joke played on men by nature in order to perpetuate the race? The normal man takes his lumps and grins. He isn't interested in tragedy. He'd rather chuckle at a dirty joke. His work is more important to him."

"Women know these things."

"Yes," I said. "But I don't think women understand their own instinctual demands as well. Although they know of sexual differences, they tend to accept the masculine definitions and try to fit into them, which of course won't work. They have not been able to define for themselves their own goals quite so clearly. Take the act itself. Take that word 'orgasm,' which is a nasty little word that I don't like."

"Kinsey says——"

"Kinsey makes me sick," I said. "Kinsey would have turned Freud green. Kinsey started as a statistical specialist on insects. Human love is no more than that of the spider, fly, and cockroach? In the latest Kinsey Report, the one on women, there are some sixty-three references to orgasm in the index and not a single reference to love. He never even mentions love anywhere in his work."

"I wonder if it's so important."

"Love?"

"The other word that you don't like."

"Betty, that's just what I'm talking about," I said. "It takes nine minutes to satisfy a man. It takes more than nine months for the woman. For her, there's something more than momentary spasm of the muscles. It begins, I should think, when she feels a quickening of pleasure at knowledge of the man's eye upon her. It doesn't end until she suckles a baby at the breast. The subject is one of my favorite peeves. Mind if I blow off a little steam?"

"Blow!"

"Modern woman feeds her infant from the bottle and thereby deprives herself of the climax of her act. Why? Because bottles are more convenient? Who thinks it's convenient to boil up formula in the middle of the night? Is the bottle better for the baby? Of course not: any honest pediatrician will tell you that the breast-fed baby is tougher in both mind and body. No, Betty, the true reason is that the woman is afraid to lose her shape. A breast is a secondary sexual organ; we have made it a primary fetish symbol. My profession encourages this perversity. Physicians conspire with brassiere manufacturers, editors of girlie magazines, and advertising geniuses to make sex neurotic and commercial for the sake of making a buck! I wonder why? Are doctors afraid they would go out of business if women stopped being neurotic?"

"That white stuff coming from your ears is steam, I suppose?"

I grinned. "Sorry. The diatribe is over."

"You get pretty worked up over things like this."

"I get worked up about the waste and futility of human unhappiness," I said.

"What can you do about it, Dan?"

"Not much in general, but one hell of a lot in particular," I said. "Every time I make a sick person smile, every time I beat a little common sense into the sick stubborn stupid head of a patient, every time I can puncture superstition, ignorance, false ethics, arrogant pompous morality, I . . ."

". . . get a little older, Dan."

"Yes. I suppose," I said with a sigh.

"You're cute, Dan."

"Cute?"

"Would quaint be the better word?"

"How about antique?" I suggested. "Archaic? Victorian? Born a century too late?"

"You'd have been a most unpopular Victorian," she said. "That's what I love about you, Dan. The passion."

"Nobody ever accused me of being passionate!"

"In a tight icy restrained New England way," she said. "Vigor in a strait jacket. Fire under ice."

"That's the Puritan in me. I'm a pilgrim who has made no progress, Betty."

"If I remember my Bunyan," she said, "you have left the City of Destruction but have not yet arrived in the Celestial City, and therefore you are stuck fast in the Slough of Despondency."

"Otherwise known as Juniper Island," I said.

"Have you ever seen a slough so beautiful?" She waved her hand in an arc to include the blue ocean and the blue sky and the dark green evergreens and the white birch bark and the incredible flaming foliage.

"I know what you mean," I said.

* * *

I've heard it called the anniversary syndrome. On the date of some traumatic episode in the past, the patient develops subconscious symptoms of anxiety, in remembrance of the bygone date. I guess I had it on Hallowe'en. I kept expecting to see a man and his wife die side by side and to feel the necessity of doing an autopsy on both of them.

It was the usual cold rainy Hallowe'en. Branches scratched at the windows like the fingers of skeletons. All the little spooks visited me that year. After having tricked-and-treated the last of them, I waited for the phone to ring, but nobody called me that night.

They waited till the following morning. One of the fishermen came dashing in and told me to get in the *Mary Jane* and go quick to Hog Island. In his speed and anxiety, he had not identified the place for me properly, even though he had given its proper name.

"What's the trouble?" I asked.

"He's committing suicide, Doc. And likewise he's set fire to his house."

"Who is?"

The fisherman looked at me as if I were crazy. "Willie Harpswell, of course."

Of course. Harpswell's Island was called Hog Island on the charts. I went in a hurry. I was disturbed and upset, for Willie was a friend of mine, but I was not surprised. Suicide is a hazard of the manic-depressive, particularly when the patient is in a despondent, depressed phase. There was a whole cluster of fishing boats anchored off Willie's island: all of the Juniper Island volunteer fire department, as a matter of fact. Fortunately it was a calm day and the bay was still, for there was no good anchorage, and a good deal of the time nobody could make a landing except intrepid Willie in his dory. As I nestled the *Mary Jane* among the crowd and threw my own anchor overboard, I saw a good deal of smoke. When I got ashore it was obvious that the smoke was pouring out of the upstairs rooms. Although the roof might go, there seemed no danger to the house itself. There was no flame among the smoke, as far as I could see. I was about to go dashing into the house, looking for Willie, when I almost tripped over him. He was on a stretcher on the lawn. A tarpaulin had been pulled over his face. I gathered he was considered dead.

Peeking under the tarp, however, I knew an error had been committed. Willie wasn't dead. He was sound asleep but his breathing was regular. I applied painful stimulus in the form of a good hard pinch; he didn't wake up, but he stirred and groaned and his eyelids fluttered.

"I thought somebody said this was a suicide," I remarked.

The volunteer fire department was milling around, too busy fighting fire to pay very much attention to me and Willie, but somebody thrust a piece of paper in my hand. It was written in Willie's characteristic wild violent scrawl. It was, without question, a suicide note and it informed me that Willie had consumed sixteen one-and-a-half-grain Seconal capsules at six o'clock in the morning: three hours earlier. Quite a goodly slug of barbiturate; it could have been fatal under certain circumstances, but Willie was pretty tough. Perhaps he would have died if he hadn't been discovered. I got a stomach tube out of my bag and thrust it down Willie's gullet and washed out his stomach. I got back in the returns a number of chunks of undigested red gelatin capsule, so I could be sure that the total dose had not been absorbed, despite the time interval. Actually, as I later discovered, although Willie had written the note at six in the morning, he had not ingested the Seconal until much later, no more than an hour earlier and perhaps even less. A few of the firemen-fishermen watched me, but most of them seemed to find stomach-pumping slightly gruesome, or the fire more entertaining, or something. After Willie's stomach was well and truly washed, I gave him an intravenous dose of picrotoxin. This is a central nervous stimulant supposedly specific for barbiturate poisoning, which I carried in my bag for just this purpose. I don't happen to believe in it; I think it may do more harm than good; but the stuff is recommended in the books, and therefore I don't dare not to give it, even way out on an island.

Willie had a brief satisfactory convulsion, woke up long enough to look at me wildly and cuss me out convincingly, and fell back to sleep again. He slept until the middle of the afternoon. By then the fire had been long out. The firemen-fishermen had moved Willie's belongings back into the house from the lawn again and had returned to the lobster fishing of the day. I had been sitting by Willie's bedside for some six hours, bored to distraction, with nothing to do but count his pulse and respirations from time to time and wait for the son of a gun to wake up. Towards the end of it, I thought that he was faking, just having a gentle snooze at my expense. My last therapeutic act was to go to the well and bring up a bucket of nice cold water and throw it in his face. Worked better than picrotoxin. He woke up.

He grinned at me and he said, "Doc, I'll bid six no-trump."

I gave him back a few of the cuss words he had previously used to me.

"Pretty foolish of me, wasn't it?" he said.

I agreed. I advised him next time to take enough of the stuff to finish the job and not just enough to tie me up all day, a day's work for which I did not expect to be paid.

"What did you do?" said he. "Why should I pay you?"

"For bringing you back across the river Styx and returning you without apparent gratitude to this vale of tears."

"And how'd you manage to accomplish this miracle, Doc?"

"Ice water and picrotoxin," I said, "and if I hadn't gotten to you with the stomach pump in time, twenty-four grains of Seconal might have been enough to do the trick. Living out here alone on this blasted hunk of rock, you were pretty damn lucky that anybody found out that you were sick. The fact is, nobody would have known if your damned house hadn't been on fire." It was only then that I happened to think of the incongruity of the situation. Just how in the hell had his house happened to get on fire in the first place, at a time when he was lying unconscious and needing help, and the smoke from his burning house could conveniently be seen by all the fishermen all over the bay?

He looked sheepish. "I set it myself, Doc."

Indeed!

"Willie, you're a fake," I said. "You didn't intend to kill yourself. You made a cheap melodramatic gesture. You wanted us to know about, and feel damn sorry for, your lonely miserable life."

"I've done many a foolish thing in my day, Doc."

"Well, I forgive you," I said, "but don't let it happen again."

"You suggest that I actually kill myself next time?"

"I do."

"Wouldn't you miss me?"

"Only on Friday night when we need a fourth for bridge," I said.

"Tough guy!"

"Willie, you can be pretty tough yourself. Don't soften up on me."

Willie had a psychosis, manic-depressive disease, and suicide is a common result of the depressed phase of this condition. However, Willie was not in a depression; the way he came out of his slumber, garrulous and social, informed me of this. His theatrical gesture was neurotic in nature. Can a psychotic also be neurotic? I think so. I'm not sure psychiatrists are yet aware of this fact.

"You want me to explain myself, Doc?" said Willie.

"Not especially," I said, "but if I don't listen to your sad story, I suppose you'll be gulping more sleeping pills, and I'll have to wash out your stomach all over again tonight. Quite frankly, I don't enjoy washing stomachs."

"I was married once, Doc," he said. "We didn't get along. In order to keep peace in the family, we broke up the family by mutual consent. There were no children, thank God! I'm a thoroughly useless personality type, over and above the creative work I do. I don't get along with people very well, and people bother my creativity. I work best and live most constructively alone, except when my crazy spells break over me. When I'm in a manic mood I go to New York. I always used to see my wife on such occasions, and we used to have a ball. She is, you might say, rather wild herself. Her psychotic tendencies match my own."

"A year or two ago, right on this particular date, your wife committed suicide, I suppose."

"No. Three years ago today my wife married somebody else."

"I understand. Since you are a person with a certain reputation, Willie, it would get into the papers if you committed suicide. And your wife might read the papers. So this was a sort of swell anniversary present for the lady, huh?"

Willie smiled. "As you know, Doc, I'm the sweetest sort of guy!"

"Well," I said, "there's the explanation. I don't like it; I don't approve of it; I don't know if we can accept it fully at face value. It'll do for me, however. I've no particular desire to go diving any more deeply into the mess of your subconscious mind, Mr. Harpswell. There is, however, one thing I still don't understand."

"Yes, Doc?"

"Your paintings. Why did you try to put them to the torch?"

"I don't know, Doc."

"You weren't as crazy as all that," I said. "How many paintings do you have in the house?"

"I don't know. Couple of hundred or more."

"Your worst?"

"No, Doc," he said. "My best. I don't sell any but the worst of them, and then only when I need a little cash."

"And when you and the house and your best creative work burn flat to the ground," I said, "what's left of Willie Harpswell?"

"Doc," he said, "just as I was gulping the last of the capsules, this very thought occurred to me. I stopped gulping pills and ran around and tried to put the fire out. That's the last I remember before I went to sleep."

"Because no woman would ever be worth destruction of the genius of Willie Harpswell," I said. "This leaves us only one more enigma. Why did you set fire to the house in the first place?"

"Well, Doc, nobody comes out here. There's no good anchorage to moor a boat. And besides, if anybody steps ashore, Willie Harpswell might take a shot at them. So if I destroyed myself peacefully, who would ever find me? My body might lie around for weeks or months. And then the lady would never have heard about it in time for her anniversary."

"And that's why you set fire to the house!"

"Now, Doc, you understand why it's best for me to live alone?"

"Yes, Willie," I said, "I think I do."

* * *

In November, I caught a stiff nose cold. As a general rule, I seem to be immune to respiratory disease, but this time I sneezed till I nearly tore off my head. My nasal turbinates swelled like poisoned pups, and behind the swelling my sinuses were boggy swamps of pus.

"Doc, you should see a good doctor," I advised myself.

But doctors can't cure the common cold. We can only hope it develops into pneumonia. Pneumonia we can cure.

"Doc, you should go to bed," I advised myself, but like any patient I ignored the doctor's advice. I was too busy to go to bed. Whenever I bent down to tie a shoelace I thought the top of my head was falling off. On minimal exertion, I was bathed with prickly droplets of perspiration that felt hot and cold at the same time. My head was light and woozy. My balance sense was insecure. None of my muscles hurt very much, but there wasn't a single one that didn't hurt.

"Doc, I feel absolutely wretched. I think I'm going to die," I told myself.

The doctor, as usual, laughed at the patient for making such a hell of a fuss about a little cold in the nose. The patient, as usual, resented being laughed at.

"Dan," I said to myself, "there's a moral here. Sick folk ain't got much of a sense of humor. Later on, when you recover—that is, if you ever recover, which seems somewhat unlikely at the moment—do you suppose you can remember this?"

The nose cold became a chest cold. I coughed and coughed and coughed until my face turned purple and I retched, a nasty dry tickling cough, bringing nothing up, it seemed, but chunks and scraps and pieces of the epithelial lining of my bronchial tubes. I coughed all night. Slob frequently slept under my bed. Now he moved downstairs. I was keeping him awake. If he had been a wife he would have complained. Since he was merely a dog he moved downstairs.

"Rats always desert the sinking ship," I said.

I began to have shaking chills.

"Maybe I've got malaria," I told myself, and I even went so far as to do a thick smear of my blood, looking for malarial parasites.

I began to have raging fevers.

"Maybe I've got a brain tumor," I said, and I wrote out my last will and testament.

The doctor who treats himself has a fool for a patient, they say. The simple and obvious diagnostic opinion that I might have pneumonia never even occurred to me. I walked around with it for a few days, grouchy, miserable, and shaky on my pins, not too sympathetic when asked to see patients far less sick than I was and getting no sympathy whatever when I tried to tell the patients my symptoms while they were telling me theirs. Finally, one night, while making a house call, I collapsed. Somebody had the common sense to call the Widow Gideon.

"Never," I shrieked in protest. "She's no doc. She's just a stupid smelly drunken old Indian squaw. She's only good for one thing, delivering babies, and this, I am God damned sure, is not about to happen to me."

"Well, Doc, we can run you across the reach to Rockport Falls. They got good doctors there."

"Never," I said. "Not in my condition. I'd never make it. I'd die half-way across."

"Just lay still, Doc. The widow's coming," they said soothingly.

"Leave me alone," I said. "I'm all right. Just a mild touch of leprosy. Let go of me! I'm fine. I'm going home."

I tried to get up and promptly blacked out and collapsed again. I just very vaguely remember the shadowy fat aromatic presence of the Widow Gideon. I don't really remember at all how they carried me over to my own house and tucked me gently into my own bed. Rumor said the Widow Gideon picked me up and threw me over her shoulder like an empty flour sack, but personally I don't believe it. I think four or five of the boys must have rigged up a stretcher out of blankets and boat hooks and carried me across. At any rate, when consciousness returned, I was in my own feather bed, naked as a jay bird, and the Widow Gideon was sponging me off with rubbing alcohol.

"Get out of here! What the hell do you think you're doing?"

"Shut up, Doc!" she said amiably.

I reeled off a string of explosive obscenities that I learned in army barracks, but she just smiled and kept on sponging me, and when my remarks concerning her ancestry grew a touch too personal, she poured some rubbing alcohol directly over my private parts, which took my breath away and stopped my conversation rather effectively.

"Okay, okay, I'll co-operate. You outweigh me by a hundred pounds, and I'm not exactly up to par. And please keep that stuff in more decent portions of my anatomy, madam, and I'm your slave for life."

"Why don't you save your breath, Doc? You ain't got a hell of a lot."

"Why don't you go home?"

"For one thing, Doc, you got yourself a temperature of a hundred and five. For another thing, you got nobody to take care of you. No woman in this house."

"It's nothing," I said. "Small cold in the nose. I'll be fine after a good night's sleep."

"Doc," she said, "if you ain't got a lovely case of galloping pneumonia, my name is John the Divine!"

As a matter of fact, now that she mentioned it, there was something in my chest that seemed to be galloping. Every time I took a breath I could feel the rattle of little hoofs.

"Doc," she said, "I suppose you believe in penicillin?"

"And I suppose you don't?" I said. "I suppose you've got some Indian gurry made of skunk scent and whale liver and the juice of a three-day clam that works very fine for pneumonia?"

"I got a remedy," she said. "Sassafras. Juniper berry. Witch hazel. Spruce gum. You put 'em together and melt 'em down in a bottle of rum. There's only one trouble."

"What's that? The patient gets delirium tremens?"

"Three days later the patient dies. All of my people die of congestion in the lung. The lung of an Indian ain't very powerful," she said. "There ain't many of us left."

"In that event, why don't we try penicillin, just for laughs?" I said. "Whether you believe in it or not."

"Nothing but bread mold, ain't it?" she said.

"Yes, madam, but awful powerful potent God-filled bread mold. What say? Shall we give it a try?"

So I told her how to find my penicillin, how to dilute it, how to draw it up into a syringe, how to give me a deep intramuscular injection in the buttock. This pained her more than it did me. Surprisingly, she was afraid of the needle. Immediately after she had given the injection, I thought she was going to faint.

"Well, Doc, maybe we can try that again tomorrow," she said with relief.

"Like hell," I said. "We do it every three hours."

After two or three more jabs at three-hour intervals, she had mastered her squeamishness and had become quite adept.

"You'd make a good practical nurse," I told her.

"Doc, I'm only a midwife in a day and age when midwives is going out of fashion. Indians is also going out of fashion, except on television, and there we always lose. I don't reckon I'll be missed."

"I'll take you over the next three women I ever met," I said. "Madam, will you marry me?"

"Sonny," she said, "where do you keep your gin?"

I told her. Within six hours she had vanquished my cellar, and reinforcements had to be sent over from her place.

"Doc, you may have heard I got some weaknesses."

"Yes," I said. "I understand you're fond of gin."

"The other thing I'm fond of," she said, "is marriage. I like to marry smooth clean-shaven perky sweet-smelling cocky little pale men. Just like you!"

"Madam, you don't frighten me a bit," I said. "But I hope you don't mind waiting for me just a few more days. Let me get back a little of my strength."

She studied me. "Nope, Doc," she said at last. "You ain't quite the type."

"Why not?" I said, feeling as if my potency had been insulted. I never met poor Gideon, but I had heard the stories. Seemed to me anything he had done I could do better.

"I ain't never married a useful feller yet," she said. "I'm a bit too old to change my ways."

I was intrigued by this. "You mean you prefer the drifters and the bums, the flotsam and the jetsam and the old dead floating logs?"

"When I want me a man," she said, "I want a man for me. I want him in the house where I can keep an eye on him. I don't want him hanging around the waterfront, getting into trouble, losing money in a poker game, flirting with other people's women, under the justification that he's making us a livelihood. I earn all the livelihood necessary in my house. The only things a man is good for, Sonny, is consolation, tenderness, and back-scratching after the work of the day is done."

It seemed to me I understood why Gideon and the others didn't last so very long.

She sighed. "So maybe that's the trouble, I suppose," she said. "That kind of a man ain't much of a man, is he? No wonder all us Indians got weak blood. In them ancient days, when there were as many of us here as stars in the midnight sky, the brave was a brave and did the fighting and the killing and the praying; the squaw cooked the meat and kept the fires going. Then the braves got weaker and the squaws got bigger. That's the true reason, Doc, why the Wabanaki tribe clean vanished itself away. It wasn't the paleface and the white man's God; it wasn't alcohol or taxes; it wasn't even them peace treaties. That should be a lesson to your nation, Doc. When a squaw gets too big for her breechclout and a brave gets too small to defend his tribal privilege, the future has already become a part of the distant past."

"Madam," I said, "a matriarchy is a dangerous thing. Think what happened to the Amazons! You're right. That's why I'm not married."

"Roll over, Doc, and pull down your pants. It's time for another shot."

"Hey!" I said. "Isn't this a little early? Are you getting to enjoy this procedure?"

"Roll over," she said.

Although my fever was down, I had about as much strength as a wet dish mop, so I rolled over and pulled down my pants.

"Doc," she said, "you want some small words of advice?"

"Madam," I said, "from you I would welcome any advice, large or small."

"If you don't get yourself married pretty soon, you're going to become like Gideon, may all of the smaller gods rest his soul in peace."

"This is good?"

"This is not good," she said. "Gideon was a friendly little man. Gideon was full of tenderness and back-scratching after the sun went down. Gideon was well liked. But Gideon was no damn good. He had no enemies. A man without enemies is like a clam without a shell."

"And marriage will make me enemies?"

"Marriage will make you, Doc," she said, "and that's the long and short of it. You gotta stop drifting back and forth with the tide."

"Well," I said, "and who am I supposed to marry?"

She knocked the top off a fresh bottle of gin and took a healthy gulp and said, "For a smart man, Doc, you surely can be stupid! You've known whom you were going to marry since long before you come to Juniper Island."

"I see."

"You see just about as far as the end of your nose and no farther. Open your mouth, Doc. It's time for us to take your temperature."

I made a good recovery. Thanks to penicillin, gin, and Indians.

Part 7

Dr. Dan's Retreat

THIS TIME she kept me waiting. I stalked back and forth on the Municipal Pier at Rockport Falls, bitterly regretting the whole damn thing. I was alone on the wharf. Anybody with any sense would have stayed out of the blizzard. It wasn't a blizzard yet, but the glass had been falling all morning, and the weatherman on the radio had been making ominous remarks. In general, I disregard the prognostications of weathermen, who never seem to have sense enough to look out the window, but anybody looking out the window that afternoon could tell that it was going to snow like crazy for three or four days, starting any minute now. What more could you expect for December twenty-third?

It was only two o'clock in the afternoon, but on this, one of the shortest days of the year, it would be dusk within an hour and a half, even on a sunny day. The sun had gone south for the winter. The clouds were low hanging and driving and threatening to sop up land and sea. The sea was muttering and growling and stirring itself around. The wind was rising. I'd had no difficulty getting across the reach in the *Mary Jane* at noontime, and the getting back still looked possible, though perhaps implausible. However, give it another hour, with darkness coming and a blizzard and wind reaching full gale intensity, and the reach would be classified as impassable even for sturdy nautical types and stubborn damn fools like me. Once cut off, the island was likely to remain cut off for the rest of the week. I could shack up in the small commercial hotel in Rockport Falls and spend my Christmas in those dismal surroundings, praying that the *Mary Jane* wouldn't break her mooring lines or swamp and sink. But there were several sick people from whom I didn't wish to be cut off for a matter of several days.

I glanced at my watch. "Fifteen minutes," I said to myself. "Absolutely no more. Because I'm going to get back out to the island tonight or drown, and after fifteen minutes I would surely drown, and no woman ever made is worth that sacrifice. My mother didn't raise me for crab food, thank you just the same."

Just then the snow came swirling down, as if somebody had thrust a knife into a feather pillow, and in the same moment a Thunderbird convertible, buttoned up tight, came whistling out of the snow cloud, down onto the pier, and screeched to a stop beside me. June rolled down the window.

"Good afternoon, Clark," said June quite cheerfully.

"Good afternoon, Hedy," I replied. "It isn't, but this is the best we can do for it in these latitudes."

"Do you think it's going to snow?" said she.

The blast of hard tiny little particles, blowing like a dust storm, was so thick we could hardly see each other, even though we were face to face.

"Could be," I said. "Frankly, the weather was better an hour ago. Didn't I ask you to meet me here at one o'clock?"

"Chum, at one o'clock I was slipping and sliding around that long stretch of ice facetiously called a turnpike. I'm lucky to be here in a piece. Dan, you've lost weight."

"I had pneumonia last month."

"Then what are you doing out here?"

"Waiting for you," I said. June got out of the car. "Haven't you gained weight? Are you pregnant?"

She laughed. She explained to me that she had on woollies and woollies woollies plus three flannel shirts and four pairs of pants and sweaters on top of that. Abercrombie & Fitch, not the Tailored Woman. All decked out for dangerous expeditions to the top of Mount Everest.

"Where's the ocean?" she said.

"Out there."

"Everything's gray."

"The wet lower part is the water," I said. "Maybe you can't see it, but you can hear it if you stop talking. It's snarling like a hungry lioness at the moment."

She walked, cautiously, over to the side of the dock and looked down on the poor little *Mary Jane* below, jumping and pitching and crashing into the pilings of the dock. June came back to me, icicles in her eyebrows, her face wan, pinched, and slightly terrified.

"Don't worry, darling," I said. "I wouldn't expect you to make an ocean trip this afternoon. They have a small inn in the village here. I think you'll be perfectly comfortable."

"Fine."

"I'll see you in three or four days," I said. "As soon as it's safe."

"Won't you be at the inn, Dan? Where?"

"Home," I said.

"Out there?" she said, incredulous, pointing at the easterly segment of the roiling gray snowy nothingness.

"Why, sure," I said. "Do you think you can find the hotel by yourself?

It's beside the village green. Because I better get going right away, before the conditions become even less favorable."

"You idiot! I absolutely forbid it! Why do you want to go out there?"

"Because," I said, "I live out there. I work out there. There are sick people who need me out there. I can't abandon them. This will likely be a three- or four-day blow."

Her face became a little more wan, a little more pinched, and considerably more terrified.

"Then get my bags out in a hurry, Dan! Please let's get going. If it's going to get worse later on, although frankly I can't conceive of anything worse."

"June, you're not coming with me!"

"Dan, I am coming with you."

"You're not!"

"Then you're not either!"

"I have to," I said.

"Then so do I," said she. "Anywhere you are going, I am going too."

I had great admiration for her courage at this moment. Inside, I was in a panic state about the voyage myself, but obviously I couldn't let it show. I carried her baggage down the icy ladder to the pitching icy treacherous decks of the *Mary Jane*. This was not easy, I might say. Then I tried to help June down the ladder, although it was all I could do to keep from falling off myself. We made it. I had a problem then about the mooring lines. I couldn't unfasten them from below. If I cast off above, the little pitching pea pod containing my beloved would be swept out into the Maelstrom forever. An experienced seaman might have held the vessel against the pier, but I wasn't sure I could do it myself and I scarcely wanted to ask June to try. So first I started the engines. And then I cut the mooring lines with a knife. And then I grabbed the wheel and headed out into the middle of it.

"How are you?" I shouted over the engine and the wind.

"Petrified," she shouted back.

"Seasick?"

"It hadn't occurred to me. Too damn frightened. How are we? I mean what are the chances? Are we any kind of a decent insurance risk?"

"For about ten seconds we were in bad shape," I said. "If we'd smashed hard enough against that piling before I could get her off, we'd have had it. Now we're in fine shape."

"I'll bet!"

"No, really. The *Mary Jane* won't sink. We've got enough gas aboard to get us halfway to Portugal. No sweat. No problems. We'll get home."

June glanced at the mass of gray-black snow-filled nothingness everywhere.

"But how can you see where you're going?"

"I can see the radar screen," I said.

I showed her the screen with the green revolving line and the passing blips. I demonstrated the high beam and the low beam. I showed her the silhouette of the dock from which we had just departed and that of the island to which we were going, even the mouth of the harbor, which was our immediate destination.

"Fascinating!"

"Also lifesaving, now and then," I said.

"What's that?" She pointed to a blip, ahead of us and off to the right about a quarter of a mile.

"Another fishing boat. Probably headed for Juniper Island too."

"You mean we're really not alone out here?"

"Oh no. I imagine it's Cyrus Lunt. I'll find out."

I turned on the marine radio to the fisherman's wave length. There was the usual caterwauling of static screeches and bellows and blasts, but I got through to Cyrus. I told him we had fresh fish aboard. He told me it was a great night for cats. We signed off.

"That was Cy," I said.

"I couldn't understand a word you were saying, what with all that noise."

"Shall we telephone your mother long distance to tell her that you've not yet drowned?"

"Could we?"

"Sure."

I switched over to the Boston marine operator. The reception was much clearer here. The operator and I exchanged some friendly social words. She said it was raining in Boston but it would turn to sleet shortly and she was wondering how she was going to get home to Brockton. I said it was thick of snow out here. She wished me Merry Christmas. I told her I had June aboard, who was going to visit with me over the holidays. The operator said this was fine and she hoped I married June before long. I then signed off before the conversation should become too personal.

June had heard every word of this. "She knows me?"

"Certainly. The fisherman's world is small. Everybody knows everything about everybody else out here."

"It's sort of fantastic."

I agreed. It was sort of fantastic. The elements roil and roar, and man is puny and weak but the thin thread of his lifeline persists and extends and endures. And over the miracle of his electronic creation comes not talk of the cosmos and matters eternal but the simple banalities of the Monday wash, the Tuesday bridge, the Wednesday marriages, and the Thursday child.

I looked at June and grinned. "In New York," I said, "you live in an apartment house with a thousand people, not one of whom knows your name. And yet five thousand fishermen from Eastport to Boston know as much about you as I do."

"I better watch my step," she said. "This would give a lady pause."

We had negotiated the stormy reach and were entering the harbor. Wind and weather were less of a problem here, but the radar had lost its effectiveness, for the obstacles were crowded too close together. I had to pick my way through the harbor by hand, like a man in the dark going downstairs in his own house. After the perils of the icy ladder at Rockport Falls, another icy ladder at Juniper did not seem to bother my beloved. She went up it like a spider of experience. I passed the luggage up to her, buttoned down the *Mary Jane* against the storm, and slogged on home through the inch of accumulated snow. My little house felt wonderfully dry, snug, cozy, and comforting. The pretty Christmas tree, which Slob and I had decorated the day before, twinkled at us. Slob greeted me with vast affection and was gracious enough to extend at least small courtesies towards June. She went upstairs and I could hear the bathtub running. I prepared the drinks. That night, I thought, hot buttered rum would be appropriate.

June returned, a delight in a filmy frothy dark green evening gown.

"By golly," I said, "if I ever did climb Mount Everest with you, I swear you'd dress for supper like a million bucks."

"Out here, I sometimes feel overdressed," she confessed.

"Never mind," I said. "I like it. I presume this is for my benefit."

She wrinkled her brows over this one. "No, Dan, I don't really think so," she said. "It's for mine."

We consumed our hot buttered rum, which lined the gastric epithelium with a warm radiant glow. Then I cooked supper. I had laid in some of Wellington's choicest tenderloin. After supper we did the dishes. Then we sat before the fire. I smoked my pipe. Slob lay on the tiles. June settled back in her armchair, eyes closed. She almost fell asleep.

"You've changed in the last year and a half, Dan," she said.

"Apologies are in order, I presume?"

"You have acquired a certain solidarity," she said. "Peace and strength. You've put down roots. You know, when you came out of the army, you weren't very sure of yourself. You were a good kid with a sense of humor and a certain light touch of the intellectual, but no professional self-confidence. You acted like a well-trained young doctor, but if I had been sick I wouldn't have wanted you. You would have made me nervous, Dan."

"And now," I said, "I put you to sleep."

"You know what you're doing, at least. I wish I did."

I was wondering what would be the most strategic time, place, and technique for a proposal of matrimony.

She opened her eyes and stared at the ceiling and said, "So therefore I release you."

A startling comment. "Huh?" I said.

"You've become one of the most solid and substantial bachelors I think I ever met."

"Oh," I said, "damnation!"

"I tried to tell you in a letter," she said. "I didn't know how to phrase it. Everything I said seemed fatuous and foolish. I didn't intend to hurt your feelings and I didn't want to jar your pride. I wanted to tell you that I like and admire you better this way than I did some time ago when I thought I might have been in love with you. I was angry at you then. You made me wait so long and I turned down several golden opportunities, but you were right. Usually you are right. I'm glad we waited. Aren't you, Dan?"

A surge of latent violence welled up within me.

"So when you wrote and invited me here over the holidays," she went on, "I was delighted. Even though this isn't the easiest spot to reach at this season of the year. But this way I think we can end things neatly and nicely and remain the best of friends. Any letter from me would have turned you into an enemy. Your friendship is very valuable to me. In fact, if I ever got sick, I think I might want you to come down to New York and take care of me. But I suppose I could never pry you away from your devoted fishermen."

"What in the hell are you trying to tell me?"

She removed her line of vision from the ceiling and looked directly at me. The gray iris grew so wide it looked as if she had taken belladonna.

"Why, I thought I said it very clearly, Dan," she said.

I wanted to punch her in the nose.

"What's the matter, Dan?"

I was inarticulate, a condition in which I seldom find myself.

"Dan," she said, "have you a tendency to high blood pressure? Your face is getting awful red."

Slob had woken up from his dreams of rabbits, steak, and bitches, and was also staring at me strangely. I couldn't sit still. Nor did I think it a neighborly and friendly thing to do to slug her in the eye. So I went into the kitchen. I took the largest of my dinner plates out of the cupboard. I raised it over my head. I threw it down on the floor as hard as I could. It shattered with a satisfying smash. I walked back and forth over the fragments several times, crunching them into the floor. Then I went into the cellar, looking for gin. No gin: the Widow Gideon had consumed all of it. So I got a bottle of Jack Daniels Black Label Tennessee sour mash sipping whiskey instead. But I didn't sip it. I drank a slug of it raw. Then I brought the bottle back without a glass. June was wide-eyed, apparently wondering whether she should summon the police. Slob also was alarmed. Although he didn't like June very well, he had put his head into her lap for mutual consolation and protection, and, though she didn't like him, she was patting his head. I sat down on the opposite side of the fire. I put the whiskey bottle down on the tiles with an audible clink.

"All right," I said ferociously, "give it to me straight!"

June didn't say anything. Slob gave a soft whine. June scratched his ears.

"Come on," I said. "Who is it? Who are you marrying?"

"Oh." This came out of June, sounding a mouse squeak.

"I won't bite you," I said.

"Don't you think you'd better sweep up that broken crockery in the kitchen, Dan?" she said.

"This is my own house, and if I want to leave smashed crockery on the kitchen floor I have the right to, haven't I?"

"Slob might cut his paw."

I hadn't thought of this.

"I'll sweep it up later on," I said. "First, let's settle this."

She got up, came over to my chair, shoved at my hips with her hips in a twisting motion, and insinuated herself into the seat beside me. These were close quarters. She leaned across me and picked the Jack Daniels off the floor. The quarters were closer than ever. I was aware of breasts under green filmy cloth brushing by my shirt and my nose was full of that distinctive perfumery of hers and if her thermostat needle had varied just the slightest bit towards the side of the dial labeled "hotter" I would have jumped on her. But her thermostat was very steady and her effect on me hadn't occurred to her at all. She was worried. She was concerned. It was an impulse of Florence Nightingale thrusting up those breasts of hers and not that of Cleopatra of the Nile.

She placed an impersonal motherly hand upon my forehead. "You aren't running any temperature," she said.

"Well?"

"Well what, Dan? Dear, what's the matter?"

I got out of the chair and I took the whiskey bottle out of her hand with some ferocity and headed towards the kitchen.

"Please, Dan, no more plates," she said.

"I'm going to get a glass," I said. "Do you mind?"

"Don't break it."

"Wasn't thinking of breaking it," I said. "I can't drink whiskey off a plate."

"Bring me one."

"A plate?"

"You jackass!"

I came back from the kitchen with two glasses and ice cubes and a pitcher of water. Then I remembered I had left the whiskey in the kitchen. I went back for it and returned with it and also a saucer. I poured a little whiskey in the saucer and put it on the floor for Slob. I made two reasonable sipping drinks for me and June. I sat down. Slob sniffed the whiskey, looked up at me as if I were crazy, stuck out a tentative tongue and took a lap, jumped back as if the whiskey had bit him, started to retreat, had a second thought, went back to the saucer, lapped it all up avidly, looked to me for more, starting running wildly around the room, acting drunk and crazy, chasing imaginary rabbits, hiccoughed once, looked astonished at himself, hiccoughed again, looked dizzy, staggered towards the fireplace, collapsed before he reached it, and fell very sound asleep, snoring away like fifty buzz saws. By the time this ridiculous performance was completed June and I were both laughing fit to kill.

"Oh, Dan, you shouldn't have," she said, wiping tears from her eyes. "Perverting the innocent."

"He'll have a hangover in the morning," I said. "Where were we?"

"I'm afraid I don't remember," she said.

"I'm afraid I do. Who are you going to marry?"

"Why, nobody," she said.

"Oh."

"What do you mean?"

"Wasn't that what you were trying to tell me?" I said. "Before Slob hit the primrose path?"

"I don't think so," she said.

"Oh. Well then, I broke a plate for nothing."

"Dan, I don't think I need to marry anybody all that badly."

"June, I think I do. The Boston marine operator thinks I do. Little Martha Drinkwater thinks I do. The Widow Gideon thinks I do. Betty Winkle from the library thinks I do. I've proposed to you half a dozen times in the last half dozen years. I've proposed to Betty Winkle, but she won't have me. I even proposed to the Widow Gideon. I haven't proposed to little Martha Drinkwater yet, because I really should wait a few more years, but I don't think I'm able to wait a few more years."

"Why don't you propose to the Boston marine operator?"

"That's a thought," I said.

"Dan, where are you going?"

"To the telephone, of course."

"You nut! Come back."

Three minutes later I came back from the telephone. "It's snowing in Boston now."

"Dan, you didn't really do it?"

"Sure I really did it!"

June was half aghast and half delighted. "You're a lunatic. Will she have you?"

"She's married."

"Too bad. The best ones always are, Dan. You wasted a long-distance conversation."

"I didn't waste it. The lady had some excellent suggestions."

"Such as?"

"That I should woo you first and ask you later, instead of the other way around. I told her I thought you were marrying somebody else. She asked if you had already married. I said I thought not. She said then that it didn't make any difference whether you had other plans or not, under the circumstances. I asked what circumstances. She said, a three-day blizzard, feather beds, and no chaperon in the house. I said I had a fierce blood-hound for a chaperon. She said, give him a sedative. I said I already had. She said, then what in the hell was I waiting for, Christmas? I reminded her that Christmas was only two days off. She said that ought to be plenty long enough. I thanked her, hoped she got back safely to Brockton, wished her a Merry Christmas, and hung up. That was worth a dollar and twenty cents of my time, plus tax, wouldn't you say?"

"All I can say is: Dan, you're crazy."

"You're lovely," I said.

I sat down in her lap and kissed her long and ardently and began to define with my fingertips whatever it was under green filmy cloth that had seemed to be bothering me.

Finally I backed off to catch my breath. "What'd you say?" I asked June.

"How could I say anything?" she said. "Under the circumstances?"

"Your lips were moving."

"You should know!"

"What do you think of the advice of the Boston marine operator?"

June's pupils narrowed down into tight pinholes. Her lips moved as she phrased a remark, but there was no breath behind it.

"I didn't hear you," I said.

"Why don't we try it on for size?"

We started up the stairs together. Slob woke up. He started up the stairs after us. I kicked him back down again.

"Dan, that's cruelty to animals."

"We need," I said, "no drunken witnesses."

"He's just curious. He wants to see what's going on. He wants to be with us, Dan."

"Very touching," I said. "But he can't."

"Then he'll never know the details."

"Do you think he's old enough?"

"Everybody wants to know those details."

"Okay." I took a book down from my bookcase, opened it, laid it on the floor in front of Slob, and went upstairs with June.

"What was the book, Dan?"

"The Kinsey Report," I said.

* * *

She woke me up saying something. From the depths of my subconscious, a learned voice informed me that it was just as well to listen, or pretend to have been listening, whenever one's beloved speaks.

"Yes, dear," I therefore said, and I rolled over.

Said my learned inner voice: "Dr. Dan, you're ninety-three per cent married already when you make a remark like that."

I stuck out an exploratory toe and discovered that she was not with me in the bed. "Hey! Where the hell are you?"

"Over here," she said, and my radar located her as somewhere in the immediate vicinity, say ten feet away. More precise localization could only be accomplished if I opened my eyes, and I didn't feel like opening my eyes.

"What time is it?" I asked.

"Tomorrow," she replied.

I thought about this, and, since I was a man, my thinking followed the cool clean comforting paths of logic and I said: "Impossible. Tomorrow never comes. It's always today."

"December twenty-fourth," she said.

"Let's home in on the target closer, dear. What time is it?"

"Ten."

"A.M.," I said, "or P.M., or what?"

"From here," she said, "it's a little hard to tell."

I thought I'd better open my eyes in self-defense. Sounded to me as if my beloved was in a difficult condition. Shouldn't have been, not if my memory for immediate past events was correct; she should have been all pleasantly comfortable and glowing and all that sort of thing, but with women you can never tell. Or at least I can't. So I opened my eyes. She was standing by the window, all wrapped up in a thick woolly robe. The house was cold. Not unnaturally, since nobody had been down to turn up the heat. The room was a vague grayish shade. I then knew what she meant: it was difficult to tell whether this was morning or night.

"I hope you've got food in the house," she said.

"Why?"

"Because, dear friend, it's still snowing like hell, and it's up to the rafters already, and I think it'll soon be over the roof. I won't be getting out of here till February."

"Perhaps," I said with pleasure, "you won't be getting out of here at all. This is once when you can't kiss and run and be gone the following day."

"It's a trap," she said darkly. "I'm hungry."

"You know where the kitchen is, and if you can't find it Slob will gladly show you the way. And while you're there," I said, "you can make breakfast for me. Couple of eggs, toast, coffee. That'll be fine."

"Dan," she said, "you know I can't cook."

"Not even eggs, toast, and coffee?"

"I live next door to the Automat," she said.

"Well, to hell with it," I said. "Come on back to bed. I'll make brunch for us both later on."

"Don't you have work to do?"

"Me? No, I don't think so. This isn't the summertime," I said.

"But I thought you had all those sick people you didn't want to be cut off from during the storm."

I looked at the telephone. It was resting peacefully. "They know where to find me," I said. "Obviously they're all right, or else they're dead."

"Or else the wires are down."

This was a thought. I picked up the telephone; there was a reassuring buzz; the wires were okay. Now that my beloved had pricked my conscience awake, I called a few numbers just to be sure. The kid with the tonsillitis was better: fever down. The kid with the measles wasn't any worse than I would have expected. The man with the cardiac decompensation had had a hard night; I told the wife to increase his digitalis. My two neurotics were anxiously expecting me but know very well that neurosis must wait for a snowstorm and that it would take me most of the day to get myself dug out. I hung up and yawned.

"Come on back to bed," I said.

"Do they have little elves around here?"

"Do they have what?"

"Little men with red pompon hats and red mittens and snow shovels who come around burrowing through mountains of snow, digging people out?"

"You're drunk."

"There's one out there right now, working his way in this direction. In fact he just reached the back door, I think."

I thought so too. I could hear the shovel scraping the door, and the door itself being opened, and Slob letting out loud squeals of delight to welcome an old dear friend.

"Go see who it is, Dan."

"I know who it is," I said.

"I must get dressed. Get out of bed."

"Why?"

"Because this is my room," she said. "Come on, Dan, move along."

"Not yet ready," I said. "If you want to get dressed, please do so. Don't bother me."

"I can't put on my clothes with you in the room."

"Why not? You took 'em off with me in the room."

"Don't be disgusting and indecent. I'm going into the bathroom."

She scooped up a tangle of clothing and started to open the door but then slammed it hastily again as the patter of little feet could be heard in the corridor outside.

"Dan," said June, wide-eyed, like a fawn encountering a hungry bear. "It's the little brat. The one who lurks."

I yawned. "I thought so."

"But she's seen the bedroom doors!"

"I imagine Martha has seen a bedroom door before," I said.

"But, Dan! The door to your room is open, and she knows you're not in there. The bed is made. She can see you haven't slept in it. She can also see this door is shut."

"Simmer down, June," I said. "Martha isn't a child any more."

"I'm going to get dressed right here and now, I don't care what you say."

"I didn't say anything. Help yourself."

"Keep your eyes shut!"

"Oh, naturally," I said.

Naturally, I had my toes crossed under the covers, but I might as well have shut my eyes. With a variety of contortions and swift secret motions and a swirling of cloth that would have done credit to a bullfighter, my beloved was decently dressed and I had seen nothing of indecent interest. Then she went to the bathroom and when she returned, *mirabile dictu*, the Tailored Woman! Now all her moral confidence had returned. She could face Martha now and deny everything and even convince herself that she had spent a proper night, if necessary. Ah, woman! Thou can bend the truth and cloud the issue and remain irreproachably virginal and proper, provided the costume is correct!

"Get up!" said June.

"I am getting up," I said.

"Nothing I can notice."

"I have my own technique for getting out of bed," I said. "A little at a time. Prevents shock, you know."

June, not interested in preventing shock, rudely tumbled me the rest of the way out.

"Now, get dressed."

"I am dressed," I said.

"Pajamas?"

"Covers more of me than a bathing suit," I said.

"You go into your own room and put on your clothes. Right away," said June. "What's that I smell cooking?"

"Fresh coffee," I said. "And toast, and scrambled eggs. My small lurking friend can cook."

"Anyone can learn," said June. "I'm going downstairs."

"I'll slip on a robe."

"You'll slip on your clothes, all of them," said she. "If you come wandering down indecently clad, Daniel van Dine, I shall divorce you, I swear to God!"

"How can you divorce me?" I protested. "We're not married yet."

She didn't hear me. She was already down the stairs.

*   *   *

"Morning, Dr. Dan." Martha, domestic in an apron, was matter-of-fact about the situation, as if it always snowed to the rafters and she always cooked my breakfast and there was always a tailored woman at my breakfast table.

"Good morning, dear," I said.

"Morning, Dr. van Dine," said June, casual, as if we hadn't met for two or three years.

"June," I said, "this is Martha. Martha, this is Miss——"

"We've met," said June.

"Your breakfast is on the stove, Dr. Dan," said Martha. "I've turned up the furnace and shoveled the back drive all the way out to the road. I've cleaned up the office and the waiting room. Want me to go upstairs and make the beds?"

"No, dear, I'll do that," said June hastily.

"Then I reckon I better go home and cook up breakfast for Poppa and John," said Martha.

"You haven't gotten breakfast for your own family yet?" I said.

"Menfolk always sleep late in a snowstorm." She put on the red wool cap with the red pompon and her red mittens and white snow boots. " 'By, Dr. Dan. Awful glad to make your acquaintance, miss."

"Good-by, dear," said June and, when Martha was out the door, she said, "She's sweet."

"Indeed," I said.

"Does she take care of you this way all the time?"

"Lots of the time," I said.

"How did you manage to bewitch her?"

"I've a great deal of natural charm," I said.

"She told me Dr. Dan was a swell feller. She said Dr. Dan needed a woman in his house. She advised me to marry you quick. She said that if I wouldn't marry you nobody else would either; and that if you didn't get married you were likely to become a slouchy grouchy mean old bachelor. I believe those were the exact words."

"Good advice."

"I'm considering it," said June.

After breakfast I went out to shovel snow. Martha had done a mighty job, but it needed to be done all over again; the stuff was coming down as fast as I could move it. Then I made my house calls for the day. When I returned I found that June was entertaining Betty Winkle over sherry.

"Sherry in the morning, ladies?" I inquired.

"This isn't morning, Dan," said June. "We're well into the afternoon and it's getting dark again."

"I didn't bother to open the library today," said Betty Winkle. "As a matter of fact, I couldn't get to the library to open it."

"Not much point," I said. "You ladies have found a subject of common interest for discussion?"

Silly question. Yes, they had a subject of common interest: me!

"Have I been sufficiently dissected?" I inquired.

June looked at Betty; Betty looked at June; they both looked at me. Yes, I had been sufficiently dissected.

"What conclusions did you reach, ladies?" I asked.

"Dan," said June, "do you really want to know?"

I thought about it. I decided: no, I really didn't.

"Dan, I must run. I've got to help with the children's Christmas party over at the church," said Betty. "It's been nice visiting with you."

"You haven't been visiting with me," I pointed out.

"Good-by, June dear. We'll be seeing a lot of you, I hope," said Betty, drawing on her snow boots. I didn't attempt to help her. She still had good legs. So did June. Betty kissed June on the cheek, and me too, and took off into the blizzard.

"You've got quite a rooting section here among the female islanders," said June.

"What did she tell you about me?"

"Several matters of considerable interest and practical importance, which are none of your damn business," said June.

"I see."

"Why haven't you married her, Dan?"

"She wouldn't have me. Females may be rooting for me, but nobody marries me. I'm undesirable."

"You've really made a place for yourself on this island, Dan, and I now agree they really need you here. It would be a shame to tear you away."

"And who's going to tear me away?" I asked.

"And who's going to make me live out here?" said June. "It's all right in the summertime."

"This sounds like an ultimatum."

"That's the damn trouble with matrimony, Dan: the compromise. Isn't it too much to ask? I mean, what the hell am I going to do out here? I enjoy the theater. Once in a while a night club is fun. I have an interesting job in New York. I make as much money as you do."

"What kind of a job do you have in New York?"

"You really know a hell of a lot about me, don't you?"

"You're an editor or something."

"Or something," she said with a very wry smile. "On a fashion magazine, or something."

"Must be interesting."

"I'm fed up with it, if you really want to know," said June. "I'd quit tomorrow if I could find something better to do."

"I've a good suggestion," I said.

"The woman, I suppose, is intended for the kitchen and the bed. You know how I am in the kitchen. And please don't feel it necessary to make the next obvious remark, Dr. Dan!"

"Who's making remarks?" I said.

"Woman serves. Her life is indirect. Her achievements and accomplishments are solely those of the man she services. One long life: one small man: this man, and the man alone, is supposed to fill the whole of it?"

"Please don't mount a feministic attack on me," I said. "I'm not responsible for the inadequacy of the second sex."

"But you'd have plenty of answers to the problem, I suppose."

"It's my theory," I said, "that all of us, man and woman, must compromise and that adjustment to the dream that won't come true is the source of greatest strength, and in strength lies happiness."

"This is what I mean!"

"Well, it's my opinion, but, gal, you've got to make your own opinions for yourself."

"This," she said, "I know!"

"Well, it's going to snow for a couple or three more days, so I'm going to enjoy you while I can. I have you in my power. You can't get away." I gave my version of a lascivious leer.

"Damn it, you do, and you don't know how you do, and I don't know what to do about it, damn it!"

"That's a lucid remark. You're not making sense," I said.

"Yeah. Let's sit around for two or three days, leering at each other and making lucid remarks."

"Let's go to bed."

"Let's not."

"What's wrong with feather beds?"

"We tried it already," said she.

"This sort of thing can be tried more than once."

"I suppose the nearest movie is a mile of wild water away from here?"

" 'Fraid so," I said. "We can always turn on the television set."

"The last gasp of expiring humanity. There's nothing else to do, but we can always turn on the television set!"

"Why don't we go to church? This is Christmas Eve. There's a lovely little service for the children at three o'clock and a party with the community Santa Claus afterward. It's sort of fun."

"I would feel out of place."

"I don't think so," I said. "You are never out of place with children at Christmastime. The service is mercifully brief and then they have the Christmas pageant. The boys look nervous and sheepish, dressed like shepherds in their sandals and flour sacks. The big boys horse around in the back row. The little boys are solemn and forget their lines. The girls are dressed like angels. They giggle and they blush and you know the chances of their growing up to be an angel are remote, but the hope of the future is in the eyes of a child. As long as there are children on Christmas, we can never lose!"

There was something funny about June's eyes. "You like children, don't you, Dan?"

"They seem to like me," I said. "In the pageant last year, the chief speaking role was that of the Angel Gabriel and they gave it to a girl, the biggest girl in the class. She was too big. She had to deliver her oratory from a platform on top of the stable roof, and the stable wasn't any too secure. Cyrus Lunt built the scenery and I think he was drunk at the time. At any rate, in the middle of her best speech, the platform gave way and the poor damn girl fell through the roof. She landed on the cradle. She almost extinguished the Infant, who was really a light bulb under red tissue paper."

"Please don't get blasphemous, Dan. I've got sort of a thing about Christmas."

"So do I. No blasphemy intended. Christmas Day is children's day, and the Man we worship was a child. I don't think He was a good sweet perfect child. If I thought He was anything else but a normal child, I would change my religion. He Himself always put the little children first. He taught us to cherish the child in all of us. We are only the children of God. Any other concept is sheer hypocrisy."

June's eyes looked funnier than ever. "You ought to have children, Dan."

"Yeah," I said, "and I figure the only way is——"

"Oh, shush!" said June. "Let's go to church."

June enjoyed the children's service fully as much as I did. Afterward I said to her: "Did you notice the big girl in the congregation, the buxom blonde in the front row?"

"The pregnant one?" said June. "I suppose she was last year's Angel Gabriel who fell through the roof."

"Sixteen years old," I said. "And not married."

June touched me on the arm. "The ironies, Dan!" she said. "The bitter heartbreaking ironies everywhere! That's why it's so very hard to learn to live, isn't it?"

I think I felt closer to June at that moment than I ever had before.

"June, would it offend you if I said that I think Jesus was an ironist? That all of His remarks have a double edge? Or do you prefer to take Scripture at simple face value?"

"I'm simple that way," said June. "You have to have something solid and simple to lean on."

"Well, I don't know. This is not a simple world."

"But riddles and paradoxes do not explain the irony."

"I don't think we are intended to boil everything into a simple formula," I said. "Truth is beautiful. A candle flame is beautiful, but there is also beauty in the mysterious changing shadows on the dark side of the room. He Himself had to die before He could be sure that He was right. I think we all do. I think we should welcome the opportunity. For me, June, if things are simple, and if Jesus was a simple person, then His simple philosophy is inadequate for a complicated world. I am quite sure He understood the subtle nature of the paradox."

"Do you suppose He had a sense of humor?"

"Can you love children without a sense of humor? I know perfectly well He did."

"There's something else," said June. "I don't like to think of it. I don't think it's right to think of it. But if He loved children, Dan, then why none of His own? And what does this mean about the body of a woman? Dan, is this dirty? The virginal state is the only righteous thing? And woman by her nature is shoulder deep in original sin and by her own female condition therefore damned? These are surely strange foundations for the kingdom of God. Dan, I don't go to church very much. Churches mostly seem to be filled with manless women."

"I think Freud would have been appalled by Kinsey," I said, "and I think Jesus would have been appalled by John Calvin. Wait just a minute. . . ."

I went up to my room and consulted the Bible on my bedside table. I came back down and I said: " 'But from the beginning of the creation God made them male and female. . . . And they twain shall be one flesh. . . . What therefore God hath joined together, let not man put asunder. . . . God is not the God of the dead, but of the living. And when the multitude heard this, they were astonished at his doctrine.' I quote with some accuracy. The multitudes are still astonished. And, to put it bluntly, they do not understand."

"Neither do I."

"And neither do I. But, June, this is my opinion: when the doctrine of a church is set up to sweeten and rationalize the sanctity of manless woman, it really isn't much of a church."

"Do they have other services out here on Christmas Eve? Something for grownups? A midnight carol service or something of the kind?"

"Sure," I said. "What do you think we are? Uncivilized?"

"And nothing but virgins in the congregation?"

"The church will be literally packed," I said, "with womanizing fishermen."

"We're going. Aren't we, Dan?"

"I always go. Every year," I said.

* * *

When we got back from church June said: "I want to marry you, Dan."

"It's about time!"

"Do you know why I want to marry you, Dan?"

"Because I'm irresistible."

"Because I want to have your children."

"Then it'll be much more appropriate if you have married me," I said.

"I'll even live out here."

"Since I live out here, you'll more or less have to," I said.

"For a little while."

"Hold on!" I said. "Let's have no strings to the bargain."

June smiled at me sweetly. "But we only live for a little while."

"Okay."

"I can't wear white."

"This is a matter of importance?"

"Yes. Strangely enough, this is," she said. "So we won't get married in church."

"This is fine by me."

"And you'll have to leave your precious island long enough to marry me in my father's home."

"They got along without me fine for several centuries," I said. "I guess they can get along without me for a few more days."

"Weeks?"

"Two weeks," I said.

"Okay. And there's something else."

"Too many strings."

"This is an absolute condition."

"I don't accept absolute conditions."

"Maybe not, but I won't permit you to perform obstetrics on me, Dan."

"I haven't the slightest idea of performing obstetrics on you or anybody else," I said. "The Widow Gideon delivers all the babies on Juniper Island."

"That's what I mean," said June. "I absolutely, positively, and incontrovertibly refuse to let the——"

"—Widow Gideon deliver you?" I said.

"Right, Doc!" said my beloved.

"We'll worry about that when the time comes," I said.

"We'll get me to a good modern hospital when the time comes."

"Weather permitting," I said.

"Weather or not, even if I have to go there weeks ahead of time."

"Okay," I said.

"Good night, Dan."

"Good night. Hey, where are you going?"

"Into my own room, of course."

When I tried to go with her she shut the door and locked me out. I didn't get back into her bedroom until after we were married. Women are strange. I don't understand them. It didn't seem to me that this would make any difference, but it made all the difference in the world to June.

She reappeared in the morning, Christmas morning, fresh and radiant after an undisturbed night of slumber. I must confess I felt radiant myself. We exchanged Christmas presents and a kiss.

"Changed your mind?" I inquired.

"Nope," she said. "And you?"

"I'm still here. When do you want to get hitched? We can probably get the blood tests back from the state lab by the end of the week."

"March," she said with some finality.

"Hey," I said. "That's a hell of a long time away from now."

"I can't leave 'em flat in the office. I've got to give them notice and stick around to break in my successor. After this, I've got to go to school."

"School?"

"Cooking school," she said.

I laughed.

"Then there's a lot of things to be done," she said. "Plans and arrangements and wedding invitations and——"

"Hey, I thought this was supposed to be a small wedding?"

"Not a church wedding," said June, "but there's not going to be anything small about it."

"Couldn't we just elope?"

"No," said June. "We could not just elope."

So I was hooked. A man has small control over the events of his own wedding, as any husband knows. She said we would be married in March. So we were married in March. I'm afraid I don't remember the details. In fact I can never even remember the date. I know it had something to do with the first day of spring. When I left Juniper Island it was snowing like hell. When I reached June's family home in Virginia the daffodils were out. When we returned to Juniper Island after our two-week honeymoon it was still snowing.

I carried June across the threshold. Slob greeted me with great enthusiasm, being delighted to see me back. He greeted June with polite but distant puzzlement; he wondered what she was doing here again. I caught a brief look of puzzlement on the face of my bride, as if she also wondered what she was doing here.

"So they lived happily ever afterward," I said.

"It's not automatic," said June.

"We'll work it out," I said.

"Complications do not end at the altar, dear," she said. "In fact, I think, the love story has just begun."

"Good. I like love stories," I said. "Why didn't we get married years ago?"

"You always seemed reluctant, dear."

"It always seemed to me that you were putting me off," I said.

"Frankly," said June, "I was afraid that I would have to put too much of myself in cold storage in order to become just another housewife."

"Well, in equal frankness, I think I was afraid of women," I said. "I really don't know why. My mother is very nice. I had no sisters, but I've always been greatly attached to a sweet variety of aunts. My first contact with sex, long years ago, was not traumatic. Frankly, I like sex."

"I know."

"I don't think I'll fear women any more. I think I'm about to discover that there really is a human being hidden underneath those disconcerting sexual appendages."

"I think I may discover that a woman never does accomplish anything," said June. "It really makes no difference what we do. The important thing is what we are."

"Well, let's get to work on constructing a good marriage," I said. "As an initial step, I suggest we go to bed."

"As an initial step, I'm going to cook dinner first. Is this the kitchen?"

"Can't you tell?" I said.

June's first attempt at dinner was, frankly, pretty horrible. Like a brave gentleman, I cleaned my plate without a word. With practice, though, her cooking improved. I put on ten pounds of weight between April and July: right between, right around the middle, if you know what I mean!

Part 8

The Second Summer

CHANGES IN THE WEATHER, and changes in the sea, and inevitably a change in me: I remember thinking, as the summer of 1955 approached, that, no matter what happened next, I would never really be a bachelor again.

Chintzy curtains and potted plants blossomed in my waiting room and the magazines were always up to date. I wasn't spending my free time down at the waterfront, chinning with the boys; if I had a free moment I was fixing the back steps. My bicycle was given away on the grounds that it wasn't dignified. In front of our house stood a Thunderbird convertible: June's, or, as she preferred to call it, "ours." We had had to hire a barge to get the thing across the reach. There was scarcely enough length of road on Juniper to get it into high gear.

Martha Drinkwater no longer did her homework in front of my fireplace. To see Betty Winkle, I had to go to the library. I still played bridge with Drinkwater, Willie Harpswell, and Holy Joe Brown every Friday night, but I was always the first to break up the party at midnight and go home. Slob no longer occupied my waiting room. In fact, Slob took off for the summer several weeks before the summer came.

"Regrets?" said my wife.

"I think not. I have compensations," I said.

Such as warm feather beds, for example, although, after novelty wore off, this was no longer a number one subject of life. Perhaps one of the great advantages of the married state is that you have time and emotional energy for other things. It was nice to cook without can openers; my pretty little cook was getting better all the time. And it was nice to have somebody in the house with whom one could talk freely and frankly, although I am not entirely convinced that man and wife ever talk completely frankly and freely with each other.

I hoped that June would be as happy with me as I was with her. Sometimes I thought I could detect in her eyes the dim memory of lights on theater marquees.

"And you? Regrets?" I said.

"No, Dan," she said, as bravely as I had.

"I'm afraid there isn't much for you to do around here," I said. "For example, what do you do in the mornings?"

"It makes no difference what a woman does. I used to think so," she said. "When I was working in the office I used to wake up in the morning tense and jittery."

"Why?"

"I think I was waiting for the Day of the Great Collapse," she said.

"What's that?"

"Dan, I think women live behind a false front. The fashion and perfume, the brassiere and girdle, the cultural fads and fashionable cults are only part of the act, assumed for this single purpose."

"To attract the male."

"No, I think not," she said. "The cosmetics and the calico are there to conceal the inner she, a formless pulpy ineffectual glob underneath. We keep expecting that everything will all fall down some horrible day, and then everybody will know!"

"We all feel that way: men too," I said.

"I wore smart clothes and tried to keep fashionable partly because it was expected of me at my work but mostly in order to keep up the act. As I was walking to work, somebody might whistle at me. Naturally, I would ignore the whistle, but some morning nobody might bother. The elevator boy would smile at me. In the powder room, I would inspect the other smart chic young women just as sharply as they were inspecting me: we were wondering which one of us would show it first. Somebody always placed fresh roses on my desk. Two of the older male executives, both very much married, would angle with the other to see which one would take me out to lunch. One day I'd have the choice of eating with the girls or alone. Dan, you know that ad about being caught naked in one's Maidenform bra? I am sure that this must sell a lot of lingerie, because it puts the finger on the crux of female anxiety, fear of the approaching day of being caught naked in Macy's window without the brassiere, the day of All Fall Down and the Great Collapse."

"Men fear it too."

"Not in the same way, I think."

"Well, of course, we don't wear brassieres."

"And don't have to," she said.

"But nobody whistles at us," I said. "We buy our own roses at the risk of being considered queer. The other men are watching us, waiting to cut our throats and use our bodies as a steppingstone. That's why I decided to live on Juniper Island, where nobody is peering over my shoulder, where nobody has enough training and technical knowledge to understand my mistakes. I won't drag anybody down with me when I fall. I'll collapse all by myself."

"Isn't it worse alone?"

"Willie Harpswell wouldn't think so," I said. "Nor Holy Joe Brown. Nor any fisherman named Rast in a lobster boat. You go fishing every day, no matter what the weather. The wind blows and the waves run high, but you're strong and smart and the radar works, so you get home that night, since God is willing. If God is no longer willing, then you fall overboard and drown, and the crabs eat you. When those crabs die, other crabs eat them, and other fishing men put themselves into God's pocket overhead. This is the way of things out here. The individual is responsible for himself and to himself and God alone. This is the only honest way for a man of pride to live."

June put her hand on mine and looked at me. I had always been susceptible to the effect of June's eyes. I could see twin smoky opalescent pools at least a hundred and fifty feet deep: a man could get rapture of the depths down there and, coming back out, he could get the bends.

"A lobsterman is not responsible for the pain and suffering of others," she said.

My wife had the knack of touching spots that troubled me, so I defended my position. "I don't like modern medicine; we've made big business out of it," I said. "We treat patients in great clinical factories along the assembly line. We send them around a circle of interlocking consultants. We treat them in groups, like a committee. You've heard the definition of a camel, haven't you: a horse constructed by a committee? The individual physician is afraid to assume responsibility for any individual patient and the patient hasn't got a family doctor any more. The patient doesn't know who to trust, and he doesn't trust anybody, and I don't blame him."

"Out here, they trust you."

"They do, or else they go off the island to somebody else," I said.

"They have to trust you because they don't have anybody else out here."

I knew that this was true.

"I like looking at your ocean, Dan," she said. "I've caught your habit of looking at it every day. I'm beginning to see more than a mass of restless salty water out there too."

"Good."

"Have you looked at it long enough, Dan? Do you now understand the meaning of suffering and pain?"

"No," I said. "I don't understand except that some things are inevitable; that everything inevitable has a pattern of beauty; that all beautiful patterns change; that change is necessary for this beauty; and that the inevitable changing patterns of nature will continue to be heartbreakingly beautiful even when there are no more human hearts to break."

"That's quite an answer, Dan."

"A lousy answer," I said, "but the best I can do at the present time. Better than the attitude of nihilistic violence that seems to prevail these days. Our nihilistic skeptics haven't even seen the ocean, although they may have sailed their ships of fools on the surface of it. They seem to know nothing of the depths."

"Your answer is cynical also, isn't it?"

"I don't know."

"Is it enough to accept the transient beauty, and the inevitable change, without conceding any unifying force behind the patterns?"

"I don't see much unity," I confessed. "Perhaps I haven't known sufficient suffering and pain."

"You tend to laugh at things you don't understand."

"Laughter is the best defense against fear," I said. "It's the fishermen's defense. They always laugh at the vagaries of the wind and tide. They laugh at pain. I've seen them laugh at the face of death. My chief danger might be that I might lose the ability to laugh and take myself too serious."

"You think the whole damn thing should be a joke?"

"No, obviously not," I said. "Then there would be no point in doing anything."

"There's a Bible on our bedroom table."

"I've always kept one there."

"I haven't seen you reading it."

"I don't," I said, "but it gives me comfort to know that it is available should the need arise. That's why they put 'em in hotel rooms, isn't it?"

"I've developed a small routine," said June. "I finish the bloody damn boring housework first; then I sit down and smoke a cigarette. I sit in our bedroom, on account of our million-dollar view, and then I watch your magnificent ocean, which never looks the same twice."

"I don't own it," I said.

"Often I read a few pages in your Bible."

"Our Bible."

"It was given to you by your mother when you were eight years old, according to the inscription, Dan. I doubt if she had me in mind."

"All right."

"Have you ever read the Book of Job?"

"Yes," I said.

"Did you understand it?"

"No, I don't believe so," I said.

"Unless I am mistaken, most of the answer you are looking for lies right there."

"Job sounds as if it were written by three drunken philosophers having an argument," I said. "Each of the three puts up propositions that he can't support, and no one of the three listens to the other arguments."

"When you came out here nearly two years ago, Dan, you came looking for the answers to just these questions."

"You think I should have stayed in the interesting city, reading Job in a hotel room?"

"If a man can't find the answer in one place he might consider looking somewhere else."

"You'd be surprised, June," I said. "I've considered this."

Despite my independence and my pride, despite the sense of belonging and being needed way out here, the obvious limitations of island medical practice had occurred to me. You can go just so far on an island and no farther. The time would soon come, if it hadn't come already, when Juniper Island would have no more to offer me. Then I must choose: settle for what I had got, or strike out on broader, wider, longer pathways. I couldn't be sure just then. I'd give it a little bit more time.

* * *

I'm never sure whether time is the eroding enemy or the healing friend: something of each, I guess. Time heals almost everything, but the remaining scars are the reminder of the loss and injury.

Just when I was beginning to feel the pinch of bankruptcy in the pocketbook, and now having another dependent to support, a dependent whose tastes were not always the simple ones, summer sprang on us again and I was making money. I like to make money. I'm never sure I quite like summer on Juniper Island though. The place was crowded as by a colony of ants, and most of them seemed to get sick. My phone started ringing night and day. I saw the heart attacks on the golf links and the fainting women on the dock, the sprained ankles from high heels on slippery rocks, the infected black-fly bites, the demanding millionaires, the wounded and exhausted travelers.

Michael Vladimir returned to occupy the medieval castle for the season. He brought a wife with him and, strangely enough, it was the same wife whose name was Dolores. He seemed to regard this as something of an accomplishment. Dolores was better adjusted to the permanence of her position as Mrs. Vladimir, by which I mean that she was threatening to divorce him only once or twice a month. Mike didn't feel the need to consult me so frequently that summer. Dolores consulted me on one occasion.

"Doc," she said, "I've missed a couple of my periods."

"Good," I said.

"You think it's the change of life?"

I studied her, this glamorous creation surely not more than twenty-four years old, filling the purple twin-mounded sweater and yellow toreador pants to the bursting point. If she had reached the menopause, woman's period of fertility had become depressingly brief, I thought.

"I get queasy at the breakfast table," she said.

"I think we ought to do the urine test for pregnancy," I said.

"Okay," she said. "I think so too. Then when can you do the abortion?"

I was shocked by this suggestion, and offended, and I threw her out of the office rather rudely. Mike came to see me shortly thereafter.

"Dan, I know you're not an abortionist," he said.

"Thanks."

"I also know this procedure is illegal. Some doctors, I suppose, would stretch a point for the very large sum of money that might be offered in this case, but I know you can't be bought."

"Correct."

"I can't entirely understand your aversion to the dirty dollar," he said. "Sometimes you seem like a Boy Scout in a den of wolves. I have no particular admiration for unrealistic honesty, but I do appreciate your integrity and I don't like to jeopardize our friendship. I think Dolores was very foolish to put the proposition to you. You must be aware that she is young and flighty and that she comes from a chorus line."

"All right," I said. "Perhaps we can persuade her to accept her condition. She is a healthy mammal and perfectly constructed for this sort of thing. Furthermore, I have a feeling she is maternal at heart. She'll make a good mother, Mike, when she accepts the idea."

Mike gave me a wry smile. "Dan, you don't understand."

"What?"

"I don't expect you to do this yourself. I came to ask you for a name. There must be some reliable man in this area. Just give me a reference, and then we'll forget it and deny that we ever spoke of it."

I was doubly shocked and doubly offended at this suggestion from him and I threw him out of the office more rudely than I had ejected his wife. I would have thought that a son and heir was just exactly what Mike Vladimir needed and desired.

I should have retained professional confidence in the case, especially since my wife was a friend and social intimate of the parties concerned, but the problem bothered me, so I discussed the situation with June.

"I just don't get it!" I said. "They want to destroy the one thing that could seal the marriage, the one thing their money can't buy."

"There's something you don't know about Dolores," said June.

As a matter of fact, I knew almost nothing about Dolores.

"She was married once before," said June. "She had a previous child. It was deformed and lived only a few hours."

I could see that this sort of thing could make the woman fear the consequences, but somebody should tell her that congenital deformity is usually not inherited and that the odds are good for a normal child next time around. "But how about Mike?" I said. "This I don't understand. He's had a lot of wives, and no children, and he's getting along in life."

"He's had a lot of wives before, and no children, and he's getting along in life, but she is young and desirable. Maybe that's it."

Maybe so. This hadn't occurred to me. Maybe Mike was not the father in the case.

"You see the evil in people, Dan," said June. "You see it, but you don't accept it. You really don't believe in it."

I wanted to protest.

"No, Dan, this is true," said June. "You like people too much. There's almost nobody you don't like. You want to take people at face value, at the valuation they offer you for your approval. Whenever they disappoint you, you're shocked and offended, and you tend to get mad at them."

Maybe. "Well, for a doctor this is a weakness, then," I said. "Because the good physician must accept people as they really are and not as he would like them to be."

"It's a charming weakness, Dan," she said, "and in it lies most of your particular kind of strength."

I don't know how many husbands have this experience. I often had the feeling that my wife was older and wiser than I, despite her frequent lack of logic, despite the foolish things she sometimes says and the silly things she does. Maybe Adam was created from the rib of Eve, or maybe it was Lilith who really did come first.

By the end of the summer Dolores Vladimir obviously wasn't any more pregnant than she had been at the beginning. I don't know what happened. Maybe it was a false alarm. Maybe Nature took charge of the situation. Maybe they found somebody in Rockport Falls. It could have even been the Widow Gideon, I suppose. I didn't inquire. I think perhaps my wife might have told me, but I didn't ask.

* * *

One question is impossible. No doctor can ever answer it. The patient asks you, "Why?"

You can give a learned discourse on the dynamics of disease, but this isn't what they mean. They mean, "Why did this horrible thing have to happen to innocent *me?*"

For example, why was it Willie Harpswell who had to go blind that summer, Willie the painter of bold color who needed his vision more than the rest of us and whose color sense was the only important thing to him?

Willie made an appointment in the office: his first, last, and only one.

A small boy, son of one of the fishermen Rasts, led him in, and it was obvious that Willie was almost totally blind.

"I hardly expect you to do anything about this, Doc," said Willie.

"I'll do what I can. You know that."

"Doc, I think you're out of your depth here," said Willie.

This was true. He called for help too late. I couldn't give him back his sight. Knowing this himself, he was therefore coming to me for encouragement, consolation, moral support, and hope, which is the only true reason people come to me at all.

I began to investigate the condition at the fundamental level with a history and physical, as we always do. Willie had been blind in his right eye since he was ten years old. Although I must have been subconsciously aware of this disability, I never really noticed it through fifty or sixty Friday night bridge games. It wasn't obvious blindness on this side, meaning that the eye didn't look dead. There was no cataract or superficial injury and Willie's right eye moved and sparkled and seemed to see. Internally, there had been retinal detachment.

"Kicked by a mule, Doc," he told me. "A typical accident for me. My father told me never to stand behind this mule. Partly because I never took my father's best advice and partly because I felt superior to the mule, I bent down in back of the animal's hind end and dared him to kick me and he did. I never could see out of that eye again."

"What did the doctor say at the time?" I asked.

"I told nobody. I saw no doctor," said Willie. "Nobody knew but the mule and I have outlived him."

"Inheriting some of that animal's stubbornness," I said. "Willie, it is possible that eye surgery could have restored your vision at that time."

"Who knows this at ten years old?" he said. "Besides, one good eye has served me well enough, until last week."

"What happened last week?"

The blindness on the other side also might have been preventable. The week before, Willie had had an attack of acute glaucoma in his good eye. In acute glaucoma, pressure within the eyeball rises until the vital structures are literally squeezed to death. This sounds painful and it is, one of the most painful afflictions of mankind, fully comparable to squeezing a testicle in a vice.

"For Christ's sake, why didn't you call me then, Willie?" I asked.

"I've no telephone," he said.

Willie, of course, had no communication to the outer world from his small island. That night must have been a horrible one for him.

"Doc, in perfect frankness, I could have reached you," he said. "Though blind in one eye and with hellfire roaring in the other, I still could have crossed the reach. As any fisherman can tell you, I can row across it blind-folded. I rowed it this morning alone and didn't hire my small friend to lead me until I got to Juniper."

"You suffered alone by choice?"

"We have no choice, Doc. We all suffer alone," he said.

"Needless suffering and useless waste, Willie," I said. "There's nothing anybody can do for it now. That night, I could have eased the pain at least and probably saved some vision."

"When you live alone you get fatalistic about that sort of thing," said Willie. "Death and disability are a calculated risk in any way of life. I'm not the sort of man to get his appendix removed before an ocean trip to avoid appendicitis during the voyage."

"Spartan courage is a virtue, I admit, but I hold no brief for useless, needless disability," I said. "In fact, this sort of pigheaded stupidity al-ways makes me mad."

"Getting mad at me won't help me now," said Willie.

"Nothing I can do will help you now," I said. "So why did you bother to consult me at all at this late date? The damage is done."

"I want your opinion, Doc. That's all a doctor has to sell, and at least half the time he isn't right."

"At least half the time the patient isn't right," I said. "It's my opinion that you've paid a heavy price for the stubbornness of pride."

"Give me hell, Doc," said Willie, "but give me back my sight."

"I can't," I said. "It's hopeless now."

"No hope? That's all I wanted to know," said Willie. "Thanks very much for your opinion."

"What now, Willie?" I said. "A real suicide this time?"

He gave me a sightless grin. "On the contrary, Doc," he said. "Now I have something to live for. I'm going to lick this thing."

So Willie went home and licked it. The ability of the blind to compen-sate has always astonished me; they seem to have radar; they use some special senses the rest of us ignore. Willie kept his small boy on hire for a few weeks but no more than that. No seeing-eye dog for Willie Harps-well, no tapping white cane. He learned to find his own way around his house and island. He continued to astonish the fishermen, rowing back and forth across the reach in any weather. He continued to play Friday night bridge with us with only a single concession: our cards were marked in braille. Willie couldn't paint any more, so he took up sculpture: wild violent sinuous shapes, flowing with dynamic motion.

"Willie," I said to him one night at the bridge table, "I admire you tre-mendously. What great faith kept you going?"

"Faith in nothing but my own stubborn pride," he said. "The Greeks had a word for it. Hercules helps those who help themselves. I hope you didn't waste too many prayers on me."

"I didn't waste anything," I said.

"Out of waste comes beauty," he said. "I was getting bored with painting anyway. I would never have attempted sculpture unless I lost my eyes."

"What happens when you're bored with sculpture?" asked Drinkwater.

"The Lord provides several sets of eyes," said Holy Joe Brown.

"Light the candles later, boys," said Willie. "I bid six clubs."

He made his little slam in clubs, of course.

*   *   *

Betty Winkle came into the office for her appointment. I thought she had been crying: her eyelids were slightly red and swollen, the conjunctivae suffused, the nasal passages watery. I guessed it was more than a cold. From the wrinkle on her forehead, I thought she might be in pain.

"Old devil migraine again?" I asked.

She tried to snap my head off, her voice crackling at me like a bull whip: "Don't be so damn humorous, please!"

What was so humorous about migraine? This had been a complaint of hers and I had cured it in the past. But the doctor should never expect to get credit for problems solved in the past: the present complaint only is the one that counts.

"What's wrong, Betty?" I said as gently and sympathetically as I could.

"I'm in love." Her tone of voice was fully as somber and doomed as if she had said she had cancer.

Trying to inject a note of levity, I said, "Please, not with me, I hope! I'm a married man and not now available, you know."

She slapped me. A good roundhouse smack on the left cheek. The first time I have ever been slapped in my own office suite, although I have slapped a patient myself upon occasion: this is good therapy with a certain type of hysterical female if the timing is proper. Then Betty burst into tears. I sat still and let her cry. I didn't even offer her the Kleenex box. When they cry in front of you, the only thing to do is nothing: sit still and patient and let them cry it out. Any word or gesture from you will merely prolong the flood.

"Sorry, Dan," she said finally, and then I offered her Kleenex.

"All right," I said. "I'm still here. Ready to offer the other cheek as well as Kleenex if necessary."

"Did I hurt you?"

"No."

"But your cheek's all flaming red."

"It will fade," I said. "Want to tell me about this thing?"

"I'm not sure that I do."

"All right," I said. "But love is supposed to be a joyous thing, I thought."

Very quietly she said, "I'm in love with Michael Vladimir."

"No!" I should have repressed that remark, but it slipped out against advice of the physician. Then I was prepared to take it on the other cheek. But her need for violence had expired.

Still quietly, she said, "I'm afraid so. Isn't it horrible?"

Either astonishing or horrible, I thought. "Well, he's quite a guy," I said.

She offered the understatement of the season. "He's been married before."

"He's married now," I said.

"Well, I don't think really. Dolores wants to divorce him."

"I wonder if she would?"

"I wouldn't let her. Marriage is out of the question. Absolutely."

"Not for him," I said.

"For me, Dan."

"I like Mike Vladimir," I said. "He's a complicated gent. I don't understand him, and I surely don't pretend to approve of the things he does, but I enjoy his company and find him attractive. Women surely must. It can't only be his money."

"I've no interest in the money."

"Betty, what's love? Can we define our terms?"

"Well," she said, "one knows. Who cares about the definition?"

"Physically?"

She blushed.

"Betty, we've got to be frank and honest, if you want me to give you any help."

"This is painful to me," she said.

"Surgery often is," I said. "I try to use anesthesia."

"What do you expect to do, Dan, cut him out of me?"

"Better than leaving him in to fester, wouldn't you think?" I said.

"I've not had the feeling since the man of mine was killed on Normandy," she said. "Not really then, I don't believe."

"Physical?" I asked again.

"Very much so," she said, with prim tight lips. "Though I didn't especially enjoy myself, and neither did he, but he was urgent, and I was there, and it was accomplished before we knew what we were doing. You'd have thought he'd have known what he was doing."

"Yes, I'd think so," I said.

"Now marriage. He's very urgent. Very strong pressures. As soon as Dolores has divorced him and set him free."

"Why?" I wondered aloud.

"Dan, that's just it! Why? What in the devil could he see in me? I'm not on a chorus line. I don't even have good legs."

"You do have good legs," I said loyally.

"A middle-aged librarian?" she said.

"It is just possible," I said, "that a middle-aged librarian could offer him more than anybody from a chorus line. Like sympathy and tenderness. Like understanding. Like intelligent companionship and sensible taste."

"Like a mother?" she said.

"He's a little old for that," I said. "But a quiet sensible person might be more important than a chorus shape after a certain time in life."

"Whose side are you on?"

"Yours."

"You're giving his arguments," she said.

"I'm afraid they're good arguments," I said. "What do you see in him?"

"A charming spoiled attractive aging little boy with too much money and expensive taste and a sort of whimsical appeal. I don't really believe in him. He doesn't seem to me real."

"How about the Normandy man?"

"What about him?"

"Was he charming?"

"And spoiled and attractive and whimsically appealing?" she said. "Yes, Dan. He was."

And this was it. A ghost had not been laid, even though, to phrase it crudely, Betty Winkle might have been.

"Don't do it," she said.

"What?"

"What you were thinking of," she said.

"And what was that?" I said.

"Having a talk with Mike. Don't threaten him off. Please don't mention it. Please respect his privacy, and mine, and that of Dolores too."

"All right."

"One thing I'm not going to do. Hurt his feelings."

"Well, he hurts others freely enough," I said.

"No. He's gentle and considerate."

"It doesn't show."

"Only his blindness shows. He can't get out of his own inner circle. And that's his trouble, poor dear. He needs no more pain and suffering. Not from me!"

"You'd buy for yourself a great deal of pain, to save him minor injury of the feelings."

"Surely," she said. "I'm a woman in love."

"It's only a word," I said. "Frayed and battered and fading and sadly misapplied."

"I wish I could think I was haunted by nothing but a word," she said, and she placed three dollars on my desk and took her departure. I hadn't helped her a hell of a lot. I could not help her, I thought. Because I didn't really believe in the genuine existence of her problem. Betty Winkle and Mike Vladimir: this combination was incongruous to me. That he might reach for any woman reflexly: this I could understand. That she should take him seriously and feel pain and consider herself in love with him: this, for me, was unacceptable, even though I thought I could see the cause: some vague resemblance between Mike Vladimir and a man who died on Normandy. She had never really known that man. All these years she'd been living with a dream. Mike was an extension, an auxiliary nightmare.

One thing I didn't doubt. Betty Winkle did know pain. And this was my business, wasn't it? To alleviate pain?

I woke up around 2:00 A.M., suddenly, in the black hour of the morning with an answer of sorts that had erupted from my subconscious mind somehow.

Betty Winkle was in love with pain. And had always been. And so I asked the old impossible question: "Why?"

"Why what?" said my beloved from the bed beside me.

"Excuse me," I said. "I didn't realize I was speaking in my sleep."

"Well, I'm awake, so let's have it," said June.

I lit a cigarette and got up and stood at the bedroom window looking out. It was an overcast night, so black I could not see the reach.

"I'm waiting," said my beloved.

"All right," I said. "So why are women masochists?"

"For the same reason men are sadists. The lock fits the key. The oracle of Delphi speaks. In the usual riddle."

"There are so many manless women, and this is the trouble with all of them."

"Poor Betty Winkle," said June.

"How in hell did you know I was worried about Betty Winkle?"

"I'm not exactly blind," said June.

"And read me like a book," I said.

"A nice book," she said. "Full of chuckles and warmth of heart."

"And it gets dull as hell when I'm worrying about reasons for suffering and pain."

"Betty Winkle and her kind have made a choice: to live with it and engorge themselves and thrive. You don't."

"Reckon that's the reason women live longer than men."

"Reckon maybe so," she said.

"It's so useless," I said. "So wasteful. And the trouble is, damn it, the pain of hysterical women is contagious and it spreads around and infects everybody in the area."

"You consider she's hysterical?"

"The word 'hysteria' is from the Greek root meaning uterus," I said. "All women are born with it. The definition of the sex: tears and periods."

"Me too?"

"You're married," I said. "Happily, I think. Betty and her kind are not."

"This is your prescription, Doctor: marriage equals solution to womanhood?"

"Well, damn it, it's the prescription doctors would be inclined to dispense," I said. "But I know you can't get it in drugstores."

"Then call her up and advise her accordingly."

"It's two o'clock in the morning," I protested.

"Oh, I imagine she's awake, soaking her pillow with tears," she said. "Advise her to marry Mike Vladimir and come on to bed and we'll all get a little sleep."

"That would only make it worse."

"If Betty loves suffering," said June, "and if marriage to Mike would make that suffering worse, then your advise will show her the way to more love, won't it?"

"Oh, go to hell!" I said.

"Don't have to," said June with a chuckle. "Being female and carrying my own private personal one around with me all the time."

"Oh, phooey!" I said.

"See you in the morning with circles under your eyes," said June, rolling over and making like asleep.

I padded back to bed. I stared blankly at a dark ceiling. "Gee, I'm glad I married you instead of Betty Winkle," I said.

June grunted and then said, "So am I."

"But I'm sorry for Betty," I said. "And for all of them. There are so many of them. What can we do? Shouldn't we make love to them? Even though so many of them are unattractive and difficult to love?"

June sat bolt upright in bed. "Absolutely we should not!" she declared.

"All right! I'm not going anywhere," I said.

"We should respect their privacy. We should leave them damn well alone."

"Okay, already."

"Small pain protects against the greater pain," she said. "Adjustment to private pain is the art of learning how to live. Public pain is degrading. One should not degrade oneself in public except for great causes, and little manless women lack great causes. We love them best by respecting their right of privacy for small sufferings. In other words, Dan, we love them best by leaving them alone."

"Good night," I said.

"Good night, Dan."

Some weeks elapsed before I saw Betty Winkle in the office again. When she came, it was not to consult me, not to ask me anything, but to tell me something. She sat down in the patient's chair, comfortable and relaxed, and smiled at me.

"Dan," said Betty, "I am wearing a small sign. Can you read it from there?"

"Huh?"

"It says KICK ME! Would you like to be the first? Shall I bend over and assume the proper position here and now?"

I grinned. "Don't tempt me. I'm a married man," I said. "Do I presume that you have made a recovery from the Vladimir disease?"

"Love is for idiots," she said.

"Well . . ."

"No. There shall be no arguments," she said. "To live alone is comforting. Men are all right, as stray inhabitants to populate the scene, but who wants to live with them?"

"About love . . ." I said.

"I doubt it," said Betty Winkle.

"Oh, now, come," I protested.

"What I mean," said Betty, "is that I doubt that lust, cohabitation, and the itch have very much to do with anything. If by love you would tend to imply that one must have a deep and tender regard for every stranger who lives next door and put his interests before your own, I would say this is wonderful, and it isn't at all easy for most of us. If I try occasionally, more credit to me. But if you ever see the signs of the itch on me again, Dr. Dan, kick me in the podex good and hard. I'm sure your wife wouldn't mind."

"Podex?" I said. "I don't seem to recall that word from *Gray's Anatomy*."

"It means just what you think it means," said Betty. "Thanks for your wisdom, comfort, and support in a recent hour of trial."

"But I did nothing," I protested.

"Sometimes that's the best thing to do, isn't it?" she said.

* * *

In late August a high-pressure cell in the upper atmosphere moved over Juniper Island from Canada. The air was crisp, clear, dry, and frosty cold.

Summer vanished overnight. Just before departing for warmer, sunnier climes, Mike Vladimir dropped in to see me.

"You've had quite a summer, haven't you?" I said to Mike.

He looked puzzled. "I've been in good health. I haven't had to consult you very frequently."

"How's your wife?" I inquired.

"Dolores? Very well."

"And Miss Winkle?"

"Who?"

"Betty Winkle from the library," I said.

"Oh," said Mike. "Good kid. I'd like to marry one of that kind. Matter of fact, I wish I'd met an example of the type some twenty or thirty years ago. Perhaps things might have been different."

"Mike," I said, "I——"

"I think I know what you're going to say, Dan, and please don't say it. Moral strictures and puritanical suggestions are really not required."

"I was merely wondering whether your casual meddling accomplished very much," I said. "And whether you were being fair to any of the women in the case."

"Look, Doc," he said. "If a man comes in to see you with syphilis or tuberculosis or something, do you blame him for the disease he's caught?"

"Of course not."

"His disease is contagious. Do you blame him for that and condemn him as a public nuisance?"

"I would try to isolate him," I said. "As a public health measure to protect the community."

"But, since being sick is not a crime, the law gives him the right to run around loose."

"He should have sufficient personal standards and enough responsibility not to infect everybody he meets," I said.

"Now wait just a moment," said Mike. "Betty Winkle's not going to marry me or anybody else. From what I hear, you know this as well as I do. So, she's a lonely frustrated old maid. Why not give her a titillation and a thrill? Liven up her dull routines a little bit?"

"And break her heart?" I said.

"Nuts. Her heart is tougher than yours or mine. You know that."

"Go to hell," I said. "Go south. I'm glad it's nearly Labor Day. I'm tired of being a summer doctor anyway."

"That's the only kind you'll ever be, isn't it?"

"I regret the fact that I happen to like you so well, Mike," I said. "Otherwise I'd be delighted to make you an enemy."

He grinned. "How's Willie Harpswell coming along, by the way?"

"Poor Willie is blind," I said.

"So I heard."

"But making a surprisingly good adjustment, considering his inner weaknesses and the rather nasty nature of the disability," I said.

"Well," said Mike, "and so is Betty Winkle from the library and so am I, as a matter of fact; don't waste your pity on any of us. You have helped us; you give us consolation and support; but you shouldn't push your luck. Don't try to reform your patients, Doctor. If you rock the boat, somebody might drown."

I suppose a doctor learns from all his patients. That's the only way he ever can learn, I suppose.

"See you next summer," I said, "and I hope you're still married when I see you again."

"I will be," said Mike.

"I meant, still married to Dolores."

"I don't think anybody can see that far into the future," said Mike Vladimir with a grin.

*　*　*

It was Labor Day. On the wings of a stiff cold northeast wind, over a bay of shriekingly loud violets and greens flecked with whitecaps, a trim white beautiful yawl sailed into our harbor and dropped anchor. A young man rowed ashore, and I had a visitor. It was a memory from my past: Jake, the young physician who had gone through internship and the Korean War with me. We greeted each other with happy shouts and ribaldries.

"What are you doing in this neck of the woods?" I asked him.

Jake gave me his lopsided leprechaun grin. "They even let surgical residents out of the cage a couple of weeks a year," he said. "I'm spending this vacation cruising on my uncle's yacht. Can't stay for more than a few minutes, Dan. We've got to beat our way back to Boston by the end of the week, and a breeze like this can't be wasted. My uncle didn't want to stop at all, but the chart said Juniper Island, and I thought I knew somebody way out here. I wasn't sure you'd stuck it out, but I remember you for a stubborn man with short thumbs."

"I'm still here," I said. "Are you still a surgical resident?"

"Hell yes, I've got another year to go," said Jake. "And I'll probably take a fellowship after that."

It seemed to me a small lifetime since I had last seen Jake; ergo, Jake had spent a small lifetime in the teaching hospital.

"When do you practice what you've learned?" I asked him.

"This one sometimes wonders," Jake admitted. "What have you been doing with yourself out here all this time?"

I thought back on my two years on Juniper Island and wondered how to describe it. "For ten weeks I'm busy," I said. "I'm a summer doctor."

"And the rest of the time?"

"I sit around looking at the ocean," I said. "I'm married, by the way."

"So am I," said Jake. "My wife's out on the boat. I think I got your wedding invitation."

"I think I got yours," I said.

"I hope we sent each other presents."

"The women would know," I said.

Then, quite suddenly, Jake and I ran out of things to say to each other. "I'm backward, primitive, and behind the times," I said. "What's new in the city?"

"Same old baloney. You've not missed anything," said Jake. "Dan, I envy you out here. The air, the sky, the magnificent scenery: if we ever have a sunset in the city, I never notice it. Our hospital is full of interesting cases, but I don't know any of the patients. Out here, you live right next door to them."

"I haven't seen an interesting case in years," I said. "Incidentally, my wife doesn't care for island life."

Jake laughed. "My wife doesn't care for city life," he said. "I've got only one question, Dan: where's your bridge?"

"Beg pardon?"

"You told me there was a bridge connecting Juniper Island to the mainland. So that you could escape at any time."

"The bridge blew down long ago. I guess I can't escape," I said.

"What happened to the Thunderbird?"

"We have one," I said. "It sits in front of the house."

"Last Christmas my wife gave me a canoe, for that camping trip we're never going to take," said Jake. "It sits in the garage. I nearly run over the God damn thing twice a day."

"Jake, I do miss the excitement of the teaching hospital, the challenge of the puzzling case, the meeting of the minds. I can remember when medicine was fun. Now I see nothing but neurosis, psychosis, and the common cold, except for the occasional desperate emergency that I'm not equipped to handle."

"Dan, I'm so sick of staff meetings, committee meetings, and hospital politics that I could vomit. I can remember when surgery was fun. Now I wonder if I'll ever have a patient of my own."

We looked at each other. "Maybe we should swap places," I said.

"Our wives would like that," said Jake.

"Yeah," I said. "But unfortunately we wouldn't."

In ten or fifteen years, I thought, Jake would probably be professor of surgery somewhere. In ten or fifteen more years I would be the most backward, dangerous, primitive old country horse doctor you ever saw. Jake's future lay ahead of him. I had gone about as far as I could go: all that lay ahead of me was more of the same.

"Nice seeing you, Dan, but I've got to run," said Jake.

"See you again some other year," I said, but I thought it extremely unlikely that I would.

*　*　*

On Tuesday, the morning after Labor Day, my wife said, "There's a dirty and disreputable creature scratching at the kitchen door. It carries many fleas. Should I let it in?"

"Don't be fooled by the exterior," I said. "There's a golden loyal heart beating underneath."

"So loyal that you don't see him all summer."

"He doesn't like me in the summertime," I said. "And I can't blame him. I'm glad he's back."

"Dan, you love that animal more than you love me!"

"Stop talking like a wife, June," I said. "You know I have never taken the animal into my bed."

"You don't let me slop around your waiting room."

"Dear," I said, "you know that you could never slop around anywhere!"

"All right, Slob, come in," June said to the dog. "This is your home too, I suppose, damn it!"

Slob walked in as if he owned the joint. Summer was over at last.

Part 9

The Season of Discontent

I woke up with uneasiness, which might have been called premonition, and at first I didn't know why. It was a beautiful cold golden morning in late October. Everything was a study in fire and ice: cold flaming foliage, glittering sunshine without warmth, cold sparkling sea, frigid crystalline air. I got up vigorous and fresh, feeling as lively as I always do in the autumn of the year, only slightly older and sadder every fall. This was a day for accomplishment, but I was afraid of it.

Then June told me it was the morning of Hallowe'en.

"I'm not exactly superstitious," I said. "It's just that I've noticed how everything falls into recurrent patterns."

"Well, don't just sit around the breakfast table waiting for it to happen," said June. "Busy yourself."

So I busied myself. I had a few calls to make. My hand hesitated before each knocker and bell button, but I found no catastrophe behind a door. I did everything that needed to be done, and a few little chores that didn't, and then I ran out of things to do. The summer doctor isn't very busy in October.

"Well, for Pete's sake, don't just sit there quivering," said my wife.

"I'm waiting for the phone."

"Which will never ring while you're staring at it," she said. "Watched pots, and so forth. Come on, it's a wonderful day. Let's go and enjoy our million-dollar scenery, which we have almost to ourselves these days."

I permitted myself to be led forth into the sunshine, accompanied by wife and hound dog. Slob roamed in joyous circles, scratching under things, snuffling into piles of dead leaves, working up all kinds of imaginary rabbits.

"What a useless hound," said June.

I defended my companion and friend. "Why is it necessary to be useful all the time?"

"Most dogs in this vicinity are busy at this season of the year. They're bird hunting, doing the job they've been bred and trained for. Has that mutt been bred and trained for anything?"

"Love," I said.

June snorted, sat down on a rock, and lit a cigarette. The sparkling blue waters of the bay were crowded. Every fisherman, even the laziest, was out in his boat that morning. It was a fine day for vigorous outdoor work, and there was enough frosty hint in the air to remind a man that long deadly winter was coming when no man can work. The stiff north-easterly breeze had kicked up a disturbance in the water: not long deep-ocean rollers but saw-toothed irregular jagged waves. One lobster boat, the approximate size and shape of the *Mary Jane,* lay hove to not far from shore. She was broadside to the chop, wallowing, rolling, corkscrewing. Her captain, hauling on fifty pounds of dead weight, stood on the wet slippery deck in slippery wet rubber boots. Near a ledge, a small dory was working. White water churned and snarled and crashed on the reef; the pea-pod dory seemed to vanish every other minute.

"You know," I said, "none of those men out there can swim."

"If they capsize, you can swim out and make a hero of yourself."

"Not I."

"You wouldn't sit here on a safe dry rock and watch them drown?"

"I might pray," I said, "but there would be no point in adding two drowned bodies where one is sufficient. The strongest swimmer couldn't reach that ledge. Sweetheart, the temperature of the water is around forty-two degrees; exposure and shock set in very quickly. If a man falls overboard at this time of year, he gasps. If his head is under water at the time, he draws brine down into the larynx, and the larynx goes into spasm, and that's it: within thirty seconds he's drowned."

"That's why they don't bother to learn to swim. But, Dan, it looks as if they were having fun out there: taking chances for the sport of it, playing around like the seals and the gulls."

"They don't go lobstering for money," I said. "There's good money in it for the tough hardy worker, but they enjoy the challenge, danger, and excitement. Man pits his muscles, brains, and heart against the elemental force under the most beautiful surroundings."

"There are also challenge, danger, and excitement in the profession of medicine," said June. "Man pits his wisdom and strength against the three old enemies: fear, pain, and death."

"But the surroundings aren't so beautiful," I said.

"There's more money in it."

"Let's go home," I said. "The telephone's ringing."

"You can't hear it. We're too far away."

"I can feel it," I said.

"And they laugh at woman's intuition," said June.

When I got home the telephone was silent, but Drinkwater was seated in the waiting room.

"Sorry, Professor," I said. "I've been goofing off. I was out admiring the view. Hope you haven't been waiting very long."

"Just came for a blood pressure check," he said.

This was hardly challenging. Drinkwater had his blood pressure checked every few weeks. I opened the case of my blood pressure machine, wrapped the cuff around his arm, pumped on the inflating bulb, stuck the buttons of my stethoscope into my ears, and listened. His pressure was much higher than it had ever been: dangerously high.

"I imagine I'm breaking the current Olympic record," said Drinkwater.

"Indeed," I said. "What brought this on?"

"John."

"Your son?"

"The boy is in the county jail in Rockport Falls," he said.

I could scarcely credit my hearing. I had never paid much attention to John: a plump, quiet, colorless, well-mannered kid, some ten or twelve years old. His sister Martha had always been a very good friend of mine, but John was in the background, just tagging along.

"What's the trouble?" I said.

"The charge is assault and battery," he said.

"John beat somebody up?"

"He cut somebody up," said Drinkwater. "A girl, several years older than he: two slashes in the right breast and one in the belly. She's hospitalized in Rockport Falls, and so is the arresting police officer who took the knife away from him: John almost cut off his hand."

"Good God!"

"The deity is not always benign," said Drinkwater, "but perhaps He smiles, since both patients are in good condition. If somebody expired, the charge might be homicide."

"When did all this happen?"

"After midnight in a bar in Rockport Falls."

"For Pete's sake, what was he doing in a bar?"

"What do people usually do in a bar?"

"Who served him liquor? How old is he?"

"Thirteen on his next birthday," said Drinkwater. "Everybody denies having served him liquor, and nobody apparently saw him take a drink, but both the arresting officer and the girl maintain that he was drunk and crazy."

"I can't believe it. He's a good boy."

"The sheriff doesn't think so. There have been other moments in the past. Windows broken. Chickens killed. Gasoline siphoned out of automobiles."

"Childish pranks."

"A knife in the belly is not a childish prank," said Drinkwater.

I found this difficult to believe. As my wife would have told me, althought I have seen much of the darker side of human nature, I have trouble accepting it.

"I went to the jail this morning, but he won't talk to me," said Drinkwater. "He turns his face to the wall. Since the charge is only assault and battery, and since John is a juvenile, the usual procedure is to release him into my custody. Dan, the boy won't come home with me. He prefers to remain in jail."

I looked at Drinkwater. He looked at me.

"Why?" I said at last.

He gave me a bleak and wintry smile. "I was going to ask you that question, Dan."

"The question I can never answer," I said.

Drinkwater passed his hand over his forehead. "There are hostilities," he said. "Aggressions. Animosity between father and son. I suppose it's natural. I tried to bring him up without a mother. I'm not much of a father. Knowing Martha's case, you are aware of this."

"What can I do to help?"

"Nothing much," he said. "Unless you can give me something for this headache. I want to go home. I want to lie down."

"All right. Sure," I said. I gave him something for the headache. "I'll go over to the jail and talk to the boy."

"I wonder if he'll talk with you?"

"I can try."

"Thank you," he said, quite formally. "He was such a pretty little boy. Kind and gentle and good. And, especially, polite. I don't think I ever heard him say an angry word. Instead he sticks a knife into somebody's belly. Sometimes, Dan, really, don't you think we have the right to look up when we're saying our prayers and inquire, respectfully, 'Sir, what in the hell is going on down here? Don't you know? Or, Sir, don't you care any more?'"

"The Great Experiment isn't quite finished yet," I said.

"A man of pride and dignity would like to hope he was something more than just an experimental animal," said Drinkwater.

Glorious Hallowe'en! The day was just beginning. I crossed the beautiful cold sparkling bay in the *Mary Jane* as fast as I could travel, but I wasn't fast enough. I couldn't beat the county medical examiner. The further tragic complication of the case was almost more than I could bear. It made me physically sick. I straightaway telephoned out to June on the island.

"Can you do something for me, dear? Something very tough," I said. "Something too tough for me. I simply can't do it."

"I'm not tougher than you are, Dan."

"I'm not sure. I think maybe you are. Can you go over to Drinkwater's house? I think you'll find him in his room lying down."

"More bad news?"

"Quite horrible," I said.

"Oh dear. The poor girl in the hospital is dead?"

"No," I said. "But John is."

"What?"

"John hanged himself in the cell. They forgot to take his belt away from him. The neck wasn't broken. They've been trying artificial respiration, but . . ."

"Merciful God!" said June.

"Sometimes," I said, "one wonders."

The men at the jail were horrified. It is not good jailkeeping when the prisoner hangs himself from a bar in his cell. They were guilty in my presence, and, in fact, I was guilty myself. While a boy was strangling himself with a belt and an iron bar, I was out with a wife and a dog admiring a view. The view was still there. Was it any less beautiful?

I had to go next to the hospital in Rockport Falls. Not that the girl could tell me very much, but I seem to be obsessed with experimental curiosity. I always want to find out why.

It was a strangely unproductive interview. The girl looked pale but claimed to be feeling fine. She was a little peroxided blonde, a tart, Junior Miss edition. And seemed to know almost nothing about it. I told her what had happened to John.

"Gee!" she said. "That's too bad." Not exactly overwhelmed by tragedy, but she seemed genuinely distressed.

"This kid stuck a knife in your belly." I gave it to her roughly. "You might be glad that he's dead."

"Oh no, mister, of course not," she said. "He didn't hurt me very much."

"Just what did he do to you," I asked, "and why?"

"Don't think he meant to. I happened to be in the way. Bad habit of mine, mister: being at the right place at the wrong time."

"The boy was only twelve years old."

"Looked older than that. I never seen him before."

"Was he crazy? Was he drunk? Why did he cut you?"

"He seemed okay. Happened so fast, I didn't know."

"What were you doing to him? You never saw him before. Why did he pick on you?"

"Probably I was talking. I talk too much. Everybody tells me that."

"What did you say?"

"Nothing. Look, mister," she said, "it ain't exactly my fault. So don't blame me. I said I'm sorry about what happened afterward. What do you expect? After all, it was him what pulled the knife on me. Can't you see that I'm the injured and innocent party?"

"But why?" I said. "That's all I want to know."

"It's happened already," she said. "One of them things. Can't you leave it go at that? Ain't you got nothing else better to do, mister, than trying to put the whole damn blame on me?"

"Sorry," I said. "I was out of line. I hope you make a quick recovery."

"I'm okay," she said.

Yes, she was the injured innocent party. Aren't we all? But in this event, for heaven's sake, why?

Beautiful Hallowe'en. It wasn't over yet. My wife was trying to reach me on the telephone.

"Dan!"

"Yes, dear?"

"Come back out here as quick as you can."

"What's the matter?"

"I went to the house, like you told me."

"Yes."

"And I looked in the bedroom, just like you said."

"Yes?"

"I found him there, all right."

"Come on, June," I said. "Get to the point."

"I couldn't wake him up," she said. "He seemed to be unconscious. Maybe he was comatose."

"Unconscious and comatose mean the same thing, June," I said.

"Could he have had a stroke, Dan?" she said. "Haven't you treated his blood pressure? Wasn't it rather high?"

That morning earlier, Drinkwater's blood pressure had been so high that I couldn't record the systolic pressure over the top of my machine.

"Are you coming, Dan?"

"I'm coming," I said. "Quick as the *Mary Jane* will get me there."

* * *

Drinkwater had had a stroke. He was unconscious when I got there, and remained in coma for sixteen hours or so. I wanted him in the hospital, but I felt he was too sick to be moved at first. Later he refused.

After making my preliminary examination of the patient, I stepped out of the room into the hall where June was waiting for me. I explained the situation: a cerebral thrombosis or hemorrhage, a stroke. He was comatose and might not live. The right side of the body was paralyzed. If he survived, some recovery of muscle function might very well occur but also it might not. There were good chances that Drinkwater would be a permanent invalid.

"Everything always seems to happen at once, doesn't it?" said June.

"To them that have shall be given," I said, "and to them that have not shall be taken away."

"You have another very dirty job ahead of you, darling."

"I'd rather not. It's been a tough day. What do you mean?"

"Martha," she said. "She'll be on the boat coming back from school any minute now."

"No. I can't do it. You do it," I said.

"I wouldn't mind trying, but it must be you."

"Why?"

"Obviously, Martha Drinkwater has never been in love with me," said June.

I would have preferred to look forward to frying myself in deep fat. Telling Martha, however, didn't turn out to be difficult. Martha already knew. Not only did she know what her brother had done to the girl in the hospital and what her brother had done to himself in jail, but she also knew about her father's stroke. The Juniper Island grapevine is a miraculous plant. Martha took it very well. I don't know who started the rumor that children are fragile and delicate. In moments of stress, I find that children and adolescents are mighty tough.

"Been more or less expecting it, Dr. Dan," Martha told me.

"All of it, dear?" I said.

"Well, trouble all the way around," she said. "Poppa's had high blood pressure now for many years. He always expected that he was going to have a stroke. Time and again, he's told me what to do. Lead my own life; not to worry about him; just see that somebody takes good care of John. John took care of himself, seems like."

"Yes, dear," I said. "I wonder why? Do you have any notion?"

"You're the doctor. Don't you understand why blood pressure causes clots in the brain?"

"No. I meant all that trouble with John."

"Crazy, Dr. Dan. He's had that stuff bottled up in him for years. Just waiting for somebody to put the knife in his hand."

"But why, I wonder, did he take it out on that poor innocent girl?"

"Innocent she's not," said Martha. "She's in my high school class. You can't tell me nothing about her."

"Oh?" I said.

"She makes a thing about getting folks stirred up. Likes to throw a stink bomb into the congregation just to see the people scatter out of church. Know the type?"

What happened to my little girl? This assured and competent young female was no child: now telling me the facts of life, I guess. What happened? Had she grown up overnight while I was looking the other way? Of many losses I had suffered on this harrowing Hallowe'en, this could be the greatest loss of all. As a grown-up female, Martha might feel differently about old Dr. Dan.

"Perhaps I know the type," I said.

"Better off if you don't; they ain't much good," she said. "She'll get herself more than a couple of skin cuts one of these days, and serve her right."

"What did she happen to say to John?"

"Don't know, Doc, I wasn't there," said Martha, "but I can take a guess."

"I'm old enough," I said. "You can tell me."

"Something about Mother, probably."

"Your mother? She's dead."

"Poppa said so. John and I believe it. Maybe this little cutie suggested something otherwise. Something like that would have uncorked John, Doc, I really do believe. Can't see that it makes a hell of a lot of difference. It seems to me that the *why* of things don't make no never mind, don't really amount to a hill of beans. Why does the tide come in, Dr. Dan?"

"Pulled by the moon," I said.

"That knowledge will help you a hell of a lot if your motor dies when you're out in a boat in the middle of the reach. It's the *what* that matters, Doc, I figure, not the *why*."

"Knowledge for its own sake lifts man above the animals," I said.

"How high, Dr. Dan?"

"Maybe not high enough, Martha."

"Don't worry about it, Doc. You keep looking around in the clouds for the reasons and the whys. The rest of us will keep things in shape down here on earth while you're looking. Somebody's got to cook the meals and make the beds and wash out the kitchen sink, you know what I mean? Now why don't you tell me everything I need to know about how to take care of Poppa?"

"He's a very sick man, dear. He ought to be in the hospital. I'll move him as soon as I dare."

"Over my dead body you'll move him! He stays right here at home."

"But——"

"Don't you think I'm fit to take care of him?"

"Nobody fitter," I said, "but——"

"Ain't you got the necessary knowledge about his type of condition?"

"I know a good deal about this kind of condition," I said, "but——"

"What's the matter, Dr. Dan? Afraid? Don't want to take responsibility?"

"It's a question of facilities," I said. "He might die. He might be a bed-ridden invalid for life. He might——"

"He might come out of it pretty darn well fine, considering, what with you giving the orders and me to carry them out. What do you think?"

"What I've always thought, Martha, you're wonderful," I said.

"Oh yeah?"

"Yes indeed."

"Ain't so wonderful," she said.

"I disagree. You go around taking care of everybody, and everything, and——"

"Doc," she said, "I didn't actually happen to take such good care of John."

A shadow of pain flickered across the determined angular and beautiful young face—just momentarily, like a summer wind riffle over the still surface of the reach—and then immediately was gone again.

I took her hand. "This wasn't your fault, dear," I said.

"Doc, I wasn't claiming so."

"We can't take responsibility for all the evil, for all the horror, for every awful strange incongruous thing that may happen around us," I said.

"You do, Dr. Dan." She had shot an arrow into my heart.

"I shouldn't," I said.

"You keep worrying all the time about everything," she said.

"Well, let that be a lesson to you. See what a mess I turned out to be!"

"Actually, Doc," she said, "I figure it's enough for me to take care of things as they come up, as well as I can, without worrying why and without fussing too much about the responsibility. But I ain't about to claim that the way I do these things works out so wonderful, you know."

It seemed to me that this was a very female point of view. "You've grown up," I said sadly.

"You should have waited for me, Doc," she said.

Later June said to me, "Dan, how did she take it?"

"In a fatalistic, calm, and feminine way," I said. "My Martha is not an urchin any more. I really looked at her today. She's budding. This is a woman now."

"Fortunately, I got there first," said June. "What's going to happen to Drinkwater now?"

"If anything can happen with the help of a fatalistic, calm, and wise young woman," I said, "Drinkwater may be all right."

Drinkwater made a recovery. He remained partially paralyzed in body but his spirit was strong, courageous, and buoyant. We resumed our Friday bridge game after several weeks. Drinkwater was in a wheel chair. Willie

Harpswell needed cards marked with braille. Holy Joe Brown and I were all right, more or less.

* * *

It was in February, I guess, when I remarked to June that her cooking seemed to be agreeing with her. She was putting on weight.

"Look again, Dr. Dan," she said.

Looking again, I decided that the contours of the abdomen were less like obesity and more like pregnancy. A frog confirmed this impression.

We had a rough winter that year. It kept snowing and snowing and snowing. Everybody stayed indoors, waiting for the wolf to come in after them. The only person making any money was Cyrus Lunt, who owned majority stock in the coal and oil company. Although Wellington carried most of the community on credit for their groceries, it was necessary to pay for wood, fuel oil, and coal, spot cash, unless you wished to freeze. My volume of business in the office was low, and nobody paid me, of course. The doctor is always paid last.

I remember one Sunday morning when June must have been about three months pregnant. We were lolling late abed. Suddenly June thrust one naked leg high into the air.

"Look!" she said.

I was looking, of course. A most attractive extremity was on display.

"What is it?" she said.

I searched for words to describe what I was looking at. I was tempted to reach for the Bible on the bedside table, where the appropriate phrases might have been found somewhere in the Song of Solomon.

"Fleabites, isn't it?" she said.

I stopped looking at the forest in order to examine the tree. I saw three red dots on her thigh, about an inch apart, in a line. I thought very likely it was fleas.

"Damn that dog!" she said.

She got right out of bed and went downstairs, routing Slob from behind the kitchen stove and saturating him generously with a commercial anti-flea preparation, consisting, I believe, of DDT and creosote. This agitated Slob's fleas and they leaped into space, landing on the nearest warm body not covered with creosote, which happened to be June's. All she got for her pains was more fleabites. The more the fleas bit her, the more she scrubbed Slob down with creosote. As for Slob, the chemicals irritated his skin more than fleas would have done. He put up with this foolishness with considerable grace. Only now and then he looked at me with soulful brown eyes, as if to say:

"Boss, are these things necessary? When is that woman going back to wherever she came from? We had such a pleasant relationship here before she came along."

I scratched the dog on the ears and said, "We must be tolerant, remembering her condition. Sometimes she gets up in the middle of the night with an intense craving for sauerkraut and pickles."

"But, boss," Slob seemed to say, "her condition is of no great concern to me."

"It doesn't exactly fascinate me either," I said, "but a miracle will be the final result."

Slob put his head between his paws, sighed, closed his eyes, and tried to think of miracles. The only miracle he could think of was summer, which might come again, when he could be free and loose and the boss's lady wouldn't keep attacking him with creosote. Poor June was also thinking of summer. Then, she could get out of the house and do something and, at the end of it, would finally be released from the heavy burden in her belly. I also, I'm afraid, was discontent. Few patients, no money, and the wolf in sight. The only cases I seemed to see were the chronics with the depressing lifelong disability, for which I could do nothing, and the even more depressing neurotics, harried and crushed by their shadow fears. The neurotic has a distorted outlook on the value of life, and he tends to infect the physician, bringing doubts of the physician's own value and worth.

"Funny," I said to June. "Slob's fleas never seem to jump on me."

"Don't blame them," said June. "They might get blood poisoning."

There are times in the winter when it seems that spring will never come, and there are times when a house seems too small for the two people who have chosen to live together in it. Sometimes June and I didn't speak. Each of us was tense and irritable. We were each afraid that if we spoke we might raise our voices and say something nasty that we didn't mean. This, I think, is an occasional but unavoidable part of "living happily ever afterward."

* * *

"Seen the Widow Gideon recently?" said Wellington at the grocery store.

As a matter of fact I hadn't seen her.

"Did you put her on a diet, Doc?"

There was something incompatible about a diet and the Widow Gideon.

"She's nothing but a shadow of herself, Doc, and it don't seem natural," said Wellington. "Looks to me like she's lost a hundred and fifty pounds."

The next time I passed the Widow Gideon on the street, I knew what Wellington meant. There had been a swift and pathological weight loss.

Her clothing billowed around her like a tent; her face was wrinkled, and the wrinkles sagged. This meant only one thing to me: that her cancer had recurred and was spreading. In a way, I was hoping she would consult me in the office, as a vote of professional confidence. On the other hand, I was just as glad she didn't, since no physician enjoys treatment of the terminal malignancy. The call came for me eventually, but not from the patient. While doing a delivery, the Widow Gideon had collapsed. First I completed the delivery, and then I supervised as a dozen people carried her home. Even with her weight loss, it took a dozen people to carry her home.

"It's an old woman I've become, Doc," she said when she revived. "You'd hardly think I'd faint at the sight of blood. You'd think by now I should be accustomed to the fact that the papoose is born in the middle of blood, gurry, and pain."

"Thought you didn't believe in pain, madam," I said.

"When dealing with the paleface squaw, Doc, you gotta think in terms of the paleface manner of speech. If them ladies speak of pain, I gotta agree with them."

"Madam, you're sick. You've lost too much weight and strength," I said.

"I reckon we both know why," she said. "That old crab is eating on my bones."

"Bone pain?"

"I've been around the paleface for a thousand turnings of the moon," she said, "but I'm still an Indian. We don't know pain."

"But you hurt in the bones?" I asked.

"The bones are grumbling," she admitted.

"I have something good for that. Another paleface miracle, even more potent and full of gods than penicillin. We call it morphine."

"Don't scarcely think I'd believe in it," she said.

"It comes from poppy seed. Don't you believe in poppies?"

"The bright sassy yellow flower?"

"Yes. You use plant juices and natural herbs yourself, madam."

"I could better use a glass of gin."

So I relieved her terminal pain with gin. We put away many bottles in the next three days.

"Sonny, don't waste any sweet talk on me; I'm a dying woman," she said.

"The patient often knows this better than the doctor. You do believe in death?"

"I believe in moving out of a tepee when the tepee has rotted away," she said. "I'll sail into the sunset in a great white canoe."

"You mean a real canoe?"

"I'll see it, Sonny," she said. "I doubt if you will."

"What will you find beyond the sunset?" I said. "A great green virgin forest where all the animals are the same size and shape, full of Indians, and not a paleface anywhere? No gunpowder, no tuberculosis, no pants?"

"And no peace treaties," she said.

"And no gin?"

"Well," she conceded, "it would be nicer if there happened to be a little gin."

"So you believe in a literal paradise. This must be comforting," I said. "I don't."

"I only believe that something's there. I don't know what it is," she said, "and I ain't much interested in playing guessing games. I'll find out, soon enough, when I get there."

"You have no fear?"

"There isn't any word for fear, Doc, in the Wabanaki tongue."

"You've never been afraid?"

"I've been scared plenty in my time. We do got a word for that."

"Are you scared now?"

"Not while the gin holds out," she said.

"And this is the reason for the gin."

"Not entirely," she said. "Mostly, it's the dreaming. I've been a great dreamer in my day, Doc, and I'd rather be awake enough to know what I'm dreaming about."

"Do you ever wonder why?" I asked.

"Why what, Doc?"

"Well, why you happen to be dying now, for example."

"Doc," she said, "us Indians is pretty stupid. We never could figure out the reason why. Even our gods were stupid. They never told us anything. 'Just take it or leave it!' they said to us. So the Wabanaki took it, and we've been leaving ever since. I don't reckon we'll be missed. You pale people got no great need for deerskin moccasins and birchbark canoes. When you run out of dead Indians for television shows, you can paint up your own people with walnut juice."

"We'll miss you very much on Juniper Island."

"For two or three weeks," she said. "And when you leave the island, Doc, you'll be missed: for two or three weeks."

"Suppose somebody could tell you why," I said, "would you be interested?"

"Go ahead, Doc. I'm listening. You're a pretty smart young man."

"Not smart enough for that," I said.

"Then why worry yourself?"

"I suppose I can't help it, madam. I'm built that way," I said.

"You pale people ain't so fortunate," she said. "Your pants and your gunpowder don't do you a hell of a lot of good, and you worry so much you can't scarcely enjoy your gin. You seem to miss the fun of it. You chew on the meat, but you can't taste the salt and the juices. You won't enjoy what you got until the tribe begins to vanish, and you lose it."

"You think my tribe will vanish?"

"Yeah, Doc, in a great big orange fireball," she said. "I don't happen to believe in atoms, but it sends up one hell of a large smoke signal, so I hear."

"You may be right," I said. "I do happen to believe in the atomic bomb. I may not accept the evil in individuals that I meet, but I am a great believer in the vicious and stupid destructivity of people in political and social groups. Soon there may be nothing left but red rock."

"And clams, Doc."

"Radioactive clams, madam?"

"And lobsters and cockroaches," she said.

"The radioactive cockroach shall inherit the earth."

"And people too, Doc."

"You think any people will survive?"

"Not your tribe," she said. "It'll take more color to the skin. Black-faced people will survive. They got more drum beating, singing, praying, speed of foot, and joy in the blood than any of your people got."

"You may be right again," I said.

She grew rapidly and visibly weaker as the hours passed, and for an entire day she didn't talk to me.

"The light's getting dimmer," she finally said.

"The sun is setting."

"Darkness is creeping into this room."

In point of fact, it was not dark in the room. Her bedroom window had a westerly exposure. The rays of the setting sun, reflecting off white snow, blue ice, and green water, lit the room like a searchlight. The widow suddenly sat up in bed, facing the blinding rays.

She said in a loud voice, "It's orange. This is the eye of the gods. They are all much bigger now. This is the middle of the heart of the sun."

This strange declaration took most of her remaining breath, and she spoke to me no more. She died a few hours later, just as the gin was running out.

I have attended many deaths, and death itself does not disturb me. It is only the dying process that I fear, and pain, and suffering. Death is just and merciful, it seems. The suffering is for those left behind. I was glad that the Widow Gideon had found her white canoe. I was sorry for those of us who remained on Juniper Island. The place wouldn't be the same.

On my way home a perverse thought occurred to me. Some literal Christian might have interpreted her final words as meaning that she was sailing into hell. Certainly her list of major sins and minor vices was long enough, and there was no evidence of deathbed repudiation of her sins.

"Well, maybe," I thought to myself, "but if so, she'll enjoy it. She'll drink up all the gin in hell."

When I got home I told June all about it. My hardheaded wife said to me, "You're a sentimentalist, and unashamedly romantic, Dan."

"Maybe so," I said. "But, you know, I loved that smelly stupid one-mounded old Indian squaw."

"So I gather," said June.

"Old mother earth," I said. "We should never get so virtuous and intellectual as to deny the healthy animal nature of our instincts. Women especially. That old dame was the most basic female I ever met."

June's eyebrows did a twisting contortion that almost unscrambled her face.

"Nothing personal," I added.

"Thanks," she said with some formality.

"After all, you're pregnant," I said. "This is as female as anyone can get."

"You're welcome," said June. "Who's going to deliver the babies out here now?"

I hadn't thought of this.

"Please don't look at me," said June.

"I imagine it might be difficult to get another midwife."

"Fancy so," said June.

"I'll send them to Rockport Falls when I can," I said. "And I'll cope with the rest as well as I can."

But it occurred to me that Juniper Island might be an even more lonesome and frightening place without the Widow Gideon.

* * *

Of my steady neurotics, Holy Joe Brown was the steadiest: the curious fisherman with the clerical costume. Except in the summer, I saw him two or three times a week. I was beginning to get a trifle weary of him and his imaginary problems. There was something old-womanish about his multiple complaints, and I sometimes wondered if the best therapy might not be a swift kick in the pants. Holy Joe might have been the prototype for the boy who called, "Wolf, wolf." With the complaining hypochondriac, there is always the danger that the real organic disease might be missed.

However, I did happen to be listening when the real disease occurred. There was something different about him that day. In part, it was his color; the complexion was poor. In part, it was his conversation. He was not discussing physical symptoms for a change.

"My father died last week," he said. "I just got back from the funeral."

"I'm sorry to hear it, Joe."

"And left his financial affairs in a terrible muddle. I have always considered myself a rich man's son. He used to send me generous amounts which I didn't need and which I gave to charity. I took false pride in philanthropy, I'm ashamed to say. I will not be able to donate any more."

"I'm sorry," I said again for lack of anything better.

"Everything always happens at once, doesn't it? My wife finally got around to divorcing me. I received the papers this morning."

I didn't realize that Joe had ever been married, since he lived alone on Juniper Island. Yes, always, everything happens at once. It would be ironical if this one time I discovered physical disease in Joe. On account of his color, I did a blood count, which was strikingly abnormal. He could have had the benign condition, infectious mononucleosis, the so-called "kissing disease" of young adults in colleges and camps. But Holy Joe Brown was not young, and surely he didn't kiss. The other possibility was leukemia.

I saw no point in withholding the diagnosis, so I told him. He accepted the news. He had been expecting serious physical disease for years and now he seemed almost visibly relieved. He voiced only one protest.

"If only this could have happened some other week," he said.

I reassured him as well as I could. The type of leukemia he had often carried a relatively good prognosis, and the patient would often live without symptoms for many years, although the condition would kill him eventually. I explained the possibilities, but Joe wasn't listening.

"Van Dine, have you ever read the Book of Job?" he asked me.

"It's a favorite of my wife," I said. "I don't think I understand it."

"This is the book about not understanding," he said. "This is the answer to the irony of fate. The Calvinistic doctrine of original sin, of punishment for the sins of ancestors, is one answer, but I consider it untenable. Job has the only other one."

"This is not my field of expert knowledge," I said, "but I thought the answer was on the Cross."

"The victory over pain and death is on the Cross, but not the reason," he said. "Recall what Jesus screamed in His agony? 'Eli, Eli, lama sabachthani.'"

" 'My God, my God, why hast Thou forsaken me?' "

"Job screamed the same thing when covered with boils and confronted with total material loss."

"But God gave it all back to him, I think."

"Not in response to a prayer," said Holy Joe. "Not in response to the scream for help or mercy."

"That's exactly what I don't understand," I said. "If God is responsible, He should show mercy. The guilty should be punished; the innocent should go free. In medicine, you see punishment of the innocent every day."

" 'The Lord answered Job out of the whirlwind . . . Where wast thou when I laid the foundations of the earth? Declare, if thou hast understanding!' "

"We are deprived of understanding, Joe," I said.

"That's the answer, Doc," he said. "When Job acknowledged his lack of understanding and in his human ignorance girded up his loins like a man to face the ashes and material loss, then and only then was everything given back to him. I think it always is."

"Be proud, in other words."

"Not quite," said Joe. "Our pride is our susceptibility to total loss."

"Show courage, then, in the face of material loss. We must get rid of fear."

"According to the Book of Job," said Holy Joe Brown, " 'Upon earth there is not his like, who is made without fear . . . he is a king.' We are only the children of pride."

Some things I didn't learn in medical school. Some things my patients have taught me—Martha, the Widow Gideon, even Holy Joe Brown—during the winter of my discontent.

Part 10

A Seasonal Physician

I WAS LOOKING FOR SPRING, but as usual I didn't look quick enough. Memorial Day was muggy and hot, and the foliage had leaped into tropical exuberance.

"Is something the matter with us?" asked June.

"The matter? What do you mean?" I said.

She approached me. "Dan, you don't seem happy here," she said.

"Me? Sure I am. We made it through the deadly winter. Summer's just around the corner now, and I'll be busy, and we'll make money, and you'll have some social life for a change."

"I think I misadjusted you," said June.

I didn't follow.

"You were settling down with roots, solid and substantial, carving out a place for yourself in this funny little community, before I came along," she said. "Now you seem restless and dissatisfied."

"It isn't Juniper Island exactly," I said. "It isn't that this place has something other places lack. It isn't the ocean. Life's purpose might be greater than staring at the dynamic mass of restless salty water. It's the people. They count for most of it. But, June, it seems to me already that they've gone away, and I haven't been around three years. No one will replace the Widow Gideon. Betty Winkle has locked the door on her own inner circle, and she's not going to open it again. Martha Drinkwater has grown up. Willie Harpswell's blind, Drinkwater is paralyzed, Holy Joe Brown has leukemia. It doesn't seem to me I took such very good care of them."

"But, Dan, you can't take responsibility for everything that happens to your friends!"

"Now why can't I?" I said.

"You're not in charge."

"Somebody ought to be in charge," I said.

"It makes you restless. I don't like to see it, dear. This is one problem, I'm sure, you can't learn to cope with here."

"Maybe I could cope with it in the city," I said. "You know, I get the impression that in ten or fifteen more years Juniper Island is going to be uninhabited. Nothing but fog and the sea gulls."

"Except in the summer," she said.

"I'd sort of like to be a full-force working machine fifty-two weeks a year and not just ten," I said.

"If I did this to you, I'm sorry," said June. "I wouldn't have married you if I had known."

"There's nothing in the life out here for you," I said. "It isn't fair to you. You deserve to go to the theater every now and then."

"You wouldn't leave on account of me?"

"No, I'm afraid not. I'm selfish. I'd only leave on my own account," I said.

"Well, I'm glad of that."

"Because there are certain limitations, and I've gone about as far as I can go."

"Because," said she, "if I forced you away, this would stand between us for the rest of time. You would always blame me for the decision. And whenever anything went wrong somewhere else, and you'd think of the fog, the ocean, the sea gulls, and the fishermen, you would look at me with resentment in your eye."

There was something surprising to me in her attitude. "You mean you don't care where you live if I am satisfied in my work? You'd even live out here if I wanted to? With four-wall fever, and a nine-month winter, and nothing to do?"

"I'm directed inward," she said. "It's better in there."

June patted her bulging tummy where a small creation of ours was stirring itself around.

"This, I guess, I couldn't understand," I said, "because I couldn't live inwardly."

"They got along without you fine for several centuries, Dan. The point is not so much what you have given to them. You've served them: very good service. But there's more to a doctor's life than the service that he gives."

"There shouldn't be," I said. "It's a service profession."

"To each new patient you give more than service. You give them an accumulated lifetime of experience. To each new one you give a little from all the patients you have seen before. This is what a young physician can never give; and you can't learn it in medical school; and you can't hide it behind a beard. This is what Juniper Island is good for. The soil, the fertilizer, the sunlight, the water, to make you grow."

"If I can't grow any more, then I should leave."

"You'll serve any community you live in, Dan. You can't help it," said June. "But I don't think it's selfish, and I do think it's important, for you to inquire: in what manner can this community now serve me?"

"I think I've probably gone about as far as I can go."

"Why?" she said. "Because your teachers have died, or left childhood, or become firmly set in their own disabilities?"

"There's not much scope."

"The scope, Dan, is inwardly directed."

"I'll have to stay one more summer," I said. "After the long winter, we have no money and we can't afford the move. But in the fall . . ."

"I wonder," said June.

"You wonder what?"

"But you must make the decision for yourself."

I don't understand women, even though I now was living intimately with one. Her speech was cryptic, like the Sphinx, like the oracle of Delphi. I couldn't exactly understand it, except to interpret it in my own way, but I thought she was trying to persuade me to remain on Juniper Island, she who had always been dedicated to digging me out of there. Probably this was a clever female trick. To obtain her heart's desire, she pretends to take the opposite position, to give the male his chance for argument, to let him win the argument and hoax him into the original position as if it were his own.

Trick or no trick, I thought, I had made my decision. I was going to go. I would leave Juniper Island, have myself a refresher residency, and then set up in some promising suburban center in the metropolitan East.

But I couldn't do it immediately. One more summer first. A little business, a little cash, to pay my debts and spring myself.

Pleasure craft began dotting the waters of the reach. The phone began to ring. Slob took off for the summer, looking for glassine envelopes, imaginary rabbits, and maybe, here and there, a bitch. Maybe, this time, when Slob came back looking for me in the fall, he wouldn't find me. I might have gone down to the corner for a loaf of bread, and getting back might take me twenty years and more.

* * *

The medieval castle was still occupied by the family named Vladimir, and Mrs. Vladimir was still named Dolores, and she was pregnant now. Have you ever seen a woman seven months pregnant, wearing tight orange slacks and a purple blouse? Dolores Vladimir looked like a gaudy hippopotamus.

"Refuses to wear a maternity dress," said Mike. "I think she's proud of the condition, as if she was the first female ever to have found herself that way."

"My own is the same size and shape," I said.

Invariably, Mike Vladimir and I had to compare notes. His wife and mine were at almost exactly the same stage of the condition, the expected dates being within a couple of weeks of each other.

"Does yours go for banana splits and cherry sundaes?" asked Mike.

"More inclined to be pickles and sauerkraut," I said.

"How is the disposition? Dolores is placid as a cow. I don't believe she's even mentioned the word 'divorce' for six or seven months."

"June is a little bit withdrawn," I said. "Edgy. Sometimes unapproachable. Developing interests in abstract lines, such as philosophy and religion, and very little interest in the externals. Doesn't even read the theater section of the Sunday New York *Times* any more. Put her fashionable clothes away in moth balls. Wears maternity dresses of the most drab colors, and sometimes slouches around in a bathrobe all day, without even getting dressed. As long as the factory seems to be working, I have no right to question the personnel or management."

"Has anybody ever done a psychological study of pregnant husbands?"

"Of what?" I said.

"Well, you know what I mean. Having performed his functions long ago unknowingly, he becomes useless and unnecessary. The woman carries on by herself, and for the first time since puberty she has no use for the male whatever, and doesn't care who knows it. What does the husband do in the interim? It lasts for months and months."

"I don't know about you," I said, "but . . ."

"On me it has a singular effect," said Mike. "I'm faithful. Although I can't prove it, I don't even think; I don't look anywhere else. For the first time that I can remember, I am not conducting a survey of the opposite sex."

"Mike," I said, "last summer you——"

"It's this summer, Dan," he said.

"But I——"

"Dan," he said.

"Yes?"

"That's none of your business."

He was right. A doctor comes to feel that everything personal, everything intimate, everything secret about the entire population has become his business. It might be good medicine for the doctor himself if somebody regularly told him where to draw the line.

"Who delivers the babies out here on Juniper Island, Dan?" Mike asked me.

"We did have an old Indian midwife," I said. "She died of cancer of the breast, unfortunately, several months ago."

"That's not the answer to my question, Dan."

"I send them all in to the hospital in Rockport Falls whenever possible,"

I said. "Obviously it isn't always possible. There's the sudden unpredictable element in obstetrics. And, as you know, we're sometimes cut off out
here for days at a time during a storm. I've had to deliver three or four
women since the death of the Widow Gideon. I'm keeping my fingers
crossed. I haven't killed anybody yet."

"You don't sound any too confident about your obstetrical abilities."

"I had good obstetrical training. I had some experience during my internship," I said. "But I didn't do any deliveries in Korea, obviously, and
only a handful out here since. The tools get rusty if they're not kept in use.
And I'm not certain that the home delivery is justifiable in this day and
age. It's far from being ideal, and not altogether safe."

"But many a delivery has been done by a cop in a taxicab?"

"Sure," I said. "Many a delivery has been done by midwives, by unqualified physicians, by husbands, and by the woman unattended. But this
could not be classified as ideal. On an island, you do the best you can to
meet the circumstances. There are hazards in the life out here."

"What are your own plans?"

"June is due in late September," I said. "Around Labor Day we plan to
move her in to Rockport Falls. She will stay in the hotel there two or three
weeks, I imagine. September is a tricky month for hurricanes and line
storms."

"Dolores is due on Labor Day. What do you suggest?"

"The same policy maybe," I said.

"Are they any good? Any specialists?"

"No Board-certified obstetricians. They're general surgeons, but they're
good. Two or three men I trust implicitly."

"I don't know," said Mike. "We can afford the best. I'm not sure I want
to entrust my wife to the tender mercies of small-town medicine and a
rural general hospital."

"Then you'd better go back to the city in August."

"I hate the city in August," said Mike. "And so does Dolores. Dan, would
you be willing to take charge of her case?"

"Only with extreme reluctance," I said. "Look, I'm far less qualified than
the small-town surgeons."

"You're something rather special, Dan. She trusts your judgment. So do
I."

"I'll tend her in the prenatal visits. That's easy. Just a question of blood
pressure and urine and so forth," I said. "But no more than that, Mike. I'm
sorry."

"I'll pay you a great deal of money."

"No," I said. "No money would justify that responsibility. I'm sorry,
Mike, but for once I must give you a flat unqualified rejection. You must

make other arrangements. And please make them now, Mike, early in the summer. Let's not leave anything to chance and the vagaries of the wind and tide."

"All right. If that's the way you want it, Dan," he said.

The arrangements that he made were not those that would have occurred to most of us; few of us, in fact, would have had the means even if we had had the inspiration. He engaged a hospital architect. He then had constructed, within his large medieval castle, a complete and fully equipped modern labor room, delivery room, and nursery. It was a rush job and he paid extra to have it done quickly. I shudder to think of the expense. It was completed before the end of July, and Mike invited me to inspect the result.

"Anything missing, Dan?" he asked me.

"Gee, it's wonderful. It's perfect," I said. "I wish we had available facilities out here like this all the time."

"We'll only use it once, then tear it down," he said. "In the meantime, providing Dolores is not there, feel perfectly free to use the facilities yourself if you ever have the occasion."

"Thank you. I will do that," I said. "Who's going to staff this imposing one-woman institution? Have you engaged one of the men in Rockport Falls for the occasion?"

"I have engaged the best man available in the country," said Mike, "and six of the best nurses. The whole crew's coming early in August. And the contract specifies that they'll stay here until the job is done."

I was wondering what sort of obstetrician could be hired on this basis. I was thinking it might be some sort of a fringe man, long on charm and social graces, short on technical skill and ability. I was therefore astonished when Mike gave me the name. I had heard of him. Everybody would have heard of him. He was one of the big names in the field, co-author of a textbook, head of the department of a famous university. Because this was not his name, I'd better call him Smith. Since this was during the summer vacation period, he would be more available, and his stay on Juniper Island would provide him with a pleasant paid vacation, combined with one simple professional assignment. Teaching physicians do not receive very large salaries, and most of their regular work is concerned with teaching and research projects on charity patients in the medical schools, where no fee is involved. It is reasonable for such men to accept an occasional wealthy private patient at a lucrative fee, justified by their international reputations, and from a small number of such cases to earn money on a level with those reputations. Such men, in a sense, are summer doctors too. Just for curiosity, I asked Mike Vladimir what fee was involved in this case. The sum was staggering. I think I'd better not repeat it. I don't think quotation of the occasional astronomic fee is particularly helpful to the public relations of the medical profession.

So-called Smith arrived in plenty of time, a good three weeks before the expected date of term. He inspected the setup at the castle, pronounced it excellent, and settled down to enjoy himself, spending most of the daylight hours on the water in one of Mike Vladimir's several pleasure boats and, in the evening, being a social lion among the millionaires.

Mike invited June and me over to the castle for cocktails, soon after Smith's arrival, to meet him. He was a smooth plump pink-cheeked specimen with a little wax mustache. Charm and social grace were spread all over him, but he had a manner of authority underneath so that you could tell damn well he knew what he was doing.

He took one look at June's silhouette and beamed with positive pleasure. Another of the specimens especially created to be attended by the famous Dr. Smith.

He took one of June's hands in both of his and he said, "My dear, when are you due?"

She told him.

"Too bad," he said. "Couldn't we arrange to have it a little earlier? Because then I would be delighted to attend you, my dear."

June whispered to me later, "I hope not, Dan. I would have even preferred the Widow Gideon. I don't like him. He fawns. His delight at the grotesque nature of this condition is insulting to the dignity of the feminine position."

But Dolores liked him, and this was the point. Smith then turned his charm on me.

"Practice out here, Doctor?"

"Yes, sir," I said.

"Must be pretty lonesome in the winter."

"I'm a summer doctor, sir," I said.

"Have plenty of time for hunting, fishing, and winter sports, I suppose."

"I'm not much of a winter sport," I said.

"Obviously, you do obstetrics, Doctor."

"Not when I can avoid it," I said. "I send them in to Rockport Falls when possible. That's the small community on the mainland. They have a nicely equipped community hospital, and the men are quite competent."

"Emergencies arise, I presume."

"They arise, and so do the wind and tide," I said. "For many years they had a midwife here."

"Really?"

"An old Indian woman. Surprisingly enough, she was quite competent. She died a few months ago, and I feel lonesome without her. She did all the obstetrical work when she was alive, and I was very happy to let her."

Smith looked down his nose at me. "Where were you trained, Doctor?"

I told him. He seemed surprised. He expected, I guess, that I had received my training from some second-rate diploma mill, if I was prepared to admit that an old Indian midwife was better qualified than I am. I attempted, then, to engage him in technical conversation, taking this opportunity for an informal postgraduate refresher course, to learn of the new advances that had been going on since I left the city. He wasn't very helpful. Maybe there had been no advances, or he hadn't heard of them, or else he wasn't interested. He gave me the identical answers I would have received as a junior in medical school nine years earlier. Some doctors need to review their medical school years periodically, I suppose. I have a fairly good memory myself. I can recall a lot of what I learned in school. What I can't remember I can always look up in the books. What I want to know is the new stuff and more especially the very old stuff that they can't teach in school.

I would have liked to ask him, "Doctor, do you have any thoughts on the psychological meaning of labor pains to the pregnant woman?"

Or, "Do you think breast feeding is of any psychological importance to the mother?"

Or, "Do you think there's any physiological reason for post-partum depression?"

Or, "What part do masochism and the need for humiliation play in the sexual response and fertility potential of the modern American female?"

But I didn't try. I touched a note of interested response only when I was tactful enough to inquire about his special field of interest in research, and then he bent my ear for nearly an hour on chorioepithelioma of the laboratory mouse.

To his credit, though, he made a generous offer that I accepted. He placed himself, his nursing corps, and the well-staffed one-woman lying-in hospital at my disposal, in case there should be any deliveries on Juniper during his brief residence. I sent him three cases, and at his invitation I watched him work. He was a smooth and clever operator with great technical skill. Since obstetrics is a technical speciality, that's all anyone could ask. Probably a psychologist would have no place in the delivery room.

* * *

Martha Drinkwater made an office appointment. There was a young man sitting with her in the waiting room.

"This here is William," said Martha. "Maybe you don't remember him."

"I do," I said. "William is the boy who's mighty tough, but you used to push him around. You conked him on the head with a pop bottle once, I recollect."

She pushed him again, straight into my office. "You first, William," said Martha.

William and I found ourselves together behind closed doors. He was a tall gangling youth who would be strong when he was mature. His face carried a generous crop of acne pimples. His clothes were dirty and his neck unwashed. He was the silent type, but he had a pleasant grin, and I liked him.

"What can I do for you, William?" I inquired.

"She didn't tell you, Doc?"

"No, she didn't."

He looked embarrassed, searching for the words before he found them: "The blood tests, Doc."

His words were disturbing. "Premarital blood tests, William?"

"You can't get married without them, can you, Doc?"

"You're marrying Martha Drinkwater, son?"

"That's the plan," he said.

"But she's much too young," I protested.

"Sixteen on her next birthday."

We had reached a difference of opinion. To him, sixteen was a marriageable female age. He knew, and I also knew, that a third of the girls in the high school class would marry at that age, and that half of the rest would be married within another year. From my point of view, sixteen was impossibly young, especially for a young person I hoped might grow to be a lady, for a possible Vassar candidate.

"How old are you, William?"

"Going on eighteen, sir. I'm graduated. I was on the basketball team."

"Good for you, but you can't support a wife playing basketball," I said. "No college?"

"No, sir. I'm fishing out of my father's boat."

"Son, can you support a wife?"

"Just as good as anybody else out here," he said, and I could see the validity of the remark.

"How about Martha? I thought she was going to college?"

"This is just as much her idea as mine, Doc, maybe even more."

Maybe so. I studied young William for a long moment, a moment so long as to be cruel to him. He began to flush. He was a good kid and he would make a good lobsterman, a Juniper Islander. I always felt that they don't come any better than that. But William was out of his class. Martha was more intelligent than he, subtler, shrewder, deeper. He would never understand the patterns of her personality. She would run him like a trained mule. Martha would be telling William when he could and when he could not hang around the waterfront with the boys, just as she had apparently told him that this was the time to be married, even though he might not have been ready for it yet. He'd make her a good husband and provider. She would make him a good housekeeper and breed him strong tough kids. But, when Martha got tired of housework and breeding, she might also get tired of William. William hadn't reached his full physical growth, but Martha would keep growing in other ways. Perhaps Martha might learn to occupy herself in the mornings, but what would they have to talk about at night? There's a long length of life between sixteen and seventy-six.

"William, one question," I said. "Who'll wear the pants in your family?"

"Doc, I . . ."

"You'll be the means of depriving this young woman of her chance for growth and further education," I said, driving in the barb a little deeper.

William had had enough of this now. Still flushed, he put the trumpet of youthful defiance to his lips. "You better take that blood test, Doc," he said. "Or, if you won't do it, reckon I can get it done in Rockport Falls."

So without further argument I drew the blood sample and dismissed him, asking him to send Martha into the office. She appeared, fire in her eye, dressed in full clanking armor and ready for mortal combat. I fooled her, refusing the challenge, setting about my work wordlessly. I wrapped a tourniquet around her arm. I swabbed the antecubital area with alcohol, inserted a 20-gauge needle into the vein, and withdrew a 10-cc sample of fresh fiery young blood.

"I send the specimens to the state lab," I said. "And they'll send me back the certificates by the end of the week. I sign the papers and you take them to the town clerk, who issues the marriage license."

"Dr. Dan, Poppa knows all about this," she said.

"I should hope so."

"He's got no objection. He admires William."

"I admire William myself," I said.

"So therefore, if William and I want to get married, and Poppa don't care, what business is it of yours, Dr. Dan?"

"Do I act as if I were making it my business?"

"You act like you don't even care," she said.

"I care," I said. "And I'd guess your Poppa does too, even though you think not."

She had left a small chink in her armor, approximately over the heart, a dangerous area to leave vulnerable in mortal combat. "He just wants me to be happy," she said, too loudly.

"So do I," I said. "Is your Poppa very happy?"

"Well, you know Poppa. Always in a gloomy frame of mind. Maybe he thinks I'm a little young."

"Aren't you?"

"Doc, most of the girls out here——"

"—will never go to Vassar," I said.

"Really, Dr. Dan, do you see me as the Vassar type?"

"Maybe not," I said, "but we do have an excellent state university at Orono."

"Can't see the point of college. Why?" she asked me.

That good old question again!

"In the first place, you'd have a lot of fun," I said. "Secondly, you'd have the opportunity to grow. And most important, your education, a chance you'll never get again."

"What good is an education, Dr. Dan?"

"Well, obviously . . ."

"Look, Doc," she said. "I'll be cooking meals and raising kids and scrubbing the kitchen sink. Who needs education for that?"

"A woman's life should be more than meals, kids, and the kitchen sink."

"In the evening we can turn on the television set."

"Exactly!" I said.

"Dr. Dan, you got my best interest in mind, and I thank you for that. It was you what taught me the facts of life, and I'm grateful."

"Couldn't teach you enough. Didn't have time enough," I said, "and a little knowledge is a dangerous thing."

"But I got my own life ahead of me, and I want to start living it. I done already made up my mind."

"Your mind, William's mind, and your Poppa's mind," I said, "but not the mind of good old Dr. Dan. Good-by, Martha."

"What do you mean, good-by?"

"What do you think I mean?" I said.

Perhaps I put it too roughly. I did not mean that I would stop being her friend on account of this decision. I did mean that our relationship could never be the same again.

"Dr. Dan, I never really could have married you!"

"Of course not, dear," I said.

"Even if you tried to wait for me, which you didn't."

"We've always been in a different generation, dear," I said.

"So there!" she said. "So you got no cause for jealousy."

"Jealousy?"

"William is a good boy," she said. "So won't you come to the wedding, Dr. Dan?"

I relented. "Sure I'll come to the wedding," I said. "Take care of William. Treat him with tenderness. And, Martha . . ."

"Yeah, Doc?"

"Don't try to wear the pants. Don't push him around too much," I said. She gave me a funny look. She started to make a remark but bit it off and left the office. She didn't want me to misunderstand, coming as I did from the prehistoric generation.

Since Martha's father had not consulted me on this problem, I suppose I should not have consulted him, but I went over to Drinkwater's place anyway.

"Sorry, Dan," said Drinkwater, almost as if he were apologizing to me.

"I am sorry too, Professor," I said, in apology to him.

"Martha may be young, but she's far older than her years. Born wise, I think. William is two years ahead of her, but she's ahead of him in certain ways."

"And will always be, I'm afraid," I said. "It's that, more than calendar age, that bothers me."

"Funny," said Drinkwater. "I'd swear William would prefer to wait a few more years. It's Martha who's gone ripe, not William. In fact, Dan, I'm not sure that William wouldn't prefer the daughter of a fisherman, and I'm not sure that Martha wouldn't marry anyone who happened to be available and lived next door."

"Why the urgency? She's not pregnant, I hope?"

"I think not," said Drinkwater, "but, frankly, Dan, she might not hesitate to use that weapon if she needed it. This is one reason I didn't try to talk her out of it. The other reason is, of course, I couldn't. Martha is a determined person when her mind is set. Since she has arrived at the decision, we accept it as well as we can."

"I don't quite understand."

"Maybe I do. There's a rumor, Dan, that you are leaving Juniper Island in the fall."

"What if I do? How does this affect your daughter?"

"It affects her deeply, Dan. When you depart, Martha's sun goes down."

"Come now, Professor," I said. "Martha wouldn't remember me two weeks after I left."

"She has determined to forget about you now. Therefore William, and the kitchen sink, and children of her own as soon as possible."

"Ridiculous," I said. "I don't believe it."

"I'm the other factor in the case," said Drinkwater, smiling with the only side of his face that could smile. "It's no fun living with a gloomy paralyzed old man. She needs to escape from me, and I can scarcely blame her."

"I don't think you need to feel that you have failed her in any way," I said. "And neither do I."

"So, Dan, we give our blessing and we wish them luck. Being so young, and so lacking in formal education, they'll need plenty of luck, I think."

"I wish I really didn't feel responsible," I said, "but I do. I was paid to teach her the facts of life."

"Teen-age marriage is a fact of life," said Drinkwater.

"So is incompatibility," I said.

"Don't worry about Martha, Dan. She's made of iron. There's something in her that makes everything work out fine."

"I know. I won't worry," I said.

But I did. I woke up in the middle of the night. I lit a cigarette, got out of bed, walked to the window, and stared into the darkness.

"What now, Dr. Dan, the worrying man?" asked June.

"Didn't mean to wake you up."

"You worry in high voltage, lighting up the room with greenish sparks," said my wife.

"It's Martha Drinkwater," I said.

"Pregnant?"

"Soon," I said. "I did a premarital blood test today."

"Who is it? William, the boy next door?"

"Poor William, selected just because he happened to live next door."

"I don't feel sorry for William," said June. "The fun of chasing Martha might only be exceeded by the pleasure in catching her."

"She mousetrapped him."

"Usually," said June, "we do."

"June, the girl's not yet sixteen years old."

"I was born when my mother was sixteen," said June, as if this were the answer to everything.

"I am aware of the biological possibility," I said.

"Isn't it a pity, Dan, that you can't draw up a life schedule for all your friends and neighbors, like school rules?"

"Now, June!"

"Sorry, Dan, but sometimes . . ."

"That little brat!" I said. "She was suggesting that I might be jealous of William!"

June laughed.

"And her father suggests that this might be a reaction on her part against my leaving the island in the fall," I said.

"You don't have to go," said June.

"Well, I can hardly change my life plans on account of Martha Drinkwater. But it's true, June, the longer I stay, the harder it is for me to go. Why don't we leave right now?"

"Now, dear, in the middle of the night?"

"Start packing first thing in the morning," I said.

"This is only August. The summer isn't over yet."

"September is coming," I said. "The tricky month with hurricanes and line storms. If we delay the wind might begin to blow. When the wind blows we're trapped out here. Once trapped, we might stay trapped for life."

"Everybody's trapped," said June.

"I'm doing my best to get you out of this one," I said.

"The prisoner must learn to love his cell."

"We move. First thing in the morning," I said. "Before that eternal wind begins to blow."

But we couldn't move fast enough. You can't pick up and leave a medical practice in a day or two. There was the house to be taken care of, and the *Mary Jane,* the furniture, my office equipment, and the Thunderbird. I had to plan where we were going. All the while, summer business was overwhelming me, and the phone kept ringing.

"One of these days you'll have to ignore that telephone," said June.

"I can't," I said. "Somebody on the other end might need me."

"Soon there'll be nobody here."

"I must give service as long as I'm still available," I said.

Time was sneaking by, as it always does when you're busy, and it was almost September now, season of the equinox. Weather experts, searching the Caribbean area, noted small circular disturbances of wind which they labeled with the names of ladies. Some of these disturbances, like ladies of the evening, disappeared harmlessly, but others produced complications. One began heading in our direction. Our local weather experts made ominous prognostications.

As usual, the fishermen ignored the warnings on the radio, but they did not ignore their own internal barometers. The sky grew gray and the sea was misty. White clouds massed below the higher gray cloud cover. There was humidity and tension in the atmosphere, and the wind began to blow from the northeast.

The fishermen wet their forefingers and stuck them in the breeze. Then they attempted to arrive at a decision. The wise old ones and the smarter younger ones pulled their traps from the water in order to avoid loss during the approaching storm. The lazier and the greedier men decided to ride it out and take a chance. I had contracted for a barge to move our Thunderbird across the reach the following day, but I began to wonder. If the wind kept rising, the reach would be mighty rough. I was afraid the automobile might break from her lashings and plunge through the rail halfway across. The following morning, the wind was a good fifteen or twenty knots from the northeast with occasional gusts to thirty or forty knots. I decided to wait one more day, hoping it would blow over. It blew over, all right: straight over Juniper Island with full gale force.

"It was a day like this, right at this particular season of the year, that the Juniper Island bridge blew away," said Wellington to me at the grocery store. "Nineteen forty-nine, I think."

" 'Fifty," I said.

"How do you know, Doc? You wasn't here."

"I'm interested in history," I said.

"It was an interesting moment," said Wellington. "She began to creak, strain, and stir around as fifty-foot breakers crashed against the span. She began making noises like the flapping of a window blind. Then there came along a great big one. Boom! Spray flew up a mile high, it seemed like, and in the middle of the spray was these hunks of iron girder, like flying toothpicks. Then in a moment the wave had gone, and you couldn't even tell where the bridge had been. I remember remarking to my wife that the wet hand of God had wiped out this mighty work of man with a single swipe of the almighty paw. Some of the women cried, I recollect. It was a lonesome feeling, knowing that we was cut off out here permanent. Yet it was comforting too. I don't think the good Lord ever intended for Juniper Island to be connected to anything."

A gust outside struck the grocery store, rattling windows in their frames, rocking the structure on its foundations.

"This is not the day to put a Thunderbird on water," I said.

I fought my way homeward through the fury of the wind and driving horizontal rain and bits of flying wet dead leaves.

"It's building up towards a full hurricane, June," I said. "We're stuck right here for the next few days."

She smiled. "We can endure, Dan," she said.

I went out again and fought my way to the waterfront. I battened down the pitching, tossing, bucking *Mary Jane* against the blow. The waterfront was a bustle of wind-blown activity as everybody was busy battening down.

"I'm sort of concerned about old Cyrus Lunt," one of the Rast boys said to me.

"How come?" I asked him.

"He ain't in yet. He's still out there somewhere." Rast pointed into the raging roiling gray nothingness beyond the harbor mouth.

"Probably he's at Rockport Falls, cut off for the rest of the week," I said. "Cyrus Lunt's a smart old codger. I don't think he'd let himself get caught in this."

"Lunt considers himself smart about the dollar, Doc, but everything else is strictly second rate," said Rast. "Before a blow, he can't never bear to pull his lobster traps. When she's already weathering heavy and it ain't exactly safe, then he can't bear the thought of letting his traps alone and losing 'em. You might think, what with his coal and oil company stock and that damned enormous bank account of his, that he could stand to lose a dollar now and then, but old Cyrus Lunt might prefer to lose himself a life. He ain't heard that theory about not taking it with you, Doc. I think he plans to try."

"Don't worry," I said. "He'll be all right."

"Us islanders are the worrying type, Doc."

This was true, strangely enough. The way of life of the islander would scare hell out of any city man, and the islander wouldn't live anywhere else, but he worries just the same. I fought my way home again through the hurricane.

"There may be a fisherman out in the middle of the reach," I told my wife.

"Nothing you can do about it, dear."

"I hope Willie Harpswell doesn't try to row his way through this," I said. "I hope he's got enough provisions for the week."

"Don't worry about Willie."

"Can't help worrying. I'm an islander," I said.

"Then call him on the telephone."

"Willie doesn't have a telephone," I said. "I wonder where Slob is?"

"Slob? Are you also worried about that mangy hound? You haven't even seen the animal for months."

"The summer is over and Slob should be home," I said. "I don't like to think of him weathering a hurricane."

"Well, Slob doesn't have a telephone either, Dr. Dan," said June, "so why don't you sit down, safe and comfortable, and compose yourself?"

I tried to compose myself. The wind was still rising out of doors. Our little house was creaking on its old foundations, and in the gusts it seemed to jump and jitter. Cold wet air was blowing right through the walls as if they were cheesecloth. I was thinking: if I raised a flying jib from the roof peak, the damned house would take off and sail across the reach all by itself. At three in the afternoon a large tree in the front yard went down, crushing part of the front porch. A half an hour later we lost our television antenna and part of the chimney too. The plaster on the northeast exposure of the house was soaking through and it crumbled to the laths before morning.

The phone rang. I picked it up.

"Hello?" said a voice. "Are these damn wires down?"

"No, the damn wires are not down, though I don't know why," I said. "This is Dr. van Dine."

"Mike Vladimir, Dan. How's the weather over there?"

"Wet and windy," I said.

"It's a hell of a whirlwind over here," said Mike. "I think we just lost a battlement. Is this an example of your winter weather? Does it blow like this till spring?"

"Only intermittently," I said.

"I'm glad you're still here, Dan. I heard you were leaving the island today."

"Nobody leaves for several days," I said.

"Think we're cut off?"

"I don't think you could get a battleship across the reach right now," I said.

"Well, I'm surely glad I made my arrangements well in advance, and the doctor and his nursing staff are safe in here."

"How do they like hurricanes?"

"I don't know, Dan. They're busy. Dolores has started into labor."

"Oh?"

"I thought you might want to know," said Mike.

"Thanks. I do. Keep me in touch. Everything under control so far?"

"I can't tell," said Mike. "They won't let me into the delivery suite, and nobody tells me anything. It's a nerve-racking experience, Doctor. I'm crazy for the sound of a human voice. I don't consider the butler human, by the way."

I laughed. "Phone me any time. I imagine I'll be right here," I said.

I hung up and went into the kitchen where June was cooking soup.

"Dolores Vladimir has started having labor pains," I said.

June looked at me, sort of funny.

"What's the matter?" I said.

"Dan," she said, "so am I."

* * *

I thought this might be false labor. It was three weeks or more prior to my wife's due date. The circumstances of the storm, of our being cut off, might have given her sufficient psychological justification. The pains weren't very frequent. At least twenty minutes apart. But they were fairly strong and they were steady. Shortly after supper her bag of waters broke.

"Well, June," I said, "this is it, I'm afraid."

"Naturally," she replied.

She seemed very calm and matter-of-fact, the typical feminine reaction under stress. I was nervous and jittery: the male stress reaction. No wonder women live longer!

"June, there's no possible way we could get you across the reach to the hospital," I said.

"I know it."

"Here we are: stuck!" I said.

"Dan, I'm chiefly worried about the child. Isn't this awfully early?"

If our calculations had been correct, the child would be premature. On the other hand, June was quite large. I thought it likely we had made a one-month miscalculation in our dates. I was much more concerned about June herself.

"Maybe it will blow over in time," I said.

She laughed. "What will blow over, Dan? The storm? Or me?"

My remark had been silly. Obviously the only thing that might blow over was our house. No use to dream about reassuring possibilities, Dr. Dan: reality is here, so cope with it!

"A very unfortunate choice," I said. "I wish the widow was alive. Now it's me or the well-known Dr. Smith."

"You," she said instantly.

"I'd rather not, June."

"All right. Then Dr. Smith," she said, equally fast.

"Damn it," I said. "A hell of a situation, but I might have known. I should have gotten you out of here weeks ago. It's my fault, June. I don't know how to apologize."

"Oh, sure, all your fault, Dr. Dan. You caused the hurricane. You started my labor pains. Now you've done your worst, so have yourself a drink or something. Settle down! You're making me nervous."

"We ought to be doing something."

"What?"

I really didn't know.

"We can wait awhile. Then, at the proper time, you can take me over to Dr. Smith."

"There may be trees down across the road."

"We'll get there, dear," she said calmly.

The phone rang again. I hoped it might be Mike Vladimir, so that I could explain our problem to him, but it was one of the fishermen named Rast.

"Doc, you got a minute?"

"What's up?" I said.

"We got some trouble here."

"You got trouble. I got trouble. We all got trouble," I said.

"Well, if you're busy, Doc, we won't bother you."

"Rast, what's the problem?"

"Well, Doc, it's Cyrus Lunt."

"Isn't he in yet?" I asked.

"You know that hunk of rock off the eastern tip of the island? They call it the Mad Lady Reef."

I knew it: a wicked and dangerous ledge, even in calm water.

"Cyrus is out there right this minute, Doc. His boat is hung on the reef, if she hasn't already broken up. His radio's still working and he's calling for help. The Coast Guard is coming, but we figger by the time they get here there won't be anything left of Cyrus Lunt. He's in bad shape now, Doc. You can imagine. Furthermore, it sounds like he's hurt. Broken legs and stove up in the chest, I reckon. Just betwixt you and me and the kitchen stove, Doc, I don't think he's going to make it. I ain't convinced we can reach him. If we reach him, I ain't convinced we can get him out of there. But we can't just let him go, so we'll give her a try. He'll be in bad need of medical attention. Can you be standing by?"

"Want me to go out with you in the boat?" I said.

"Doc, it's dangerous."

"No more dangerous for me than you."

"Well, it would be handy to have you aboard, but the decision is up to you."

"Let me think it over," I said.

"Don't think long. We ain't got much time."

"Give me your number. I'll call you right back," I said.

He gave me the number and I hung up.

"June," I said, "fifty-foot breakers are crashing on an ugly reef a quarter of a mile off shore. There's a lobster boat caught on that reef, breaking up. Hanging to the remains of the boat is a stubborn stupid no-good thief and pirate by the name of Cyrus Lunt. He is badly hurt already, and he won't last long. The Coast Guard won't reach him in time. So the fishermen are going to have a crack at it."

June turned pale and put her hand to her mouth. "Are you going with them, Dan?"

"I haven't got much time to think it over," I said. "Of course, I should stay here with you."

"I'm all right," she said.

"You're in labor, on a cut-off island, during a hurricane."

"There's a trained obstetrician and a modern delivery suite just down the road."

"Nine miles from here, in the opposite direction from the harbor. It would take me the better part of an hour to make an eighteen-mile round trip during a hurricane. Cyrus Lunt wouldn't live that long."

"Then go get him," she said. "I wouldn't have the baby for many hours yet, would I?"

"Your first child and the pains not very strong so far," I said. "No, I don't think you'll deliver until morning."

"Then stop jabbering. You're wasting time. Your primary obligation is pretty clear, I should think."

"I can't abandon you under these conditions. I can't let you fight your way nine miles through a hurricane."

"Don't worry about me. I'll make it."

"Alone?"

"What about Mike Vladimir? He's not doing anything. He has a Cadillac. They ferry it on a barge back and forth across the reach each season. If he's afraid of the wind, he can always make the butler go."

"Would you trust Mike Vladimir?"

"Sure. What could he do to me in this condition?"

I laughed, proud of my wife and her courage. I phoned Mike and hastily outlined the situation. Mike had some courage too. Hell, he wasn't afraid of a little wind, he said. He'd set forth immediately. He'd take along the butler, and a chain saw and a block and tackle. If there were any trees across the road the butler would clear the way. And if they happened to get stuck or anything, why, hell's bells, they could make it on foot easy. And if June couldn't be brought to the doctor, the doctor could be brought to June. Nothing for me to worry myself about. Take off. I thanked him and hung up.

"Mike's coming," I said.

"Then you're going," she replied.

I was still hesitant.

"Dan," said June, "are you afraid?"

"Frankly," I said, "yes."

"For me?" she said. "Or for yourself?"

"Both," I admitted.

"But you know I'll be all right."

"And I know I have to go," I said. I phoned Rast and told him I was on my way.

"Make her snappy, Doc. Time's a-wasting," said Rast.

I hung up and kissed my wife.

"For God's sake, Dan, take care," said June.

"You too," I said.

And I set off into the teeth of the hurricane.

Was I afraid out there? Brother, let me tell you: I was terrified! My mother didn't raise her son to be any hero type. I have been terrified before. Our unit was strafed in MIG Alley once upon a time. This was just as bad.

There were about a dozen of us in two boats. We were all afraid, but we didn't mention it. Heroes save their breath. If one of us had started jabbering, all of us would have started jabbering, and we would have infected each other with our fear. Silent, we appeared to each other unafraid, and thus we kept up our morale. We were less afraid once we got under way. There was plenty to do and we were fighting for our lives. Then we didn't have time to be afraid. A man in an emergency forgets everything except the matter at hand. I even managed to forget about my wife. Furthermore, when you're right in the middle of catastrophe, there's a strange atmosphere of unreality. You can't quite believe it is really happening, and you can't accept the fact that it is happening to you.

When I think of a storm at sea I think of the marvelous Hollywood photography that we've seen so often in the movies. Actually it isn't like that at all. There is no wind machine, no convenient lightning to flicker the actor's face, no stage hands throwing buckets of water. It would be almost impossible to really photograph a hurricane. You couldn't hold the camera still or keep the lens dry. And in a storm at night there's nothing to photograph. There's really nothing to see. It's enveloping blackness and inclusive noise, and it's a revolving sensation of the balance center as if you were caught in a centrifuge. Enormous masses of black, green, and white roll up, roll over, and roll hissing by. The sound is a demon's orchestration of shrieks and wild animal sounds. We were in the barrel, going over Niagara Falls.

We could not have gone across the reach. In the shallow funnel between islands and mainland, where the tide was running one way and the hurricane the other, the cross chop had the effect of a buzz saw and would have broken any ship in two. The Mad Lady Reef was on the tip of the island and, using the island's lee as a shield against the main force of the blast, we could creep very close to it, as a hunter might creep through brush on his belly towards the game. We had to commit ourselves to the full force of wind and weather at our destination. We lashed our two little boats together. We used the lead boat and sea anchors to keep the rescue boat in some sort of position and we edged as near to the reef as we dared. We couldn't actually see the reef. We could see it on radar, and feel it, and hear the cannon fire of the breakers thundering over it.

I did not witness the actual rescue. The boys seized me and thrust me into the relative safety of the cabin.

"Don't want you to wash overboard, Doc," they screamed in my ear.

"We're all in the same boat," I tried to scream back.

"Doc, you're too valuable," they said. "We got plenty of fishermen and we can spare a few of them, if they wash away, but there's only one of you."

In theory, it should have been I, perhaps, who was first at the side of the patient to give him aid. But they wouldn't let me, and I put up no argument, for I knew they were right. Physically, I lacked the conditioning, the experience, and the seamanship, and I would have jeopardized the entire expedition. The best man was selected: the strongest and quickest. Also, he happened to be one of the oldest, and his name was Rast.

We had a cannon and breeches buoy aboard. Somehow we got close enough without being entangled in the undertow. The cannon was fired; the line shot out into the wind; with luck (or with the assistance of a merciful deity), the line was secured on a pinnacle of granite on the reef. Somehow Rast got out there on the breeches buoy; somehow he found Cyrus Lunt. Cyrus was unconscious. Rast disentangled him from the wreckage, scooped him up, and carried him back on the breeches buoy. They dumped him in the cabin for me, and started fighting back towards home again.

Cyrus Lunt was seventy-five per cent drowned. I worked on him all the way back. I managed to get him breathing again with artificial respiration, which didn't do his stove-in chest much good. He had smashed ribs and lung injury; his right femur was shattered; so were his left humerus and his pelvis. When we got back to the harbor we put him in a basket, like a mess of fresh-caught lobsters, and hauled him up from boat to dock with the fisherman's block and tackle. We moved him out of the weather, into the dock shed, but no farther than that. I worked on him there for the rest of the night.

He was tough, stubborn, too cantankerous to die. By morning he was awake, cheery, full of ginger, cussing me out. I cussed him back. I gave orders for the boys to carry him home on a stretcher of blankets and boat hooks. Later on, when the weather permitted, I would hospitalize him in Rockport Falls.

Then, exhausted, broken-backed, and grainy-eyed, I stepped out of the fish storage shed for a breath of air. A wan pale watery sun was trying to peep through, and the wind was falling. In the reach outside, the devil's orchestration was still in full cry, and would be so for several days, but in the shelter of the harbor there was relative peace. The emergency was over. I had coped with it as well as I could. Now it was time for me to pick up the routine affairs of a mundane world, but first I needed rest.

"Hi, Doc!" Wellington from the grocery store greeted me.

"Hi," I said.

"Give me a cigar."

"I don't have any cigars," I said.

"Gladly sell you a box, right here and now. Your credit's good. Pay for it next week."

"The last thing I need right now is a box of cigars."

"On the contrary, Doc," said Wellington. "You just become a father, so I understand."

My mind came rushing back to my personal affairs. Although a nagging subconscious anxiety had been with me all the night, the immediate urgencies of the business at hand had completely possessed the surface of my mind. Now I was suddenly concerned about my wife and child.

"How's June?" I asked anxiously.

"Better shape than you are, Doc," said Wellington.

"And the baby?"

"Six pound ten, and screaming for the teat already, so they tell me."

Six pounds, ten ounces? Then the baby wasn't premature after all. We had made a miscalculation on the dates.

"That fancy specialized baby doc had a busy night himself," said Wellington. "Mrs. Vladimir come through too last night. She had herself a boy. What are you going to name yours, Doc?"

I didn't know. I hadn't thought of that. "Dan, Jr., I suppose," I said.

Wellington laughed.

"What's the matter? That's a pretty good name, isn't it?" I said.

"For a girl, Doc?"

A girl? What did I want with a girl? Like all men, I wanted a son.

"Well . . ." I said.

Overhead, the sun burst through, and the glory dawned on me. A girl? A girl! A wonderful little mutty urchin child, female, who would grow up to be a woman and who even might, with luck, grow up to be a lady too!

"I wonder," I said. "Do you suppose we'll ever get her into Vassar? Have a big cigar, on me!"

Part 11

In Each Season

"Okay, June?"

"Okay, Dan?"

"Darling, you look wonderful," I said.

"You look simply horrible," said June.

We laughed at each other and kissed. Everything was under control.

"You're quite a gal, quite a woman," I said. "An island woman. They don't come any tougher, braver, stronger than that."

"You're quite a man."

"Who? Me?"

"You! I should think you might be eligible for a Carnegie Medal."

"I didn't do anything," I said.

"I heard differently," said June. "You couldn't get a battleship across that reach. You did it in a tiny lobster boat."

"They did it. I just went along for the ride," I said. "We only did what we had to do. They'd do it for any man out here. It's part of the island life. I'm only ashamed that I was afraid."

"What if you'd all gone down together?"

"We didn't," I said. "We're too damn stubborn for that."

I went down and gave my thanks and my congratulations to the famous Dr. Smith.

"Lifesaving, sir," I said. "I don't know what we would have done if you hadn't been out here."

"It was interesting," said Dr. Smith, as if discussing some new phenomenon of chorioepithelioma in the laboratory mouse. "We lost our lights right in the middle of everything."

"We lose them rather frequently," I said.

"Next time, I might advise Mr. Vladimir to install an auxiliary dynamo. I never did a delivery by flashlight and kerosene lantern before, let alone two of them. Both ladies came to the point at about the same moment. Had to do a breech extraction on Mrs. Vladimir, and at the same time your wife started to bleed. For a moment there was too much going on at once. I even asked one of the girls to give you a ring and see if you could come around and give me a hand. They tell me you were otherwise engaged."

"I was otherwise engaged," I said.

"It'll make a good story for my memoirs if I ever write them," said Dr.

Smith, "but I'll be glad to get back to the city, I must confess. It's a touch too primitive for me."

"Sometimes," I said, "it is also a touch too primitive for me."

I tried to look up Mike Vladimir, thinking we might exchange mutual cigars and congratulations, but Mike was asleep, under heavy sedation. Dr. Smith had found it necessary to give Mike sedatives just about the time the lights went out.

I visited Dolores. She was perky. I saw the children. Two pink wrinkled bundles of small hungry humanity. My wife thought they were beautiful. Personally, I disagree. The newborn is a kind of a little slob, in my opinion.

There's no gain without loss. I went on home, and there I found Martha Drinkwater waiting for me, bearer of bad news. Of course, we spoke of the good news first. Cyrus Lunt doing very well; the babies well; the mothers fine.

"I'm sorry, Dr. Dan," Martha said then. "I gotta tell you."

"Tell me what, dear?"

"About your dog."

"Slob?"

"He was trying to come home, but he didn't make it, Dr. Dan."

Yes, Slob had been a hurricane victim. In a sense it was his own fault. He should have started home before the storm. But, like Cyrus Lunt, like a stubborn islander, he had waited a bit too long. He was caught when a tree went down.

"Smushed him up. He don't look pretty," said Martha.

"Show me the body. I'll bury it," I said.

"Buried him already for you. Didn't think you'd want to tackle that particular nasty job, Dr. Dan."

"Thanks, dear."

Her consideration touched me. Typical of Martha Drinkwater to think of a thing like that. And I was sad at the loss of Slob, useless companion, faithful bum. I could scarcely practice medicine on Juniper Island without that hound in my waiting room. But then, I was leaving the island. It was time to close my office and my waiting room.

June and the baby, Dolores and her baby, both did very well. In two weeks famous Dr. Smith and his retinue had departed. I tried to pay him, but of course he would accept no remuneration. Mike Vladimir, Dolores, and Michael, Jr., were ready to go south.

"I don't know how to thank you for getting my wife through that hurricane," I said to Mike.

"It was nothing," he said modestly.

I made a bet with myself that it was a good deal to Mike, that he would tell his story again and again, that his mission of mercy would grow longer and longer and the dangers of falling trees and ferocious winds more dangerous with every passing year.

"I've made arrangements to tear down the labor room and delivery suite," said Mike.

"That seems a shameful waste," I said.

"Yes," he said, "but I wouldn't be using it again. At least not for another year or two."

"They could use the facilities out here," I said.

"Well, I offered to leave it in for you this winter," said Mike. "Next summer there would have to be other arrangements. I couldn't live in a part-time summer hospital."

"The offer was generous, Mike," I said, "but there is no point in it. There'll be no doctor here after I go. I couldn't find a substitute. This is not generally considered a desirable location. There'll never be a midwife here again. So what use is a delivery room?"

"You're definitely leaving here?"

"Yes."

"A shame."

"I have my own professional future to consider," I said.

"Look," said Mike, "if it's a matter of money, I'll——"

"Mike," I said, "you still can't purchase me."

"I've a suggestion," he said, his face brightening up. "I'd be glad to build you a small hospital here. A nice modern clinic. What do you say?"

"Get thee behind me, Satan, I believe would be appropriate."

"Well . . ."

"Sorry," I said.

"Okay. So am I," said Mike Vladimir.

* * *

It was a beautiful sharp crystalline day in late September. The waters of the reach were mirror-still. A baby could have paddled a canoe across. This was a perfect day for our departure. Our Thunderbird had already been shipped over on a barge and was waiting for us on the civilization side. One final trip in the *Mary Jane* would do the trick. It was time to lock up the house and go.

"What's the matter, dear?" said June.

She was standing patiently, just outside the door, holding the baby. At the threshold, I looked beyond her, across the reach, to the soft blue hills of the mainland in the distance.

"It's beautiful," I said. "And the city isn't beautiful."

June sighed, came back into the house, sat down on the arm of a chair. The baby smiled, gurgled, winced, and produced a small blast of gas.

"Are you ready to go, dear?" I asked.

"As ready as you are," said June.

"I guess there's nothing more to be done," I said. "Cyrus Lunt is recuperating nicely in Rockport Falls. I've paid up my bill at Wellington's. I've said good-by to Drinkwater, Willie Harpswell, Holy Joe Brown. I'm sure they can find another fourth for bridge. I've been down to the library. I wonder how long Betty Winkle will stay on here?"

"Indefinitely," said June.

"Poor Betty. She didn't change. She's just as lonely and frustrated as if I had never attended her."

June did not comment.

"We're going to miss Martha's wedding," I said, "but we sent her a lovely present. I've put a little permanent marker on Slob's grave. Is there anything I've forgotten?"

At this moment the telephone rang.

"Yes, indeed," I said. "The lights and the water are turned off, but I forgot to have them disconnect the phone."

"Don't answer it," said June.

"I'm not answering it," I said.

We watched the telephone. It rang five times and stopped.

"I hope that wasn't an emergency," I said.

My wife said nothing.

"June, give me a push," I said. "If I don't start now I'll never go. My roots are hurting me."

My wife offered me no help. I got up, grabbed suitcases in both hands, and started out the door. Then, finally, June figured she might as well say it, I suppose.

"How many doctors in the city where we're going, Dan?"

"Thousands and thousands," I said.

"Are you sure they need another one?"

"Here's the point," I said. "I'll serve any community I inhabit. A life in the city is worth just as much as a life on Juniper Island. But I have the right to inquire: in what manner can this community now serve me?"

"You've not found anybody to buy this house. Nobody's bought the *Mary Jane*."

"To hell with it," I said. "I arrived here with nothing but a Thunderbird three years ago. I'm leaving with a Thunderbird, a wife, and a child. I came out ahead of the game. I'll earn some money later on."

"You made more than that," said June. "These three years were valuable. Dan, you've been growing up out here."

"I hope I'll not stop growing."

"I hope not. There are a few things you haven't quite solved as yet."

"Such as the reason for suffering and pain?"

"Such as the matter of responsibility for others, for example. I don't think you'd be content in any small community if you felt totally responsible for everything that happened way out here."

"Whereas, in the city, responsibility must be shared?"

"That's true, Dan."

"On the other hand, everything is shared out here."

"Yes, Dan."

"Well, come along," I said. "Let's not jabber till the sun goes down."

June got up; we left the house; I locked the door. Then I heard a distant voice.

"Hey, Dr. Dan! Hey, wait a minute! Wait for me!"

It was little Martha Drinkwater, running towards us up the hill. She arrived, disheveled and out of breath.

"My dear," I said to her, "a lady never runs."

Martha grinned at me. "Ain't exactly a lady yet," she said.

"You're getting married next week. You'll have to be."

"Nope," said Martha. "Haven't you heard? Where have you been? The wedding's off. I ain't getting married after all."

"Indeed?"

"William's gone away to Orono."

"Oh?" I said. "To college?"

"Yep. Poppa's helping him. We figure to marry eventual, but we done decided to get ourselves a little education first."

"Wonderful," I said.

"So I brung back that present, Dr. Dan."

"Keep it, dear."

"Ain't earned it. You keep it, Doc. Give it to us again in six or seven years." Then Martha turned toward June. "Lady?"

"Yes, dear?" said June.

"That's a mighty pretty baby you got there."

"Thank you," said June, quite pleased.

"But, lady," Martha went on, "you're making one hell of a large mistake, you know?"

"Is that so?" said June, less pleased.

"That's so. I'm speaking of your ring."

"Ring?"

"That ring you've got hooked into the nose of good old Dr. Dan. Lady, stop tugging it!"

"I don't understand you, dear," said June.

"I figure you do," said Martha. "You have no right to drag this man away from Juniper Island."

"I'm not dragging," said June.

"Are too!" said Martha.

"Am not!" said June.

Two rather subborn female minds were tugging away at each other here.

"Look, lady," said Martha. "You know damn well Dr. Dan ain't going to be happy anywhere else but here. If he ain't happy, you ain't going to be happy. And if you ain't happy, that poor sweet baby's going to grow up to be the damnedest little brat. So you got no decent right to take him away."

"I'm not taking him," said June.

"He damn well ain't leaving on his own desire," said Martha.

They were mad at each other now.

"Ladies . . ." I said, but they ignored me.

"My dear," said June, mad as hell inside, cold as ice to cover it, "I know that my husband has been happy here. I know he will not be happy in the city. You people need him. He needs you. Since I need him, I want to stay."

"Then why don't you make him stay?"

"Because he's stubborn," said my beloved. "Because he would not listen to me. Because that decision would not work unless he made the decision for himself."

"Then decision him!" said Martha.

"I am not a prize fighter," said June.

"Then you ain't a lady neither," said Martha. "Because any lady worth the name can make up the mind of the man in love with her at any time. This leaves you nothing but an ordinary common stupid dame!"

"Ladies . . ." I tried to say.

All ladies present, including the baby, ignored me.

"HEY, YOU DAMN DUMB DAMES!" I yelled at the top of my voice.

Now they looked at me, all three of them.

"I wish to insert a few words in here," I said quietly. "Edgewise. Would you mind?"

Apparently they didn't mind.

"Ladies," I said, "I have just exerted that prerogative not limited to women and changed my stubborn mind."

"What do you mean, Dan?"

"Where are you going, Dr. Dan?"

"If you don't mind," I said, "I'm going home."

I picked up the bags, turned in my tracks, walked back to the house, unlocked the door, walked in, and went to the telephone. I phoned the water company. I phoned the electric company. I told them I was planning to stick around a few more decades, or something of the kind. There was no argument from any of the ladies in the immediate vicinity.

That night June said to me, "Look in the baby's crib, dear."

I looked. "For God's sake, what's that?"

"One of those small objects is your daughter," said June.

"Obviously. What's the other? A dog?"

"More or less. A puppy, just been weaned. The bloodlines seem to be mixed."

"What's he doing in there?"

"He belongs to us," said June. "A gift from Martha Drinkwater."

"But, June! In the same crib with the baby?"

"I don't think they're hurting each other, dear."

The baby was curled up, sleeping against the puppy. The puppy was curled up, sleeping against the baby. They didn't seem to be hurting each other.

June put her arm around my waist, rested her cheek against mine, and whispered in my ear: "Don't you think we ought to call him Slob?"

I did. This seemed appropriate.